Aggressive Behavior

Book Four of Freelance Familiars

Daniel Potter

FALLEN KITTEN PRODUCTIONS

Copyedited by Nicole Evans & Andrea Johnson

Cover by Ebooklaunch.com

DanielPotterAuthor.com

To everyone who needs solace and sanity in these days of pandemic and panic.
Stay safe, stay healthy and be brave.

I

"Ready to run the gauntlet, Thomas?" O'Meara asked, giving the top of my head an affectionate scratch.

I shook, making my ears slap against her fingers, clearing out the daydream of being in a tree, gnawing at a haunch of fresh deer meat. I don't get much alone time anymore.

"Uh, we got everything?" I turned to look at Rudy, who was busy tucking something away in my brand new harness—totally black, and embroidered with two words on either side in golden thread: "The Boss." It felt weird to be in charge of my own life, let alone the lives of others. Yet it was a point hammered home multiple times every day.

The gray squirrel popped up and put on his most innocent expression, which is about as innocent as a burglar with his hand stuck in a safe. "We're missing the Wizard Phooey Mark Four!"

I rolled my eyes, "We are not bringing a grenade launcher to the council meeting. Besides, I don't think I can fit through the doorways with the Mark Four." Seriously. It had its own wheels, otherwise it would break my spine.

"Okay, okay, so maybe I got a little carried away with the Mark Four, but the Three isn't that much bigger than the Mark Two, we could take that one." Rudy never changed, the ancient rodent lived for explosions, embarrassing predators, and making the world a better place. In that order. A good friend to have, despite the frequency of scorch marks on the furniture and myself.

"Rudy, relax. I've got more wards on this harness than there are floors in the building." I started moving, and the doors to my office opened smoothly, without even the faintest hint of a mechanical whir.

"That just means you're nearly as blind as O'Meara," Rudy grumped.

"Nobody is going to jump us on the way to the meeting with the Council of Merlins, Rudy. Relax," O'Meara said, and then added, *At least while we're bonded,* mentally.

They should be educated on that bit by now, I thought back as I shoulder-checked her thigh. Despite my two hundred pound bulk, O'Meara withstood the affectionate blow like a mountain. Nearly six feet tall and built like a brick oven, O'Meara had spent a lifetime being thrown at nasty problems. She'd survived, but her familiars hadn't proven as resilient. Out of utter desperation, I'd bonded with her. That temporary arrangement sprouted deep roots of love and trust. Although my particular talent allows me to bond with any magus that I choose at any time, I had no desire to forge a mental connection to anyone other than her.

We walked toward the elevator that waited for us about thirty feet in front of my office's doorway. That elevator marked the border of our sanctuary in the MGM casino—which we had claimed as our own six months ago, after the previous owner had succumbed to a hunger demon. Three heavy wooden doors faced the antechamber. The one we stepped through depicted myself and O'Meara heroically battling a giant maw in colorful mosaic tiles. The scene animated if you stared at it long enough, and we smote the monster with a burst of blue and red flame. A gift from House Hermes. The second door, which stood to the right of mine, depicted a Phoenix bursting from a spent torch in wooden inlay. No magic animated this one, but the flames seemed alive through the sheer artistry of the artwork. Opposite of O'Meara's door stood a potted artificial tree. In the shade of the tree stood a door five inches tall, painted yellow and black stripes, with red letters warning that a blast zone lay beyond. O'Meara and I had given it to Rudy as a joke, but he had insisted on using it. Behind each door sat our respective offices, and beyond them lay our private wing with sleeping quarters, labs, a library and everything else we needed on a daily basis.

If I didn't think about what enabled all of this luxury, then it'd be so easy to never leave. Instead every time I passed through these doors, I forced myself to remember the huge pit in the basement, where horrors fed on tiny slices of the tourist hopes and dreams. So far as we knew, the harvesting didn't hurt the tourists long term. Nobody had been eager to perform a clinical study to find out for sure.

A light boot to the rear jolted me out of my thoughts. "Stop ruminating on your belly fur and keep moving. Hiding up here isn't going to solve anything," O'Meara said.

I made a disgruntled huff and moved into the elevator. It's always annoying when your partner calls you on your internal BS.

"Ahh, stop worrying, Thomas, it gonna be fine." Rudy bounced a bit on my back as we boarded the elevator, and O'Meara hit the button for ground on the upper panel. The elevator had three – one normal sized and positioned for humans, a second one a foot from the floor with over-sized buttons for paws, and a third panel, so small that I had to squint to see the numbers on the buttons.

As the floors ticked down, the tension ratcheted up along my spine. I hated this part. I focused on keeping my ears forward. O'Meara's knuckles cracked and I heard her inhale.

A sharp babble of sound rushed at us as the elevator doors opened. A combination of the electronic slots announcing their riches and the blended noise of human voices. There were several hundred feet between ourselves and the door where the car waited. Eyes found me. They didn't belong to the majority of the population, but there were more than enough of them. After a gulp that sounded too loud to my ears, I started to move.

"Mister Thomas! Please! A moment of your time." A woman in a bright pink suit pounced first, stepping up beside me with a desperate smile and a teal green parrot on her shoulder.

"I do not have it right now. Please make an appointment." I said, glancing up at her only briefly. She was definitely a magus.

"My apologies sir, but I have a new bid for your casino retrofit. If you'd just take a look." An envelope thrust into my path.

"Bids are closed, Sophia," O'Meara answered coldly.

"Will you perhaps be embarking on another expansion soon?" A new voice, belonging to a short man with a dark beard, said. "Maybe a security overhaul? Those wards you're sporting are very nice, but I see you're still using some of Death's wards around the casino. They won't last too much longer."

"Shove off!" Rudy told the man.

Another joined the fray, opening up a cloak filled with bangles that glowed with magics. "I have some very interesting commissions that are currently unpaid for."

"No." My ears went back and my voice dropped to a growl. "We have no work for any of you at this time." I bit my tongue before it could add "I'm sorry." Their plight wasn't my problem, I reminded myself. I can't fix the consequences of decades of embezzlement overnight, even if I wanted to. Magus Lansky, the magical world's largest banker, had turned into a hunger plane-aspected monster and consumed the majority of the tass he'd been entrusted with. There was no such thing as banking insurance. More than half the magi in Vegas found themselves suddenly destitute, making me a fat turkey waddling among hungry wolves.

They fell back and a new wave approached. These did not have the bright glow of foci hidden in their clothes, but each were distinctly inhuman. A group of satyrs clopped forward, their leader sporting a grey beard down past his belly. They all wore white shirts – unemployed servants.

O'Meara handled this group. "Positions will be posted when they are available, Gerard."

"You've got cows and pigs dealing cards, madam." Gerard bowed his head. "It's not an efficient way to turn over the tables. I've got folks with years of experience... and hands."

"Do not make me repeat myself," O'Meara said. We were getting close enough to the door that the doorman, a tall spelldog named Nathan, pulled it open. We had almost made it.

"That's it, rush off. Forget all about us less fortunate souls." A new voice stopped me dead. A voice I very much recognized. The owner of which I had last seen being tossed through a portal after attempting to murder me. I turned, mentally triggering all of my wards to blossom into their highest settings, to find an orange tomcat sitting square on the patterned floor tile. He had changed, thinning considerably, although he still wore the same smug smile. It didn't quite reach his eyes. More than anything else, Jowls' eyes were dimmer than I remembered, and the bottom eyelids drooped down, giving him a haggard, tired look.

"What are you doing in my casino, Jowls?" It took a monumental effort to keep my teeth concealed. "This isn't a safe place for you." Any deeper than the lobby and he'd start running into employees who had lost family to the callous scheme with which he and his bond had tried to grind up Grantsville and everyone in it for tass.

"I need to talk to you, Thomas." Jowls looked down at his paws.

Easy, Thomas, O'Meara soothed. *He's got no magus.*

I sat back on my haunches and did my best to smooth out my puffed fur. "You can make an appointment. But it will be short. You and Jules killed people, Jowls, lots of them. Then, you sold me out."

"It's so gracious of you for being willing to talk to the peasants, but your audiences are booked solid for the next three months. And that will be too late. I go up for auction in less than a month," Jowls said.

"And I should care why?" I didn't bother keeping the hostile hiss out of my voice.

Jowls kneaded at the floor. "I don't want another bond, Thomas. It's too soon. I'm too young to be a TAU officer and I didn't develop any knack from Jules anyway. Oric's not willing to bend the rules for me, either. Let me freelance with you. Please, Thomas!"

"Then he'll just spy on us for Oric," Rudy grumbled. "Don't go soft, Thomas."

Rudy needn't have worried. I still remembered Jowls' wicked taunting over the loudspeakers as I lost friend after friend to their spells; how he hadn't seen the people in the town as anything more than resources to be expended and used. "Best of luck on your auction," I said and walked around the orange cat.

He lunged, ricocheted off my wards and scrambled after me. "Thomas, I'm sorry! Jules' ambition blinded me. We were wrong. Give me a chance!"

"Should have led with that, Jowls," I said as his claws somehow latched onto my outermost ward and dragged him along behind me.

"I'll make amends! I don't want to go to House Erebus, Thomas. Take pity on your old pal!" he begged.

After dislodging him with a foot, we hurried out the door toward the waiting limo, Jowls continued to call after us. "You're going to need friends, Thomas! All the friends you can get to take on Oric!"

I had to pause as one of the chauffeurs, a capybara, hurried to open the door. I couldn't resist the urge to snarl back at

Jowls, "I have friends! We have friends that are a lot stronger than you, Jowls."

He hollered back, "Friends and money are very different things, Thomas! I know that now! I know that real well now!"

The door shut as soon as I pulled my tail inside the car. For a moment, silence settled on all three of us. Slowly, we all exhaled a breath.

"Well, that was a truckload of bitter almonds." Rudy poked at the quiet.

I found that my heart seemed to be louder than the limo's engine as the driver gunned it into the traffic. Doubt was already beginning to take root in my mind.

Should have killed that one when you had the chance, brother. A deep voice rolled out from the back of my mind. Bone Whistler, the being at the other end of my soul. The apex predator spirit whom I'd swapped bodies with when I'd awakened into the magical world, had started talking to me again.

Maybe. I admitted. Bone Whistler was a fan of solving problems permanently. Preferably by eating them. Eating Jowls might have indeed saved me some trouble, but keeping everything from the Grantsville incident wrapped up tightly would have required killing magi who'd surrendered. As violent as I'd turned out to be, that was a line I wouldn't be crossing. I felt Bone Whistler's presence fade. Due to the way we were connected to each other, our lives proceeded in rough parallels. When I am fighting for my life, so would he be, although the reasons for it could be completely different. Regardless, if his attention had been required elsewhere, there was a better than good chance I needed to pay attention to my own surroundings.

O'Meara had pulled out a three-ring binder from the briefcase she carried. "Forget about Jowls. Let's focus on this meeting we have in front of us. He was probably sent by Oric to rattle you, Thomas."

"Or goad us into something stupid," Rudy added as he hopped up onto his own tiny seat and buckled himself in. "That owl's barney, anyway."

"Is that cuz he's a barn Owl?" I groaned.

Rudy simply grinned.

2

A SMOOTH, UNEVENTFUL RIDE took us to Vegas' second strip, where magic took the place of neon and money. Befuddled tourists wandered the sidewalks gaping up at the impossible architecture erected by the Council of Merlin and every House that could afford the real estate. They'd googled futilely to find explanations. Outside of Vegas, the Veil would replace all their memories of these buildings and anything magical they witnessed, like talking mountain lions stepping out of a limo while the door was held open by a capybara wearing a tiny hat. The fifty-story tall black obelisk bore cracks and livid white scars from the battle between the Council of Merlins against hunger plane demons six months ago. The white flame that crowned it had been relit, but only with a basic spell of shaped light, no longer a pyre of raw tass so bright that it pained magical eyes. The only serious magic the tower displayed were structural reinforcements to prevent the damage from getting any worse.

A whiff of decay hit me directly in the back of the throat as we walked into the lobby across a floor so black, I feared we might fall into it. In fact, that could probably happen, if the defenses activated. We drifted towards one of the three lines that led to the gilded reception desks.

"Thomas Khatt and company?" An imperious looking white stag intercepted us. A huge pair of elegant antlers rose above his head.

"Yes," I said, making the mistake of inhaling through my mouth instead of my nose. He absolutely reeked of cervine musk. For him, it was probably a desperate to call out to any sentient lady deer in a hundred-mile radius. For me? An apex predator from the same ecological biome? It was as if he'd rolled himself in melted butter and hung a sign on himself that said EAT ME. I swallowed back a mouthful of drool.

The Stag regarded me as if I were a bug that required stamping on. So tall and long his neck stretched that he could look O'Meara in the eye. It would be so easy to lock my teeth down on his trachea. My stomach nearly howled.

Thomas! Get it together. He's a servant of the Council, you cannot eat him! You don't eat people, remember? O'Meara scolded.

Right! I thought back, clawing back control. I had eaten before we left. But it hadn't been deer, just leftover carnitas, which wasn't venison, hot bloody venison.

The Stag nodded. "Follow me. The Council is expecting you." And he turned his back. *A strange pressure clamped down on me and clarity came. MEAT!* My blood sang. My body coiled to strike.

Thomas! A hard yank lifted me into the air, ruining my jump as I found myself dancing awkwardly on my rear paws. My heart was thundering in my neck and ears. *Not food!* O'Meara shouted into my head.

The Stag looked back at me as O'Meara let me down on all fours, his ear flicking quizzically. "Is everything alright, Master Khatt?"

"Fine. I tripped," I said, lying as I suddenly realized that I had gone feral mind for a moment. I heard distant laughter from somewhere, but I felt okay now.

"The floor can be slick, even for cats." A playful smile flashed across his narrow muzzle before resuming his walk toward the stairway, displaying his still delicious looking rump.

"Easy, big guy." Rudy patted my neck.

O'Meara worried at me. Flaming *ash and crispy critters, Thomas, you went dark there for a second.*

We agreed to talk about it later as we followed the buck up into the tower. The structure had been built assuming that magic would always be available to its occupants. There were no elevators, only portals, even for transitioning from the lobby to the main portal room on the floor above. Now that had been considered an expense too far. Mr. Delicious led us up a stone stairway that had recently been carved out of the wall of the tower. We emerged onto the second floor where the five portals were housed within stone arches, arranged in a semi-circle. Only two were active. Large ovals hung in the air, connected to the stone by thin threads of purple magic. One had people solemnly trudging in and out of it, papers and briefcases clutched tightly in their diverse appendages. The majority had arms of some type or another, but there were also tentacles, giant crab claws, wings, and one briefcase hung on the branch of a crystalline tree that tiptoed past on its roots. These were the mythics, the working class of the magical world. If they'd lived outside Vegas, outside the border of the shallowing that made up most of the valley, reality itself would nibble on these people until they were gone, unless they could pass for human. The portal they used flicked between cubicle farms, controlled by a single magus attendant with a small green lizard sitting perched on his hat.

The stag guided us to the other portal, which revealed nothing about its destination. Matte black filled the oval within its frame of purple energies. I caught a worrisome flicker of purple energy dancing over the stonework. The stag tilted his head, listening for a moment before casting a wary glance at the portal attendant. Once the attendant looked down at her clipboard, the Stag kicked the portal with a rear hoof. The purple flashing between the stones stabilized into a steady glow. The Stag bowed, sweeping his antlers in a graceful arc. "They are expecting you, House Khatt," he said without even the hint of amusement, which I appreciated. Rudy snickered, as usual.

As we went through the portal, the darkness rippled away and resolved itself into a room that aped an American court-room, minus a jury and with far more judges. The Council of Merlins. Those who were left towered over the vast expanse from a row of boxes across the back wall. Seven booths, three on each side, with the central one elevated a modest foot higher than the others. Only four seats were occupied, the ones furthest from the center.

On the very left sat Dominicus, the lanky and feared arch-magus of House Hermes. Arms enfolded within his purple robe, he looked down on us with a twinkle in his eyes and a pleasant smirk on his lips. He seemed to tremble on the precipice of laughter. Despite all the stories of his ruthlessness and schemes for power, the man was difficult to dislike. On the very opposite sat the archmagus of House Morgana, Morrian, a squat shape that barely poked above the rim of the judicial box. Her pear-shaped face sagged from the sheer size of her scowling frown. These two were the closest things I had to allies on that bench.

The man next to Morrian, clad in a black suit, a black shirt, and a black tie, had a desiccated look to him, empty eye sockets occupied by the tiniest pinpricks of light. Michael, the second of House Erebus, regarded us with the impassive cool of a corpse. The last of the Archmagi, Fibalt of House Picitrix, didn't look at us at all, his impressive beak of a nose pointed at a notepad where he scribbled furiously, lips rippling without a single sound. Instead, his familiar studied us, as I might study a small animal to determine if its meat content equaled the effort of catching it. A not unfamiliar expression to encounter in Vegas, but I had never seen a fat raccoon pull it off so well. That would be Cherri, the only familiar we could see. The rest were there, no doubt hidden within the boxes.

We walked towards the Council down an aisle framed by empty seats. There were no witnesses for this meeting. I had been half expecting an audience to further intimidate us. But no, this would be a deal that the council wouldn't want public.

A desk sat in front of the Council's bench. A chair sat central, and beside it, a marble cube which in other settings might pass as an end table instead of a stool. O'Meara and I debated switching them, but if the cube turned out to be solid rock, it would be impossible to shift without magic. Channeling during a council meeting would be an excellent way to commit suicide.

Rudy leapt up onto the table as O'Meara and I took our seats. "Wow, never thought I'd make it in here." His quiet aside filled the empty room. Sitting up in surprise, he tilted his head, listening. "Oooo, spells that force talking spells to mimic the acoustics. Fancy."

Dominicus snort-chuckled.

"Right, right! Formalities." Rudy's tail waggled as he swaggered (as only a squirrel can) up to the front edge of the table. "Glorious Merlins." He started with a tone that contained only the slightest hint of mockery in it. "We of House Freelance have gathered before you at your request."

"According to the file, the official title is House Khatt." Michael's voice slithered out from an unmoving jaw.

Rudy shot me a sharp look, as this slight error may have been my fault. "An unfortunate typo on the form. We've filed the proper amendment."

The pinpricks of light in his sockets danced briefly. "I have not heard of this filing, perhaps it was lost. Until it is found, you are just a House Khatt."

You petty little matchstick of a wizard. O'Meara ground her teeth together. *Two groat says it is lost in his desk drawer. We should get up and leave now if this is the game they're going to play.* A groat was a low ranked magus' monthly salary. Outside

Vegas, it'd be considered a pile of cash. But here, it was little more than pocket change.

He's Erebus, I soothed. Still, the other archmagi weren't leaping to our defense on this one.

"Whatevs." Rudy dismissed the name thing with a wave of his paw. "House Khatt," giving the word a sharp Germanic emphasis, "is happy to loan the Council, with a very low interest rate, I might add. On the previously arranged conditions."

O'Meara pulled out a scroll from her briefcase and laid it on the table. The contract.

"This agreement is entirely unacceptable. Those funds belong to House Erebus in the first place," Michael said.

"Now, now," Dominicus leaned toward his colleague. "Let's not relitigate that. It's a settled matter."

"Not to mention," Cherri tapped her paws together, steepling her dexterous digits. "Death didn't even will his riches to his House. The way I sees it, O'Meara and Thomas heres stopped all that tass from being no use to anybodies." Tass is essentially the dryer lint of the universe, small particles that are scraped off when realities rub together. If you wanted a magical spell to last longer than a minute, you had to build it with tass. It served as a sort of currency, in the magical world. Realities rubbed together and generated tass in two ways: transitions, naturally temporary overlaps, and shallowings, which were permanent. The entire valley of Las Vegas sat in a massive shallowing.

"For now." Michael's head swiveled toward Dominicus. If the council was broke, House Hermes was well in the negatives. Lansky had held all their House's wealth. All archmagi were required to front the council a significant amount of tass every year, more than our vaults could contain at maximal capacity. All of Lansky's casinos had been taken over by various factions in the city, from the council bureaucracy to the minor Houses who had enough muscle to repossess a casino. That left them with only the tass the House had in their pockets at the time and a few ancient shallowings in Europe. That tax would come due in a month, and House Hermes could be forced to give up their seat. But if that happened, the Council would be without a quorum and dissolve entirely. However, it took four votes to approve a new archmagus. Scuttlebutt, meaning Rudy, told me that Dominicus was withholding his vote for new council members unless the Merlins bailed his house out of its difficulties. The council had no money to do so.

"And that claim on House Khatt's territory does not concern us today. Any future council should honor precedent and new leadership does not wipe away the debts," Morrian harrumphed. Should Dominicus relent on the block, only Houses Picitrix and Erebus were in a position to pay for additional seats. The seventh seat would have to go to one of the larger minor Houses, but with the finances so scrambled, nobody knew which it would be. "The terms of this loan are more generous than other offers. It will give us the means to begin the repairing of both the building and the council's reputation."

That's one vote, O'Meara thought, and we both let our hopes rise a bit.

Cherri tilted her muzzle back, looking up into the starless dark that covered the ceiling of the council chamber. Perhaps imploring some being to smite Michael, and failing that, she tapped her claws together. "The interest rate is good, Michael. But we sees trouble with the terms. Too much trouble. The TAU is an institution with a long history of contribution."

"We're not asking you to abolish it. Merely permit a competition model." I flung the words at Cherri. I had to get three of them to support the deal. The loan's interest was so low that I'd probably lose tass on the deal. It appeared that only Morrian would pass it with a wink and a nod. *Are they fishing for more tass?*

Probably? Not like I play politics well. A mental image of Grantsville passed through O'Meara's mind, as if we were driving through it at high speed.

Dominicus leaned forward to peer down at us. "House Hermes recognizes that the auction system is distasteful to younger magi, and the number of familiars who stand for pairing, while voicing reluctance, is increasing. But authorizing a House of Magi to train familiars is to hand you a privilege no other House has."

Rudy's tail went full bushy and waggled with frustration. "We're only a House because you lot forced us to be! We've only got one magus."

"That's the problem we see. You have a magus, which means you cannot be a mythic guild, like the TAU. To control a valuable asset such as a casino, you must be a House. But only a mythic guild could be allowed a function that would serve all the magi impartially." Behind Cherri, her magus momentarily looked up from his scribbling, and gave me the most tepid of smiles before resuming his doodling.

My jaw fell open. They weren't going to allow us to build a network of freelance familiars because we owned a casino? Only my utter astonishment prevented me from hissing like a feral cat at the panel of archmagi. Of all the bureaucratic nonsense!

Rudy chittered angrily, "Dems the terms. If you didn't like 'em, ya could have sent a text and saved us a trip."

"Give up the casino and I will change my vote, allowing you to incorporate as a competing familiar guild," Michael said.

I opened my mouth to say something, but closed it when I saw the glare that Cherri cast in the death magus' direction. Interesting. I thought.

Cherri's enjoying her moment of leverage, she's not usually the deciding vote. I think Michael made a joke. O'Meara thought.

Funny, nobody laughed. Although Michael's eyes might have twinkled a tad brighter.

Cherri turned her muzzle towards us and smoothed her whiskers. "We are personally not opposed to the terms. The Auctions can be..." She reached out in grasping motion with a fingered paw, "...an unfortunate tradition. But the way we sees it, it's not the time to change traditions. The paperwork alone would cause a ripple. We cannot be seen as bending to an individual with your unique history."

Ashes and dust, O'Meara swore, and I joined her. It is so much easier to act composed when you have a secret room in your head to shout and scream in. Truth is, I hadn't thought about the perceptions of the deal. Two of the council's seats had been emptied by the Dragon I'd freed a year and a half ago. It wouldn't look good if they now rewrote the rules for us. It would be an acknowledgment of how weak they were. Not that I really cared.

"That's still a no," I said. Next to me, O'Meara swept the scroll up off the table.

Dominicus held up a hand as I rose. "Wait, a moment, please. Cherri has a counter offer from Fibalt that she needs to get around to."

The raccoon huffed while Fibalt flinched, pushing his nose deeper into his notebook. "Thomas, you have risen faster than any member of the... community has within mortal memory. If we grant you the terms, we foresee your fall as equally rapid. While some are eager to hasten that day," Cherri's left ear flicked toward Michael, "we would rather you become a more stable presence here in Vegas. Build up your ties and, in a decade or two, we can revisit the treatment of familiar issues."

A snarl that very much wanted to happen made my lip tremble. The long list of very rude things to say piled up on my tongue. A light squeeze on the scruff of my neck distracted me from picking the most acidic among them. She's *got a point, Thomas*, she thought.

*They're down, O'Meara. We have leverage at the moment.
They need the money. I can't give it to them as a show of
goodwill. They're Magi!*

*Yes, they're Magi, Thomas. They'll die on that hill of pride,
but it goes both ways. Without the council's legitimacy, House
Erebus will take the MGM back by force. Even if we survived,
we'd be chased out of Vegas. O'Meara's hand slowly began
easing the scroll out of her satchel.* In her mind, the three of
us stood on a shrinking island encircled with sharks.

Why was it always my pride that had to be swallowed? With
a grumble of assent, O'Meara placed the scroll back on the
table.

Rudy looked from her, to me and chittered under his
breath. "What are you guys doing?"

I ignored him and stared directly at Cherri. "We will revise
the terms, removing that offending clause, but the size of the
loan will be halved and the interest rate trebled. Turning the
loan from a bribe to an investment, which is thinking more
long term. Don't you agree?"

Cherri turned to glance back at her bond, who didn't look
up.

"It is reasonable to me," Dominicus said. "The original offer
was far too generous. But you didn't hear that from me."

"Triple the interest and half the money is not..." Cherri
trailed off, grasped at the air in front of her.

"It will insure Houses Picitrix and Erebus get the best familiars for now," Morrian grumped.

The black nose dipped as Cherri's paws rubbed together in
a vague washing motion. "We sees it," she muttered to herself
before looking up. "This is acceptable. Goodwill is a process."

3

"Goodwill, my fluffy tail. That's highway robbery, That's what that was," Rudy groused as we climbed into the car.

"They'll pay it back, with interest. It's not like we loaned the tass to House Hermes or anything." I said.

"And as long as the council thinks we are playing their game, those three will keep House Erebus off our backs." O'Meara settled into the limo's leather seating.

"Game? We just gave those four oily nut clusters a fourth of our tass reserves. Fifty thousand groat. You'd be better off betting it at the craps table downstairs." Rudy chittered, tail dancing with irritation.

I laid down and covered my eyes with my paws. Fifty thousand groat? Is that how much it was? It was unimaginable. A year ago we were in a desperate struggle over a mere hundred.

"I don't care if we have 5 groat or 5 million," O'Meara declared. I winced as I felt her thoughts pivot onto other worries. "Thomas, what the heck happened to you and that deer? You were going to kill him!"

"I mostly wanted to eat him." I hunkered down further but hiding isn't very effective when you're trying to hide in a lap.

"And you would have if I hadn't grabbed you! I've never had a familiar go dark like that before. Just gone." O'Meara was looking at Rudy, who watched me with a thoughtful expression.

He then shrugged. "It's meat brain thinking. It happens sometimes to a lot of awakened animals who are way outside their home turf. He is probably super stressed. Maybe he needs a vacation."

"Well, he has been thinking an awful lot about hunting in a forest lately." O'Meara frowned and cut off my objections to this analysis with a well-timed ear scratch.

I rolled onto my side to let her nails dig through my thick neck fur and sighed. "Too bad this job doesn't seem to come with vacation time."

"It barely comes with breathing time. But if this gets any worse, I'm taking you to see a head healer," O'Meara said.

"Maybe I should let Rudy run the casino?" I looked at the cashew-devouring rodent.

"Nuts to that!" He shoved a cashew half into a cheek pouch. "I got my paws busy figuring out what to do with all our tass before you two give it all away!"

"No exploding the city, Rudy, we talked about this." O'Meara conjured a blue flame into her palm.

"Finefinefine. No exploding the city. You keep your sparky fingers out of my lab."

The flame dissipated. "Now do you actually have anything useful to contribute?"

"We can do anything we want if we use that tass. Magi in this city are so busy trying to get it, that they forget what they can do with it. Most tass is used to stop other magi breaking into tass stockpiles," Rudy sputtered.

I sighed. "While Death owned it, the MGM only made a groat or two a day in profit. Maintaining wards, the extra dimensional rooms, employing a few houseless magi goons, and keeping whatever is in the library powered up siphoned most of his income. He made the majority of his wealth acting as a bookie for wagers between magi. There are hints he might have also created immortality chambers for other Magi in return for very large sums of tass."

"Immortality and power seem to have been his only interests." O'Meara shivered. The sensation traveled through the link and went down my spine, bringing with it memories of the very gruesome collection of artifacts that sat in Death's 'toy' vault. Worse, there were definitely souls entrapped in some of those devices. But, after a close call with a trapped device, neither of us was eager to experiment further. We both batted the images away as O'Meara resumed her thought process. "That and desperation. He was always pushing others to see how far they'd go, how badly they wanted something, who'd they hurt or kill in order to get it. The larger his pile of tass and the more fearsome his reputation, the more untouchable he was. He extended that protection to a few friends who shared his interests— namely Ghenna, who styled herself after the worst depictions of the Mayan empire. Never mind that she was British."

"Well, barring us getting into the bloodsport bizzness, we're up to five groat a day, with O'Meara and I doing a weekly inspection of all the wards," I said.

"I wish we could get that space bending ward more efficient. Every time we look at it I wince. No ward should take more than a groat a month to maintain. It's as if we spackled the entire casino with tass mud," O'Meara huffed.

"I told ya to outsource it." Rudy said.

"We can't trust anyone with our anti-Oric war, Rudy. If we don't build it ourselves, we can't be sure that there isn't a back door or something in there. And we don't know enough about it to check another's work thoroughly." I tried to keep the frustration out of my voice, but telepathic links ruin any attempt at hiding one's feelings. The petting stopped and I found my muzzle rudely shoved off O'Meara's lap.

"Oh, quiet, you. I don't see you spending much time study-ing the gravimetric parameters of space, either. Those books make us both cross-eyed. I'm a fire magus; bending space ain't something I've ever tried to learn before, and Picitrix, the House that actually writes books on this stuff, treats us like cigarette burns on a coffee table. Grace and Alice being the sole exceptions."

"I didn't say-" I started to object, but O'Meara clamped her hand around my muzzle.

"I know you really want to rework the raw deal familiars get, Thomas. But we still don't have the basics grasped on how bonds work. With time, knowledge and tass, we can do anything. So they say. Right now, we've just got tass. We can't recreate Mr. Bitey without some serious learning and some tutelage. We're stumbling around in the dark. Cherri was right about that. We need time. Recruit a proper Cabal, preferably somebody connected to a plane that lends itself to bonding work."

"There ain't no magi who space bending comes easy to," Rudy said, his voice muffled by the cashew in his cheek. "A plane is a place that embodies a concept or an energy type, or it's simply a reality. Bonds and portals are all manipulating those places. It's never easy. Sometimes a magus will have their anchor in a plane with wildly different rules about how things move, but that's real rare. Oric developed his talent working with one of, I think, three different magi who had a knack for it."

"Where are they now?"

"Dead or gone. It's tough to tell with those types. They pop in and out of magi social circles and then just stop showing up. Everyone assumes they finally got themselves into a reality they couldn't get away from. Course, you all know who was the best at the whole twisting space thing?"

"Who?" O'Meara and I asked simultaneously.

"Archibald." Rudy grinned.

"Archibald had a conceptual plane? But Scrags dribbled acid as his knack," I said. Familiars who stayed bonded to a magus for ten to twenty years often developed a knack, a single ability drawn from their magus's anchor plane.

"Yeah, Archibald's anchor was to a reality that embodied poison. Nobody expected him to be much more than a battle magus when he was younger. But after a hundred years he apparently got real tired of watching people's bones turn to jelly. He didn't use his anchor much after that. Focused more on how to ascend from our reality. He dreamed of the entire world awakening to our precarious existence. He got the manifest destiny bug real hard. Wanted humankind to expand into other realities. Very noble, but it's a dangerous universe out there and all that." Rudy did jazz hands for emphasis.

"That don't help, Rudy, unless that portal trick you pulled back in Grantsville can go through time, too. Archibald's entire library is in the belly of a Dragon." I shivered, remembering the sensation of being reassembled and being semi-conscious for almost the entire process.

A sly look entered Rudy's eye as he itched an ear. "A Dragon that you probably still have a few threads of connection to, I bet. With a little effort I bet you could find it again. Maybe if you're nice, feed it a few treats, you could turn our insurance policy into something a bit more than the empty threat it is?" Rudy's tail whipped behind him, his eyes narrowed as he clapped his paws together. "What does a Dragon want? Maybe it likes the taste of Owls?"

O'Meara and my thoughts meshed together. "Absolutely, one hundred percent no, and never," We said as one.

Rudy flinched, "Woah, total mind meld, no? Aaah, it was just an idea. But why?"

O'Meara and I gave each other the side eye and pulled back into our respective heads. I focused on Rudy's question. "Rudy, that Dragon wants nothing to do with this reality, it's as far away as it can be right now. There is nothing we can do to bring it to our earth, or any earth, for that matter. It's hunting deep in the black."

Rudy cocked his head at me. "You... know that. Don'tcha?"

I blinked. "I..." My voice faded out as I probed my internal thoughts, searching for where those words had come from. I didn't find the source, but they rang with a certainty that felt like a foundation of bedrock. "I do. That Dragon is never coming back here. Not if it has a choice, and it will fight very hard against anything that attempts to take away its choice in the matter."

I breathed out and gave a small huff. "Let's talk about something else." I recollected my thoughts from the scattered winds and shook my head. "Right, so..."

A phone rang, a high pitched doodley dee song. I looked to Rudy, whose phone was sitting on the seat next to him, blank and silent. Instead, O'Meara dug around in her satchel and pulled out a black phone that buzzed in her hand. Glancing at the screen, I felt her surprise dance down the link at the words Riona Calling. She thumbed the button and put it on her thigh.

"O'Meara here," she said with all the tact of an armored tank.

"Hey, hots! You and Kitty T busy at the moment?"

O'Meara snatched the phone up and pressed it to her ear lightning fast, but still slower than the blush that spread across her face. "Riona, I'm with the boys."

"Kitty T? Hots!" Rudy giggled so hard he fell over, the impact shot the cashew out of his cheek pouch and into the air. It only made him laugh harder.

O'Meara's dagger-like glare suggested that I not say anything further. Instead, I pushed my way into her head to listen in.

"Oops, sorry, Mistress O'Meara." You could hear the wink in Riona's voice. "Hi, Thomas! Tack says hello, too." Of all the Blackwings, it had been Riona we'd seen the most of over the months since acquiring the casino, and the only one with any interest in helping O'Meara figure out how bonds work.

"Listen, I got an idea about those Fey chains I really want to try."

O'Meara peered through the tinted windows, mentally plotting out where we were. "Don't talk about it over the phone. We're nearby, though. Mind if we pop by for a visit?"

"Uh—" The line went dead silent, muted for several seconds before the static outside Riona's voice returned. "That's cool. Gimme a few minutes to set the stage, right?"

"We'll be there in about five. Maybe ten," O'Meara said as I pawed at the intercom button. A chime rang in the front of the limo, barely audible to my ears. The mirrored window that separated the passengers from the cab rolled down, revealing the profile of one of the Capy brothers as he peered at us with a brown eye. The other brother would be down below, operating the pedals. Gnome-style driving.

"Yes, sirs?" The capy asked, probably Henry, his lisp stretching the word out into a whistle.

"We need to swing by House Morgana, please," I said.

"Certainly, sirs. Be our pleasure." The window rolled back up as O'Meara and Riona wrapped up.

4

To everyone's surprise, the Capy brothers had us to House Morgana's Tower within five minutes.

House Morgana has only one commonality. All of its Magi are women. There are no rules against male magi visiting the house or even working for them. And yet in the dozens of times I've gone in and out of the building, I could count the number of two legged men I'd seen on the tower's stairway on a single paw. I wouldn't need all the digits.

As I exited the limo, I noticed that the count went up by one. I probably wouldn't have done any more than that, but he froze, like a rabbit caught in the open, one foot hanging over the next down step. This isn't terribly unusual, people are often startled when a mountain lion steps out of a limo. Still, the pause drew my predatory eye and the self-satisfied smile that broke across his stern face set off alarm bells. I have a fairly good head for names and faces, but this man, tan with a chin a rodent could bungee jump from, and wearing a shiny black leather suit, wasn't someone I'd easily forget. A refugee from the dimension of 90's rock.

I don't know him, either. My attention to him had drawn O'Meara's. *Is he a magus?*

Dunno, I thought. In order to tell, I'd have to drop the majority of my wards.

He continued down toward me, swaying as drunkard might, before stopping in front of me. "Do I know you?" I hazarded.

"No." He made the word sound like its opposite as his eyes traveled along the length of my back and wobbled as they followed the lash of my tail. "But I have to thank you anyway."

"Thank me for what?" The only folks who generally thanked me were the Grantsville refugees, and as most had been converted into employees over the last six months, that gratitude had transitioned into grumblings that I didn't pay them enough.

"For being you. And doing what you do. You're so much better this way. Makes it all worth it." As he talked his eyes slid off me, to somewhere else. He stepped around me. "See ya around, Kitty. Gotta go now." Turning, he began to walk down the sidewalk, wobbling slightly as he placed one foot in front of the other as if he walked an invisible tightrope. To top it off, he began to hum.

He disappeared into the thick current of tourists that wandered Vegas' second strip, blissfully unaware that any memory of it would be pulled from them the moment they left the city's limits.

"Weeeeirdo," Rudy said.

"You know him?" O'Meara whispered.

"Nope! Never seen him before. Probably some Morgana magus' fling or toy. Come on, you two. We're famous now. Stuff like this happens when you're famous." Rudy bounced up and down on my back.

"Rudy, I think the proper term is INfamous," O'Meara said as I tried to shake off a nagging sense of familiarity with the strange man. After glancing in the direction he went in one last time, I headed into the tower.

O'Meara and Rudy argued over the nature of our fame up to the 11th floor, where the Blackwings' suite was located.

A scrabble of claws against hardwood floors greeted me as I stepped up to the door. "Thomas!" I heard my name shouted through the wooden barrier as I listened to the scrape-clicking of several locks being undone.

"That was fast!" Riona exclaimed as she threw the door open, displaying a wide smile almost brighter than her rainbow-colored hair that had a plaid pattern twisting through two long pigtails. Her clothing was comparatively mundane, blue jeans with a black t-shirt commanding the viewer to scream. "Hold on, Tack. Let them all get inside," she said as she stepped aside, simultaneously herding her familiar, a large German Shepherd whose tail might be approaching light speed, away from our path into the room.

"So, what's my name?" Rudy asked as the door swung closed behind us.

If Riona deigned to answer him, I missed it. Instead, Tack bounded around his magus and stomped on the floor directly in front of me, growling in challenge. Disabling my wards so they wouldn't punt him across the room, I batted at his nose. He swiftly ducked my paw and charged me, driving his head into my shoulder, hard. I landed on my side, and instinct rolled me back up to my feet with an angry hiss. "What the hell was that?" I hissed.

Tack's collar glowed yellow with kinetic energies as he grinned doggedly. "Um, evening the odds. Morie's not here and you're twice my size. S-So there." He glanced up at Riona, who nodded her support. I had one guess where this idea came from.

"Sooo," I growled. "You have strength equal to mine with that little toy?" To be fair, I'm nearly four times Tack's size, but I'm a cat and I'm not interested in fair fights.

"Uh – Maybe more." He nodded to himself. "I'm gonna get ya this time." He assumed that universal play posture that dogs do, bowed down, front paws splayed out.

Thomas, don't hurt him, O'Meara warned.

"Think so?" I allowed myself to grin as I settled back into a pounce-launching stance.

"C-Come and get it, cat!"

I launched. He dodged to the side. Smart, but I hadn't aimed for him. I sailed over him, hit the wall behind him with all four paws and leaped down at him. I struck him mid-turn, wrapping my forelegs around his torso, and biting down on the scruff of his neck.

"Hey!" He yelped as my weight slammed him into the ground.

"Gotcha, dog!" I declared, springing off him and back onto my feet.

"Stupid cat!" He growled and charged again. The tussle began in earnest. Riona's focus did make Tack much stronger, but it didn't increase his mass, so it still wasn't much of a contest. Till I got tired. Then Tack managed to get his teeth around my throat. The claws came out.

"Alright! You're done!" A fist seized the scruff of my neck and hauled me into the air. "Fun ends if somebody has to wear a cone collar." I hastily resheathed my claws.

"I – waaa." My tongue hung too far out of my mouth for me to complete the words.

"Take a break before your brain melts." O'Meara let me go and I melted against the cool floor as the adrenaline ebbed. Tack flopped down next to me, tongue lolling out of the side of his mouth. His stupid dog tail still softly thumping against the floor boards.

"Wow. It kinda looks like something exploded in here." Rudy said with a whistle of admiration.

"Tack and I can fix the couch, but that TV's a loss. I hope he remembers the Netflix passwords, because I don't." Riona said. "When did Thomas take up parkour?"

"If you had to deal with half the paperwork we do, you'd be running up the walls too," O'Meara chuckled. I lifted up my head to see what they were talking about and stared. The Blackwings common area appeared to have been hit by a tornado. Every piece of furniture had been overturned, the couch sagged, white fluff bleeding from numerous gashes in the black leather. The communal TV had tipped forward off of its undersized stand and cracked. "Wow," I said. "I-"

Don't apologize, O'Meara snapped in my head. *They boosted Tack. He's very lucky you didn't hurt him.*

I had to chuckle, answering her with an image of a huge fiery momma bear. In real space, I finished my sentence, "-had a good work out." Then I let my chin fall back down to the floor with a soft thump, pressing my ear against the cool tile. Most other magi and familiar pairings would probably do a cooling spell at this point, but when you're bonded to a fire Magus, you have to give up on magical air conditioning.

Tack, for his part, seemed totally unabashed by the destruction we'd wrought, and somehow managed to exude a bit of pride despite the awkward angle of his tongue. Little brat probably thought he'd won, conveniently forgetting that half dozen times I'd pinned him and then let him go. Dogs... so dumb sometimes.

"Let's get them some water," Riona suggested.

O'Meara followed her into the kitchen and I listened via the mental link. "So, you lured us here with some sort of idea for the new bond we're working on. Or was that just an excuse for Tack to try his new toy?" Rudy bounced over to the kitchen doorway, listening out of direct sight of the magi.

"They both needed a good romp. With the rest of the Blackwings in Italy for a week, Tack's been a bit of a lump."

Tack gave a snort at that but didn't move as his magus filled two bowls with water. "But yeah, I got an idea that might help."

"They left you here? Again?" O'Meara opened the fridge and handed Riona a tray of ice cubes.

The punky magus shrugged before cracking the tray and putting a few cubes in each bowl. "Diplomatic thingie, murderers not invited." The ice crackled as her face hardened. "They can leave us behind anytime. It's the only way we can work on other projects. I've got an actual gig tomorrow."

Tack whined, "And I'm not allowed to come."

"You show up with me and everybody knows I'm a magus, and once they figure that out, it's all plastic smiles and false cheers. That's the worst. I'll take boos over that." Riona and O'Meara snagged a bowl each and carried them out to their respective familiars.

"I guess we're off the hook then, too." O'Meara placed the water down in front of me and I lapped at it gratefully.

"Rudy could come. Nobody would even notice him pretending to be stealthy and all," Riona said.

"Hey my ears are still ringing from the last time I listened to one of your 'songs,'" Rudy quipped, jumping up on the back of the couch as the two woman drifted toward it.

Riona rolled her eyes. "How was I to know you were inside the robot? Besides, it's not like I do death metal."

"Are ya telling me you ain't at least as loud as your hair?" Rudy asked.

"Oh she is sooo much louder than her hair." Tack said before Riona could protest, her pale skin flushing pink.

"Sooo, that idea I had," Riona said as the laughter began to subside.

"Aaaw yeah, lay this brilliance on us, Lady Loud." The rest of us stilled to silence.

Riona looked around. "I really hope you haven't thought about this before or I'm going to feel very silly."

"Stop stallin'!" Rudy crunched a cashew.

"Here's the show, then." Riona took a breath. "We've all been stuck on figuring how a familiar bond works. You got this grand scheme of making the TAU irrelevant, but you can't do anything until you create a new bond type. Till you can, the Freelancers are pipe dreams and you two are a wealthy but essentially Houseless magus and familiar pair."

"Yeaah," I ventured.

"But, if you had a way to make the sort of bond you want now; you could get magi used to the idea of independent familiars," Riona gushed.

"We have a way, technically. Fey chains," O'Meara said.

She grinned. "But nobody will use Fey chains because of the fragility."

"That, and it still hurts like a gaping wound when you break a Fey chain bond," Rudy said between nibbles.

"It's not that bad, so long as you break it gently," O'Meara said.

"But it's much closer than what you want, isn't it? With the amount of tass you have access to for modifying the existing Fey chains, you could ward them against physical damage, making them much tougher to break. You could do that. Right, O'Mistress of Wards?"

"Yeeesss," O'Meara said, both of us thinking furiously. I'd originally made it my goal to acquire as many Fey chains as I could get my paws on.

Riona tapped a focus on her wrist and an acoustic guitar appeared on her lap with a flash of green. "I think a lot about that night in the desert, the peace of that song and the silver threads."

"But I didn't do that," I protested, remembering how a strange bird had been spun to life from the outpouring of the Blackwings' emotion as they reconciled. "That was something inherent to that plane."

"Someone told me that the secret of making magic isn't just power, it's inspiration." She began to play and magic glittered along the strings. Her aura didn't swell with light, Tack's did.

The song had no sound, but O'Meara and I heard it, softly plinking through our minds, as a sensation of calm steadied our breathing into each other. I searched for the source in my head, and at first I thought it was through the bond itself, but instead I found it below that, burbling forth like a happy spring along the silver strands. Those very threads that Lansky had fed on six months ago, the natural bonds of relationships. Her song played out directly on the silver threads that bound us together.

"Stop it," Rudy sniffed, blinking rapidly as he clutched his tail. "Stop playing!"

Riona stopped, and that feeling of calm began to lessen. "What's wrong?"

"Uncooked cashews, don't screw around with those!" Rudy sniffled. "At least not mine!" he said, his voice gaining strength.

"It's just a song," Riona said, her tone a trifle defensive. "It can't change anything."

"It's stirring up my memories!" Rudy tapped his head as if it were a shaken up coke can.

"That is what music does." O'Meara smiled, her mind already pivoting to practical uses. "So, could that be recorded? Soothe the soul as a Fey chain bond is broken?"

"With a little tass, I could rig something up. Plus a bit extra for my troubles." Her eyes glittered. Her House didn't give her any tass for her own projects, since she was on a parole of sorts.

O'Meara nodded, a grin spreading on both our faces. "This could work."

"Sure, we don't have permission to start up the freelancing biz, but it's not like the council has forbidden us," I echoed O'Meara thoughts. "Nobody will object to a pilot program."

"Except Oric," Rudy grumbled. "Possibly violently."

"And if he does, you can blow him up," I quipped.

Rudy brightened immediately. "I can? Oh! Of course I can!"

5

HOLD IT. HOLD RIGHT there! O'Meara strained as she channeled power into an intricate network of spells we'd spent the last two days constructing, or rather, constructing and then exploding.

My brain felt like mush as I struggled to keep the design of the spell in my head. In reality, all magi and their familiars were physically wired together, it's simply that the wire existed fourth-dimensionally. Normal bonds were incredibly tough, far tougher than the being on either end. Most spells, even if they got a hold of the bond, would be attempting to saw through a steel cable with a pocket knife. A Fey chain's bond had the comparative tensile strength of a silk thread. In addition to being physically vulnerable to say, a werewolf snapping the chain, a magus with a passing familiarity with space magic (aka not us) could snap it with the same ease as O'Meara could crisp a critter.

To protect the thing, we had to make a transdimensional slinky, armor it, and then paint it with camouflage. It would never be as tough as a natural bond but unlike them, it would bite back.

If we could get the dang ward to hold together. I'd never seen a spell with so much tension in it. O'Meara capped it off and the pressure on my head redoubled. The spell tried to jerk away, but I dug my mental claws into my anchor and held on. *Hurry!* I pleaded to O'Meara as she shifted herself from a power conduit to a needle and thread, sewing together all the seams on the spell that threatened to burst.

"Hey, Thomas!" Rudy's voice leapt through the void of my concentration.

"Not now, Rudy!" I said through the side of my muzzle. My jaw began to ache from the strain of clenching it. In my head, I had the spell held in my teeth.

"Your girlfriend's here. You're thirty minutes late!" Rudy sing-songed.

"Girlfriend!?" My concentration wobbled. The spell slipped in my hold. "What girlfriend!?"

Thomas! O'Meara scolded. *We've almost got it this time! Don't you dare let go!*

"Ya know the really big one that you reeeeeally don't want to see angry. S- something. Sasha? Sarah."

"Ah crud! Shina's here!" I swore as my stomach flooded with panicking butterflies. Shina was on the do-not-piss-off list, for multiple reasons.

"If I have to do this spell again, I'm going to light both your tails on fire! Tell her five more minutes, Rudy!" O'Meara resumed bending the spell into position. Almost there.

"Not unless you let me feed her firecrackers. I can hear her stomach rumbling."

"Order her something from the kitchen, then." I said as my body began to shake.

"Dude, it's Wednesday, all we got for cats is tofu and I'm not serving Shina tofurkey. She'd eat the staff."

"For the record..." O'Meara tied off half of the spell. "I told both of you that meatless Wednesdays were a bad idea."

"You're lucky we negotiated it down to only one day," I grumbled, taking the lead from O'Meara on the spell stitching. "They threatened to sue for a hostile workplace environment because they were on the menu. Rudy, Go up to the office. I have a stack of burgers under a time ward."

Rudy's eyes narrowed as his voice pitched to indignant squeak. "You have a time ward?"

"It's in the mini fridge of my office."

"This I gotta see." Rudy scampered off, a gray streak in my peripheral vision.

I thought we agreed not to tell him about that, O'Meara huffed, but we focused on finishing the spell instead of arguing further. Five minutes later, we both collapsed to the floor, every muscle in our bodies screaming in relief as the weight of the magic disappeared. The Fey chain that lay in the circle between us looked no different, a thin simple chain with a collar on each end, but to my eyes, its thin purple line was now sheathed in golden scales that contained their elemental reprisals. A dangerous sculpture forged of neon colors.

"Not bad, not bad at all." O'Meara studied it via my vision. I had to agree as a proud purr poured out from my throat. While I would never call the process of spellcraft pleasant, there was something satisfying about the end result.

I got a brief pet and hug from O'Meara before she patted my rump and said, "Alright, go see what your girlfriend is hawking today."

"Don't you start." I would have growled had I not been angling for an ear scritch.

"I know what you think every time you see her."

"That's she's big?" I ventured.

"Mmmhmmm and..." she murmured, indulging the itch right next to my ear.

"She's big in a nice way." I pulled away, closing the link before she could tease me further. "Why don't you try to rustle up some volunteers to test this thing."

"Ugh."

"Oh finally have time to see me, little cat?" Shina said as I slinked into my office. The only sign of my emergency burger stash was a faint scent of meat in the air.

"Sorry, got tied up working on a project." I hopped up on the chair. "I hope you made yourself cooo-"I looked up to see all of Shina and my brain locked up in mid-sentence. She's a lion, the African kind, but that doesn't do it justice. Lions you see in the zoo generally laze around all day. Take a depressed zoo lion and feed her Captain America's super soldier serum, that's Shina. Her skin ripples over moving tectonic plates of muscles whenever she moves. So to see her, belly up, sprawled across the width of my office, tufted tail softly beating against the wall like a house cat in a sunbeam, well every part of me had to pause to appreciate the view. I fletched, pulling her scent in and tasting it against the roof of my mouth. Her vibrant musk screamed her health while whispering of loneliness and so much more that I couldn't quite grasp. The scent language of cougars and lions didn't quite meet up. With the only other intelligent cougar in the world currently being imprisoned for murder by the council of Merlins, my mind was more than willing to look beyond species.

"Quite comfortable, little lion. Heated floors are a very nice touch. Your office is full of nice little touches. Just like you." She rolled onto her side, deliberately rubbing the side of her muzzle against the floor. Spreading her scent, marking the space as hers. The staff would have to scrub down the entire office with nature's miracle or anyone with a better than human nose was going to get the wrong idea about my relationship with her.

"Well..." I swallowed, trying to flush her from my mouth, but it made no difference. "Glad you weren't too inconvenienced."

"You should make it up to me." She pushed herself up into a sitting position, her golden eyes meeting mine on the same level despite the fact that I sat on an ottoman behind the desk.

"My very busy schedule is all out of whack today because of you." I'm not sure how a maw that big can produce a small mischievous smirk, but Shina managed it.

"Uh huh." I tried to act casual, opening my laptop by hooking a lower fang in the groove that separated the keyboard from the screen, getting another snoutful of her scent as I did so. She had definitely marked my desk directly. "Important naps and such, I'm sure," I said, annoyance at her territorial encroachment beginning to overcome her charms.

"Sounds like you need more shut eye, Thomas. Are you trying to keep human hours? You're cranky."

I gave a hint of a warning growl. O'Meara and I had taken a short nap in the middle of last night, but that had been it. Extending the force hands from my anklets, I pretended to look up what exact reason Shina had come. "Right, so what sort of wonder have you brought me today?"

House Hermes needed tass so badly that they had been selling non-essential magical artifacts to anyone with ears to hear the sales pitch. Once we had the casino, I had to fend off six of their agents at a time. I got very good at saying no. That is, very good at saying no to everyone but Shina. A small yellow purse lay next to her on the floor which she took in her mouth and placed on my desk with a faint metallic jangle. I reached for it.

"I had to do a lot of digging to find that. It spent nearly two hundred years in a vampire's sock drawer." Shina's eyes glittered with eagerness.

Taking the bag with my force hands, I shook it gingerly until the contents fell out. A thin chain with two collars lay in front of me. The magical patterns along its length are an exact duplicate of the object I just spent all night warding. A Fey chain. It would be our third. We had two so far, but with three, something special could happen. Three felt like the smallest number we needed to make the freelance familiars finally work. No force on earth could have prevented me from licking my chops at that moment.

I reached out my paw for the chain. "Name your price." But a paw twice the size of my own slapped down, covering it entirely. Looking up, I found her eyes, still laughing.

"Fredrick wants a thousand groat," She said.

"Done," I agreed, far too quickly. The paw didn't budge. It took me a few moments to figure out what she waited for. "And what does Shina want?"

"I want you to come hunting with me. On the savannah of Shangra-la." That little smirk of triumph came back.

My imagination took flight, seeing us stalking deer shoulder to shoulder through the crisp foliage, dragging kills up into trees to share. The freedom of the hunt, the simplicity, it tugged hard, and I batted it away. Chiding my own imagination, honesty, hunting shoulder to shoulder with Shina? It would be more shoulder to elbow. Plus, there were no trees in a savannah. Instead of letting my pent up meat brain romp, a hunting trip with her would only stress me further. Besides, "I'm not going anywhere unbonded," I told her.

"O'Meara is welcome to join us. Not like I can be unbonded at all. It's safe. I'd die before I let a guest of mine come to harm. You must see what I'm trying to save, Thomas. Shangra-la is so much more than a stronghold of House Hermes. It's bigger than that. You need to see it." A desperate shine coated her eyes. "Don't you want to see it?"

"Of course I do! Look, O'Meara and I are the only magi we have protecting this casino. We could maybe slip away for a day," I offered.

"That's not a hunting trip, that's a drive through a game park," she growled.

"Shina, I'd love to go, but if I'm going to leave for that period of time I need more magi willing to fight for the MGM, and to get that I need more familiars and more Fey chains," I said, my own ears folded half back.

"Basing your expansion on the number of Atlantean artifacts you can acquire is foolish. And besides, don't you have
a hundred barnyard animals ready to be bonded?" Her tail
flicked, a smug movement.

"And how many apprentices does House Hermes have who
are overdue for their familiars?" I asked.

She swayed side to side in a leonine equivalent of a shrug.
"Not my problem. I have enough of my own without dealing
with apprentices."

I sighed. "I can give you a day, Shina, and I'm going to be a
nervous wreck being gone for that long."

"You're letting Oric put you in a box. I want a week," she
countered with a snarl.

I snarled right back. "And when I can get away, I'll give it to
you. But I can't say when, I have to put Oric in a box first. The
date gets closer now that I have that chain."

A growl rolled forth from her fangs, an engine of threat
that could rip me in two. "If you won't take my favor, it's four
thousand groat, little half lion."

I challenged her with a rolling scream-hiss which sounds a
bit like two alley cats in a fight to the death. Snagging a thread
of power from O'Meara, I lit my hackles on fire for an extra
flair. "Fifteen hundred!"

She roared, showing me all those glorious teeth, "Thir-
ty-five hundred! You thick-skulled male! Any feline in Vegas
would kill for a week's hunting with me."

I couldn't compete with the roar so I just pinned my ears
back and held my ground. Any more heat and I might trigger
the sprinkler system. "Two grand! Typically you start with
dinner and a movie, not come to my private island for safari."

"Oric will give me two grand for it. Three thousand. Why
start small as you are, little lion? Besides, I hate popcorn! It
gets stuck in my teeth!" she shouted.

"Twenty-five hundred groat and no more!" I hissed back at
her. "And who said anything about popcorn? There's a theater

downtown where you can get deep fried mice. And I start small because the last cat I wanted to date was Feather, and everyone knows how that went down."

"Fine!" She lifted her nose into the air, assuming a regal pose and sliding the Fey chain across the desk at me. "I pick the movie."

I stopped the chain with a paw and immediately started to groom it. "Fine! I have no idea what's playing anyway."

"Seven tomorrow at Graboli's. Since you'll want to go to the Auction tonight," she said as she continued to pretend to study the ceiling.

"Hrrrm?" I exaggerated a shake to clear my head. I had not known about an auction tonight. Only one organization would have an auction and not invite me nowadays. The TAU.

Dammit. "I'll be there," I told her.

She looked at me with a smug smile. "See you there, little lion," and bumped her nose to mine.

I watched her leave, tail swinging, as O'Meara burst into laughter on the other side of the link. Reaching for the flaming mane had meant letting my magus in.

Hate to break it to you, Thomas, but she is only interested in you because we're rich, O'Meara mentally elbowed me.

Keeping on her good side is good politics, I thought back. *And, she's fun.*

Only cats would declare that conversation fun. She still chuckled. *Anyway, let me get Rudy. We have some planning to do.*

6

"I KNOWS TROUBLE AND you reek of it, cat," the black bear said as he gazed down at me over his graying muzzle. He stood on his hind-legs, forelimbs braced against a podium on which held the guest list. "Members only," he rumbled.

"We are House Freelance. We have a right to watch the proceedings, Bernard," O'Meara said smoothly. She stood next to me, in a flowing crimson dress long enough to hide the ass-kicking boots on her feet.

"I could go get Rudy. He's a member," I offered innocently. The bear, Bernard, fixed me with a glare that told me he knew the rodent personally. Never seen an ursine with an eye twitch before. I might be trouble, but Rudy is trouble crystallized. He'd been surprisingly amenable to staying behind, declaring, "Just call if you need me! I'll make you an extraction zone in two seconds flat." The way his black eyes glittered left no doubt on the method of extraction he preferred.

"You're lucky Oric isn't here. Don't make me call him," the bear grumbled and jerked his head through the double doorway. Curiously, his gaze remained fixed on O'Meara, not me.

O'Meara bit back a nervous chuckle, but let it flow through the link. You *might be on Oric's naughty list, but I'm the boogie man to familiars.* Her thoughts carried the sharp tang of guilt as we stepped through the doorway into the ballroom. A rush of sound met my ears as the door opened into a crowd of colorful people and familiars. Pressing my tongue to the roof of my mouth, I sorted through the scents as O'Meara sized up the gathering and identified escape routes. I found Shina's scent right away, although neither of us saw her. More familiar scents mingled on the air-conditioned currents. Veronica and Gus, along with her Archmagus Morrian, yet also Dominicus, the Hermes Archmagus. Was the entire council in here?

I'm counting about thirty magi and familiars, O'Meara thought as she watched the majority of the magi edge away from us. The room was divided in two parts. The area near the door, where most mingled, was a bar serving drinks and waitstaff of various sizes wove through the crowd, bearing smiles and hors d'oeuvres. In the other half, a small stage faced a phalanx of chairs. A whisper-thin woman whose head barely reached my shoulder thrust a silver platter at my nose. "Bacon-wrapped scallop, sir?" Her voice dripped sweetness as she offered one of the morsels to me on the end of a stick.

"Sure," I answered, the scallop thrust closer, and I pulled it off the stick with my teeth. Swallowing, I opened my mouth to say thank you, but she had already moved on, somehow skating toward a cluster of house cats surrounding a silver furred main coon. The plainness of the room struck me as odd. Usually Vegas magi surrounded themselves with opulence and clear magical displays of wealth. Yet, if you took out the inhabitants, this appeared to be little more than a corporate meeting of some sort.

"Hey Thomas. How you been?" A familiar voice called out and Gus broke free of the sea of gowns and robes to trot towards us.

"Good, Gus. The Blackwings done anything interesting lately?" I asked as he approached, but the small black cat didn't stop at the normal polite distance. Instead, he continued past my front paws and circled to my haunch and leaned against it, nearly panting. "Something wrong, Gus?" I asked.

"Naw. Perfectly fine. Good to see a friendly face or muzzle in here, ya know." Even as he talked, he peeked around my back and I heard him give a mew of distress as his tail puffed. "Lord Almighty, here they come."

I turned to follow his nose to find pure trouble heading my way. The part of that trouble that contained Jowls was bad enough, but matching him step for step was a green eyed calico, Esmeralda, Madam Morrian's familiar. Why would Jowls be palling around with an Archmagus' familiar?

This doesn't look like my scene, O'Meara thought, stepping out towards the bar. *Too many tails to step on.*

Some help you are, I grumble-thought back as the two cats stepped toward me, Jowls lightly supporting Esmeralda with a shoulder.

"Well, well, well. This is the last cat I would have expected to see here," Jowls said. "Haven't you had enough of venturing into the lion's den? Planning to tweak his tail feathers?" He chuckled with amusement, no trace of his earlier desperation anywhere in his body, all orangey warm charm.

Esmeralda said nothing but opened her mouth in a scenting grimace. Her glossy fur gave her an almost kitten-like aura, but it did not match her eyes which, while bright and green, had a sunken look to them, as if they were far too heavy for her skull. Those ancient eyes looked directly through my rump at Gus.

"Not planning on tweaking tail feathers tonight," I said, mostly meaning it.

"Liar." Esmeralda's voice creaked as if rusty and she cleared her throat, her eyes glancing up at me before returning to the cowering Gus.

"Haha, Subtle as an arrow. That's Esmeralda," Jowls said.

"He will ask me for a favor soon. Once he figures out precisely what to ask. Also the answer is still no to your question, Jowls."

The orange tom's jovial mask fell. "I-I didn't..."

"Don't need to."

Jowls covered up his mortification by thrusting his nose into the air, but he couldn't hide the fact that his tail looked like a fuzzy baseball bat. "Well, I'd never work for a Morgana magus anyway," he exclaimed and stomped off into the sea of robes.

"Liar," Esmeralda sat, her long tail curling in front of her paws. "Come out, Gus. We are not done."

I felt the little cat gulp and he timidly poked his head around my rear to stare at the ancient calico. My curiosity as to what Gus had stepped in this time stopped me from intervening.

"I don't haveta do what you say. You're not my magus," Gus said, hiding behind the base of my tail.

"You don't have to do what Veronica says, either," I butted in. "No matter what she expects."

"Easy for you to say Thomas. You're a friggin' mountain lion," Gus grumbled.

"True. On many levels. You are not Thomas and to your fortune, will never be him," she said. I started to protest, but her eyes flashed a warning. "Now come. I will not have a member of House Morgana afraid of his own shadow. Veronica deserves a..." she glanced at me, "partner who does not telegraph weakness."

Veronica's false smile flashed in through the link with O'Meara. Idle chatter flowed from her lips. Over her shoulder, I saw my half folded ears. She wouldn't be swooping in to save Gus from Esmeralda as he bared his tiny fangs at her.

"I am not weak! I train every day. Magically and physically. Verony and me will wipe the floor with anyone." As if to prove it, he stepped— well, more climbed—over my tail, puffing strand of hair on his body. Which gave him even more of a stuffed-kitten look than before. I swallowed back a snicker.

"Liar," she said, licking her paw in a dismissive gesture. "You rudely ran away from Jowls. He's unbonded. Harmless."

"He was gonna bugger me!" Gus hissed, then he cast me a pleading look. "You know what that cat did! He's evil. He ground my home into hamburger. I'm not gonna take that!"

"Liar." Her gaze bore into the small cat. Gus looked down at his paws.

"Actually, that last part's all true," I said. "Jowls paraded himself into evil territory pretty solidly."

"We are all predators. Compassion is the responsibility of the magus, not the familiar," she said. "That isn't the reason you ran."

"He loomed." Gus sulked. "I hate it when people loom." With a deep sigh, he moved to sit beside her. His head barely reached her shoulder, and her long multicolored tail formed a half circle on the floor around him.

"Good." Rewarding Gus a gentle prod with her nose. "Now. You're going to go talk to Shina and you're not going to run away."

"The lion?" He squeaked.

"Familiars gossip, especially between rival Houses. It's part of our duties. If you run away, you'd embarrass Veronica."

"But— If I never."

In an eye-blink, Esmeralda had seized Gus by the scruff of his neck and lifted him from the floor. His eyes went huge as the paralytic reflex made his entire body sag in her jaws. After a second, she dropped him. "If you must fear... fear me," she whispered so low that I barely caught it. "Now get up."

Distantly, I saw Veronica still chatting pleasantly with O'Meara. The smile even more fixed, worry etching into the folds around her eyes.

Gus stayed down until his eyes refocused. Then he stood up, shook himself and stomped off toward the back of the room, where the chairs were set up.

He disappeared into the forest of dresses, robes, and legs. I rose to follow, because no way I wanted to miss this, but Esmeralda's gaze settled on me like a leaden weight. "Yes?" I ventured. "Is there some lesson for life you want to teach me as well?"

"Many." She said. "But you are not Morgana. Although you should consider joining us."

"I've already got a House," I said with caution.

"Liar. A House is more than a legal loophole. Independence is expensive. Your wealth will be under siege constantly. How can you change the world if you spend all your time clinging to what you have?"

That statement hit pretty close to home for someone I'd just met. I stared off with a thoughtful expression while I took a closer look at her with my magical sight. I saw nothing at first, before noting the faintest glimmer of power in her plain leather collar. My own wards prevented me from getting a better look. Certainly didn't see any trace of mind magics. "The services of House Freelance need to be available to all Houses," I said with a huff.

"I haven't seen you offer to rent yourself out recently and there are no fliers on the chairs." Esmeralda lifted herself from the floor and together we began to walk toward the stage.

Giving her a hint of a smile. "I'm not planning on making any trouble tonight. I've never been to one of these events before."

The magi parted for us, revealing the show in all its shabby glory as well as Shina and Gus. Shina lay in front of the stage, positioned like a sphinx, as Gus sat six inches from her paws, hackles up, tail poofed, but holding his ground. Positioned on the stage were three animals. Two sat within white circles. A golden retriever cocked his head at the pair, ears perked, while a gray tabby kept his eyes averted from the lion, idly clawing at the vinyl flooring. The third contestant on this sell-your-life show apparently couldn't be trusted to stay within a circle and had been placed in a dog crate. A long shape huddled under a thin blanket, a weasel of some type stared balefully out at the scene surrounding her.

"In Shangra-la, we don't use cars. Force chariots are much simpler. No hands required and no nasty oil leaking all over the place like my last Jeep," Shina told Gus.

"Oh that's so... interesting. About Shangra-la, I mean. Wait, you had a jeep? When? The old jeeps were great!" Gus's eyes gained back a bit of their amber shine as he focused on his one love on this earth, cars.

Shina looked up to stare at the pitted white drop ceiling thoughtfully. "Would have been 1956 or so."

"That would make it a real classic! Simple to maintain one of those. You could with paws and teeth I bet. Do you still have it?" Gus leaned toward her eagerly.

Shina wrinkled her muzzle in disgust. "Touch a car's innards with your teeth? Oh yuck. Blech. Haven't you ever stepped in oil and tasted it when you go to groom?" Turning her head, she feigned a retch. And saw me. "Thomas! You came." She grinned and stood abruptly. Gus scrambled backwards to get out of her way, spine arching in a threat display, but Shina gave his antics no notice. In three steps, she loomed up in front of me and thrust her forehead into mine with enough force that a bystander probably heard a clunk. We exchanged scents in a less than formal manner as she broadcast a possessive purr-growl.

"Hey, hey, now. I'm not your territory marker, lay off a bit," I murmured.

"I'm big, bold and beautiful. You love it," she said as she settled next to me.

"And now everyone in the room knows of your alliance," Esmeralda sniffed, she had circled around to my other side.

"My time away from Shangra-la is limited. Thomas is worth investing some of it in," Shina said, purposely laying her tail across mine.

"Shangra-la is ludicrous opulence that no one can afford. Even if Thomas gave your House the entire MGM, not a penny of it will go to save your precious herds," Esmeralda said.

"Your herds?" I asked Shina.

"They are magnificent." She said with a faraway look in her eyes.

"15 minutes until the auction begins!" A voice rang out.

I decided to shift the subject. "So why are either of you here today?"

"For the weasel," Shina whispered. "She's listed as depressed and uncooperative. We're hoping to get her for a groat or two." I wanted to say that she had over two thousand groat in her pocket, no need to be that cheap. However, I kept my mouth shut.

"Liar." Esmeralda drawled. "She'll go for at least fifty. What you're hoping for is Thomas will buy her for you as a gift, in exchange for that terrifying smile you have."

Shina lifted her head to bare her very large chompers at Esmeralda over my shoulders. "Careful little elder, all that bile you're holding back is starting to stink. Maybe you want to toss a hairball at my feet and be done with it?"

"I'm not buying anyone a familiar," I said, cutting off Esmeralda before she could reply. "This whole thing is awful. I'm observing tonight. I can't bid anyway; House Freelance would need a certified apprentice to do so."

The weasel poked her head from beneath the blanket and stared at me with accusatory eyes. Familiars on auction weren't supposed to eat or talk to the buyers. The circles were a warded to block sound. Examining the circle, I found it flawed. It blocked sound to be sure, but it didn't block mind magic of any type. Familiar speech is technically telepathy that mimics sound. The weasel could hear us and our bickering perfectly well. I glanced at the other circles. They were less hasty, more permanent things. I prodded O'Meara. She'd been hovering at the edge of Veronica's conversations.

Yeah, the weasel was a last minute addition, her name is Carey. Lots of folks complaining that Oric is holding back all the talented familiars for the next auction, hoping tass will be less tight later on. Folks are joking about hiring you if the supply doesn't improve.

I stared at Carey, idly wishing Rudy had come with us. He'd bust her out without a care. Fifty groat. It wasn't nothing, but I had just traded over twenty times that for a single artifact. *What is the point of all our tass if we sit on it?* I asked O'Meara.

Oh no. You're as bad as Rudy sometimes. You know that? She thought back as the inkling of a plan began to solidify.

Some hot headed fire mage you turned out to be, I joked, even as she took the plan and filled in a few holes with her own ideas.

Do this right and we won't have to have Rudy blow a hole in anything yet.

He's going to be so disappointed, I thought.

Tell him handling Oric afterward is his job. That will perk him up.

O'Meara chuckled suddenly, startling Veronica and several magi from House Morgana that were in their circle across the room. I'll *get Veronica on board. You handle Shina and House Hermes.*

"What has your little tail twitching so eagerly?" Shina rumbled next to me, bringing me back to the tug of war where I was the rope.

I leaned into her, enjoying the small shock of surprise that rippled through her body. "So, how'd you like to help me make a tiny bit of trouble?"

Esmeralda gave a wheezy laugh. "And here come the favors."

7

I RETREATED TOWARD THE other side of the room in a probably vain attempt to keep my paw prints off the bidding after I concluded my negotiations with Shina. I got my first look at her bond, Fredrick. A heavy set man, whose neck had consumed his chin, sported a buzz cut and thick black glasses. He grinned, winked, and gave me a thumbs up in the manner of a fraternity bro. I nodded as I passed him, surprised at his appearance. I'd expected the best interdimensional engineer to be more...otherworldly.

Bernard lumbered up onto the stage, scanning the crowd until he found me and O'Meara standing near the door, away from the bidders. Seemingly satisfied that we weren't going to toss a bomb or anything, he ambled up to the podium. "Welcome. Let's get started. You all know the rules. No channeling, no sealing your competitors lips closed or stealing their paddle."

The assembled magi tittered and flashed smiles that acknowledged shared memories. O'Meara placed her hand on my head. Hopefully, *we're the only ones up to mischief tonight.*

I gave her a small nudge with my shoulder.

"First up is Carey, a former human from the east coast." A pair of granny glasses materialized on the bear's nose. "Common weasel. Carey is—"

A small bang sounded. "How dare you do this! Let me out right now! I'll fucking tear your balls off and stuff them into your nostrils! Then I'll... I'll feed your head to your mother!"

O'Meara lent me her eyes, allowing me to see over the heads of the magi. The cage had tipped, so it now extended over the circle of the wards. That part now contained the second most irate weasel I'd ever seen. The entire cage rattled as she shook the bars. "Whoever buys me! I'll kill you! You hear me?!" She hissed and bit at the enclosure.

The bear rushed over and swatted the cage upright. Carey's protests were muted like a TV volume. A husky rushed up from behind the stage and steadied Carey's enclosure with two paws as Bernard returned to his podium. "It should be noted that Carey has not murdered anyone yet. Although not for lack of trying."

Thomas, you're growling, O'Meara gently prodded me.

Noise and her pack had put me in a circus cage, and watching the weasel had thrown me right back into it. I shouldn't be doing this. I shouldn't participate in any way. This was what I had been fighting all this time against.

The term here is necessary evil, Thomas. We're saving them from the system.

You're right. I swallowed down the bile that had risen up in my throat.

"I'll open the bids at 5 groat," The Bear said. "Do I have five?"

A paddle came up.

"Erebus' got five," The Bear pointed, launching into a professional auctioneer patter. "FivfivfivdoIgottengimmieten." No takers. "Nineninenine, eighteighteight."

Fredrick's paddle shot up. A ooooh rippled through the crowd. "IOUs won't do!" Someone jeered.

The Bear ignored the peanut gallery, zeroing in on the numbers. It went back and forth, with several minor Houses getting in on the bidding war. But the outcome was never in doubt.

"And sold to Fredrick of House Hermes for 47 point seven groat. Sleep with a light on, sir." The Bear tipped an imaginary hat and the Husky threw a black cloth over Carey's cage.

"Next up, we got Tilly, who's a dang good boy. Perfect for any apprentice who's comfortable doing most of the work."

"At least he'll try. As long as there are no squirrels, butterflies, or motes of dust to chase," a lackadaisical voice chimed in. The tabby cat had stepped out of his circle.

I'd never seen a bear roll his eyes before. He did it very well. "Midnight. We'll get to you soon. Please step back into your circle."

"My proper name is Black Shadow that Strikes at Midnight So Silently That They Never Hear Death. Please use it if you have a request."

The bear looked down at his podium and appeared to ponder its suitability as a cat hammer. Apparently deciding that he'd need a less clumsy weapon against the cat, he took a deep sigh. "Oh Black Shadow That Kill At Midnight So Silently That They Never Hear Death, please wait in your circle."

"Heh. Words are fun." He stepped back inside the circle and lay down, keeping one ear poking through the ward.

"Now do I hear 8 groat for Tilly?" The bear opened the bidding as Tilly still sat in his circle, looking hopeful and rather stupid. The bidding was less than fierce, he went for 7 groat to Veronica.

Why so low? I asked O'Meara.

Good boy is code for dumb as a brick. Not capable of complete sentences. Scent magic is tough enough to learn when you have a familiar able to guide you through the nuisances of the scented world. Without that, it can set an apprentice back several years compared to their peers.

I nodded and the bidding tried to move on, but Midnight had moved out of his circle without anybody noticing. Amid the hubbub, I noticed him on the buffet table attacking the bacon-stuffed mushrooms.

"There he is!" The bear pointed from his podium.

Midnight gulped down more bacon and looked back at the bear. "Yeeees?" he asked, tail hooked like a question mark. I chuckled.

"You were supposed to wait on the stage," Bernard growled.

"I did. Then I got tired of it," Midnight said with all the affectation of a high school math teacher.

"Whatever. He's there. He's a very cat cat." The Bear swept his claws in Midnight's general direction. "Win the bid and he's your adorable problem. Not mine."

"Do not call me adorable! You-you very large dog thing!" Midnight went from sleek to puffy.

"Do I hear 100 groat?" The auctioneer asked.

Nearly every magus in the room shot up a paddle. I winced. This one was gonna be expensive. Grinning, the bear took bids at 100 groat increments. Only north of five hundred groat did the crowd begin to thin. Veronica, my bidder for this, stayed down for now.

"You really want this one? He doesn't seem to like directions," a Jersey-accented voice called up to me.

I looked down to find Gus standing at my rump.

"Gus, you shouldn't be near us until after the auction," O'Meara whispered out of the side of her mouth as she repositioned to hide Gus. Not that it took much; her boot was bigger than he was.

"Eh, everyone and their mother will know where we got the tass. There aren't many options," Gus said. "Then Oric's gonna use all that tass against you."

I sighed. "Doesn't matter. Think of all the cats Oric's sold in the past. It's a drop in the bucket. The TAU spends some on their own enchantments, but they don't need that much. When Oric attacked me last year, O'Meara blasted their office to shreds without a bond. Oric is sitting on as much tass as a major House. If he wanted to, he could replace Lansky as the major magus bank." He also could have loaned the council the tass they need to rebuild, but he hadn't so far as I knew. What if that was just it? Dammit, I bet the council were playing us off each other. My loan to them wasn't public, but Oric's wouldn't be, either.

The bids were creeping up now, cautiously, a few groat at a time, as the total amount neared 800. An Erebus and another magus were dueling. Midnight kept one ear on the proceedings as he continued to eat the filling out of the mushrooms. Daring someone to stop him. Nobody did.

"Eleven hundred," Veronica voice rang out.

The crowd inhaled together.

"Well…" Bernard's auctioneering paused to appreciate the jump. "A new challenger? Anyone want to dance? Eleven hundred and ten."

Five sets of eyes flicked towards me. I innocently licked my paw. Between the loan to the council, the Fey chain, and these familiars, we were about half as wealthy as we had been last week, but they didn't know that. Death's fortune had been just as much his rep as his money.

Nobody else bid as the auctioneer pattered halfheartedly.

"Going once, going twice, aaaaaaaand, Sold! To House Morgana," he concluded. The crowd clapped politely.

"Puh, numbers," Midnight muttered. He had moved from the bacon and now stood on the tall brown coffee dispenser. "Later." With that he leapt straight up. Slammed into the plaster panel above with enough force to pop it out, and disappeared into the drop ceiling.

So many eyebrows raised simultaneously, that it produced a small sound perceivable by feline ears.

"Charlie?" Bernard inquired as he stared at the hole.

"Yeah, yeah." The husky that had covered up Carey's cage trotted out onto the stage and stretched out first his front legs and then his back. "I'll get him."

"Charlie," Bernard said with the tone of a reprimand.

"I see him. I see him." The husky made a show of cracking his neck before settling down into a languid doggy play stance, tail up and wagging, head lower. "Time's up, Kitteh!" he called out before literally exploding into motion, a nearly blinding flash of kinetic energy propelling the dog over the magi and into the ceiling. The entire room shook with the force of the impact. Those directly below the now dog-sized hole casually threw up wards or channeled in ways that shuttled the falling plaster dust to the side. A few more junior magi waited for the dust to settle before simply brushing it from their shoulders. Everyone waited.

A muffled yowling of protest sounded. Another crack shook the room as Charlie's knack fired again somewhere above us.

Thirty seconds later, Charlie trotted through the door, Midnight hanging by his scruff, gripped tightly between Charlie's teeth. White plaster dust clung to Midnight's coat and I winced in sympathy. That stuff tasted awful. I'd rather clean sand out of my fur. Charlie took the cat directly backstage.

"And that concludes our auction today. All parties have twelve hours to settle the accounts." Bernard announced. O'Meara and I were first out the door.

8

FOR ONE JUBILANT MOMENT, I believed we were going to make it out of the building without incident. The automatic door to the airlock that helped to keep in the precious cool air of the casino had swung open. My nose neared the threshold. I had begun to think that since Bernard did not know me personally and the auction had gone smoothly—too smoothly—that he didn't perceive my throwing around our ill-gotten gains as trouble. Therefore, he had not deemed it necessary to contact Oric. Therefore, I might, just might, have gotten one to three familiars that I could convince to freelance for me before Oric canceled or otherwise altered the deal.

A flash of purple, the pop of an owl-sized quantity of displaced air and my fantasy deflated into a more complicated reality.

"A word, Thomas," said Oric from about ten feet to my left. O'Meara reached for her anchor, subtle as a nuclear hand grenade, a sentiment she enjoyed.

Bad cop is so much easier, she thought as I turned towards the bird, sitting on my haunches as I did so. He sat on the floor ten feet away, eyes narrowed and head cocked so far that those eyes were almost perpendicular with the ground. His expressionless beak nonetheless gave an impression of a frown thanks to the same spell that allowed us to talk.

"Like it?" I asked, knowing he was examining the very fine anti-teleportation ward woven into my harness. It been contracted to an expert ward weaver. Nobody would notice it unless they knew to look for it. I'd have bet Oric had been bouncing off it for the last couple of minutes or so, trying to teleport much closer. To most, the barn owl, wearing a black bowtie, looked small and unthreatening, but the merest sight of him twisted my guts into knots as they recalled the abject terror of freefalling over the city.

"Hrrm," he grunted, and gave a little hop back from the ward's border. He'd be powerless within it. "Let's go somewhere more private to chat."

I smiled politely, curling my tail around to cover my claws. "You're welcome to make an appointment. I'm very busy, but for you, how's next Tuesday?"

He fluffed his feathers, and his wings lifted from his body for a split second before he caught himself and his feathers rippled back smooth. "I'm not precisely informed on the deals you've woven with the winners of the sales today. But I am not afraid to invalidate them and fine all the magi involved."

Very deliberately I yawned, covering my teeth with my paw. "I fail to see how that concerns me, Oric. Per the bear's warnings, I did not cause trouble. But go ahead, anger the great Houses; make them even more aware that the TAU is outmoded."

Oric mirrored my yawn by preening, "The TAU has rules about the transfer of familiars to unauthorized parties. The buyer would be fined and the unauthorized parties would have considerable bounties posted on their heads. I've been doing this a long time, Thomas. You're not the first would-be competitor, nor will you be that last."

"No," O'Meara spoke with the crackle of a furnace. "Blood and Ashes, you two, you both could make a mint giving posturing lessons. I want to make one thing clear, Oric, then you and Thomas can hammer out the rules of this game. If he disappears, I will end you. I will end the TAU and reduce all the elders to crispy fritters." I heard all the AC in the entire casino click on as they struggled against the waves of heat radiating from my fire magus.

"I am not afraid of you, Ashbringer," Oric hooted calmly. "No familiar will aid you other than Thomas, and without one, you're an impotent match."

"I wouldn't be so sure of that if I were you. I've had seven familiars, Oric. I know how to use magic, by scent and by sound. From rodents to bats, I've learned them all. I'm a former Inquisitor; I know how to get through wards. Before you start threatening our family, you'd better see that you have one of your own to lose as well." She reached down and raked her nails through my head fur in a possessive gesture. "I'll be in the car. Play nice. I'd rather not reduce the entire building to slag," she said to me, loud enough for everyone else to hear. With that, she headed out of the building. Other words, other secrets she knew about how familiars really worked, floated between our heads.

Oric and I watched each other until the automatic doors closed.

"You!" Someone barked from behind me as the yellow of kinetic energy flashed from the same direction. Instinctually, I flung myself to the side.

Too slow.

My kinetic ward flashed, entombing me in golden light and I felt it shudder.

The husky, Charlie, flew back from the cracked surface of my ward, a ward built to withstand anything short of an artillery shell. Another flare of his knack and the dog righted himself in midair, landing on his feet. O'Meara howled in my head as she wheeled around mid-step, grabbing her anchor, and igniting her aura to rival the Vegas sun.

Purple flared and the snicker-snap of displaced air sounded. Charlie disappeared as a beam of superheated plasma cut through the spot where he'd been standing, sending the scattered ring of magi and familiars who'd been watching the scene between me and Oric either shrinking away or empowering wards. Charlie landed, sitting on his rear. Oric reappeared a bit farther down the bank of glass doors. The doormen had done an entirely mundane disappearing act. "Not smart, Charlie. Apologize to Master Khatt," Oric said as a glittering ward enveloped them both, this one tuned to heat.

The Circus Circus was nominally owned by a minor House, and used as neutral turf. Only minimal wards protected the property. About thirty feet outside it, O'Meara casually held a ball of fire that had enough energy in it to level the building.

The dog grinned. "Sorry for cracking your expensive smelling ward, Khatt. That is you right? Only cougar standing in town, right? The guy trying to muscle in on our turf?"

"That's right and if your boss weren't so fast, your brain would be baked potato," I growled.

"Believe it or not, I'm quite used to this." Oric deadpanned. "The familiars will be transferred per the contracts."

"But if they're not where they're supposed to be and you're muscling in on our turf, it will be just like right now. You're never gonna see us coming, cat," Charlie's tail wagged.

"You really want a war then, Oric?" I asked. "I know his trick now and I can defend against it all day."

Oric sighed. "Let me introduce you formally to Charlie, otherwise known as Crash. He is one of the ten officers of the TAU. He and Bernard are in charge of the Vegas offices. Enforcement of TAU rules, which are agreed to at the time of auction, falls to him. He's a hundred years old and knows the city better than you know the taste of your toes. This is who you're going to be pitting untrained familiars against in what, Fey chains?" He looked over at O'Meara and back at me. "Why bother coming after you directly? You and O'Meara are a potent king and queen combo. Ask yourself." His eyes narrowed. "How many pawns are you willing to lose to my knights? Pawns you have to pay me to get."

"The TAU works because we can protect our members, Thomas. We're so good at it, that nobody really tries anymore. That is the heart of the TAU. You, yourself, are well protected and you're a survivor. I give you a nod for that. But can you keep others safe?" His head tilted. "That's the real business. Goodbye. I have to deliver some familiars to Houses Morgana and Hermes." With a purple flash and a snicker snap, they disappeared.

With a haughty chuff, I took a look at the still-curious onlookers. Shina, in particular, watched me with an ears-half-back expression, worry plain on her huge face.

I gave her a cocky wink and walked out, tail lashing with the confidence that I almost felt. We were entering a new stage of the game.

O'Meara played her thoughts close to her chest until I stepped into the van. As soon as the door closed, my scruff was grabbed, I was roughly hauled into her wide lap and then hugged until something popped. She released me with a heavy sigh as the car started to move. I reached out and found none of the anger I had been expecting. There was anger, but all of it pointed at a certain owl.

"Okay, what happened?" Rudy demanded, bouncing up and down on what appeared to be a cannon mounted so it could pop up through the roof. We ignored him for the moment.

Why would I be mad? she asked, as she ran her hand along my side.

Because I've done something rather rash and stupid? I countered.

You saw an opportunity and took it. You do that. We also panicked Oric to the point he confronted us without backup. We could have killed him. All it would have taken is a small lunge forward while he scryed the ward. He'd have been cut off from his little trick and been dead meat.

And this Charlie?

"Stop cuddling and tell me: WHAT DID YOU DO?!" Rudy leapt down and landed with his sharp claws in my ear. "Why are we sending House Morgana over a thousand groat! Are you two trying to spend all our tass in a SINGLE DAY?"

O'Meara laughed. "Most of it's going to Oric, but they get a 100 groat commission."

This distracted Rudy enough that I could pry him off my muzzle. "You went and bought familiars?! When we've got a dozen studying their brains out?"

"We need some headliners," I said. "I figure we'd get the freelancing business going since I can't loan myself out. And none of them seemed too happy about being a familiar. We can give them options."

"You know how many assassins you can hire for a thousand groat? Lots, like dozens probably," Rudy said.

"Well, I think Oric's trying to in-source things first. Apparently this Charlie wants a piece of us," I said as I pawed him off my head. "How you feel about pulling security duty on new recruits, Rudy?"

Rudy's tail, which until this point had been waving around as if trying to beat out an invisible fire, went still. "Charlie, that dog would be smarter if you replaced his brain with peanut butter." He mumbled and began to rub his hands together. "Ooooo, maybe I could finish the Anti-wizard Phooey Mark V." He looked up, his beady black eyes shining.

O'Meara and I glanced at each other, an image of the giant hole in the building that had been the product of the Mark IV replaying in our minds. "There's a Mark V?" I asked.

"Not yet!" Rudy grinned.

9

ORIC LET THE DEALS go through. Although he issued some stern warnings to both Houses. Which gave them an excuse to ask for more tass to put up with the trouble of being chewed out by a half-pound owl. By morning, two small pet carriers arrived with unhappy cargo. Tilly, the last to arrive, came in under his own power on a leash held by Fredrick.

The golden retriever gasped as he entered the large vault-like room we had brought the carriers into. "Friend!" He immediately bounded up to Midnight's carrier and doggy bowed. "Is cat friend! They tell Tilly not see cat friend again! But here is Cat Friend. Hello, Cat Friend! How are you?!? I am Well! Do you want to play? Let us Play!"

"Hello, Dog," Midnight returned the greeting with a voice thick with sarcasm.

A rumble of disgust rolled from the weasel.

Tilly turned. "Ooh! It long, angry friend! Hello, Long Angry Friend! Do you want to play?"

"No! I want to see this magus who bought me so I can test out these teeth on the bastard," Carey growled, although it was a high-pitched one and sounded more cute than intimidating, at least on this side of the bars.

O'Meara ushered out the magus, leaving me and Rudy in the room.

"Wanna explain this to them?" I asked Rudy who stood on my back.

"Nah. It's much more fun to watch you stumble around. I'll give ya the support if you need it." I heard Rudy click his small zippo closed.

"You big cat," Tilly said, noticing me for the first time. He put himself between Midnight and me, tail still wagged, but weakly.

"I am that," I conceded. With a wave of my paw, I triggered my magic hands, which floated out and opened the cages. Tilly sniffed in the wake of one. After the doors were open, Midnight flowed out of his and peeked around Tilly at me. Carey stayed at the opening of her carrier, long back bowed, ready to spring. "I am also the one who financed your exit from the auction house."

"Where's your magus?" Carey growled. "And this apprentice?"

"Fortunately, I don't have an apprentice for you to kill. Instead, I'm hoping you all will be my apprentices of sorts."

"I don't work with anyone who keeps me in a cage!" Carey said.

"I don't really see the point of working at all," Midnight commented.

"Will there be treats?" asked Tilly.

"There will be treats," I said.

"Oooh I like this big cat, cat friend. He has treats!" Tilly's tail blurred like an airplane propeller.

"The name is Black Shadow That Kills At Midnight So Silently That They Never Hear Death. I made it myself," he declared with pride.

"Yes, yes I know. Is cat friend. I only have one cat friend. Maybe big cat is friend?"

Both Carey and Midnight glared at Tilly, who didn't seem to notice. They turned back to me.

"There will be treats, beds, salaries, and even some days off," I said. "It's a bit better deal than the one you were expecting.

Carey perked up at the word of salaries. Midnight just yawned. Figured the most expensive one would be the toughest nut to crack.

"That door behind you is still closed, Mr..." Carey squinted, examining my harness. "Boss? Oh real classy there, Booooss."

"Trust me, he's got more class than sense, that's for sure," Rudy said.

Midnight cast his eyes at Rudy while Carey's gaze remained locked on me. She stepped cautiously out of her cage and began to edge sideways. "Look, look, I'm sure you buying us was generous. But you still fucking bought me. I got no interest in any of this bullshit magic and all that. I'm going home!" She zipped toward the door and launched herself up to the door handle. Like every single door handle in the casino, this one was L-shaped, for easier access with paws and mouths. Although I don't recommend biting them. People put their feet on them.

The door swung open. The weasel fell, paused, staring up at the door handle in shock. She glanced at me and then back at the open doorway, which opened into a security office. O'Meara lounged behind a grey metal desk, boots propped up, nose in a book.

Her long body puffing, Carey hesitated, lips drawn in an uncertain snarl as she scanned the room for something or someone to fight. O'Meara slowly put her book down and smiled at the weasel. "Hello, Carey. I'm O'Meara. Can I help you?" She laid the Irish accent on thick.

Carey flinched as if O'Meara had hit her and then straightened herself out before rearing up to her hindlegs. "I want to go home."

"Alright. I'm sure you've heard all the reasons that's a bad idea, but we can do that." O'Meara frowned at her.

"Take me home," she demanded, although there was a slight waver to her voice.

"Very well." O'Meara offered a heavy sigh and looked at me. "Thomas, if you'd assist. This lady would like a trip home."

She didn't even let me get my pitch in, I grumped and made to enter the office.

Well, for what it's worth, I think you're impressing Midnight, O'Meara thought.

I glanced back to the tabby cat who watched me with definite interest. "We will return in a moment," I told him.

"Out?" Tilly asked. "I gotta go pee. And treats! You said treats. I remember! You said treat."

"I will come as well," Midnight said. "Best to verify your word."

"Aw, are you sweet on the murder tube?" Rudy asked.

Midnight's tail went slightly puffy but Carey beat him to the punch. "I AM NOT A MURDER TUBE! FIGHT ME, SQUIR-REL!"

"Any day of the week, princess, but I'm working now," Rudy said and then, in a lower tone, continued, "Oooh maybe if she doesn't work out as a freelance familiar, we can start a mecha battle arena. She'd be a great pilot."

"Now, now, no blood on the floor today, please. Come on, boys, let's get this field trip done," O'Meara said, summoning up her practiced bartending charm.

"Freelance Familiar... you are him, aren't you? The one we were warned about." Midnight paused at the door, tail bending over his back.

"Yes, I can bond anyone I want. Anytime I want. O'Meara is my bond by choice." I sat on one side of the exit door.

"Because she's the only magus willing to put up with him," Rudy quipped.

"Rudy!" I warned. "Is there an actual reason you're here?"

"Yeah. To eat these popcorn kernels," Rudy literally pulled a popcorn kernel from his cheek pouch and nibbled at it. O'Meara snorted.

"Less talking! More home," Carey demanded.

"Right, lass," O'Meara sucked in a breath and touched the door frame with a hand and I laid a paw on the opposite side. Runes flared beneath the gray paint. While O'Meara was rubbish at bending space, Death had been pretty good at it, and several of these emergency exits were in strategic locations around the building. It had been a simple hack to alter their exit points.

"I don't need magic to go home! I live in Vegas," Carey huffed.

"You've been with the TAU for months, dearie. Your apartment is long gone." O'Meara opened the door to reveal a large two-story house with a white picket fence running along the sidewalk. The house gleamed in the morning sunshine, and dew twinkled across the manicured front lawn. A suburban dream made real. Yet something about the house hinted at a mystery within—black trim and shutters were like too-heavy eye shadow while the red of the front door perfectly matched the color of humans I've ripped open.

Carey shivered, her little tail tightly tucked between her back legs. "That's my sister's house."

"Would you prefer your parents?" O'Meara asked.

"How the hell do you know!" Carey snarled.

"I'm an ex-Inquisitor. I know how to find things." O'Meara smiled.

"Ooooh, good smells!" Tilly stepped over Carey and onto the sidewalk. He bent his nose to the base of the fence and sniffed rapid fire. "Oooh! There's a human, another human, pretty human, old human, Poodle bitch!" He jumped the fence without effort and squatted.

"Tilly, don't you dare poop in my sister's yard!" Carey scrabbled up on top of a picket and squeaked fiercely.

"Is okay! Is grass," Tilly said. "I good boy."

"Your sister is home, Carey," I said. "Go ahead and try to talk to her. I just sent my parents a long email explaining it. They never wrote back."

Carey looked at me. Doubt had entered her eyes for the first time. "They forgot you?"

I did my best impression of a shrug. "It... worked both ways. For me at least."

She opened her mouth to say something and then decided against it. Swallowing, she hopped down from the fence and walked up to the front door. O'Meara and I touched and wove a quick spell, unlocking the bolt and pushing the door open a crack. It would be best if her sister didn't see both Carey and the crackling portal we stood in. Cold prickles danced down my spine. A friendly warning from the Veil to not push our luck in this neighborhood.

"Woof," said Tilly with relief. "Treats now?"

"Sure." O'Meara pulled some jerky from a pocket.

"Oooo good treat. I take mine. Cat friend's too. Hold for him." Tilly hopped back over the fence, tail a-wag.

"Hey, where'd Midnight go, anyway?" Rudy asked, shifting around on my back.

"Oh, he in the house," Tilly said, mouth full of jerky.

I didn't see the tabby anywhere. "How'd he do that?"

"Sneaky cat is sneaky," Tilly swallowed. "Very good at cat-ting."

"Stay," I told Tilly, activating my invisibility charm, and stalking toward the house.

"Okay," Tilly said.

Is this really necessary, Thomas? O'Meara asked as I nosed the door open.

Hopefully no, but I kinda want to see the inside. She's a doctor, right?

Cardiologist. Her thoughts trailed off into illustrations of the various ways cats paid for their curiosity. Rudy hunkered down on my back. At least he couldn't quip while we were in stealth mode.

The house stank of filched hospital cleaning solutions and the floors shone in a way that only a borderline neurotic neat-nick could maintain.

"Hey, sis." My ear caught a whisper, swiveling to find its origin.

The shriek that followed it proved much easier to track.

I hurried upstairs and found Midnight peering into an open bedroom. Carey's voice pleaded through the bedroom door. "Hey, hey, Melissa. Calm down! Please!"

"You sneak like one of the metal beasts with indigestion," Midnight grunted as I joined him at the doorway and peered into the room. Inside was an office of sorts; papers were scattered all over a large L-shaped desk with a tiny little laptop dead center. Carey stood on her hind legs, front paws raised and open.

"Look, I know it's strange! But you gotta listen! Please, Mel!"

Wedged in the corner of the room, clinging to a wall so tightly that she might pass as a human limpet was Melissa, Carey's sister. Short-cropped hair, wide dark eyes and a very professional spray tan over skin that didn't have much opportunity to see the real thing. I watched as she gathered her courage, snatched up a framed diploma from the wall and swung it edgewise at Carey.

It caught Carey in the ribs and hurtled her from the desk with a light crunch. That had been no plastic frame. Carey gave a cry of surprise and pain as she rolled to a stop on the floor.

"Rotten walnuts," Rudy swore.

"Oh fuckity fuck fuck FUCK. Should have dodged that," Melissa mumbled to herself as Carey found her feet. "Early stage rabies? Or are you a pet?" She brandished her diploma in a sweeping gesture. "Either way, OUT! Out! Out of my house." Carey scrambled out of range but instead of being driven toward the door, the weasel leapt into a sparsely populated bookshelf. Melissa slammed her diploma over it, trapping

Carey within. Melissa ran for it then and I had to scramble to get out of her path. The door slam bit my ears and echoed through the house.

Melissa whipped out her phone and demanded Google to dial Animal Control.

All the while, Carey pleaded through the door for her sister to recognize her. "It's me! Please! I need your help, sis. One last time, PLEASE!"

Melissa cocked her head at that line. Recognition briefly emerged on her face before she dismissed it with a shake and lifted the phone to her ear. "Hello, Animal Control? There is a weasel trapped in my office. No, it's not a ferret. It might be rabid. No, it didn't bite me but it's acting real weird. I might have hurt it."

Should I rescue her? I asked O'Meara.

Wait for her to ask if you can. She counseled. *If Animal Control shows up, the Veil here might close the portal on us. We're too close to New York City for this sort of magic.*

"Thirty minutes? Fine." Melissa said into her phone, gave the address and hung up. Then dialed another number and walked down the stairs. "Hi, Hal? I'm going to be late. No, I don't know how long. Do you know how long it takes to catch a weasel? Yes, I go on leave tomorrow. No it's not a vacation. Vegas is never a vacation."

Hiccuping noises drifted through the door. Our spells mimicked human facial expressions, but sobbing remained a human thing. No matter how much a former human needed to do it, it came out rather odd.

"Not that I care, but that was what they told you would happen," Midnight said from the other side of the door. He'd ducked inside.

"Shaddup, Midnight. Go somewhere else," Carey hissed.

"Black Shadow That Strikes at Midnight," he corrected. I noted he had shortened his name a bit.

"How 'bout fuck you, Midnight," the hiss became an angry squeak.

After a pondering pause, Midnight replied, "I'm a cat, you're a weasel. It wouldn't work."

"Fuck you to hell and back," she said, with much less force. "They could have mind-fucked her like they do in the casinos. Have you seen that? All those spells whispering into people's heads?"

"No, but I didn't see any glow on Melissa. Did you?"

"No," she said, with deep bitterness in her sulky tone.

I reached up and turned the door knob, using my magic thumb spell and flicking off my invisibility. "Time to go," I said to Carey's glare. Midnight had pulled his *not here* trick again.

"Make me," she dared.

"No," I told her. "I brought you home as you requested. I'm not here to make you do anything. I'm looking for help to give the TAU a big middle paw digit. In Vegas, I can offer you some amount of independence. Now, you can stay here and see what happens to an injured weasel in a place with very little magic at all. Or you can come back with me." I looked over the room and saw no Midnight, but addressed him anyway. "That goes for you too, Midnight. I could drop you off wherever you wish, where the game is thick or thin. But you'll get bored with that soon enough."

"Oh yeah," Rudy interjected. "Nothing quite like talking to norm animals. It's like Tilly, but way worse."

"Maybe." Midnight strode out from behind the bookcase. "Can I learn your invisibility trick?"

"Certainly," I said, deploying my magic hands into a platform for carrying an injured weasel. She looked at them dubiously. "Get on, I don't care if you think you can walk it off or not."

"How rude," Midnight said as Carey climbed aboard. "You're definitely not a natural cat. You stalk like a dog and

point out injuries... Rude. I'll have to come to make sure you
know these things."

I groaned. Every cat I meet seems to think I'm not doing it
right.

10

Ooooh! I KNOW THIS one! It's got pointy bit. So triangle. Tilly thought with heartbreaking enthusiasm as he pointed his nose at a laminated card with a red square on it.

I placed my paw over my eyes and took a deep, steadying breath and thought as gently as possible. No, *Tilly, count the corners.*

His entire mind shuddered as the scent of panic rose. *No? No? I did wrong? Am I bad?*

Mentally slapping myself, I reorganized the thought. Count *the corners, Tilly. Then tell me.*

Tilly's chest heaved as he sniffed desperately at the card, trying to pull more information from it.

Eyes, I urged. U*se your eyes.*

He whined, but obeyed. Staring intensely at the image, he counted. O*ne. Two, Three... Can I go outside? I gotta pee.*

Tell me what it is first.

Triangle?

I resisted the urge to ram my own head against a wall, instead slumping down onto the floor. I could only stare into the matted mess that was the Golden Retriever's mind. Everyone else's mess made some sort of sense, it contained metaphors, images, and memories. The forms were different, but I could find my way around. Yet Tilly's was this solid ball of strands. It wiggled and shivered with Tilly's emotions but other than that, I couldn't fathom the dog's thought process at all. Pushing into it, all I got were a bewildering variety of scents without any context; they simply were. The only benefit to bonding him was that I could keep him focused for a smidgen longer. But only a smidgen. And that smidgen was definitely up.

I broke the connection. Tilly's face twitched as he looked down at me but otherwise showed no sign of distress. "It's a square, Tilly," I told him.

"Ooh, sure. Yeah, square." He squinted at the card. "Definitely. I knew that. Can I go out?"

My temples began to throb. "Go use the grass."

He went, doors opening for him automagically, exiting my library towards the balcony where we'd grown a small spot of lawn for him. Everybody else used the toilet. We were in my quarters, which I'd been sharing with the three potential freelancers for the last three days. My only break from training them had been my date with Shina. That had gone well at least, a dinner of raw imported antelope and a Bond movie. Shina's critique of the martial arts sequences were relentless and had me snorting. The chemistry wasn't quite what I had with Noise, but we had fun together. It was the meal that really was really seared in my memory though, warmed and spiced nearly raw meat that almost tasted like the fantasy deer that my meat brain kept going on about. Although the few deer I had caught in Grantsville before the disaster hadn't lived up to its lofty expectations. Shina promised me even better food up in Shangra-la and gave me a few training tips for my own apprentice. None of which had really worked.

Midnight wasn't bad but kept normal cat hours, sleeping most of the day away. Tilly was Tilly, and Carey needed more time.

I wondered if Oric had known or suspected my plan and had offered up three lemon familiars to me on purpose. To make matters worse, my security had spotted several magi in black surveying our wards. House Erebus might be on the brink of mounting some sort of attack. Peeling myself from the floor, I went in the opposite direction, towards the kitchen, fully prepared to stress eat an entire cow.

"You're wasting your time," Rudy sing-songed, echoing my own thoughts. He sprawled out on my kitchen counter, which was only about a foot off the ground, his iPhone laid out width-wise in front of him, texting someone.

I ignored the comment, pulled open the fridge using the leather strap tied around the door handle, and pulled out a slab of beef that was officially contraband in the building. I employed twenty cows and mostly cow people. Pork was safer, I only had a handful of pigs and they were less organized. Guilt was a constant flavor of my life and the light flavor of bovines clutching pearls in their hooves would be something I had to endure.

"Just send them out," Rudy said, as I tore off a chunk of red flesh.

I had a pang of longing for the backyards and wooded corridors of Grantsville. The last time I'd felt actual earth under my paws had been when we found Jet dead in the desert.

"Hey, earth-to-space brain." Rudy stood up from his lounging.

"Yeah, I heard ya. They're not ready. Hell, they're not even committed to the whole mission. Tilly will do anything for a treat and praise. I'm not sure where the hell Midnight is, and Carey's in the depression stage of grief last time I checked on her."

Rudy flicked his tail toward the bedroom. "She's still there, making my favorite pillow all soggy." It had been about 24 hours since we'd brought Carey "home." O'Meara and I had healed her injuries, but afterward the little weasel had curled up in a ball and refused to do much of anything.

"And you want me to send them out, bonded. Untrained? With me and O'Meara going on a trip to another plane of existence on Friday, two days. Oric will renounce TAU protections for Midnight, and then it will be open season for anyone trying to make some tass."

"It's Black Shadow who Strikes at Midnight!" A gray tabby head poked out from behind a row of empty cashew cans sitting by the sink. "If you're going to use my name, use it correctly!"

"Ah ha! I knew you were in this room!" Rudy crowed.

He glared at me. "And I don't need your protection, Mr. Thomas."

"You think you can handle Charlie on your own now? Or how 'bout half a dozen like him?" I ask, smirking a little.

"Charlie is an a-dog-mination. No dog can move that fast. It violates the natural order."

"Hey, look. Charlie's not the one you gotta worry about. Fact is, we paid a lot of tass to spring ya. You ever see a western? The ones with the horses and gun duels?" Rudy asked.

"The picture shows? I suppose," he conceded.

"Well those with the bounty posters, dead or alive? Where endless dudes with guns come outta the woodwork? That's gonna be what happens. Not only will there be magi after you, but every single mythic who lives in Vegas is gonna be looking at you and thinking, that thousand groat would be worth an awful lot of magi favors."

Midnight's tail gave a flick of unconcern. "And if I recall, all those desperadoes were killed. I shall have no trouble at all."

"Assuming you have a gun," I snorted. "Which in this world means a magus."

"I could get any magus I'd like," he said.

"True, an unbonded magus would probably agree to bond in a heartbeat. A few might even kill their current familiars to do so. But then you'd be bonded for the rest of your life. You'd never get to change your mind," I said.

"And the snake allows you to do it?" His eyes narrowed.

"Yes. And I have other snakes, one of which I will loan to you, provided our house gets a cut of your earnings. Formally, you will be part of House Freelance and under our protection."

"You have made my life very complicated, Mr. Thomas. I don't need this magic. Before that Owl, I was the king of all I could walk in a day. I hunted when I wanted, and when I didn't, a scratch at a door produced more food than I could eat. I was no one's pet." He lapsed into silence. "Yet, I was bored. Both you and the Owl knew that. The Owl caged me with it. This cut you want, is another sort of cage, isn't it?"

I caught his meaning. "Yes. Welcome to magic society, a series of interlocking cages. If I hadn't intervened, you'd be shoved into a cage with very little consultation. I'm offering you a cage with much sharper edges, but you have your own set of keys." I waved a paw and opened up several cabinets for dramatic effect. "My bars are made of the choices I've made, the friends, family and everyone who's helping me fight to break some of the locks that Oric has put on the system." I felt my metaphor creaking, so I stopped talking.

"That shouldn't make any sense," he hissed. "That is human thinking. All knots and circles."

Rudy giggled. "Aww I love it when house cats realize they ain't tigers."

"I could still snap your neck, squirrel," he growled, but it was more of a grump.

"They all say that," Rudy said.

"If this is where I must start to be a king of what I survey again, then I will take your snake and do this magic thing," he huffed.

"Awesome!" Rudy dived back to his phone and started swiping and typing. "I've got you a client this afternoon."

"What?! We still have to figure out security, Rudy." My own tail went puffy.

"Oh don't worry about it. It's on the premises, gotta tech-nomagus who wants to be able to see her spells for once. Couple days. Maybe we can rotate in Tilly for some firsthand experience."

"Tilly's definitely not ready." I started grooming.

"You should stop trying to train him. Have O'Meara bond him. She knows how dogs work." The squirrel's beady eyes twinkled.

"I-I- was." Something rather strong and angry gripped my heart. "Eventually." I looked away from the rodent even as my mind snarled possessively at the thought of other familiars bonding MY magus. *I'm such a hypocrite.* I told myself. Didn't make the possessive feeling go away one bit.

Rudy flashed me a grin and turned back to Midnight, who had started washing a rear paw. "Right. So, Thomas explained about circles and stuff, but this is all about spell engines and wards. Did the TAU explain that stuff to you?"

"Maybe. I didn't pay much attention. Too busy figuring out how they found me every time I managed to jump out a window," Midnight said.

"Right, crash course time!" Rudy flipped up his phone up-right, propped it against a mostly full canister of salt, and launched into an audiovisual presentation on how magic basic spells worked. To complete the shock, the tabby cat seemed to pay attention.

As he did, I noticed that the small squirrel door inset in the door to the bedroom moved. Carey's pointy face poked out the side. She listened to Rudy for a minute or so, and then withdrew without a word.

An improvement, at least. Maybe this could work, after all. As Rudy continued to lecture, I finished my steak and settled in for a quick nap.

I woke to Rudy saying, "Alright that's all of it. Let's go meet Big Stompy!"

II

IT's PROBABLY A PHYSICS fundamental. Given enough resources, a place where reality doesn't apply, and unmonitored free time, a squirrel with a love of explosions is going to make a giant robot. Still, I had not connected the fact that our second biggest stage had closed for renovations soon after we took control of the casino with Rudy's dreams of city-wrecking robots. The mortal company that legally owned the building (and kept the lion's share of the mundane profits) generally handled the entertainment. I had only met our big star, Mr. Copperfield, once, and he assumed I was part of a traveling animal show.

The stage had been stripped down to its studs and converted into a science-fictionesque vehicle bay with one particularly tall vehicle in it. Big Stompy, who looked like the aftermath of a tryst between a red corvette and a fun house mirror, judging from the amount of chrome that spread between all the car parts. The robot stood over fifteen feet tall, and sported gleaming fists bigger than me with sword sized spikes jutting out of the knuckles.

His name came from the giant red boots constructed from two halves of a sports car.

"Rudy, how did you..?" Then I saw the answer. The scaffold was absolutely teeming with rodents of all shapes and sizes. Hundreds of them, passing wrenches and screwdrivers and all manner of parts to each other.

"Cashews coated in toe jam and spread on toast!" Rudy exclaimed. "You guys were supposed to clear out ten minutes ago! I've got a magus coming in here any minute."

Squeaks of alarm rippled through the horde of rodents. A high-pitched voice rang out. "Code 5! Code 5! Emergency Evac!"

Another voice called out. "Call the cleanup crew!"

Rudy jumped up on my nose and hollered out to his fellows. "No cleanup crew! These guys didn't see nothing!" He whirled on me. "Did ya, big guy?"

"Uhh, nope," I said, tearing my eyes off the swarm. "Don't see anything unusual here, just a giant robot on a stage, where it belongs. Nothing on the scaffolding at all. It's all naked metal."

Midnight's eyes looked about ready to explode from his head. "Yes. What he said."

"EMERGENCY EVAC NOW!" The swarm called out in a high-pitched chorus, and I watched as three purple windows opened parallel to the truss that ran along the top of the stage. The rodents streamed into them, the smallest mice riding the largest rats. They moved with uncanny speed and precision, disappearing into the portals within the course of a single minute. It shouldn't have been possible. With the exception of the door portals in the basement, the entire building was warded against all teleportation spells.

"I have questions," I whispered through the side of my muzzle.

"Later," Rudy growled back and bapped me with his tail. When he hopped back onto my head, I saw that not all of the rodents had left. A single beaver watched us with a wary expression. His two incisors glinted with the shine of metal.

I approached with caution as Rudy spurred me on. "Right, Thomas and Midnight, meet Jeri Chrome Tooth. An old friend of mine. He's got just a couple of assistants that might be around. Take no note of those guys."

"Pleased to meet'chas," Jeri said, his whistling voice tinged with suspicion.

"Hellos!" A new voice rang out from behind.

"Aw, nuts. She's early," Rudy said.

I turned to find a portly woman sticking her head through the front door to the stage. "Mr. Rudy, are you here?"

"Yeah, I'm down in front," Rudy called back. The beaver stared at me with a squinting eye, head turned so to see the full effect. It took me a moment to track his eye and realize it was Rudy, on top of my head, he was giving the, *This is entirely your fault*, stare to. Meanwhile, Rudy practically vibrated. Perhaps trying to contain a rebuttal??

The moment passed as the woman jogged up to us with a "Hello, hello. Ah, Master Rudy, Master Thomas. Pleased to meet you." She thrust her left hand out, bare skin, the other bore a gauntlet that looked like it could punch through a concrete wall.

"You're Madam Whizzbang?" I asked, which earned me a stomp from Rudy.

A look of momentary confusion as Rudy rushed in. "Madam Pumpernickel, an expert on technological power sources."

"Ah," I sniffed the offered hand politely. Ozone clung to her skin, along with the acrid scent of burned motor oil. "You going to explain why we have a giant robot, Rudy? You skipped that part and I think it's rather important."

"Right. Right." Rudy leapt down from my head. "I figured one of us oughta focus on bringing in tass instead of spending it."

I looked up at the robot's grinning face. "What you gonna do with it? Walk it around the city with a giant sandwich board advertising our fake meat burgers?"

"Nooo. We're going to build another one and make'em fight! Tell me that won't be a blockbuster! Folks place bets on the outcome when they come watch. We put those hope and dream harvesters in the stadium seating and whammo we gots even more tass. Be the best thing since the invention of peanut butter. Jeri here is a mechanical genius. He's designed it with all these crumple zones, so it'll get beat up real good and still keep trucking. Stompy will be our good ol' original. An underdog the people will cheer for. Wait till you see the design for Crush bot. The eeeeevil dude." Rudy grew more and more excited as he talked, pantomiming a boxing fight with his paws, eyes shining so brightly that it's a wonder they didn't spontaneously combust.

"You're building a giant robot fighting arena," I stated. My headache announced its imminent return.

Rudy had raced up to the thing's shoulder. "YES! And it's gonna be awesome!" he declared, and then raced around Stompy's head, burning off excited energy. He stopped. "Well, it will be awesome once we get it moving." He looked pointedly at Madam Pumpernickel, who was looking the robot over with a thoughtful expression.

"Did you leave any room for an engine?" She took off her pink fedora and scratched at her scalp thoughtfully. She had long hair the color of clean motor oil, drawn into a ponytail that disappeared down the neck of her trench coat.

"Of course." Rudy kicked something and Big Stompy's chest split open to reveal a complicated meshwork of mechanics.

Pumpernickel whistled. If there was room for anything more than a car battery in there, I didn't see it. "I suppose you'd rather it didn't rip off its limbs when those hydraulics activate, too?"

"Uhh." Rudy suddenly looked uncertain. "The mechanics should be okay?"

"Hmpf. You know what they say. Anything's possible with time, tass and knowledge. I've got plenty of the first and the last, provided you've got plenty of the creamy center of this cookie." She looked toward me. "Now, I don't need a familiar for this, but it would make this much faster. Dare I say a week instead of months. If you would please bond me, Master Thomas?"

"Oh! You're not working with him." Rudy said. "You get one of the new guys."

Miss Pumpernickel frowned with disappointment. "New familiars?"

"Yeah, whatisname at Midnight," Rudy said.

"Black Shadow that Strikes at Midnight!" called out a huffy voice. "Get it right! You remembered her name fine!" My eyes followed the swivel of my ear to see Midnight, chest thrust out, on top of the same truss where the portals had appeared. With impressive grace he executed a series of leaps, landing first on Stompy's head, then to the fist, and briefly touching on the jutting kneepad before sailing out toward us. He landed on all four feet without so much as the softest of thumps.

Madam Pumpernickel's eyebrows tried to leap up into her hairline. "Well, then. I didn't see you there."

"They never do." Midnight sashayed his way towards her, before walking in a wide circle around her, looking her up and down. "You will do for my first assignment, I suppose."

Madam Pumpernickel put her hands on her hips. "Oh, will I, now?" A near silent chuckle broadcast her amusement.

"Yes. You may pet me now." He sat with his back to her.

Shaking her head, Madam Pumpernickel knelt down and stroked his fur. To my eyes the Fey chain fastened around Midnight's neck glowed silver as a length of it uncoiled. With a hiss of metallic links, it flashed up and around the magus' neck.

"Oh!" She exclaimed, eyes going wide. Then the dreamy haze of the first bonding lowered her lids to half-mast. Slowly she pulled a purring Midnight into her lap and began to stroke his side.

"You always remember the first," I commented.

"Eh, he won't get stuck on her for long." Rudy said, leaping down onto my back. "She's a total workaholic, bet he's begging to switch out for Tilly by tomorrow morning."

I recalled my first experience working magic all too well. "Let's go get him a bucket. He's gonna need one." I started walking for the exit. I could feel O'Meara reaching for me, despite not being bonded to her at the moment.

"Ain't this perfect?" Rudy sounded pleased with himself. "We can let the newbies work with Madam Pumpernickel and learn the basics. Trust me."

"Trust you and your thousands of friends?" I asked, dropping my voice low.

"You didn't see that!" Rudy hissed. "I can't talk about them. At all."

"Tell me how those portals got through our wards and then I'll forget about your friends," I countered.

"Same way the portal from Grantsville worked. Old magic networks from the medieval times. O'Meara's wards stop new bends in space from forming, It can't do anything against space that's already been bent. Now unless you want to deal with a hive of magically enhanced naked mole rats looking to make you disappear, drop it," Rudy whispered.

I chuffed, feeling uneasy. Oric was as old as Rudy. Both had been familiars of Merlin. Which meant Oric probably knew about the old magics that Rudy tapped into. I wanted to grill Rudy for more info, but I'd probably have better luck clawing open a steel vault door. Rudy had his secrets. Lots of them. Apparently, a big one was that there were far more sentient rodents than anyone suspected.

And Rudy was somehow like royalty or something to them. Something we'd never expected with his magical labors behind closed doors. Rudy ran for his quarters as soon as the elevator opened, muttering about damage control.

"I want the Cat!" screamed a voice through the door to O'Meara's office. "It was bought in my name!"

Wincing, but unable to resist my curiosity I extended the bond to O'Meara. She welcomed me with impressions of warmth and invited me behind her eyes. Two people seethed in front of O'Meara. One wore the green apprentice robes of House Morgana. The other wore a green dress and her neck was heavy with pendants. The apprentice snarled openly, her anchor manifesting itself as the wooden chair she sat in stretched out leafy branches. The other woman's anger was more of a cloud of silent spores. I *have this, Thomas, but thanks for the backup.*

"The agreement was approved by Archmagus Morrian," O'Meara said with the swaggering politeness of an Inquisitor. "I notice you are not appealing to her. The deal is done. When you are calm and able to be civil, I will be happy to introduce you to a number of our staff who are eager to meet you. To compete for your attentions."

The older woman sniffed, "What about the dog? We could buy him off you. I can manage that much."

I closed the link, wished O'Meara the best, and smiled to myself. This was going to work. Every Grantsville familiar taken in by the Houses would be another chip in the TAU's hold. Every freelance familiar, working for me or otherwise, would be a direct strike against them. There are so many things in the magical world that need a dose of equality and justice. The spell dogs, the mythics, the stranglehold of three-hundred-year-old magi on the society. But we couldn't fix everything, not all at once. It was a start.

Walking into my quarters, I found Carey and Tilly curled up on my couch. Both their eyes opened as I passed.

"Um, Mr. Thomas?" Carey asked as I nearly reached the kitchen.

"Yes?" I paused.

"Could we go out? In the city. I want to see some friends of mine."

I considered checking with O'Meara. It was a bit risky, but so long as I wore my harness and remained bonded to her we were fairly confident that I could get us all out of a bad situation. "Let me get some food and then we can go."

"Oooh Food and Walk!" Tilly's tail wagged.

"I was sorta hoping to go myself," she said. "I'll come back, I promise."

Tilly's ears drooped.

"No," I said flatly. "You need a bodyguard with spell power and that's me or O'Meara."

"If, if I decide to do this freelance thing, will I always need a bodyguard? Is that going to be my life?" he asked.

"I don't know," I told her. "But until I do everyone gets a bodyguard."

"Kay," she said.

"So I can come?" Tilly asked.

12

"SMELLS BAD," TILLY COMMENTED as we stepped out of the limo.

"So it's not the best place in town, so what?" Carey snapped defensively. "What the hell smells bad to someone who rolls in cat poop?"

"Cat poop smell different bad." Tilly sniffed the air. "This human bad."

It was certainly that. Urban decay has a scent all its own. I'm sure other cities had their own flavors of poverty, but Vegas added magic to the mix. Here among the decaying houses and fallen street lamps, you could feel the presence of the phantasms that lived under the city. These were products of the shallowing that encompassed Las Vegas and its surroundings. Creatures that fed on hopes and dreams, most of them penned up by the casinos where they were fattened up and harvested for tass. Fattened up on the false hope of riches or simply the expectation of a good time, the phantasms produced tass in pits below the casinos. However, while bound to the underground, they would congregate under anywhere where dreams were shattered, hoping to tempt the unwary down for a snack. It wasn't a smell, exactly, but a presence that made every step heavy.

"Whatever." Carey tossed her little head and walked. The locals gave us a wide berth as Tilly and I followed her past blocks of houses in dire need of maintenance. One in ten shone proudly behind a chain-link fence. Carey stood up on her hind legs at an intersection and cast her gaze this way and that. "Dammit, everything looks different from this angle."

"Need a boost?" I offered.

She gave me a sour look before gesturing at Tilly. "Come."

"Okay!" Tilly moved to Carey, and she climbed up on his back as he panted in the afternoon heat.

"There! That building." She pointed her nose down the street at an apartment building that looked marginally less dilapidated than the rest of its fellows, sporting a brick facade that was only missing a few chunks that exposed the brown wood behind it. "It's not that bad," she told me repeatedly as we approached, claws raking her whiskers, as if she could wipe the scent of the neighborhood out of them. The area had been nice once, a suburban dream back when it had been built. The nearly identical houses that had been cut from the ancient Leave It to Beaver era had since been subdivided into two to three apartments, with varying degrees of success. The yards were protected by sagging chain-link fences and "beware of dog" signs. Carey's apartment building was a mere two stories tall. You could still see a vestige of the original house in the front, the construction scars where it had been added to were unhidden. You could see its slow transformation from a single house to a monstrosity of a roadside motel. Window AC units protruded from windows that were never meant to contain them, and in some places where a window hadn't even existed before, some fed-up resident had taken a hacksaw to a wall.

"It wasn't this bad," Carey muttered as Tilly stepped over an uncapped insulin syringe lying on the driveway.

"What did you do for work, Carey?" I asked, trying to keep my tone level, but it came out with a trace of a growl.

"Waited tables," she snapped back. "I didn't need nobody's help, ya hear?"

Don't you judge. Awakenings don't always happen all at once, O'Meara thought at me. *It can take months. Months where you've got the barest hold on this reality. Lots of magi who make it to adulthood before they awaken do it places like these. Or worse.*

I conceded the point. I still wasn't sure why we were here, but I kept my mouth shut and followed Carey towards the middle of the building. We were creating a scene. A shriveled-looking man who had rows of beer bottles lined up beside him called to me. "Heeeey, we gots a circus! Hey kitty, kitty." In response to his calls, a dozen other residents peered out of doors and windows.

Somebody hushed the drunk.

A group that had been tailing us on the street waited at the gate. I checked all my wards. Tilly, proving himself to have a bit more brains than I'd given him credit for, stuck close as we approached apartment 113. The apartment next to it, 112, had a brand new door that was the wrong size for the door frame and had a one inch gap at the bottom of it.

Carey didn't bother with the doorbell or knocking; she just shouted right at the door. "Open it up, Betty! It's Carey!" No one answered. Carey scrabbled up the wall and slammed the door bell. A tinny sound like the ring of ancient telephone sounded from inside. "I know you're in there! It's before noon!"

I heard steps behind the door, and a woman's voice croaked back. "I don't talk to the dead. Go away."

Carey puffed herself. "If you don't open the door, I'll bust it in, Betty! Break all those hinges like Justin did that one time. Don't make me use this god damn crowbar!"

"I ain't opening my door. You think I don't see that lion sitting there? You think I don't know what that is? No black magic in my house. I heard you scream and die, Carey. Then those witches showed up, ripped the door off. I know the rules. I don't invite you in, you can't come in! So there!"

"That's vampires, Betty! I'm a just fucking weasel. Gimmie my phone!" Carey scratched along the hinges.

"Ha! Nice of you to admit that, Carey! And I sold your damn phone. And everything else I could find in that rat hole next door. You wanna settle up? You still owe me for that bailout. Slip that through the mail slot an' maybe we'll talk."

"I ain't into you for fat nickel Betty! You—"

"Carey!" I cut her off. Breaking my promise not to interfere, but I was tired of the eyes on us. "Front left pocket." I gestured to my harness as she turned around with a look that could have stapled sparrows to a wall.

Confusion flitted across her face.

"Climb up and get it." I told her. If I grabbed for it with my magical hands I have to extract the entire wad, and that seemed both stupid and rude in this situation.

Finally understanding, she climbed up on my shoulder and unzipped the pocket where a roll of hundred-dollar bills resided. "You walk around here with that!?" She hissed.

"I'm bulletproof, can leap up two stories and I can breathe fire if I need to." Compared to the several groat of tass I had on the other side of the harness, five thousand mundane dollars was petty cash. "No one is going to mug me."

Carey came up with two curled hundred-dollar bills. "I'll pay it back," she claimed as she hurried forward and shoved them under the door. "There!" she screamed back at the door. "You blood-sucking harpy! You want the rest? Then open the damn door!"

Silence answered her. Then, the hurried click and clanking of several deadbolts. It opened inward, and two hard grey eyes met mine, then flicked to Tilly, who had been sitting silently next to me.

"Hi!" Tilly said, giving his tail a wag.

Painted-on eyebrows nearly folded together as the woman's leathery skin furrowed. "You ain't Carey."

"Down here!" Carey called.

Betty looked and busted out laughing. "Holy shit. Those witches fixed you up real good, girl. Looks so fitting."

"Shut up, Betty," Carey dashed through the crack in the door.

"Hey!" Betty rasped. "Don't you touch my stuff." Turning back to me. "I suppose you two freaks wanna come in, too. No magic in my house." She swung the door open, displaying the black handgun she held in her left hand. She wore a cigarette-stained blue bathrobe and had her hair up in pink curlers. O'Meara pulsed with warmth in my head, letting me know that her power was there should I need it. I debated disarming Betty, but decided against it. The barrel pointed at the floor as Tilly and I walked into her home.

It was better than I expected and yet worse. The apartment was clean, yet cluttered. Prescription pill bottles covered the entire surface of a small table in the corner of her eat-in kitchen, stacks of white dishes sat in sagging kitchen cabinets, while the garbage threatened to overflow with the number of Chinese takeout cartons it'd been forced to take charge of.

Betty was still laughing. "Turned you into a weasel. Which one did you piss off, Carey? Did you sleep with one of their dog men?"

Carey leapt up to grab a drawer knob and used it to sling herself up onto the counter. "None of your business. Now where's my phone?"

"Sold it."

"It's six years old. Homeless addicts would have spat in your face if you told them it was a gift."

Betty held out her gun free hand and rubbed two fingers against her thumb. Her nails were pink and long. "You the only one with pockets, 'Boss'" she told me.

"Hmpf." I responded, pulling the roll of money from my harness, and pulling out two more bills.

Taking the money, she scowled at me. "So what, you some sort of cat hot shot? She tell ya she's a princess or something? If it weren't for her doctor sister, she'd be in the tents downtown with all the other rejects."

"I work!"

"Says the weasel. Listen, Kitty kat. Whatever she tell you, consider the source. Yeah, she worked, for about a month at a time till her mouth or her sticky fingers got her fired. Worked for me, too, some. Surprised she ain't made a mess of my inventory already, got some of her favorites in stock." She smiled, an oily expression on her rigid face as she set the gun on the table and pulled a small iPhone in a very tired looking case out of her pocket. It had been sequined once, but all one of them had fallen off. It shone in the dim yellow light of Betty's kitchen.

"Give me that phone!" Carey told her with a mixture of growl and pleading squeak.

Betty made a show of waking the phone and showing a text message through the cracked screen. "Still looking for u sis. Call me."

"Every fucking day. Down to once a day from five. But damn. My own mother wouldn't be that persistent. I can't unlock it, but I read them as they come in."

"Those are private!" Carey made a leap from the counter for the device. Betty lifted it out of her reach, and Tilly deftly moved up and caught Carey in his mouth. He set her down swiftly on the floor, where she spluttered with incoherent rage.

Betty smiled at me. "I dunno you. I dunno what you see in her. But you're not going to be the first to try to save that one. That sister of hers tries all the time, even came here to talk with little ol' me." She held out her hand for another hundred-dollar bill.

"She was he-re!" Casey hiccuped, her nose blushing so pink it might explode. "She s-s-saw."

"Two months ago, I gave her and her gentleman private eye the full tour. Told them all about how your six years of classes went. Oh, the text she sent you after she met me! That was a thrill." The way the joy lit up in Betty's eyes as Carey buried her nose into her belly made my stomach twist.

I took the phone from her unresisting hands and realized that the growl that grew into the space around Carey's sniffling wasn't mine. It belonged to Tilly.

He stepped over Carey protectively. His teeth showed only at the very corners of his mouth as he didn't know how to snarl. "You bad human." He stated with the quietest of whispers, voice trembling with a mix of emotions. "Very very Bad."

Betty flinched and covered it with a laugh. "We all are, Dog. You'll see. Now get out."

I gave Carey her phone, and she listlessly climbed up on my back, curling around it like a child with a teddy bear. Tilly backed out of the apartment, not willing to turn his back on this bad human. One stupid human tried to step in our path on the way out. I set his shoelaces on fire. O'Meara and I were having a discussion.

Carey's sister had come to Vegas looking for her two months after her awakening. Was still texting. That shouldn't happen.

It must be because Carey awakened in Vegas, O'Meara opined. *The Veil doesn't know what happened to Carey and hasn't covered it up. Maybe by bringing her out to here, we started the process?*

I had mixed feelings about that. We'd have to see, not like the Veil had an instruction manual.

O'Meara and I mused over the problem as she introduced the now sulky House Morgana apprentice to nearly a dozen Grantsville refugees. It was awkward, but things were improving once Deb, a white dappled mare, had gotten her to laugh with a constant stream of gardening puns.

We were almost back when Tilly asked me a question.

"Thomas, are you good?"

13

Tilly looked up at me with his expectant brown eyes as I realized how bad an idea it had been to bring him.

"Uh, I try to be." I answered him. "Good, I mean."

"You do bad." Tilly said. "Brought Long Angry Friend to Mean lady."

"Was that bad?" I asked back.

Tilly leaned towards me and sniffed as if the truth of the matter would be contained in the air molecules between us. "Mean Lady hurt Long Angry Friend."

"But Carey asked to go there," I reminded him.

"Could have stopped mean Lady. She small, you big." He looked me up and down. Sucking in my breath, I searched for a sentence to explain the lines between verbal and physical violence.

"I'm fine, Tilly." Carey interjected. "I got what I wanted. It's not polite to talk about me with the boss when I'm sitting here."

Tilly's eyes widen in a panicked expression, "Not polite. Is that bad? Am I BAD?"

"No, Tilly, You're fine, you're good," I said as I heard the motor that drove the privacy partition whir.

"Siiirs?" One of the Capy bros whistled from the driver's seat of the limo. "Do you hear that?"

Eager for a distraction from explaining the nature of good and evil to Tilly, I pounced on the offered lifeline. "Hear what?"

Then I saw it. A black diamond of magic rose into the sky, pulsing with an inner blue light. Even this far away I could see it was a huge spell, second only to the technologic contraption that had ground Grantsville to bits. Instinctively I brought the full force of magical sight to bear on it. Negative energy, black, wrapped around a core of mind magic.

That was as far as my analysis got before the thing exploded into a wave, a fast moving wall of darkness filled with glittering blue stars. I reached for O'Meara and together, we channeled the power of stasis. White light burst from our bodies and crystalized everything around us. Carey froze in mid swipe on her phone, Tilly's confused eyes gained a mote of panic before he froze, too. The wave hit the tops of the buildings first, the wards of the casinos flashed golden, and the blackness parted around it.

More distant wards also flared, other casinos and magi Houses, but not enough to be all of them. The magic passed over us, breaking over the stasis sphere. Out of the corner of my eyes, I looked out the window, at those in the car next to us. I didn't see its effect on either them or the pedestrians on the sidewalk. Nobody melted into goo or burst into flame. Yet it interacted with them, dark blue sparks flew in my magical sight at about head level.

Blood and ashes, O'Meara swore. *That has to be House Erebus work.*

We cut off the flow of stasis through us. What *did it do?* I asked.

How the bloody hell would I know? Hold on, I gotta deal with stuff here.

I breathed again as motion resumed around us. A horn blared behind us.

"What the hell did you do?" Carey screeched. "What the hell color of magic is that?"

"Stasis. Black magic is decay, randomness. White is order and stasis. It's a good emergency ward." I explained as I pressed my nose against the window, peering at the rest of the world. It appeared to carry on. Nobody was melting into puddles or bursting into flame. Which was good. But people were at or near the places where I had seen those interactions. It had done something. That was for sure. Mind magic. A shiver passed down all the way to my tail, making the tip twitch. Somebody had made a move. But against whom?

Tilly sniffed. "Order good magic?"

The car began to move again, the Capys driving a bit slower than usual. "Is a leash good, Tilly?" I asked.

"Yeah! Means walkies!" He smiled for the first time since we left Betty's.

"What if it stops you from getting at a really good smell?"

His face fell. "That bad."

"Magic's like that. It's not evil by what it is. It's how it's used that's good or bad."

"Oh." Tilly shut his eyes and winced with his entire face.

"Oh, my heart!" Carey abandoned her phone, leapt on to Tilly's back and scratched at his big floppy ears. Instantly, Tilly was happy again. "You're a good boy, Tilly. The best boy! Stop having existential crises. You're totally distracting me from my own problems." She scolded in that high-pitched voice that every pet loves.

The dog put his head on the seat beside Carey, floppy ears perked. "Really?" His fluffy tail wagged.

With an exasperated sigh, Carey tossed her phone to the side. "Yes, Tilly, you're too good. Way too good," she said, before putting her claws to work on scratching his ear. This quickly progressed to a full-fledged belly-scratching session.

The limo stopped, putting an end to the bonding a short time later, with both looking much happier for it. Maybe this would work out, after all? I shifted into business mode. "Alright, let's be on our toes now. No telling what that spell did to everyone."

Carey nodded. Tilly looked at his toes and made sure he was standing on them.

Chuckling to myself, I stepped out first, my body tense, and nothing happened. Well, not nothing. We got a few oohs and aahs along with pointed fingers from tourists. O'Meara waited at the door for us, her thick arms crossed. A light flame played in the curls of her hair. Anger radiated through our link. She gave me a very rough ear scratch as I approached.

"House Erebus sent a message to all the House holders that they had an incident and not to worry; the spell is completely harmless to all awakened individuals." She growled. "Nobody is objecting, but us."

"I don't suppose they are bragging what it did yet?" I circled around the back of her legs.

"Not yet," she said, then gestured to my charges. "Come on. Everyone inside. Whatever that spell was, it barely touched our wards. It's safe in here."

Inside the MGM it seemed as it always was: the electronic rings of the slots, the babble of shouted conversation (some of which was white noise played through hidden speakers). It was getting towards the afternoon and the casino soon would be packed to gills with the tourists and the gamblers. All donating a little part of their hopes and dreams to the tank of distilled phantasms in the basement.

"How'd the pairing go?" I asked as we made our way back to our quarters.

"We have a test bonding tomorrow." O'Meara's anger transmuted to smug. "Once the brat got over herself that Midnight wasn't going to be hers exclusively, it turns out she's got quite a crush on the concept of a talking horse. If it works out for them, we're going to be down a very talented black jack dealer, for somebody with hooves, at least. We'll have to armor up the other Fey chain tonight."

I made a slight groaning sound as I imagined the all-nighter ahead of us.

"It won't be that bad, we've got it to work once now," she said as the elevator doors to our quarters opened.

Once inside I heard the distinct dulcet tones of a certain squirrel. "Aw, it wasn't that bad! Ya did great for your first time!"

"Get this foul thing off my neck! I am never bonding anyone, ever again!" Midnight moaned piteously. I opened the door to find them sitting on my couch, both rodent and feline wrapped in fluffy hotel towels. Midnight's eyes went wide as I walked in. "No! You can't see me like—" He stood. Wobbled. Then dived at the plastic food bowl sitting next to him. "Oh fields of glory, not again!" he pleaded before heaving into the bowl. Finished, he rolled away from the bowl. "Just kill me now. I'm ruined."

"Naaah, you're just a melodramatic puss." Rudy shrugged off his towel. "He did great for his first time. Managed a good two hours with Madam Pumpernickel. Got a whole 20 minutes of spellcrafting in!" Rudy declared like a teacher bragging about his prize pupil. "Much longer than Thomas did for his first go around."

"And now I pay the price for excellence!" Midnight moaned.

O'Meara and I shared a chuckle as Tilly and Carey eyed the cat with unease.

"Magic takes a bit of getting used to," I told them. "When you start to feel sick, let the magus know and take a break. Don't try to power through the nausea. Why are you wet, too, Rudy?"

"Ah, he broke the bond pretty roughly on old Pumpernickel. She wasn't in any shape to clean him up, so I got the job." He grinned. "It was a grand selfie."

"Miserable rodent," Midnight groused.

O'Meara picked up his vomit bowl and made a face. "I hope that wasn't anyone Rudy knew." And took it over to the trash.

"Nah, I don't think so," Rudy said.

"Hey, huh, Rudy." Carey held her phone in two paws and waddled toward the couch on two stumpy legs. "Can you unlock a phone? I can't remember my pin. I've got one more try on this before it wipes itself."

"Huh?" Rudy turned to peer at the phone. "Oh! Sure. I mean maybe. It's an iPhone, that's a lot harder to crack than them Google spy phones. But I'm really good at cracking nuts. Come on over to my place. Maybe we can make you a harness, too."

"Really?" They scampered off towards Rudy's rooms, leaving us with the hung-over cat.

"How you doing there, Midnight?" I asked him as I jumped up on the couch. I had a huge bean bag in the corner, but there is something good about couches.

"It's Black Shadow that Strikes at Midnight," he protested, although without his usual force.

"Oh, he's definitely fine," O'Meara quipped while pulling some meat from the fridge and dicing it into cubes with a flash of superheated plasma. The dinner and nap plan in her head got nothing but agreement from me.

It pulled Tilly straight out of his funk. "Oooh! Treats!"

I woke to the buzz of an alarm. The intercom on the wall flashed red with a security alert. I lifted my head from O'Meara's lap. It was only buzzing, not screeching. Urgent, but not "OMG we're all going to die" urgent. I rolled off of the lightly snoring O'Meara and opened the panel. An oversized keyboard slid out from the wall and the face of my chief security goon appeared. "Hello, sir. We have a situation."

"What got stolen?" I typed back. This system was solely mundane electronics and could not capture my voice nor my humanized facial expressions.

"Nothing is technically wrong, sir. But if you check the cameras, you'll see what's going on," he said.

My ears half back, I pawed through the security feeds. At first I thought he might be pulling my leg. Nothing seemed amiss. No monsters rampaging through the slot machines, all the dealers stood at their tables. Tourists idly strolled across the garish green carpets. Then it hit me. I could see the carpets. It was 7 pm, according to the time stamp in the corner of the screen. People should be nearly elbow to elbow by now in the restaurants at least, and lines should be forming for Copperfield's first show.

I checked a mundane news feed, making sure there hadn't been a mass shooting or terrorist attack that would explain the sudden absence of tourists and regulars.

"What about the neighboring casinos?" I typed back.

"They're packed sir. More so than usual," he said. "You think it was the foul magic earlier today?"

"Yes." I tapped with my claws, not bothering to use my magic hands for that bit. "Carry on, and thank you for bringing this to my attention," I finished with a bit more effort.

He nodded. "I'll let you know if it changes."

I growled at myself. I'd been so focused on handing Oric his tail feathers, I'd forgotten how badly House Erebus really wanted this casino back, mistaking their patience for inaction. We had to find out what that spell had done, and reverse it fast, or our income and our ammunition would dry up.

I looked over the room. Tilly watched me from my huge bean bag bed, O'Meara snored from her upright position on the couch, nestled in a deep dreamless sleep. Midnight still lay on his back, one hind leg kicking lightly at something.

There were only a few ways I can wake O'Meara from that type of sleep. I used the almost least cruel method. Cold nose to the neck.

"AAARGH! Thomas!"

14

THE EREBUS REPRESENTATIVE WHO picked up the phone identified himself as Michael, which narrowed it down to about twenty different magi, and refused to give the name of his mentor, saying, "Just Michael, please." It annoyed O'Meara.

"What did you do to our customers?" O'Meara kept her voice so level you could stack bricks on it. She had quickly forgiven me for the cold nose after I'd shoved the situation into her brain.

"Oh? Are you attributing a drop in clientele to our little mishap earlier? What percentage would you say the drop-off was?" He didn't try to hide the pleasure in his voice. "What would you say the drop would be? 50, 60, maybe up to 70 percent?"

It was danged near 75%, is what it was. We'd bet a groat of tass, the monthly salary of a low ranked magus, that we were missing every single mundane in the city that hadn't been under ward when that wave hit. "What precisely did that spell do?" O'Meara asked.

"I'm not at liberty to disclose those details to a rival House. But the effects should be strictly short term. No doubt your numbers will improve by next week. Unless similar mishaps were to occur. This is an active area of research, after all," Michael said in the most pleasant customer service voice imaginable.

"This is a direct attack on a minor House," O'Meara said. "The council will have to order an Inquisition into this matter if it happens again."

"Well yes, if they got a majority on the matter. I suppose that to be fair. In the meantime, why don't you just build a ward over the entire city as a stopgap measure? That'd be very impressive and only a tad expensive." Translation, you need three votes on the council to stop us. Good luck with that.

"And I suppose you have another suggestion you want to tell me?" O'Meara's voice became like strained gravel.

"We'd be happy to take the MGM off your hands if the responsibility is too much of a burden. After all, I doubt you'll enjoy House Hermes' continued support without the ability to buy it." He started to laugh, but it was cut off by O'Meara hanging up.

"Well, that confirms that," I huffed as O'Meara put down the phone before she cracked the screen.

"It's a death and mind combo," Rudy said. "It's probably killed any thoughts a person has about the MGM, or degrades the eagerness of those thoughts. There are a dozen different ways they could do it."

We were huddled in my office discussing what to do. If we begged our allies for help, we'd look weak. This wasn't an immediate crisis, but if Erebus did this every week, the wards would consume our tass stores. It could also make the casino unprofitable in mundane terms, which could be another mechanism for us to lose it.

"Okay. How much is it costing them to cast that spell?" I asked.

O'Meara bit her lip and ran through the calculations. "It's complex. It has to find a single thought within a head and then kill it. But it's not a sustained effect. Depends on the anchors of the magi involved. At least a groat—probably no more than seven."

I made a disgruntled noise. "That's a pretty efficient way to kill a week of our income. Okay. How do we counter it? Rudy, could you shoot that spell down before it goes off next time? Hit it with an anti-magic bomb?"

"You want me to build a giant artillery cannon on the roof?" Rudy smiled.

"Thomas, no," O'Meara said, to Rudy's disappointment. "You and Midnight are the only ones who can see the spell go up. Both of you are too important *and prone to naps* for guard duty."

"And it wasn't in the sky very long before it went ka-bloomie." Rudy's tail flopped. "You could build an auto-mated spell..."

"Which would require a trigger ward over the entire city. Too much tass," O'Meara said.

"No wards. Our solution has to be cheaper than their attack," I said. "We gotta figure precisely how it works and design a counter spell and pulse that out after every attack. Maybe over a smaller area where our customers likely are."

O'Meara thought for a moment. "We could scry back to the point the spell hit. Watch it take effect..." she trailed off.

"Neither of us knows enough mind magic to know what we were looking at," I said for her. "I don't suppose I could bond through a scrying window? Watch their minds as the spell took effect."

"I don't think time would appreciate that," Rudy said. "Might smear your brain across the time span. Too bad we can't just ask them what happened."

A spark fired up in O'Meara's and my minds so simultane-ously that we couldn't be sure who had the thought first. She met my eyes with a grin. "Sure we can."

The word Free in combination with the word Beer works a spell all its own. Within minutes of having rustled up an artistically inclined spell dog on staff, we had a sign up with those magic words followed by an asterisk. A smaller sign declared that a short survey needed to be filled out before receiving said beer. After a bit of magic to light the words up like the brightest of neon lights, you could watch the foot traffic swerve back towards the MGM. The doorman with the ten question survey was quickly overwhelmed, and we had to recruit more staff. We got grumbling about the fact the beer required an ID check from some teenagers who then dutifully produced very fake driver licenses. I stayed near the line listening to the comments.

"Oh yeah! The MGM."

"Hey, didn't we reserve a show here tonight? Did we miss it?"

Not everyone had a positive opinion of the MGM, but the majority of the Free Beer recipients wandered deeper into the depopulated casino instead of outside. The night was still young by Vegas standards, and it was about ten when we had our battle plan. The spell hadn't gone deep. All we needed was an unexpected reminder. A quick tour through the storage vaults and a few calls to the entertainment bookers and we had two marching bands setting off down either side of the strip, one being led by a bull blowing on a tuba, and the other by a horse who'd been working on a fire-breathing act.

"Mind magic's got nothing on the unbridled power of advertising," Rudy said as we listened to the oompha oompha of the bands fading into the distance. "We'll just have corporate increase the advertising budgets and flood the streets with new acts! No tass required. Then, next week, we'll premier the robot arena! Ain't no magic is gonna wipe them out of anybody's mind!"

"One point for House Freelance," I said.

O'Meara disagreed. I didn't need the mental link to see it in the way her intense green eyes looked into the clear sky, deep blue with a few sparse stars. A thin sliver of moon hung in the sky. "We mitigated a probing blow. If we're lucky, they won't notice we're fighting magic with mundane resources." O'Meara's mind churned, arranging our resources and allies into battle lines, before doing the same for what she knew of House Erebus. "The House consists of nearly 50 magi. There is probably a single Cabal of 4 to 6 of them tasked with reclaiming the MGM. Probably one of the more junior ones for now, and ordered to avoid a direct attack. That will last until the elders get impatient or we prove a legitimate threat.

"So we hit them now?" Rudy asked. "They bought like five casinos when House Hermes went bankrupt. They don't need the MGM's income. Make them see they got more to lose than their pride if they keep at it."

"Makes me wish we actually had Ghenna's little black book. Bet that would list some interesting targets," I mused. Ghenna had been one of two House Erebus magi on the council, the one that had been slain by the Dragon I released. Death had been her friend and maybe lover. I'd managed to convince him that said Dragon had promised me protection, should he kill me. So he'd crowdsourced my execution, promising all of Ghenna's secrets to whoever brought my head to him. The contest was aborted due to his untimely, but fortunate, murder by Lansky.

The vault where we had located Death's resurrection machine had been located in the basement of the Casino. And while it had stored plenty of tass and some curious artifacts, the black book had not been there. We found later that Death had more secure holding spaces within the folded space. We made an attempt to blow it open with one of Rudy's tass bombs. The wards laughed off the bomb and nearly killed all three of us with a negative energy strike. Nobody had been particularly eager to try it again after that.

"We need more magi," O'Meara said, answering my thoughts. "We can't do it all. We need at least a full Cabal, Thomas. We're good, but we can't be everywhere at once. We have Oric waiting out there, House Erebus testing our defenses and, as soon as we start oozing blood, we'll have jackals coming out of the woodwork."

"We don't have the resources to start training apprentices!" I countered, my own voice a frustrated growl. "Besides, we'd have to find them first."

"Well," Rudy said with a sour tone, "O'Meara qualifies for both House Hermes and Morgana. They'd be happy to take you and the casino."

I was pacing now, becoming aware that discussing these things in the entryway to the MGM was perhaps not the ideal place. "Absolutely not." I lowered my voice, as if that would help. "We join a House, we become more part of this feudal system than we are already. We haven't even made the first steps toward freeing the spell dogs from that awful curse." If Noise came to town, she'd rightly gut me.

Soothing warmth flowed in through my link. *We can't fix it all, Thomas. Not by ourselves. Maybe we'd be better off trying to reform a single House, instead of taking on the entire system. Particularly when the main instrument of justice, or what passes for it, is paralyzed.*

I let her catch my harness as I stalked by and allowed her to pull me to her.

"Hey, hey, hey. No cuddling while I'm on board!" Rudy shifted back down my spine to avoid getting caught by O'Meara's arms as they encircled my neck.

O'Meara and I relaxed into each other's bodies and together we used her hand to reach down and scratch on the top of Rudy's head. He closed his eyes and leaned into it for a second or two, before brushing the fingers away.

He gave himself a shake. "Crushed candy walnuts, you two, cut it out. You're leaking gooey purrs all over the place." Stepping off my back, he scurried inside.

We sat there for a while, watching people come and go from our casino. There were all sorts of people, mostly tourists without a plan, wandering the strip. A group of satyrs exited, their shod hooves striking the concrete steps with light metallic clops. We'd won tonight, a little victory in what was going to be a long war.

Decisions had to be made soon. Compromises that would hurt. Principles that would have to be sidelined for the sake of the chance of something new. Maybe I would prove to be no better than Jowls, cackling and taunting former friends in the pursuit of ambition.

No. O'Meara brushed that thought away. *I don't think you'd cackle at all. You've got too much guilt hanging around in here. You'd be a cold villain, shutting off pieces of yourself. Probably dye your fur all black and make your tail tip glow deep blue or something. Then lurk in the shadows, muttering about plans within plans. The most gothic of kitties.*

Hey! I thought as she took that villainous image of me and put a pink bow of a collar on it.

So adorably evil, she taunted. We both laughed, She squeezed me tighter. *You keep me from leveling city blocks and I keep you from becoming a Darkwing Duck villain. It will work.*

Since when are you silly? I asked her.

When you need it, my friend.

I nuzzled her face and then we started back inside, heading toward our quarters. O'Meara's eyes went everywhere, trying to etch this place, our place, in her memory while she still could. She pushed happiness at me, at the fact that we had won something today. But someday in the future, probably sooner rather than later, there would be an offer we couldn't refuse, and the casino would be the price we'd pay before we'd give up on each other.

We went to her bedroom, mine probably being used by some of the new crew. As I curled up next to her, I had a thought. What *if we unstuck the council somehow? Gave it a fifth vote.*

Things would start moving. But I don't know in what direction.

Sleep for a cat is more like a switch, it comes and usually falls off easily. As I pushed towards sleep, I wondered if it was time to pay a visit to certain young magus and her cow named Alice.

15

WE ROSE BEFORE THE sun dared to peek over the horizon. O'Meara and I finished armoring the second Fey chain by ten, which was earlier than the 4 AM we had woken up at by Vegas standards. The distinct scent of burning beef wafted through our nostrils as we walked out of our casting chamber.

"Oh, no," O'Meara groaned before I realized precisely what that meant.

"They're in my stash!" I bolted forward, slamming through the doors of my quarters as I raced for my kitchen.

"No, no, no! Flip it, Tilly!" I heard Carey call out.

"I try! It stuck! Pan bad, not me!" Tilly answered as I pushed through the door into a scene straight from... well, maybe from a Sunday comic page somewhere. Tilly stood at my low stove, pan over a lit burner, black smoke streaming up from the steak. He held a spatula in his mouth, which he desperately attempted to get under the charring meat. To the side on the counter sat Carey, welding a two-pronged BBQ fork hooked on the edge of the pan, lips peeled back to show her needle-like teeth as she struggled to hold it in place.

"Tilly, no!" I shouted far louder than I had intended.

"Whoomus?!" Tilly swung his head around without letting go of the spatula; the steak and the pan lifted together. Carey gasped and dropped the fork as the pan flew towards her head.

"EEEEE!" Letting out an eardrum-piercing squeak, Carey threw herself into the air. The pan ricocheted off the refrigerator. Carey flipped end over end like a catapulted pasta

noodle, careening towards a very hard floor. Tilly yipped as
the hot pan clattered into his legs and I dived for the weasel
impact zone. I caught her with my face. "Oooof!" she exclaimed as she bounced back up from the bridge of my nose.
My ear stung as her panicked claws tore through the tip and
she slammed into the arm of the chair, which was much more
padded than either my nose or the floor. Her claws hooked
into the upholstery, all her limbs splayed out, like a bug on a
windshield.

My own momentum had me broadsiding the couch a moment later.

As the ringing of the pan on the tile died, Tilly's claws
scrabbled against the floor in a frantic tap dance of panic. "Oh
no! Oh no! I'm bad. I'm bad. I'm sorry! I so so so so sorry!" The
room erupted with his utter grief-stricken wail of a howl as I
picked myself up and gave my body a shake. My gaze found
Midnight who sat as still as a stuffed animal in the middle of
the couch, eyes wide and glassy.

The eyes moved a fraction, met mine and with a little sound,
a "prrrt," he lost it. "BAHAHAHAHAHAHA!" The cat erupted,
rolling onto his back, legs kicking helplessly in the air.

Tilly howled again and the contrast between it and Midnight's laughter tickled something inside of me. An involun-
tary "hee-hee" escaped between my lips as I turned to Carey,
who had climbed up the arm of the chair she'd adhered to and
looked at me with a dazed expression. "Are you," I managed
to strangle a giggle down to a small, hissing thing, "okay?"

"Yes?"

"I'M SOOO BAAD!" Tilly wailed behind me.

"What in bloody ashes is going on in here?" exclaimed
O'Meara, as she entered the room.

I was too busy trying to contain the laugh prying its way
up my throat. Midnight made an attempt. "They were—then
the pan goes—and now," was all he managed to get out before

collapsing back into laughter. It was echoed by another howl from Tilly.

"And now Tilly needs a hug," I managed, and my laugh made its escape, starting as this hoarse wheeze and growing into a mighty guffaw that left me pounding the ground with a paw.

Stop laughing, O'Meara scolded as she rushed over to the dog and threw her arms around him. "What's the matter, Tilly? You're okay now," she soothed, but the scene replayed in my head. As she watched me catching Carey with my face, a small "hee!" escaped her lips.

"It's not his..." Carey started, but it was interrupted by her own squeaky giggle, "ki-ki-ki, -fault!"

Her laugh retriggered Midnight. "What is this?! Why can't I- BAHAHAHA!"

O'Meara fought it, biting on a knuckle before making the mistake of looking into Tilly's utterly confused eyes.

"What is so funny?" he asked with absolute sincerity.

O'Meara's mind instinctively reached for the memory and we both heard Tilly exclaim, "Pan bad, not me!" She lost it, I lost it and then everyone lost it all over again to the most compulsive case of the giggles I've experienced since I was nine. All except poor Tilly, trapped in O'Meara's arms, more confused than ever.

pain was the only way out, aching chests and raw throats overpowering the mirth. *There was a period where we almost got it under control, but then a small hee!*

O'Meara was the first to shake it off with a full exhalation, "Whooooooo. Well then." She climbed to a shaky standing position and laid a hand on either side of Tilly's head, forcing him to look up to her. "You're a good dog, Tilly. And a good person. Okay?"

"Okay?" Tilly answered.

"Right. So I think everyone is hungry, yes?" O'Meara scooped the fallen pan into the sink, meat and all, before pulling out a slab of bacon.

How are you even moving? I thought at her, my own diaphragm burning with every breath.

Because I refuse to let us get totally derailed by your grade school sense of humor. She mentally huffed as the bacon began to fry. "No more beef this morning," she announced.

"Why? What's wrong with steak?" Carey said, adding in a quieter voice. "I don't get it very often."

"Because it's very bad manners to talk to someone while you have their species on your breath," I told her.

"Why am I here?" Midnight was saying as the limo approached the Luxor, House Picitrix's largest casino. He and Carey reclined on the couch opposite me and O'Meara, while Tilly sat in the corner closest to the dividing window from the drivers, nose pressed up against the window.

"Because you are the cat. You're the one they'll want to see," I said.

"How are cats better than weasels?" Carey asked.

"There is no actual difference in functionality," O'Meara said. "There is some definite anti-mustelid bias among magi."

"And the little issue of you threatening to murder any magus who attempts to bond you," I added.

"Well, it's different if I get paid," she huffed.

"I totally get that," I said as mildly as possible, remembering the crisped corpses of a few Houseless magi who had attempted that.

"Dogs different," Tilly said, without any of his usual cheer.

"Yes, that's true. I've bonded dogs before. They are better at some things and worse than others." Concern was etched into O'Meara's voice. *I don't think I've ever seen a depressed dog before.*

He'll be fine. I hoped, at least. Bonding someone randomly might have been better for Tilly, I had to concede. Innocence gets shredded quickly once you have to make choices for yourself.

"I meant, I don't see why I'm here. I won't do magic ever again," Midnight sighed.

I blinked. "What do you mean by that?"

Midnight kneaded the cushion he sat on. "I'm never going through a night like that again."

"Black Shadow Who Strikes at Midnight," O'Meara started, "It gets better. It won't be that bad again."

"I had to be tended by a rodent! A rodent bathed me." Anger covered abject humiliation. "He took a photo. And don't use my full name in that manner. It sounds silly like that."

"Rudy gets everyone, one way or another. It's just the way of life. Don't be discouraged," I said.

"Use me as... advertising if you must. You gave me choices, right?" He looked back at the black wall which was the seat back as his tail twitched with agitation.

Don't push him right nonappearance warned, patting my side.

Somewhat reluctantly, I pulled back on the thought train that contained all the reasons and responsibilities that Midnight had agreed to. His contract with Madam Pumpernickel was still valid.

"Don't worry, Middy," Carey grinned. "I'll show you how it's done."

"Middy?!" Midnight hissed.

Carey went down on all fours, in the weasel version of the playful dog pose. "Well, you don't like the full name and ya don't like Midnight, so I declare you Middy."

Midnight went full hissing puff and took a swipe at Carey, who danced back from the claws.

"Children." O'Meara was rubbish at ice magic but her voice could freeze you solid if it needed to. "We've arrived."

The limo stopped moving.

"We are on the same team and it's dangerous for everyone outside this car. Stay within ten feet of Thomas at all times," O'Meara lectured.

I switched on all my wards.

Both Carey and Midnight squinted. "Must you be so bright?" he asked.

"You'll get used to it. Come on, don't you want to meet the most graceful cow in all the land?"

"Cow?" Carey said. "This I gotta see." And jumped down into the door well as a Capy brother popped the door from the outside. Midnight followed sullenly. As O'Meara and I exited, Tilly hadn't moved from deep inside the limo's cabin.

"Tilly. Come meet new friends," I said.

That got a half wag before the tail went still. "Friends friends? Or not-friends friends."

"Huh?"

"Not-friends friends, like Betty."

"Oh. Alice and Grace are good friends, Tilly. They might be a little cheesed at me, but they're good people," I explain.

"Okay. Yay, new people." He began to amble up to the door. As he drew next to me he asked in a whisper, "Thomas? What if I not want be with people?"

"Sorry, Tilly, you don't get a choice in that." I gave him a gentle headbutt to spur him onwards.

16

WE ARRIVED AT BLIND Burgers. The name was a dirty lie. In this cat's humble opinion, it didn't matter which sense you blocked up, the burgers here would never fool me into thinking they are beef. If it ain't the smell that's off, then it's the texture. And even if they get it past my gag reflex, there's no tricking my obligate carnivorous stomach. Last time I'd forced down a meal of this stuff, I spent the next day racing for the toilet. Yet, for seeing Grace and Alice, certain sacrifices must be made.

"What the fuck is that smell?" Carey put it very eloquently when we stepped out of the limo and onto a sidewalk so hot that, even bonded to O'Meara, I felt the heat.

"Smells like treats!" Tilly did a little hot foot dance across the sidewalk and into the shade of the storefront. He'd refused the offered doggie booties.

Carey offered an indignant squeak from Tilly's back, "Says someone who can't tell the difference between beg'in strips and bacon strips."

"But they're both treats!" Tilly declared as the two continued to argue the definition of treats versus not-treats; the latter category seemed to only contain cauliflower and broccoli.

"Is this an ambush? I see a magus channeling," Midnight asked from my back, and indeed, the electric blue of a channeled anchor shone from deep within the building.

"Ah, don't worry about that one. Watch for more though," O'Meara said, stepping out behind me.

After the heat of the Vegas day, going into the vegan burger joint felt like walking into a freezer—which might be an authentic experience for a Texas burger joint, for all I knew. The decor leaned hard into transporting the customer down to Houston or something, with roughhewn table tops and wooden stools that might give you splinters. However, in typical Vegas fashion, it leaned too hard, with cartoon cows prancing around the walls, dancing around huge platters of burgers as they celebrated the end of meat. The bewildering menu of not meat-meat patties were listed within a massive speech bubble mounted over the counter, its tail pointing at the mouth of a smiling cow head with lipstick and silver horn covers. The Holstein patterns of black and white matched those of the thin deerlike figure that smiled at me from a table in the corner.

"Thoooomas!" Alice called. "Hope you're hungry! We got a new recipe for you to try. It's much better than last time, I'm sure." Next to her sat Grace, anchor pulsing within her thin elflike frame, her smile strained as she waved a greeting.

"Last time is a low bar, Alice," I said as I trotted through the seating area toward where Alice stood, smelling what was up. Buried beneath all the variations of cooking not-meat stood the curious scent of a storm god who pretended to be a cheetah. Doug was either here or had just left. It took an effort to keep my hackles down.

Look on the bright side, O'Meara thought as she followed after me. An exodus of customers were making for the door in her wake, mostly mythics of vegetarian species, goat men and a party of gnomes. Generally magi and obligate carnivore familiars weren't good signs in vegan eateries.

I hopped up on the stool that had been set out for me, lower than a human's and wider so I could comfortably rest all four paws on it. "No need for you two to dress up for me and O'Meara." I had thought, once Grace had become a full magus, she'd stop channeling all the time. I'd been wrong.

"We always want to be our best, Thomas," Alice said, rocking her head a little and jingling small bells that decorated her horns that now branched like a deer's antlers. My stomach grumbled as I informed it sternly that Alice was friend, not food.

I introduced Carey and Tilly. Midnight had pulled his disappearing act somewhere between the door and the table. Didn't even notice him slip off my back.

"Oh good! A weasel, another palate to work with." Alice said. "You'll love this too!" She turned and ran off toward the kitchen. "Bring them out, Chef!"

"What is going on?" Carey asked. "I thought we were talking about jobs here."

Grace giggled nervously. "Oh, is that what you're here for?" She looked up at me. "I thought it was a bit soon to agree to conduct another taste test."

"You could come and visit us at the MGM," O'Meara said. "You are a full magus now. You're supposed to visit other Houses. You don't have to join your mentor's House."

"Don't you think you've meddled enough in Mistress Grace's education?" Doug appeared on the seat next to Grace without a hint of magic. I did, however, feel a slight wind in my whiskers. The cheetah huffed. He wore, as usual, nothing but his spots and his collar of dark stones. Stones that somehow concealed his true nature from everyone, perhaps even his bond.

"I thought I smelled you lurking nearby. Long time no see," I said.

"With good reasons for that," Doug said, his eyes shifted toward the door.

"Come on, Doug. You supported our claim, which almost makes up for you and Ceres being first in line to kill me," I said in a slightly performative manner. We couldn't discuss the real reasons they had supported our claim in public or in front of even Grace.

Alice burst through the door, a human on her hoofed heels, carrying a platter of steaming somethings. "Here it—" Her ears fell when she saw the cheetah. "Oh, well, Doug. So glad you could join us for the tasting." The smile became a baring of teeth.

Doug glared at me, as if this were my fault. "You know Ceres believes this quixotic quest of yours: to produce the best fake meat in the city, is a waste of time and talent."

"Then she shouldn't have given us the Blind Burger if she didn't want us to make it into the best meat-free restaurant in the city," Grace said, speaking for the first time.

"It was a joke, Grace," Doug whispered with an almost pleading note, as an array of meatlike substances were slid onto the table.

"She gave us a restaurant instead of a sanctum, Dougie. It's not a funny joke. I bet House Freelance would give us actual casting circles if we asked." Grace's voice floated as a soft whisper with a hint of steel. Someone had been growing up. Her eyes went to mine.

This is interesting. O'Meara smirked as she tried some of the darker pseudo-meat and made a face.

"We do have one Atlantean circle," I ventured, "It does make certain things easier."

"Thomas, don't," Doug said. "Grace and Alice are sure to find a place among a Picitrix Cabal very soon."

"I'm sure that will happen any day, with Ceres' endorsement of our abilities," Grace's voice went tight and she sniffled. Alice had forgotten about hosting and was giving Doug a death glare.

"Aaaah." It appeared that we'd stepped into the middle of a bit of tiff between master and apprentice. I'd noted an edge of tension when we'd paid a visit last month. "Maybe we should come back later..."

Grace's eyes flicked to Alice, who animated with a waitress' honed smile. "Won't be but a minute more, Thomas. Just been so long since we've seen Doug or Ceres."

"We have been busy with renovations." Doug groomed from his elbow down to his paw.

Grace didn't let up. "Maybe we don't need Ceres' help to find a Cabal that will take us. Minor Houses can provide us with all that we need. I bet I could ask House Freelance to recruit us. They'd be stupid to say no. After all, they only have one magus. Or House Synd. I could even apply to House Morgana if I wanted to. You think sneaking into the Merlin's tower so we could bond ourselves was a scandal!"

If Grace carried out her threats, then Ceres' ambition to be the youngest Archmagus could be seriously postponed. Her House had to put forth a nomination. "I will... make her apologize, Grace."

"Then I guess I won't be accepting your offer, Thomas," Grace sighed. "Sorry."

"That's not—" Both me and the cheetah spoke the words simultaneously.

I lifted a paw and gestured for him to continue.

"That's not why Thomas is here. He's hoping you'd be willing to pressure Ceres into hiring him again. And I think you've done enough pressuring today, Grace," Doug said.

O'Meara chuckled. "Well, it does make it convenient that you're here, then. We can pressure you directly."

"I can only take so many headaches, O'Meara," Doug said sourly. "The cat would have been House Picitrix's if you hadn't intervened at the auction."

"I beg your pardon!" Midnight said, jumping up onto the table right next to Doug. The cheetah nearly fell off his stool. "I am The Black Shadow Who Strikes at Midnight! And I will not be referred to as 'the cat.'" With Doug scanning the room with wide eyes, the tabby cat bit into the nearest not-meat ball, chewed and swallowed. "That is foul," he announced, before going for another bite.

"Where?! Where were you hiding him? Is that some sort of threat, Thomas?" Doug glared at me.

I smiled. "No, he just does that. He's talented like that. And he would have gone to Erebus. Not like Ceres was involved in the bidding. The bidding would have been much hotter."

gather."

My smile turned sly. "Ceres is still on the TAU's naughty list, so that's not a real obstacle, Doug. Besides, Fibalt couldn't really object if it helped clear the way for House Picitrix's second seat on the Council."

"Are you going to say you can click your teeth together and deliver House Morgana's and House Hermes' votes, Thomas? Because I doubt you have pockets that fit a House in," Doug huffed.

"Not offering that," O'Meara said as she shoved a plate of meat stuff at Tilly. "A little work isn't worth tipping the balance of power. We'd be asking for the Luxor itself if we could do that. And Ceres would pay it."

"But I have the ears of both Hermes and Morgana," I said. "Help me out and I can add some positive noise from my end."

"You think either of Dominicus or Morrian cares what their rank and file think? Morrian only listens to the Crones of her House, while Dominicus... "Doug did a little head bobble, "has no one above him but Magus Napoleon now, with Medoci gone."

"We need protection from House Erebus, Doug. Commit to that, hire my familiars in the meantime, and if you have something that might sway this Napoleon, I'll see it delivered," I said.

"You're going to waltz into Shangra-la and see a magus who hasn't left it in over a hundred years?" Doug's eyes narrowed and I felt the prickle of a scry, as if politics could be read like magic.

"I don't see why not." With causal ease I leaned down to try a 'meat' ball, and regretted it as soon my tongue scooped up a glob. Committed, I swallowed. Feline tongues with their tiny meat hooks had no easy abort function. My stomach gurgled in a threatening manner as I stifled a cough. "What you say to him is up to you."

"Ceres and I will talk about it," Doug said. "Send us the contracts. Without the squirrel this time. He is tiresome to deal with."

"At least he knows the contracts inside and out. You'll have them within the hour," I said.

The cheetah nodded and paused for a moment. "Have you... checked in on Feather?"

My ears flicked in surprise. "No... The Council still has her, as far as I know."

I watched his spots swirl into small storms on his golden fur and then they stabilized, back into blotches of black. "I see. Never mind then. I'm sure she's secure. Goodbye." He gave a small smirk. "Enjoy your... meal."

"And here I thought I might get through two entire minutes without you being snide!" Alice snorted.

Doug laughed. "Are you cutting bits of yourself and eating it? Because that's the only way you're going to learn the flavor you are trying to replicate."

"That's disgusting!" Alice stamped her back hoof. "Are you trying to get all four of my stomachs to hurl at once?"

"Real cows do eat meat if they can catch it. Bones too," Doug taunted as Alice lowered her horns at him.

"Dougie," Grace said very quietly. "Let's not do this here."

"You're not the one who has to talk sense into Ceres after a nap," Doug moved in that too-fast-to-follow manner, bopping Alice right on her snoot. "Too slow!" he declared and then zipped back behind me.

With a bellow of rage, Alice charged around the table, a black and white blur tipped with pointy bits, and chased the cheetah out of the restaurant, swerving around a startled pair of tourists who sent their candy-colored cell phones crashing to the floor.

"At least those two like each other. Grade School affection right there," O'Meara chuckled as Grace slammed a palm into her forehead.

"Quick! Dump all this stuff before she comes back!" Carey shoved a plate at Tilly, who had been doing his level best to demolish as much food as was within tongue reach. "Fortunately, we brought a garbage disposal!"

"Is better than kibble!" Tilly declared. "It's mushy kibble!"

"It is foul, but does have a certain tang." Midnight chowed down on a particularly blackened variety. "There was a dog in my territory, Mr. Rowf, his wet food tasted similar after a day of seasoning or so."

"That's a big improvement from last time, Grace," I said, hoping I wasn't going to have two very sick familiars this afternoon.

"Maybe I will jump Houses," Grace muttered. "Or start up a vegan dog food company."

17

THE NEXT DAY THE contracts came back from Ceres. As Rudy said, "The Freelance Familiars are officially unofficially in da bizness!" There were celebrations. O'Meara had whiskey, Rudy blew up the cake. I... might have had a little catnip. Just to forget about the small red envelope addressed to one Magus Napoleon that I had to deal with.

I had to talk to Shina, but first we had to face day one and getting three somewhat nervous familiars to the safety of the Luxor.

"I fail to see why I have to come along on this fool's errand," Midnight groused from up behind the limo's head rest. O'Meara and I sat in the couch seat opposite him. Carey paced back and forth the length of the cabin in a high-speed nervous pace, while Tilly watched the door anxiously. Rudy stared out the rear window, tail twitching as he tried to pick out suspicious activity behind us.

"Midnight, you are the security while Carey and Tilly are bonded to the apprentices," I said for like the fifth time. I could have pushed it into his mind, but it seemed everyone kept forgetting the plan.

Guarding things is a dog's job. He sniffed.

It's *that or spellcraft*, I thought back at him. Even with the light touch of our minds, I felt the thread of his remembered nausea.

I had bonded him via Mr. Bitey, ensuring our link couldn't be severed, while O'Meara and I used an armored Fey chain.

So long as we stuck together, I'd know if any of the three got into trouble, and we could channel fire or stasis to Midnight, should he need it.

"No need to dig up all your nuts," Rudy said. "First day should be smooth, dog like Charlie won't be thinking fast enough to do—

The kinetic ward outside the limo flared gold.

"—anything." Rudy's tail went limp.

"What was that?" Carey asked as I looked at the point where the ward had flashed. A very tiny ding showed in the meshwork of runes.

"Sniper bullet," Rudy said, shifting to the direction of the shot. "Probing shot."

"Let's mark him." O'Meara and I cast a locator spell. The limo had a nest of wards around it, one of which traced any projectiles right back to their origin points. There were only two possibilities. The road sat between the Excalibur (owned by Picitrix) and the Tropicana (owned by Erebus) hotels.

To my surprise, the shot hadn't come from either hotel, instead it came at us from a 45-degree angle from the roof dominated by a giant cross. They were sniping from a Catholic church, not nearly as high as the Casinos, but high enough. My vision zoomed—a satyr, his long ram-like horns curling back over his skull as he peeked over the roof's lip, one eye behind the scope of a sniper rifle. The muzzle sparked and my vision flashed.

"Idiot!" O'Meara said as she jammed the switch on the sun roof. "He thinks I can't hit him from here?" The ward flashed twice more before the roof opened fully.

"Don't! Keep driving. It's a distraction!" Rudy swiveled his head from side to side.

"From what?" I asked.

"THAT!" Rudy pointed to the other side of the car from the sniper as the back door to the Honda Fit that had been driving alongside us swung wide open to reveal the revolving barrels of a minigun.

A loud BRRRRR! sounded as O'Meara spun, projecting a lash of flame out her finger tips.

It sliced through the car, the satyr, and the gun. The gun spun apart first, ripping through the cheap car before an explosion tore the entire thing apart.

"Step on it, Capys!" I shouted, leaping out of my seat a moment too late. The kinetic ward of the limo had been ripped through. And half a dozen holes showed through the seat I'd been sitting in. My personal ward had saved my life.

"YESS SIIRRS!" The Capy brothers called back from the driver's seat. The engine roared and the car shot forward.

Both O'Meara and I stared at the massive gouges in the ward we'd set up a few hours ago. Had she been a second slower, we'd all be paste.

"Less staring! More fixing!" Rudy cried, and we both started moving. Making a circle with our bodies, we patched the hole as the world outside sounded with the screeching of tires and protestations of horns. The Capys slammed on their horn and the traffic parted.

O'Meara's mind remained as calm as the eye of a hurricane while mine whirled with panicked thoughts. It hadn't even been one of the TAU! A satyr with a gun! My hold on the spell in front of us shook. Had we screwed up making the ward?

*Thomas, calm down. O'Mear*a laid a soothing hand on my neck as she scanned for more targets. *The wards worked, we're alive, nobody is bleeding and the sniper stopped shooting at us.*

Right, you're right. I saw Tilly, Carey, and Midnight staring at me, ears back as they each hunkered down. This was the world I was putting them into. Carey and Tilly sported harnesses with wards nearly as strong as mine. Midnight had refused to wear the wards as they blocked his vision. Maybe he would change his mind now. I inhaled as we turned into the Luxor's private drive. Fear floated in the air, but no blood. "We are okay. The TAU sent us a little message. Our wards worked, so O'Meara and I will send them our own message after we drop you off."

"That sounded like the M-134," Carey said, her tiny black eyes blinking.

"You some sort of expert on military hardware now?" Rudy still clung to the back window, ears twitching.

"No, it was at a party. They were shooting it at watermelons. I-I remember that sound. And what was left of the watermelons." Carey stared at our hastily patched ward and the bullet holes in the seat. "That's from Oric, right?"

"Mortal assassins are not House Erebus's style," O'Meara said. "They were most likely hired by the TAU."

"Bastard!" Carey shouted so loud that her little body lifted from the floor. "Fucking! Bastard!" A high pitched growl squeak hissed out of her as the car began to slow to a stop. "Trying to keep us in cages."

"We've arrived, sirs," the Capy brother whistled from the front. I saw Doug and Ceres speed-walking toward the limo, wards blazing. "Are we staying?"

"Yes!" Carey responded immediately. "Nobody's putting me in cage! Ever again. Come on, Tilly! We got work to do."

Tilly had curled into a smaller ball than I had thought possible, he lifted his head. "And after work, Treats?" His tail wag hit him in the face.

"All the treats! Cause you're a good boy!" Carey said. This forced Tilly to his feet, if only to avoid getting smacked around by his own tail. "Come on, Midnight! You, too!"

I couldn't see Midnight, but I felt his thoughts, I *didn't hear it coming... didn't see it, didn't smell it. Is magic worth this? So loud.*

Midnight, if you need a moment, you can come back with us. I gently prodded.

MurAGH! The sound and the thought were one and the same as Midnight popped up from between the seat cushions on the rear bench. How *RUDE!* He glared at me, lashing a puffed up tail as his mind scrambled, clumsily shutting the link between us. Chest heaving, "I'm fine. Never better. I will strike those responsible down for I am The Black—"

The door popped and the cat dove right back between the seats. It swung open to reveal a waiting Doug and Ceres. "Presenting the Freelance Familiars, Sir and Madam!" the Capy sang.

"Do any of the Freelance Familiars need medical attention?" Ceres asked.

Carey smiled as she climbed up onto Tilly. "Nope, you won't get a hurl story from us. Coming, Middy?"

There was a squrck of rubbing leather as Midnight attempted to pull himself out of the seat in a dignified manner, failed completely and tumbled out, tail going over head. He picked himself up. "If you must shorten it, the name is Midnight," he said, walking the length of the limo to the door with his nose in the air. The three exited the cabin.

Doug hopped into the car, examining the line cut through three continuous windows by O'Meara's heat lance. "Had your first encounter with a mage ripper, I see. Good thing you were with them."

Rudy chittered territorially. "Yeah. We got it handled from here, Spots."

"Do you?" Doug said with an imperious tone.

"Yes, thank ya for your offer of help," O'Meara accent had gone thick. "We will nae need your and Ceres' assistance in tracking him." And I realized that her calmness was nothing but a cool cap on an active volcano.

You... know the sniper, don't you? I asked her.

How many Satyrs with horns like that have you met? Her green eyes flickered like flame.

"Happy hunting, then," Doug nodded and left the Capy bro shutting the door behind him.

"Where's toosss?" the Capy in the front asked.

"We should go back and get Stompy," Rudy said, rubbing his paws together.

"A single Satyr merc isn't worth a giant robot." O'Meara opened up a compartment in the seat, pulling out her Inquisitorial sword and the spell ripper.

"Awww. Nuts," Rudy responded.

I pawed open another drawer, revealing the Wizard Phooey Mark II. "Gonna have to make do with your artillery instead." I looked up to the driver's window. "Take us to that church."

18

THE CHURCH'S STAFF WERE more than happy to tell us all about where they were when the gunshots started. We had a license number and a description of a black Lexus SUV that had peeled out of the parking lot about fifteen minutes before we arrived. The minster stank of fear as he led us up to the roof of the building.

This close to the Strip, one of the Houses no doubt owned the land the church sat on, Catholic church or not. Directly across from the Luxor, I imagined the faithful making a steady commute to the busy confessionals before going back for another load of sins. But that's my darker humor. The church probably did more weddings than sin forgiveness. I didn't know. I didn't really care beyond a vague sense of guilt as we let the priest marinate in his sweaty terror.

The roof was clean of most traces, no shells, no hoof marks, but I could smell him. Faint like a single rose in a field of grass, yet still that distinct ungulate flavor, mixed with a punch of humanity.

Time, knowledge, and tass. O'Meara knew precisely what she was doing, and we had the tass to make it happen. Within minutes, the spell spun up and the satyr knelt on the edge of the roof again, sighting through the sniper rifle although slightly transparent. He wore a black kilt studded with pockets, and matched it with a brown leather biker's jacket that proclaimed him a member of Hell Goats. Sweat poured off his face.

He fired, sighted, fired again. His head recoiled back from the scope, an F-bomb clearly on his lips. Hands suddenly shaky, he swiftly disassembled the rifle, pieces disappearing beyond the effect of the spell.

"You had to have known, Grugar," O'Meara told the image as he frantically scooped up shells. "Lemme guess, that was Grudge and Gullnar in the car? Was this really worth the money?"

"Who are they?" Rudy asked.

"Soldiers. Good ones," O'Meara said as the image dashed toward the side of the roof "The brothers Grim. They thought themselves so clever for that." Her thoughts were closed to me, reliving a maelstrom of memories. The image paused as it vaulted over the side. We had a lot more control of this spell since the last time we'd done it. We went downstairs, and the image resumed moving. O'Meara watched it climb into an invisible SUV and float into traffic before we got back into the limo. "Take us to the Thirsty Ermine, please," she told the Capys.

"Shouldn't we follow the spell?" I asked.

"We are." O'Meara leaned back in the seat and folded her arms. "You might as well put the Phooey away."

"You don't know that!" Rudy said. "This could be a trap. Maybe they knew you'd track them, and they're setting us up for another ambush."

"Oh, it's definitely an ambush, Rudy," I said, remembering our last time at the Thirsty Ermine. "One where all the bullets aren't going to help."

Sure enough, the assassins' image met us outside the Thirsty Ermine, the sort of bar that got sick of replacing its windows decades ago and boarded them up with plywood. The ancient ward that kept out nosey magics fried the image as it reached for the door. The black SUV was still parked down the block.

"He wouldn't still be in there!" Rudy said. "He probably came here to neutralize the tracking spell and slipped out the back."

Kill your wards, O'Meara thought at me. Tapping the bracelet where she kept her own defenses, they folded up into a vision searing dot of brightness. I did the same. *This won't be like last time. This time we really are the masters coming for a reckoning.*

"I wouldn't put any tass on that bet, Rudy," I said.

Rudy jumped on my back and started clicking a little zippo in the front pocket of his harness. "I'm still packing."

A Satyr exited the door and flinched when O'Meara caught it. You wouldn't think a bar would be crowded in late morning in Vegas but this one smacked me in the face with the scent of bacon, apples and fried eggs. You know those movies where a man walks into a crowded room and the hubbub of conversations dies? It's like walking into a physical wall. And that's precisely what happened as O'Meara stepped in behind me.

"There he is!" Rudy said and sure enough, Grugar sat, his curled black horns shining in the fluorescent lighting. "Hey, you! Ya got almond custard for brains!"

Grugar did not look in our direction. He took a long gulp of the black brew in his pint glass.

"Let me handle it, Rudy," O'Meara said under her breath. Her eyes were not on Grugar, but on the elderly satyr behind the bar. I approached it with her. "Elder," O'Meara addressed the bartender. "Would you please ask Grugar to step outside? We have business to discuss."

"So you'll kill him? Maybe after you rip the answers you want out of his head?" The Elder snorted.

"He just attempted to kill us. You know what that means, Elder," O'Meara said.

"Oh I know, You're a magus and we're satyrs. I'm sure the boy is sorry and he won't try it again. I don't see the boy's mates, so I assume they're already cinders. Maybe that's enough examples for you?"

"I'm not a boy!" Grugar growled.

"And I told you to keep your bleating mouth shut," the Elder said without taking his bar shaped eyes off O'Meara.

But I took the opening, "Not a boy?" I stepped up onto the bar. "It certainly looks like you've run home to daddy here. Hoping that he can save you? You and your band tried to make swiss cheese out of my family and friends," I hissed, letting a growl mix with the sound. Several satyrs got up from the bar.

Thomas, careful, O'Meara warned. *We do not want to alienate the entire satyr community. We have to bargain with the Elder.* Grugar had his hand in his coat, gripping a pistol, most likely.

Why? We could just grab him. Nobody here would be strong enough to stop us.

That's precisely why, O'Meara said. *Magi might not recognize any laws, but they do.*

I knew that was reasonable. I knew we were trying to be better. But I could see Grugar's blood pulsing in his neck. Blood that should be spilled.

"Easy, Thomas," Rudy whispered. "Let's not pounce in the middle of a bar. Also, you're starting to ignite."

My body had crouched, every muscle quivering in preparation for a strike. I turned with a dismissive huff back to the Elder. "You want mercy? You want him to live? Then he'd better be at the MGM within 24 hours, otherwise his name will be smoking crater."

"And then what?" The Elder straightened.

"We won't kill him," O'Meara said, deciding for me. "I believe mundane prison is six to thirty years. Don't expect less."

Now we're going to run a prison out of the hotel? I glared at her. *We can't go soft on this, O'Meara. We have to protect our familiars and if fear is the only way...*

We'll come up with something, Thomas. Calm down. She stared me dead in the eyes.

They almost got us all! With a mundane weapon!

But they didn't!

And if we hadn't been there!? If we'd sent Tilly, Carey and Midnight alone. If we had been busy.

She extended her hand and caressed my cheek. And *then we would have lost them and it would have been tragic, but we were prepared for this. You want to give up now?*

No, the thought growled and I swung my head away from her. My eyes found Grugar. "Twenty-four hours." I said and stalked out of the bar, forcing O'Meara to follow after me.

We'd taken two steps out the door before Rudy said, "Scattered cashews on a four-lane highway. Been working on your bad cop routine, eh, Thomas? I really thought you were about to rip that guy open."

"Because he was," O'Meara commented as Capybara opened the door for her.

I stopped short of the limo. Another metal box to be trapped in. My heart was still in my throat. My claws itched. "I'm going to find my own way home,' I announced.

"We're vulnerable if you do that," O'Meara said as she slammed herself down on the seat. I felt the wave of fatigue washing over her.

"I know, but I need a walk," I said.

"You do," O'Meara agreed.

"I'll keep him out of trouble," Rudy called back, as I was already moving down the sidewalk. Something in my head felt so tightly wound that it threatened to snap. The Vegas sun rose towards noon now and Rudy started to pant and suffer within five minutes of leaving the bar. After a few more minutes, he fished something out of the pocket of my harness, I heard the crinkle of tin foil. "Ahhh, much better." I glanced back to see him huddled under a small reflective blanket.

I had to get higher, had to survey my surroundings, and veered towards a three-story apartment building.

"So what's the problem, big guy?" Rudy asked. "Being a big shot's stressful, I know. This isn't how I imagined this working out, either."

I stopped, as something moderately tasty wafted through the air.

"Kinda a faaaar cry from the sleepy detective agency I'd been imagining back in Grantsville. You know, a cozy office where I'd make a nest out of unpaid bills, and we'd be weeks from getting evicted, when a leggy blond magus would show up crying about her poor snookums." Rudy talked as my ears zeroed in on the sound of yapping. It was... definitely outside, unprotected.

I leapt over the fence and bounded up onto the roof of the small two-story house as Rudy continued. "You'd bond her and then we'd figure out the nefarious plot that had led her snookums down a dangerous path of destruction. That would have been fun! But no, we landed in Vegas with responsibilities first to the refugees. Then well, you decide you wanna fix the world! Let me tell ya, life would be a lot easier if you were a self-centered jerk who pretended not to care about the world. But noooo, you keep making friends and hey, what are you doing?"

I'd crossed through several yards, and now belly-crawled across the roof of a single story bungalow. Down below, a fat sausage of a little dog panted in the shade. It was no deer, but it'd do.

The rodent chittered on my back. I ignored him as I crept down to the very edge of the roof. The dog casually watched a bug crawl through the dirt. Distantly I heard laughter, but paid it no mind.

I sprang.

"What aaaaare you doing!" Rudy's sounds crystalized into words as my paws left the roof tiles.

Hunting.

The little dog looked up far too late. I opened my mouth as Rudy's words filtered down to the next level.

Why was I hunting?

Hungry. My pads hit the packed earth with a soft whump, the momentum carrying my body forward, propelling my jaws to impact the dog's neck.

Why was I hunting someone's pet?

I froze. The dog piddled himself as I held him in my teeth. A deep malicious laughter rolled out from the back of my mind.

Good huntin', brother, Bone Whistler nearly purred.

"Drop him, Thomas! Put him down! This is not a good look for you, buddy!" Rudy tugged on my ears.

What the hell did you do! I screamed in my head as I spat out the little dog. It yipped as it bolted for the house. Five feet away from its door, he must have tripped over an unreasonable amount of stupid bravery because he stopped running and started barking.

I believe this is called showing my hand, he thought at me. *Now that I've got the technique down.*

*What tech—*Pressure shifted in my head. Abruptly, the words weren't there.

Weaver tells me interesting things about our bond. How it's unhealthy to owe each other favors. Puts us out of balance and allows one to control the length of soul between us. I can push you all the way back into that feline brain of yours.

I realized something and thoughts, memories flowed. The *deer in the council tower, the pang of hunger looking at Alice? That's you?*

And a little of the aggression at the bar. I believe my intervention helped that situation there. Everyone saw you as dangerous, instead of the overgrown housecat you actually are.

Outside my head, Rudy was telling me to move, cajoling me to tell him what was going on. I could feel O'Meara and

Midnight, but they felt distant, as if Bone Whistler had dragged me into a remote space in my own head. I started moving. What *do you want?* I asked, even though I knew. He'd asked for it while I had been bonded to Veronica. "I'm handling it, Rudy," I told him.

I want you to repay the debt. I delivered Weaver in your time of need and I demand you give me what I want.

Yes, and that worked out fine for me. I saved the life of someone who stabbed me in the back less than 48 hours later. And now you want me to do the impossible. Favors have to be things within my power. I cannot simply shove a human woman into a box and send her to you. Even if I could find someone willing, they'd fall back to their native plane within a week or so.

Do not talk to me of impossible. You are a king now. You have territory, you have servants, and you court powerful females who covet your power. You fight battles of far more consequence than your meals can comprehend. To win them, you need me.

Then give me something I can do. We were moving back toward the road now, trotting with purpose in the direction of the MGM.

Thomas? O'Meara called out to me. *What happened? Something changed.* I pushed back with a hasty assurance.

Bone whistler continued, What *was done to us can be done again.*

Archibald is gone. Both him and his work. Robbing me of my thinking bits won't change that. I cannot do what you ask.

You seek many powers, mastery over the bonds, weapons to use against your enemies. Seek one more. As you have become a predator, give me what I need to be a human. Other humans.

You don't need humans to form a family, I snorted. The only other intelligent cougar on the planet was frozen in stasis in the dungeon of the council.

We are not friends here, Thomas, I am still the Apex. I need an equal, a mate. Then children, then family. You will move toward acquiring the ability we need. Then you will do it. Or I will reduce you to meat at the moment I choose. Someone will die while you're off hunting a rabbit.

I'll fight you.

I gave you a way to cheat death. It doesn't matter if you dislike the price. I hold a favor over you. I could trade the favor back to the Weaver. Would you prefer her task? So long as I hold it, I can take thought from you. Refuse when the time comes and your precious family will have no choice but to put you in a zoo. Understand, brother?

I understand, I conceded. He had me over a barrel. How do you fight someone who can take your mind hostage? I could only hope he'd be patient. Years of research and then finding someone willing couldn't be that hard, right? Being a mountain lion wasn't all that bad. It had worked out for me so far, minus the gruesome injuries to myself and my friends.

Good, Bone Whistler purred with satisfaction. *Don't think I won't notice when you find what you need,* he warned as he slipped back to his own plane, leaving me with Rudy on my back and an anxious O'Meara hovering on her side of the link.

Somewhere else, Midnight purred. So at least someone was having a good time.

19

I TOLD RUDY AND O'Meara minimum details about the conversation with Bone Whistler. Rudy made sympathetic noises and muttered something about his anchor being crazy. When I asked who might have access to Archibald's old notes, the answer was his original House: Hermes.

Now I had even more reason to visit Shina. I spent a good hour fretting about what you bring a lioness as a gift. Roses didn't quite fit her. I went down into the vaults to peruse an assortment of minor artifacts we'd inherited along with the MGM. I found a crystalline rose under a glass dome. The flower undulated through a rainbow of colors, its wicked thorns weeping tiny granules of black sand. Beauty and the Beast came to mind immediately and I had myself chirping with amusement.

Either she'd be amused or not. Maybe she'd know what it did. There were no notes in Death's vaults. Things were barely organized. It just hadn't been in piles of especially deadly things. I had it wrapped by two spell dogs who wore face shields and gloves, just to be safe.

I put the gift in a box, and holding it by the strings, I headed over to the Hermes Tower. A modern elevator that looked very recently installed took me up to the 37th floor. High enough to be important. The elevator opened to a short hallway with a single door at the end. It had no handles, consisting of a solid slab of polished black marble on stout iron hinges. A cheap plastic doorbell had been installed next to it with a wire running down beneath the door. I could see traces of spells on the walls, but they'd all been pulled down.

I pawed at the button and heard a distant chime.

"Who is it?" a man's muffled voice called. Did they not even have security cameras?

After giving my name, the door opened an inch, revealing Shina's eye. "Thomas! This is unexpected, an unannounced visit!" Her tone was pleased as she attempted to wedge her paw through the crack, but it proved to be too narrow. She gave a frustrated chuff and pulled away. Moments later human fingers curled around the edge of the doors, and with a grunt of effort, the door opened a few more inches, allowing Shina to get her paw around it and push it the rest of the way open. "If I had known you were coming, we would have fixed this," she said. "How embarrassing. We've been on the 'no unnecessary magic' decree for six months, and we're finding out that this tower is held together with nothing but. Come in."

She backed out of the entrance. I put the gift at her feet and then slid up against her as I walked in. A grand penthouse stretched out before me, filled with a strange combination of neat Martha Stewart chic and vaguely African tribal, like they'd raided one of those free trade stores to decorate with. Bright colors mixed with stark black in beadwork and tapestries. Fredrick gave me a wave and retreated into a side room.

There were no chairs, except at a desk in the corner. All the other seats were long couches or cushions. I had not been the only one to pay her a visit recently, other feline scents mingled in the air. Not that surprising. House Hermes probably had the largest population of large cats outside the zoo. There were no windows, but a black panel took up the far wall.

"Oh my..." Shina said as she tore through the cardboard with her teeth. "The rose of Aphrodite." A focus in her collar flared and the rose floated up out of the box to hover at her eye level. It slowly spun as she tilted her massive head this way and that.

"Thomas," she sighed, "you shouldn't give me things like this. I'm going to have to sell it."

I approached, giving the rose another look with my magical sight. Tiny runes flowed within it like water. A very minor summoning effect centered on its thorns. "Really? It doesn't seem very powerful."

"A single one of those grains induces a mad, passionate love that will devolve into violence within a week. Are you trying to tell me something, little lion?" She smiled.

"No... I just thought I could do better than a dozen roses. And it was the purdiest thing in the vault that I thought might be safe to touch." I nudged her shoulder as she floated the rose over to the counter.

Her tongue ran across the top of my head. "It gets my attention. But it also makes me think you want something more than another dinner and date. Even minor Atlantean artifacts are not something to toss around."

Leaning into the grooming, I murred, "I... might have promised someone that I would talk to a certain magus who's known to be difficult to reach."

She gave something between a growl and purr. "Someone who's in Shangra-la. We could certainly work it into our trip."

"I need a quicker trip."

The grooming stopped, and the mountain of warm muscle I had been leaning on abruptly withdrew. "Heartbreaker," she chuffed. "You got my hopes up."

Gods, she was like a six-year-old impatient for show and tell. The thought made me chuckle more than anything, and I was curious to see what she desperately wanted to show me. But my House came first. I took her rejection in stride, circling around her flank and rubbing my scent along her short fur. "It will happen. At some point. When I can send out my familiars without getting jumped by satyrs."

A paw the size of my head pushed me away. "Like that's going to happen. You let one go."

Dang, news travels fast. Did I have a camera crew following me around? I thought of the thousands of rodents who had built Big Stompy. Maybe I did have a tiny film crew in tow. Still, I re-centered on the dance Shina and I were performing, pulling away, feigning my own disinterest. "Oh no, he's coming to us. He's tying up his loose ends. The satyr elders promised he won't run. I think the price that Oric will have to pay mercenaries to come after us is going to go way up."

With a lurch, two forelegs seized me from behind and her weight bowled me over. "And who do you think you are, Little Lion? The second coming of Ghenna, going to make him come to you, then feed him piece by piece to a tank of piranhas? You're a lot of things, Thomas." She playfully bit at my neck before letting go. "Intimidating, you're not."

Rolling away, I stood up into a light defensive stance, baring my teeth but keeping my ears forward. "So sure of that, Princess? Hate to get smoke damage in your home."

"Princess?!" she growled. "I'm a Queen and don't you forget about it, bite-sized lion. Besides," her tail lashed, "You couldn't hurt a mouse unless they threatened your mother first."

"Oh yeah!" No witty comeback occurred to me, and I smacked the side of her muzzle.

She roared with a lunge forward. My smaller size gave me a little more speed, but not enough. A backhand paw to my ribcage staggered me briefly as she turned. I jumped, aiming for the counter behind her. The giant lioness reared up, clapped two paws on either side of my stomach, and hauled me back to earth, suplexing me onto one of the wide cushions. The impact knocked the wind right from my lungs. I gasped for breath, helpless as Queen Shina lay down on top of me.

"You're supposed to say Uncle," Shina said, casually gnawing on my ear. Her growl purrs radiating down through me.

I struggled to breathe, period. "I... just didn't want to... mess up your place."

She laughed. "There's a lot of cats who think I'm slow because I'm big. It's alright to be wrong when it comes to me. Now who's a Queen?"

"You, I guess," I wheezed.

She rolled off me with an almost girlish giggle. "You're fun, Thomas. Got time for a flick?"

"Short one maybe," I conceded. "Gotta pick up the trio at the end of the day. You going to help me out? Or do I have to tunnel into Shangra-la myself?"

"Heh." She head-butted my shoulder. "I'll let you in tomorrow. After I see how you're handling your mercenary problem. And if you're trying to go see Magus Napoleon, then I wish you luck. But you're gonna owe me a favor."

I chirped, unconcerned. "So long as it doesn't require me to violate the central tenet of my morality, we'll be fine."

"Owe a devil a favor?" She side eyed me.

"Sorta," I said.

"Don't we all." Shina rolled her head toward the entertainment center by the black panel. "Come on."

I cracked open the bond and checked in on Midnight; disappointment rolled through him after Carey and Tilly had failed to puke while they worked with the apprentices. Good enough for me, though.

Shina and I watched a nature documentary, a one-way ticket to snoozeville. She made a much better pillow than a blanket.

No machine gun-equipped sedans assaulted us on the way home. Rudy had insisted we use his cannon-equipped van instead of the limo, and he passed the fifteen-minute trip spinning around in the firing cradle daring someone to take a shot. Tilly and Carey were too busy sleeping to be talkative, and Midnight seemed to be lost in his own head.

O'Meara and I did not get much sleep. We had an example to prep for.

Grugar and a trio of satyr elders arrived at the most ungodly hour possible on the Vegas strip, seven AM. Two hours before the arrival of the day shift. They wore white clothing, bleached to the point that it hurt eyeballs as they stood on the steps in front of the main strip entrance. I felt a pang of regret as I texted Fredrick that the show would be starting soon.

I expected at least a light rebuke but he simply texted OOW (On Our Way). Apparently, they didn't keep Vegas hours.

The four satyrs made no movement to enter the hotel, and instead stood in a circle passing a wine skin between them. Whether a ritual or simply fortifying courage, I didn't know. I had a nagging sensation that we were doing this wrong. Maybe we should have held a trial? Did the elders not believe that Grugar had attempted to assassinate us?

"You want the police to handle this?" O'Meara stated as we watched from the security room.

"Yes." I knew that wasn't the way it worked. Mythics who worked for a House were defended by that House. No employment, no protection. Houses were expected to handle their own relationships and reprisals. An assault on a magus would usually end in the death of the attacker in one style or another. We had promised we wouldn't kill Grugar, and apparently that had enough of a novel flavor that the Elders wanted to see what it meant.

More satyrs gathered, most wearing work clothes, more wine went around, and three of the satyrs poured the wine over their heads. "Funeral rites," O'Meara said. "They'll be coming inside now."

I double-checked the screen. Grugar was definitely among the three with red-stained clothing. Then I went to follow O'Meara as she left the room.

A swift walk carried us down to the lobby as the satyr crowd began to shout and stamp their hooves. Drums boomed.

"And this is the point where they light the pyres," O'Meara said as we reached our targeted position, standing in the lobby, blocking the way to the casino itself. A sparse crowd had gathered along the mezzanine railings, a few magi, all the very few satyrs we employed and a scattering of other mythics. Shina, lounging in front of a bar, yawned.

With a final boom of the drums, three wine-stained satyrs stumbled into the same section of the revolving door and got stuck. Their fellows laughed. The unstained fellow pulled one out and they managed to get it moving again. Grugar passed through first, weaving his way up to us with a mad smile. "Alrights! I'ss here! Do yur wurst, fire woman."

"And to me!" announced the second satyr, older but sporting the same black horns and clapping a hand on Grugar's shoulder.

"Lay off, Da!" Grugar twisted out of the older satyr's grip.

"Same to me," said the third satyr, so old that he looked more goat than man, two fingers ending in hooves. "You both my disgraces."

The fourth, the bar-eyed satyr, entered last. "Stand tall, the lot of ya. You drunk."

O'Meara's eyebrow raised as three howled with laughter. "What's the meaning of this, Elder? You think I'm going to burn them alive?"

"Don't know. With three fools, best be prepared in case you lose your temper, General," the Elder said, folding his arms as if he didn't approve.

"Take us instead," the withered Satyr said. "Two for one. Grugar just lost his mates."

"And he's got little ones at home," Da said, nodding. "It was just business. And he won't take a contract against ya, if you got me."

I growled, how I loathed that phrase "Just business." All the satyrs looked at me. That phrase alone seemed to be the handbasket to hell.

O'Meara made a small hmm noise. "I understand, but it's not me you have to convince. Thomas is the master of this House. It is his decision."

Four sets of thick eyebrows touched as their brows furrowed. A slight shift rippled among the gathered spectators. Plenty of magus and familiar pairs had a more dominant familiar, Archmagus Fibalt and Cherri, to name one, but it was almost unheard of to admit it to other magi, let alone mythics. I stared into Grugar's eyes and he looked back without flinching or apology. "You'd let your father and grandfather take your punishment?"

"Course he won't!" barked the grandfather. "We offer ourselves, you want time? We have it. Take double from us. Go ahead! I can join my brothers on the farm." He waggled his hooflike hands. Satyrs got more goatlike as they aged. While the younger satyrs could leave Vegas without too much trouble, the elders were trapped here.

I cocked my head, realization dawning. "You think I'm going to take years?"

"Heh, well, what else did you mean? No magus would operate a prison. That be work," he said, waving toward the tower. "Cut into the tourist capacity."

"Yes, it's much simpler to kill. Easy, clean and permanent. Running something like a prison takes responsibility and resources. I admit to lacking resources for a prison, but House Freelance prides itself on trying new things." I stalked forward as I spoke. "Frontier justice seems a little odd in civilized place like Vegas."

Somebody in the audience chuckled at that.

"You tried to kill me and my family, Grugar, but I don't think the owl—I mean person—who hired you actually intended for you to succeed. Rather, you're a pawn in a game. A probe at our defenses to find out what happens to those who cross House Freelance. And, in answer to them, a direct assault on my House is worth five years." I had circled around to Grugar's side and placed my paw on the crack between two tiles in the floor. In my magical sight the nine tiles surrounding Grugar lit up with energy as O'Meara reached back and channeled in the plane of stasis. A hold over from Death, the entire floor of the lobby could be used as a casting circle if you knew it was there. Whiteness spread over the mercenary's features, as his face froze in an expression of shock. O'Meara advanced and the other satyrs stepped away with disturbed bleats. Tass flowed between us as we tied off the spell. We'd need ten minutes or so to make it permanent, but we could do that later.

"You turned him to stone! You killed him anyway!" Da protested.

"No," I responded. "He is in stasis. His body has frozen and his mind has slowed so he will experience a day within a year. Five days to think over his life, while five years pass him by. It is very similar to what happened to Feather. He will be well cared for and displayed in the gallery if you wish to visit."

"Monster!" Da breathed. "He'll miss all the feasts!"

"Yes, he's going to miss a lot of things. But five years isn't forever," I said.

"Are you the only one that can undo that spell?" the un-stained Elder asked.

"I'm an ex-Inquisitor. You'd need someone better than me with spell locks," O'Meara said. "And several months of effort."

"I understand." The Elder nodded. "Come on, you two. It is done. You did what you could."

The satyrs left, the doorman opening the side doors for their exit. The drums started up again. The crowd began to disperse; no one clapped, but I caught a few nodding to themselves.

How'd we do? I asked O'Meara as two spell dogs came up with a dolly. Grugar would go up to the casting lab upstairs for us to finish.

Well enough, I think. Satyrs will always attempt to bargain. Offering two "useless" elder satyrs is a common tactic. Taking them in trade and allowing Grugar to continue work in and outside Vegas might have scored you points with their community, but the magi would view it as weak. O'Meara ran through the various scenarios but trailed off as Shina approached. Oh, looks like your girlfriend approves, though.

I greeted her with a side muzzle. "Well done. Collecting hostages is a smart maneuver," Shina said. "Even if you're overselling the reversal difficulty." A wink went to O'Meara.

20

"You must have a null room or two. Any sanctum in Vegas has gotta have one, they're easy," Fredrick, Shina's magus, said with a whine as he glanced uneasily down the tunnel, which was well-lit by fluorescent lights along each corner where the ceiling met the walls. The lights were overlapping, so none of the underground phantasms could hope to approach. It had taken about an hour to wrap things up after the example. Midnight and Carey had agreed to work with Madam Pumpernickel on Stompy's antagonist. Midnight had moaned a little about not wanting to do spell work, but that had stopped when Carey suggested she'd be better at it. Ceres, of course, was understanding when we told her we'd have to skip a day to focus on security measures.

Hopefully, this would be a very quick trip. We'd deliver Ceres' letter to Magus Napoleon and be back before anyone noticed we were gone. In the meantime, it was interesting to see Shina and Fredrick's relationship reveal itself.

"Null rooms are insecure," Shina sniffed. "My apologies. Fredrick is unused to the realities of living among so many unfriendly magi." Fredrick actually pouted at the reprimand but said nothing more. Shina continued, "I hope this small taste of Shangra-la leaves you wanting for more." She smiled at me and somehow when she did it, all those pointed teeth didn't look threatening at all. "Give us a few moments to set up."

O'Meara nodded her assent and the pair got to work. I had expected them to throw down a spell circle and open a portal without much fuss, but instead, Fredrick pulled out a box of metallic looking chalk sticks. They drew a three-layered circle inlaid with intricate runes. Both used force foci, similar to my magic hands, to draw on the concrete floor. Occasionally, Fredrick would flop his large form onto his hands and knees to squint at lines and make a connection. They were an absolute study in contrasts, the chiseled lioness with a magus who huffed and puffed every time he climbed back to his feet. I had expected Shina to be totally dominant in the relationship but her ears twitched with uncertainty as she studied her own work and he was the one who corrected it. You could see the respect in the way he touched her shoulders. She'd lean into that briefly, then huff and pull away.

She's still annoyed at him for something, O'Meara observed.

Is it something we need to worry about? I asked.

Maybe. I'm glad we decided to bring our toys. O'Meara said, referring to the number of weapons she came loaded with. Two were obvious. Two swords and a shield were slung over her back. These were the weapons we used to deal with Death and Lansky combined, a spell ripper shield and a force sword. The second sword, wrapped in a black scry-proof ward, was a weapon she knew as well as the palm of her hand—an Inquisitorial sword. Not O'Meara's sword. Ixey still had that with her down in Texas, but this would be close enough in a pinch.

"Ready!" Shina and Fredrick announced. They stood on opposite sides of their circle. The interlocking runes reminded me of O'Meara's own Atlantan casting circle, but their layout called to mind an entirely different circle.

"Should we turn around for this part?" O'Meara asked.

"No." Shina called back. "Memorize it if you can. I want more visitors to Shangra-la, not less."

Both Magus and Familiar closed their eyes and the interwoven rings spun. The concrete within the circle dropped a foot into the ground. Red lines burned across its surface, carving the artificial rock into equally-sized pizza slices. In my mind's eye, I saw a familiar strand of purple unfurl around the runes. I recognized the spell as the wedges began to slide away from each other. This portal was the same as the druidic portals Rudy had used. It was a vastly complex spell summoned by the markings, but no real magic was involved.

A flush of red, a flash of purple, and on the other side of the portal stood two men, each bearing arms like those of the Roman legions. Tall red shields swung in front of their bodies, and they blocked the way down with two crossed golden spears. The spear blades held so much power they outshone even the time O'Meara had nearly gone nuclear during a bad PSTD episode.

Romulus and Remus are those spears' names, O'Meara thought. *They are so destructive that the Veil will no longer allow them to exist on earth.*

"Who goes there?!? Who seeks the secrets of Solomon? Answer or face both the wrath of the sun and the howl of the void!" one guard declared.

Shina stuck her head over the lip of the portal. "Hi, Rebecca. It's just Freddy and me."

The woman pulled off her helmet revealing a narrow head that jarred with the guard's muscular features. "Oh hells, Shina! What are you doing using an unregistered portal? I'm going to have to clean all this stuff now."

"Heeeey, it was very impressive, Rebecca. O'Meara and Thomas gonna be impressed. Amiright?" Fredrick grinned uneasily at us.

"I'm always impressed by nuclear Armageddon on a stick," I quipped, "so long as it's not pointed at me." I jumped down into the portal. Gravity had a momentary argument as to what to do with me before settling me very firmly in front of the guards. I found myself on a walkway, similar to a boardwalk you'd see in a touristy beach town, except the wood appeared to be black stone slates etched with golden patterns. Instead of the beach and ocean, a river of lava flowed twenty feet below us. The stone remained cool, but even I could feel on my pads the heat creeping up between the slats.

"Got a lot of wards there, frieeend," the other guard spoke as two amber eyes stared. The spears remained crossed.

"I'm just well dressed." We had covered up the rather ostentatious golden letters that declared me THE BOSS with black fabric and oh so fashionable gold colored safety pins so I could wear my heavily warded harness without declaring myself the boss of the House of Hermes, which could be a fatal faux pas.

"Aaaand, this is a spell rippeeeer?" the same guard asked, those amber eyes dilating slightly as O'Meara's bootfalls came up behind me.

"Yes, it is!" Shina said with huff of annoyance. "They are all necessary equipment, too. Check them through, Rebecca. I dislike this bridge."

"We have to catalog it, Shina. I know you think it's silly, but I don't care how many people Bruno lets you bring on a safari, these friends of yours are packing major mojo. Fredrick, you must know what a spell ripper might do to our home."

Fredrick puffed out his chest. "It will do nothing so long as nobody casts a spell. This isn't some pocket realm. It's solid work. I made sure of that."

"For now," Rebecca conceded. I felt a prickle of a scry from the other guard, who must be Rebecca's familiar. The spears uncrossed and the guards led us across the bridge to where a pagoda floated over the lava river. Two other bridges extended to flat platforms that bore their own portals, shimmering and whirling above them. I didn't have much time to appreciate the construction of the portals, because a greater view smashed into my eyes as we made our way across.

The river of lava seemed to flow over nothing but sky and, beyond it, an entire continent stretched out before us. In the center a vast storm gathered over a crown of mountains. Passing over their peaks, it became as if the craggy mountains were mere petals of a flower, extending a white tower that held a vast castle far above the clouds. At the foot of each mountain, lands extended outwards with a different quality for each land. From one stretched red vastness, dotted with green and the yellows of parched grass, and herds flowed across it. From another rolled forth the vibrant greens of a rainforest. But something drew my eyes back toward the savannah.

"You see it, don't you?" Shina said from beside me. We had stopped about ten feet from the entryway of the pagoda. "That's what I really want to show you. All this around you? It's all magic tricks. Things happen because it is spackled with enough tass to declare that it works the way we say it does." Her eyes shone with pride. "But beyond the mountains, we finally built something real." She nosed my shoulder and got me moving again.

She hurried us through what appeared to be a museum of House Hermes's history. Glass exhibit cases held artifacts that glowed dimly with the remnants of powerful spells. Golden lettering proclaimed wonders of the great savior Medoci in Latin. Medoci had been one of the Archmagi the Dragon took his revenge on after I'd freed it back in Grantsville. Few seemed to be mourning his absence on Earth, but here would be a different story. Hence, the swords and spell ripper O'Meara carried.

"Down to the plains, my Lady Lion?" asked a young satyr whose bottom parts were more gazelle than goat. He lounged at the pilot's seat of a golden barge that floated alongside a dock at the rear of the pagoda.

The satyr looked shocked and hurried to his console when Shina told him to take us to the temple. A faint copper scent of blood wafted on the wind as the Satyr cut his thumb and wiped a bloody streak across the shining metal. Runes pressed out of the metal in its wake. I saw not the smallest trace of magic in the action.

It is not magic. Not here, O'Meara reminded me. Her mind struggled to calculate the vastness of this place and she held her awe at bay. *It's such a waste, all of this. A beautiful waste of tass. What's the point of it, other than proving that yes, you can play god. To keep this, all the tass required, it's insane.* She stared at the back of our pilot. *And what happens to him? How many like him are born of this place? Without the House of Hermes, this place will fade, this entire place is a bubble, and all bubbles will pop.*

The castle that sat on the top of the ivory tower lost any resemblance to a medieval castle as we approached. The walls formed a perfect circle that jutted out past the pillar they resided on. Carved of the same black stone, they were studded with ramparts and festooned with arrow slits. That, for sure, resembled castles of old had they invented curved bricks. But inside lay a colorful kaleidoscope of stone towers in white, red, black, and some that shifted as I watched. There were hundreds of them within the circle. Precarious bridges hung between neighboring towers and barges flitted between them like birds that had overeaten.

"Every magus in House Hermes who reaches a day over a hundred years since their awakening will build their own tower, their own home within the House, a place where they can delve into the mysteries of magic at their own pace and leisure."

I tried to count the towers. The major Houses generally kept their numbers at no more than 50. Eight to ten Cabals of magi. There were far more towers down there than fifty. "You don't take them down when a magus passes away?"

"They can be... dangerous to remove," Shina said.

"Did Archibald have a tower?" I asked.

"He did. He was a member of the Cabal of Righteous Fury, the House's third Cabal. When a member leaves, that's when we attempt to pull the tower down," Shina said.

"Do you and Fredrick have one?" I asked.

"No, we live in the temple with all the other magi who are too young to merit a tower. Technically, it's Medoci's tower but... see for yourself." She bumped my nose, directing me towards the view in front of the barge, where a grey shape loomed over most of the towers. I'd initially dismissed it as the castle's central keep. It was in the middle of the structure, rising about ten stories before it split into four towers, each angled away from the others. Between them a massive platform had been built, anchored into each of their sides. In the center of it stood a replica of the Parthenon composed solely of gold and jade.

"Well, that's a far cry from any student dormitory I've seen," I commented.

Shina's tail swished. "It's a temple to butt kissing." She dropped her voice low. "Fredrick's department."

Fredrick, whom O'Meara had been strip mining for information for the duration of the flight, flashed a quick glare before shifting back to how the prime Cabal imported a mountain from earth and then cloned it to form the ring range.

Shina hit my ear with a tongue, "That's Napoleon's tower," gesturing with her nose at one of the angled towers, the least fancy of the four. It reminded me of a story book depiction of Rapunzel's tower, having all the attributes needed for that story, being constructed of black stone, with a single white window at the top, and a little red roof.

"What can you tell me about him?" I asked, watching the tower draw closer and wondering how Ceres' letter could possibly sway a magus hundreds of years older than her to support her as an Archmagus.

"Nothing. I've never spoken to him. Occasionally, a troublesome apprentice is sent up to meet him. Usually they come back out. Usually. The only two magi who regularly enter that tower are Dominicus and Medoci." She sighed, looked like she was about to say more, but stopped herself, settling into an enigmatic smile. A vibration shook the floor; the barge had landed.

"Right, right, let's get this over with, eh, Shina." Fredrick yawned and hefted his backpack, which might have contained the lion's share of the tass I had paid for the Fey chain.

"Nothing like accounting to get my blood moving," Shina said before playfully nipping my shoulder and sending shivers down my spine. "Next time we'll have more time to play, Little Lion. One way or another, I promise."

"We'll be done in...," He trailed off into a disgruntled sound, "Five or six hours? You can either wait for us or flag down a barge to take you back to the portals. The main portal goes back to our tower in Vegas." He set off and Shina followed after a moment of reluctance. She quickly overtook her magus, forcing him to hurry to keep up. I shook off the memory and focused on Shina's aggressive stalk, particularly the way she swung that tail.

I cannot believe you let her call you that. Little lion, O'Meara thought at me as she hmphed. *She's after our tass. Nothing more than that.*

She's the reason we got in here. Nothing wrong with a few mutual wants, I hmphed right back at her. We waited in grudging silence for a moment as the barge took off behind us, me grooming, O'Meara studying the tower in the distance.

Who would live in such a ridiculous tower? she asked.

Someone who doesn't like doors. Let's go find out. I started padding toward it.

21

I PEERED OVER THE ledge. The tower extended beneath the platform on which the temple stood. Maybe the door was down there? All the other towers had obvious entrances.

Are we supposed to climb it? O'Meara mused. We started sorting through flying spells, and then the shutters on the tower window opened. A man climbed out the window.

Arms spread, he began to walk down the steeply angled tower, heel to toe as if he walked on a high wire. After a few steps, he turned sideways and began to slide down the tower. I recognized him. He was the same man we'd run into exiting House Morgana on our way to visit Riona. When he saw us, he made a sound of distress and surprise as his speed continued to increase. "Out of the way!"

We stepped apart as the man leapt away from the tower and landed right where we had been standing. His arms pinwheeled as he furiously fought to maintain his balance even though the ground or stone appeared to be perfectly flat. O'Meara offered a hand to steady him, but he waved it away. "No! No! No touch!" He wobbled up to one leg, and it appeared he was going to fall. His aura lit with...something and he got it under control. Straightening, he blew out his cheeks. "Wooo!" he exhaled. "Don't want to fall off the line. Did that once before. Never want to do that again." Using his chin as a lever, he cracked his neck.

"What's your name and how did you get here?" O'Meara demanded.

"Hi, O'Meara!" He smiled at her and then turned to me. "Hi, Thomas. Oh." He touched a finger to his chin, tapping it absently in thought. "You're here." He pointed up at the window he had climbed out of. "And you haven't been up there yet, right?"

Both me and O'Meara shook our heads.

"Oooooo, then... oops." His hand trembled as he began to count on his fingers, skipping his middle. "Aaaaaah... dammit. I'm too early." He sucked in a breath. "You don't know who I am yet, right?"

"I'd love to know," I told the man, starting to edge away.

"No, you wouldn't. Not yet. But that means I'm still on the right line. Sorry it gets really confusing this far out. Too many possibilities. For me, at least. This is crystalized for you."

I narrowed my eyes and started to scry into the man.

He rounded on me. "No! Bad Kitty! Not yet! Not yet!"

I could see the outlines of something over his aura. Something cloaking the magics inside.

"Shit! Shit! Listen, I'm sorry, he gonna be a bit mad at you, but he'll help! Just don't fall off." He made a quick gesture with his hand and it was as if my very brain had been knocked aside.

"Buuuuh!" He wailed uncertainly and burst into a sprint. A wall of flame burst into existence in front of him, but he plowed straight into it and disappeared in a burst of magic the color of which I had no name for, but one I'd only seen once on the ward that kept Rudy from aging. Time magic.

O'Meara's eyes locked with mine. Time *traveler.* The same thought burst across both our minds.

That's impossible! Nobody can walk through time! It's guarded by things the Fey fear. Every dimension is occupied by something that resents lower beings on their turf. O'Meara bared her teeth in the direction where the man had disappeared.

You haven't seen a blue British police box hanging around, have you? I asked, because it is the first thought that follows when the possibility occurs to you that time travelers might actually exist.

She gave me such a glare. Thomas*! This is serious! There is somebody mucking around with our timelines. That shouldn't happen. There are rules!*

O'Meara, there are always exceptions to rules. That didn't sound like someone who is entirely in control anyway. We have to find out what he's trying to do.

And stop it. O'Meara's thoughts were all about volition.

Mine were about possibilities. I *bet you a sack of sausage that Napoleon up there knows a lot more about that guy than we do.*

Steam visibly rose from O'Meara's skin as she reined in her anger. Not *taking that bet, but come on, let's play mailman for Ceres.* She took a step toward the tower and a dark field expanded from the stone. *Blood and ashes*, she swore. *Is that...?*

That is an anti-magic ward, similar to the ones Rudy's bombs can generate, I confirmed after a bit of scrying.

O'Meara projected a mental image of a pair of rocket boots falling into a trash can. Have *to do this the old-fashioned way then.* She tried to walk up; her boots were made for walking, but not for smooth stone set at a forty-five-degree incline. After a few moments of consideration, we melted some of the platform's rock, forged a set of climbing tools, and together we tackled the tower.

With my claws and four feet, getting to the top of the tower was a brisk walk. Definitely *a determined-student-only sort of filter*, I thought as O'Meara labored up the incline, wedging tools into the small cracks between the bricks for leverage.

He told us not to fall, O'Meara thought at me after I had waited for her for over five minutes and she was only half way up. *I'm making sure I-* A fierce wind slammed into us and only my claws biting into the wooden shutters prevented me from being flung off the tower. - *don't.*

My tail flapped in the wind as it parted my fur. Repositioning, I wedged my rear up against the roof and tried to pry the shutters open with my claws, but they remained stubbornly closed.

As O'Meara reached the three-quarter mark, driving rain joined the wind.

"Blood and ashes!" O'Meara swore as the shocking sensation of icy cold washed across her body, although one part of her marveled at the new experience. She hadn't been cold since she'd awakened. The rest of her wished the sensation to end very quickly. *I bet you a bag of sausages that he didn't make the time traveler go through this.*

My jaws chattered. I *don't care who buys I could really go for some piping hot anything right now.* Ironically, she covered that last quarter faster than the windy bit. The shutters flung themselves open for her as hail began to bite at our hides. We threw ourselves through the window without taking stock of what awaited inside.

Nothing but blackness. Although it was at least warm blackness, but that might've been O'Meara drinking at her suddenly unstopped anchor until I could hear the wet in my fur sizzle away. O'Meara! *You're gonna make me look like I've been tumble dried!*

Don't care. Warm, she responded.

"I'd offer you a towel but you seem to have that part handled."

A match lit in the darkness. Nimble fingers dropped the match into a cup and then the glow illuminated a woman's face, her white hair done up in a bun, her smooth cheeks illuminated by the pipe she puffed on, as crow's feet wrinkles nested around her eyes. When they opened, they contained no eyeballs, but tiny points of light spun unsettlingly within each socket.

"Magus Napoleon?" I asked, quite sure the man outside had referred to the magus as a he.

The light that illuminated her face did not waver, dim or expand. "You have a letter for me?"

O'Meara reached into my harness and pulled out the envelope. It burst into flame. For a moment I saw something hulking and huge in the darkness. Shock flooded from O'Meara. It had been her own anchor that had burned the letter against her will.

The woman smiled. "Silly girl. You dare come to me for petty politics? I care nothing for this Ceres. She is a thorn in the side of her House. Offered to free me from Medoci's shadow. Ha." Two more voices rang out with that note of laughter.

"So you read it while it was in the envelope?" I ventured.

"We read it as soon as you set foot in Shangra-la. We see all here. But other things require close inspection. You are the pet of the Dragon who killed Medoci, yes?" Her eyes squinted as something shifted in the dark, making the floor beneath our feet creak and groan.

Dramatic much? Using MY anchor to burn the letter after you read it? O'Meara seethed next to me. "Thomas is Thomas. If you know his history, then it's only fair we know yours." O'Meara hand burst into flame, but while I detected the heat, it did nothing against the darkness. *Stall them a bit, Thomas*, she thought as her mind slid back along her anchor.

"Trapped. That is what we are." The pipe was passed to a new face, a man with the same sparks in his eyes. "Trapped between the Veil and the Fey. Ready to explore beyond humanity. We care nothing for the Council politics. We never did."

The pipe passed again and this face was reptilian, its scales chipped stone, glittering with tiny gemstones. It had three eyes, multifaceted like an insect's, a point of light dancing within each lens. "We see the seams of your unmaking, see the marks of your rebirth, and they intrigue us. When we remade ourselves, our efforts were less than perfect. We exist between but remain anchored. To study the work of a Dragon, now that may finally free us."

"You don't get to take me apart and try your hand at re-assembly, if that's what you're asking." Having that done once by a being that was good at it had been the single most unsettling thing in my life. Letting an apparent newb or wannabe Dragon try its hand would be very high on the DO NOT WANT list.

The reptilian head cocked to the side, as if they could hear my thoughts. Hell's walnuts, to quote a squirrel, maybe they could.

"You are not going to hurt my bond," O'Meara said. "We will not be bullied. Not by a thing that has huddled in the dark. Whatever you seek, your answers are not here." O'Meara's mind braced against mine before diving toward her anchor, but stopped short and pulled power from a different plane. We had no spell prepared to contain it. The power burst from our very skins. The darkness of the room shivered as a bubble of light grew.

"You dare!" Napoleon boomed in three voices. They channeled, their aura a knot work of three anchors, throwing power back into the darkness, halting the light's progress toward them. The bubble revealed a disheveled room with dusty bits of furniture.

"We do!" O'Meara declared. "Conceptual darkness is very good at blocking all sight, magic and otherwise. But it's a cheap trick, because once set against the concept of light, it is gone." Together we spun a lens into the palm of O'Meara's hand and murdered the darkness with a flash of white.

The light revealed Magus Napoleon hunched down in front of what amounted to a magical puppetry rig that was a massive combination of draconic and insectile features. The third head approximated their true head, leaving out the scythe-like mandibles and the curiously long emerald mane of hair. An assortment of limbs decorated their snakelike torso, from human arms to tentacles to everything in between. Where rocky scales along their back gave way to pinkish skin, veins pulsed with a rainbow of magics.

"BURN!" the monster commanded. The maw opened wide and a mass of elemental magics surged out, a broad spectrum of energies that met and thundered into our wards.

The wards wobbled but held. They'd been designed to take blows like that.

"You shouldn't ask a fire magus to burn!" O'Meara snarled. "We're only too happy to oblige." She pulled on her anchor, but nothing came. Something held the flame back.

"We are far beyond your petty elements!" Napoleon's tail curled, segmented like a scorpion's. Glyphs carved among the scales lit up as a spell knitted together and ignited.

O'Meara spun, pulling the spell ripper from her back. Teeth of pure tass slid out from the edge of the circular shield and spun, turning the shield into a spinning saw blade of magic. Napoleon flung an arc of lightning that struck through our wards. The ripper tore up the spell like paste in a food processor.

"Space lightning," O'Meara said. "Cute trick. Works a lot better if I can't see it coming. Now get your thumb off my anchor!"

They snarled at each other, giving me time to take stock of the room. Books were piled everywhere. A number of complex devices were arrayed in a rack on the far side. I recognized the weave of the magical fax machine, and many other devices dominated with purple hues, that were their connections to the outside world. There was no tass anywhere. What is an ancient magus doing if not burning massive amounts of tass for research? There was barely any residue. A focus gripped in a humanoid hand emitted a silvery-purple light. I'd bet that's what blocked O'Meara's anchor.

"You're not a Dragon!" I shouted. "You're not even close. You're entirely on this plane. A casting circle built into your body is still a casting circle."

They breathed out that rainbow stew of an attack again. Both O'Meara and I sidestepped it. "We have ascended beyond you!" They hissed in at least three different voices. The armored tail smacked against the wall and the entire room wobbled. The lights in their insectile eyes danced, and I could feel their gaze scratching at us, trying to find something we were not warded against.

"Sure you have, but you still have a lot smashable stuff in the corner. Maybe you should stop hurling magic around in here."

"Get out!" They breathed another plume of magic, but you could tell their heart wasn't really in it. "We built this place. This entire plane. We will command the very rocks of this earth to chase you from this world." The bricks in the wall rumbled.

"I bet you could do that." I said. "But you'd have to leave this room. Or at least use some tass. But I don't see any in here. Did Dominicus cut you off? Or did Medoci after you did this to yourselves?"

The giant creature stared at me with no facial expression, their long torso heaving with their breath. "Medoci suggested we figure out how to separate ourselves before, we...." It looked away. "We went out again. We thought it would be a few months. We get distracted. And we cannot exist on earth anymore."

"You'll be fine in Vegas. You'd be welcome to visit our House if you wish. We have friends that might be able to get you a much more compact form. If you don't mind wings," I said.

"You attack us and now you invite us to your House?!" They issued a sort of rumbling garble of a sound. I assume it was giant abomination for confusion.

"You blocked my anchor trying to pretend you're a god," O'Meara reminded them in a very polite tone. "That might work with apprentices, but not with me. I look behind curtains."

"You said you're beyond politics, but I think you're very much people in there. Politics is people. If you support Ceres' bid, then you could attach conditions... such as supporting your own candidacy in the future if you chose," I said.

The huge magus remained silent, the sparks in their insectile eyes continued to dance before uttering a single word. "Leave."

The window opened behind us, the opening now level with the stone platform the tower rested on.

O'Meara and I nodded to each other. We had done our part here. Letter delivered. "Hope to see you around, Magus Napoleon," I said, and we exited the tower together.

22

THERE'S SOMETHING ABOUT EXPLORING a new world. Even though we told ourselves we should ask the first lift barge that docked for a ride back to the portal, we dawdled, inspecting all the towers of the first Cabal of the House and then going down to the surface of the keep and touring around the towers. O'Meara tried to match them to magi she had met before, with our curiosity spurred on by the simple fact that unless the fortunes of House Hermes reversed themselves soon, this entire world could cease to exist within the year.

Sunset had come by the time we met up with Shina and Fredrick for the trip home. It was a beautiful flight back to the portals with some light verbal sparring with Shina. I don't remember much of it. The memories flushed out of my short term memory as we walked out of the portal and heard the screeching of the fire alarms.

The MGM has a very polite fire alarm. A stern female voice says very plainly, "A fire has been detected in the building. Please exit in orderly fashion." Then it issues five ear-shattering electronic screeches to make sure you do not want to stay where you are. My ears caught the muffled sound of those screeches as I stepped out of the underground portal.

"Oh, no!" O'Meara said and we broke into a run, leaving Shina and Fredrick behind.

We came through the underground entrance to find a stream of tourists and staff flowing towards the parking garage. A small goat, Geoffrey, who had been directing traffic with two orange cones over his horns, spotted us first. "Boss! O'Meaaara! We're under atttaaaaack!" he bleated as he bounded up.

A rumble sounded from above as we asked him what was going on. "Started two hours ago! Something's hitting the wards!"

Cursing under her breath, O'Meara whipped out her phone and dialed our security. "Where's Rudy?" I asked the goat.

"He drove a giant robot out of here twenty minutes ago and told us to evacuate the building. These are all the folks who needed in-person convincing to leave." Geoffrey mimed a head butt.

"You've been under attack for hours and you're just now evacuating the building?" I asked.

"I dunno! I juuuust work here, boss," Geoffrey said. Above me, O'Meara talked with security. For a brief moment, I envied her simple ability to talk over a phone. If we could call Rudy, everything could be settled. He could text, sure, but not if he were driving Stompy.

"Rudy didn't explain," O'Meara said as she hung up. "He took all the familiars with him, though. Carey and Midnight are in the bot. Tilly's with Pumpernickel, following behind them."

"Anyone coming to assist? Maybe the Blackwings?" I asked.

"Nobody yet. But I doubt Rudy asked," O'Meara said. She looked at the goat who had been listening to the conversation. "Go on, Geoffrey, get these folks out," as we felt another shake from above.

The goat nodded numbly and went back to his flock. *Come on, Thomas, let's get to my car.*

I followed slowly, my brain tugging on an idea. Why couldn't I bond someone at a distance? Once bonded, we could stay that way anywhere in the world. Rather, I needed to know precisely where to send Mr. Bitey to bond someone. Yet as I walked down the stairway in the bowels of the parking garage, it occurred to me I did know where everyone was. Silver threads, the ties between us. The same threads that Lansky had preyed on to pull power and life from those who grieved. What if I used those? O *'Meara*, I thought through the bond, *I need to try something.*

She skimmed through my thoughts and agreed it might work. At least, it wouldn't take long to find out if it didn't. We're *not leaving until you re-bond me. Let's get in the car. I'm getting sick of all these limos and portals. Time to travel my way.*

We stepped out onto the bottom parking level, the place where we kept our personal cars, an assortment of magically armored and armed vans and limos, with one gleaming red exception. A Porsche. O'Meara's car. My stomach did a flip flop knowing the sort of ride the little car could give now. Gus and Veronica had spent two weeks restoring it, and we had replaced most of the magic the Inquisition had stripped out of it.

She strapped me in and nodded. Okay, *try your trick. If not, we'll follow the trail of squirrelly chaos.*

Swallowing, I broke the link and visualized all the people I had met in my life as a familiar, each relationship stretching into the void beyond. O'Meara's hummed with audible strength. I had to push it aside to find the others, fine thin threads, delicate things, relationships, easy to cut with mere words. Those whom I had bonded in the past shone stronger. I could grip them in my mind. I found Tilly's and Midnight's in short order, Carey's too, but it had a strained tone to it. Maybe she wasn't very happy with me at the moment. Focusing, I introduced Midnight's thread to Mr. Bitey. He sniffed the cord tentatively and then slithered out along it.

We have this well in hand, Thomas. Midnight did not even bother greeting me as I slipped into his mind. His mindscape reflected the confines of the cockpit he sat in. All the exits and entrances clearly marked, dotted escape plans so numerous it made it difficult to see the stuffed animal versions of Rudy and Carey that marked their locations. Midnight grudgingly allowed me the use of his eyes and I found myself in a space that never would have fit me at all. We looked through the head of Big Stompy. In the center, Rudy perched in front of a bewildering array of levers and an iPad showing numerous system statuses, most of which read green. Carey sat beside Rudy, opposite Midnight, both on round vinyl cushions that they each had their claws dug into as the rhythm of Big Stompy's jog threatened to fling them from their perches.

"There's another one!" Carey squeaked, her voice tight with fear.

"I heard it!" Rudy said. "Just tell me if it's coming at us. Almost there!"

"Rudy, Thomas is with us," Midnight said. "He wants to know the plan."

"Back? Peanut butter popsicles! Took you long enough! But I got this now! Gonna show these goons what happens when you mess with the Freelance Familiars." He flipped a lever and from somewhere in the mech echoed a heavy Ker-CHUNK, like a shotgun cocking, but for an artillery cannon. "I'm gonna give them a taste of the Wizard Phooey Mark Five." He laughed a high-pitched evil giggle. "And there they are!"

The mech had turned a corner and there in the parking lot of the industrial park behind the Gold Coast Hotel were great gobs of magic, the brightest of them a whirling weave of wards and force. On top of it stood a four-legged figure in shining armor, yellow-gold energy pouring off it into the mechanisms of the spell. I recognized that hue, a magical catapult powered by Charlie's knack.

Surrounding the catapult were four dim green circles, summoning magics ready to go. A black bear squatted at the edge of one as it flared to life.

"Thomas says they are summoning something!" Midnight said before I could tell him to do so.

"I hear it. Eat Phooey, magi!" A soft deep hiss slammed through the cabin, sending a huge wad of black electrical tape arcing toward the circle of magi. The whistle of wind howling around a house sounded. A cloud of green energy whipped down the road between Big Stompy and the magi, and the bomb curved like a golf ball hit into a hurricane and whizzed off course. It went so fast, we only heard the explosion.

I winced, hoping that had been something like an anti-magic bomb and not something that could kill bystanders. The green blur resolved into the fuzzy image of a butterfly with a wingspan of a trailer.

"It's not magi!" Midnight said. "They're the TAU!"

"Not much difference! Means they're working with canned spells," Rudy chittered. "Now tell me where that Wind Elemental went!"

"That's not all!" Carey point in the direction of one of the flaring green circles. Water burst forth from it in a thick torrent. It circled in on itself, twisting into a single serpentine body of water that let loose a burbling roar. Above, the blazing sun faded as clouds began to gather in the sky.

"I can see the water elemental!" Rudy said, his ears twitching. "You tell me where the wind elemental is." He flipped several levers. "They're prepped for a fight here. Projectiles are gonna be a no-go until that wind elemental goes down. Thomas, I've got one more anti-magic bomb." The big gun went up over the robot's viewpoint and Midnight heard a clunk as it hit Stompy's backside. "We gonna have, uh hey, noodle cat, what they call it in the sports ball with the guys slam together—"

"A touchdown?" Carey finished, her tone cross.

"Right!" Rudy stepped on something and Big Stompy's two fists came up into view. A spike on each burst into grey light that flowed to envelop the mech's knuckles. "All we gotta do is get close enough and blammo! No more elementals. No more magics. "

"This is stupid," Midnight said. "They are waiting for you."

They certainly were. The elementals were crouched on the other side of the road. Watching.

"Well, that's their mistake. They have no idea what they're up against. Thomas, I got this entirely handled..." His tail twisted a bit. "But ya know, a little help might not be a bad idea. I don't want to scratch Big Stompy's paint job."

We're on our way, I thought at Midnight.

"Thomas is coming and I am out of here." Midnight pawed the hatch to his side and it popped open. "I refuse to sit in a tin can while it's kicked around." With that, he leapt out.

He was on the ground within the space of a second. And *what is your plan?* I asked him.

I don't have one. Plans are for you human people, Midnight thought. He had no problem showing me only the thoughts he wanted me to see, the rest of his mind cloaked in shadow. *I simply be.* Yet I detected something gathering in there, something that he couldn't quite contain his growing mirth about.

A trumpet sounded, declaring a charge. "IT'S BIG STOMP-ING TIME!" And the mech charged forward with a speed that surprised even Midnight, who dashed for cover behind a car. We exchanged hurried goodbyes and I broke the connection as Stompy took a blast of water to its face, a shining golden ward deflecting the stream.

My mind thudded back into my own head inside my custom cougar-sized helmet. "10 groat of tass says Rudy's been watching plenty of wrestling lately," were the first words out of my mouth.

"Not taking that bet," O'Meara said.

We rebonded. And the smell of burning rubber hit me an instant before the momentum pinned me back into the seat. The car tore across the empty garage toward the spiraling tunnel that most vehicles used to ascend to street level. Most vehicles, not O'Meara's car. She touched a fist-sized crystal next to the stick shift.

I hate this part. And shut my eyes.

Big baby, she mentally cooed as the entire car lurched, rearing back. All four wheels slammed into a slab of concrete to the left of the exit. My eyes were closed, but O'Meara's looked up through a concrete tunnel with a bit of blue sky at the end. She let my dread waver a moment before she channeled. I let out a scream as the acceleration hit me like a linebacker and the walls of the tunnel rushed around us. It didn't matter that we were protected by wards that could take a punch from Godzilla, a magically strengthened car, and a helmet that had been 3d printed for my feline skull; I knew O'Meara had less than two inches of clearance on either side of this tunnel. One degree off and...

We'd still probably survive, maybe. O'Meara mentally whooped as we shot into the blue. She stopped the thrust as we exited the garage. As the casino fell away behind us, I saw the cracked and flickering wards that protected the building. Wards built to withstand O'Meara-level channeling for days on end were nearly depleted.

I waited for my stomach to catch up with us and held my mouth clenched tightly closed in the meantime. The hood of the car dipped, revealing the city below us.

"See them?" she asked.

Oh yes. Even from a mile up, I could see both the elementals and the artillery spell like shining gems between the perpendicular lines of both the main strip and the hidden strip.

Inquisitors are sitting on their thumbs, O'Meara swore. *Huge elementals in the city shouldn't be tolerated.*

Well, let's see how well the water one can withstand a Porsche- shaped meteor, I thought back, prying my eyes open.

23

"CRASHING INTO THE WATER elemental is your brilliant plan?"
O'Meara chuckled.

"Not like we can do anything fancy while you're flying this
death trap," I said. It was true. Magi could only channel one
plane of reality at a time. O'Meara's car had modifications to
help her control it, but she was the rocket engine.

"I like them simple." O'Meara waited until we reached the
top of our arc, when the weightlessness lifted me from my
seat and made her hair expand into a halo of red before she
slammed on the accelerator.

Flames roared around us and the seat slammed into my
backside. Dead center of our windshield Big Stompy and the
water elemental grew from their respective specks.

Big Stompy stood in a boxer's pose. The water serpent's
body had surrounded him, the head rearing up over Stompy's
body, mouth opening into the froth of the breaking wave.
The glowing blue orbs that were its eyes flickered in surprise before its head splashed over our windshield. My wards
blinded me as my body hurled into the straps that lashed
me to the seat. O'Meara grunted as blackness narrowed our
vision. I heard a scream like that of a tea kettle loaded with
pain. Beyond the windows were walls of bubbling fluid. It
swallowed us! I realized.

"Ha! You mean it bit off more than it could chew!" O'Meara
laughed and slammed her power through a different circuit,
heating the skin of the car to rock-melting levels. The effect

was the combination of a thunderclap and a *whoosh*. The world outside went white. "There's smoke in your eyes!"

"Steam," I corrected.

O'Meara shot us back into the air as magic lashed out toward us. Yellow, kinetic energy and something...white blasted my magical sight.

"Was that a tass bomb!?!" O'Meara nearly screeched as we pulled free of the steam cloud. The water elemental had been annihilated, but the thing's corpse was a ten-story high mushroom cloud of steam obscuring all normal sight of the battlefield. "I thought only Rudy knew how to do that?"

"Put us down!" I growled.

I couldn't see anything and if we were fighting someone with tass bombs that meant our wards wouldn't be enough. I broke our bond and sought silver cords. I seized Carey's and sent Mr. Bitey racing down it.

EEEEEEeee! Carey's thoughts were a panicked screech as she accepted the connection, all her focus on the giant green butterfly that filled her vision. "It's right in front of us."

Tell Rudy they have tass bombs. I shoved the thought into Carey's head and she repeated it.

"Now Oric's stealing my ideas!? I'm gonna feed that bird some cashew flavored buckshot!" Rudy swore as the wind howled outside the mech. I could hear gears starting to grind. "Hurry up, Thomas! I'm pinned down."

Working on it. I broke the connection and rebonded O'Meara in the space of an eye blink.

"Bloody Ashes, Thomas, warn me before you do that!" O'Meara seethed. We were not on the ground, rather we were way above the scene. The steam cloud whirled in a cyclone, the tip of the cone against the edge of Gold's Casino and the shine of wards there indicated Big Stompy's location.

The steam prevented us from getting a good view of the parking lot but the magic shone through the steam. Two nexus of light shone, green tendrils flowed out of the ursine outline along the lines of a complex summoning circle. Still brighter than that stood the complicated swirling of yellow and gold energies of Charlie's magic catapult. The intensity of the green flared as a new summoning kindled. O'Meara stuck her hand out the window and struck out with a geyser of fire, punching through the steam cloud.

A new ward intercepted O'Meara's attack. The steam rushed out of the way, revealing a wolf in the way, hovering in the air with the aid of two huge white wings. A shield hovered in front of him, projecting a golden ward into the path of the flame.

"Sorry doggie, you're not going beat me with an Inquisitor's shield!" O'Meara took her other hand off the white crystal and the beam became a blast as the car edged towards free-fall. The ward cracked and the wolf twisted out of the way. The flame struck the summoning circle and spat a tongue of glowing rock straight up. The bear manning the circle flung himself from the rippling circle of molten concrete. Bernard, the bear from the auction. We were fighting the TAU.

There's a reason we stopped using those shields! O'Meara's thoughts were jubilant as she returned thrust to the car.

But while we were dealing with the wolf and the bear, the other nexus of magic had been untouched. Now, with the steam cleared, Charlie had swung his apparatus towards us and fired, lobbing a bomb of magic the size of the car directly at us. We banked hard and the cannon ball passed harmlessly beneath us.

Harmless to us, O'Meara and I realized in the same moment. It hadn't been launched at the MGM. There wouldn't be a heavily warded building wherever that landed. Just houses.

O'Meara whirled the car around and we streaked after the spell, the acceleration rocking me back. We spun a wide turn through the sky. O'Meara cut through it with a blazing spike of power. The spell exploded in a thunderous crack that wobbled the car's wards over a thousand feet from the blast.

Rocketing back towards the industrial park, the enemy fired another shot, this one in the opposite direction, aimed directly for the heart of my old neighborhood.

"You spineless bastards!" I roared as O'Meara poured on the fuel to get within striking distance of the projectile.

On the ground the TAU were definitely doing something. Charlie continued fueling the artillery while Bernard, the bear, his aura alight with a rich green, sat among a pile of gray tass. The wolf covered him with his shield. Smaller animals were popping out of Bernard's back and landing among the tass.

O'Meara raked them with a column of flame, but a ward across the entire parking lot stopped it. They'd put up a huge fire ward. We had no time to attempt to overpower it. Rocketing onwards, O'Meara and I wove a spell between us that focused her power into a speeding disk of flame. It bisected their cannon shot as we skidded across the sky, turning around only to confront a small flock of birds rising from the ground, each containing the gray of tass clasped in their talons.

More tass bombs. They fired a third shot back towards that church. I really hoped it wasn't Sunday. O'Meara drew her sword out from behind the seat and shoved the handle into my mouth. "Light'em up!"

She pushed how to use the sword into my head. I bit down, shoved the blade out the window and concentrated. The blade had six different foci in it, two of them long distance attacks. The blade burst like a roman candle in a shotgun spray of magical globes, one took out a side mirror, but the others streaked off like missiles. They slammed into the tass bombs and exploded into searing white, blinding my magical sight. For the moment, all I had was my mortal sight. And with that I saw him. Nearly in the midst of the TAU crept The Black Shadow Who Strikes at Midnight. He was nearly to their magical artillery.

We need to open another front! Get me to Rudy! I mentally shouted as Charlie launched yet another block-leveling shot.

O'Meara swerved out toward where Big Stompy had been trapped against the building by the swirling wind elemental as my magic hands struggled to undo my seat restraints. The sword had six functions and only two of them were ranged. The blade turned black as I worked my mouth up closer to the cross guard. "Go!" she shouted.

Channeling O'Meara's power I rocketed out the window, flying across the road as O'Meara shot off towards the glowing ball.

The wind elemental hovered over the robot, pinning it to the side of the building with a torrent of wind so strong that chunks of pavement had been embedded into the wall. The black blade tore off a chunk of the wind butterfly as I passed through a great green wing.

"'Bout time!" Rudy's voice boomed through the speakers as I landed on Stompy's shoulder. "And why'd you bring that? The spell ripper would be lots better."

I fired a salvo of magic into the elemental and it howled in pain, the wind lessening as green and black globes tore through the butterfly's wings. I gripped the sword with my force hands and spat the hilt from my mouth. "Get me Carey's Fey chain! O'Meara can't keep this up for long!" I shouted at the robot's head, hoping the pilots could hear me. A gust of wind nearly tore me from my perch and the sword went spinning out into the whirlwind along with a string of my own curses. Next time, I'd commission much stronger force hands.

In the distance, O'Meara caught up to the golden shot. She launched, one, two, and three lances of flame, and the third struck home. This *is much harder without you next to me! I'm like one of those video game people!* O'Meara griped as her vision flickered black from the g-force of the turn.

The hatch swung open as a much larger flock of bomb-laden sparrows took off from the parking lot. I clung to Stompy's shoulder, claws dug into the seams of his armor. Carey stood in the opening, her eyes wide. "Rudy, take care of those birds! Carey, bond me!" I shouted.

O'Meara was rocketing back towards us as Carey flung out an open end of the Fey Chain towards me. It snapped around my neck and I felt the prickly contact of her mind against mine. I *don't see the point of this, Thomas,* she thought.

Now let go of your end! I thought.

But this one's mine!

Do it!

The birds were surging out toward us, mining the sky for O'Meara's return. The cannon coughed out a shot, smaller but still potent. Beneath me Big Stompy began to move, the wind having weakened. With a nod, Carey closed her eyes and let go of the link. My mind took it in like a noodle, akin to Mr. Bitey, but simpler. As I coiled it around my neck, the armor beneath me shifted. A compartment below me opened. The whine of a terrifying whir reached my ears.

"Stomping time!" Rudy called out before the minigun below me opened up with a solid BRRRRRR! of tiny explosions. Birds in the cone of fire exploded into bursts of red that faded into the same livid green of Bernard's aura before the white of the tass bombs rippled across the entire field.

O'Meara dived towards us as she skimmed the plan from my thoughts. We had no time for doubts. I readied my supply of tass. The car roared towards us on its tongues of flame and I flung the Fey chain upwards. As the second link opened between myself and O'Meara, I pulled Mr. Bitey from her and cast him at Midnight. It was like a yo-yo trick with minds. The juggling done, I now had both O'Meara and Midnight connected to me.

The car chased after the cannon shot.

Stop chasing after those balls like Tilly! Midnight roared into our heads. *Tell me how to get through that armor ward.* In front of Midnight, totally oblivious to his presence, Charlie stood in the middle of the catapult spell. Projected from a set of five foci arranged in circle, the spell trembled with barely contained energy being pulled from the dog in his Shining Armor. There was so much of it that Charlie's knack must have tapped into a plane that rivaled O'Meara's.

"Why bother with the pawns when I can have a king?" Charlie's laugh reminded me more of a Hyena's than any dog as he turned business end of the spell toward Stompy and me. The weakened air elemental had drifted in range of Stompy's fists and Rudy had begun to pay it back.

You don't go through that ward, you go under, I told Midnight as O'Meara poured power into the tabby cat.

"I am the Black Shadow Who Strikes at Midnight!" He charged, fur aflame, onto the pavement right outside the ward. Pushing as much heat as I could pull through the Fey chain into Midnight's paws, the asphalt didn't simply melt, it liquefied in a wave. The nearest of the five foci toppled into growing puddle with a light plonk. The entire apparatus launched backwards toward Midnight, the shot firing high into the sky.

Charlie tumbled backwards out of the thing, sending Midnight scrambling in reverse. The husky hit the bubbling goo with a yelp of surprise. But only surprise, wards rippled to life along his armor plating.

Dread rolled across Midnight's mind and mine, his of the memory of utter humiliation of hanging by his scruff in Charlie's jaws, and mine at the realization that Midnight had no wards at all. Run*!* I thought-shouted.

Stompy had begun to move forward, driving punch after punch to the elemental's abdomen, but not fast enough. I launched myself from the shoulder of the mech and let my kinetic ward take the energy of the height. I had to get Charlie's attention before--

"Why, hello there, Midnight! Funny seeing you here!" The dog was back up, shaking the black off his gauntleted paws.

Now would be a great time to teach me that invisibility trick, Thomas. Midnight turned, then ran. He bolted for a storm drain marked in his mind as a good exit, but tracking several more options. Charlie channeled and Midnight threw himself to the side. A shock of pain ripped through Midnight as the dog shot through the place he had been, the impact claiming a length of his tail.

I sprinted, my own coat extinguishing as I hit their fire ward. I felt O'Meara give a whoop as she blasted the last ball and set a return course.

The winged wolf charged at me, shield in mouth as dozens of birds, along with two more wolves burst out of Bernard's back. The bear was a one bear army.

"Nut-uh!" Rudy cried out from behind me and the air above me filled with the sharp whistle of bullets tearing into the wolf's ward (and a few in mine), bringing him to a dead stop as he braced against the onslaught. I jigged around him to see Midnight dodge another of Charlie's charges. The dog overshot, tearing up the earth in his wake, mangling the storm drain Midnight had been aiming for. As Charlie's power winked out, a simple somersault, nose to ass and he twisted back onto his feet.

He flashed me a smile. "Bernard! Take down that squirrel's tin can!" Charlie shouted and abruptly the pack that had been heading straight at me took off for Big Stompy.

I hadn't stopped running. Sheathing my claws in tass, I leapt. *Thomas, watch out! Midnight* shouted in my head, with a flash of warning as Charlie rocketed towards me. I twisted, using a plume of fire to propel me sideways. Too slow. A lance of pain sliced through my shoulder and cut upwards. In that broken moment, I could count each of Charlie's pointy teeth, inches away from my eyes. How could a husky look so vicious?

Then we were spinning away from each other. A spike of almost pure tass protruded from Charlie's breast plate.

I smelled my own blood as I crashed down. The sky and ground rolled around me, fighting over which direction was up.

"Ha! Not so tough no—" Charlie's taunt cut short as the whistle of a falling projectile grew. The sky and ground came to an agreement in time to watch Charlie charge out of the way as O'Meara's Porsche screamed through the anti-fire ward. The flames snuffed out, and it crashed down the last ten feet, hitting the pavement with a metallic crunch and flipping onto its hood.

Couldn't wait fifteen seconds, could you? O'Meara raged at me as she blew off the driver's side door and rolled out, her kinetic wards protecting her like a giant hamster ball. Beyond her, Big Stompy swarmed with what appeared to be an entire zoo of animals. Yet it didn't stop Stompy from moving forward, kicking at the pair of rhinos trying to knock his legs out from under him.

Had to distract him from Midnight, I protested and tried to stand as screaming pain bit into my mind. My left forelimb hung by a thread of muscle. Severed bone greeted the corner of my eyes.

"Time to cook canned dog sausage." O'Meara staggered up, her world still spinning from the impact and threw a wave of volcano-level heat at Charlie.

A pinprick of black opened on Charlie's helmeted forehead as he flinched, and the blast swirled into it and disappeared. It was the same sort of absorption spell O'Meara had nearly killed herself trying to overwhelm two years ago. Except now she had me. I began to drag myself toward her.

Charlie's tail wagged, he woofed in seeming surprise. "Ha! See, I don't even have to be careful with you! Not with this armor! I'm invincible!"

Too bad he had forgotten about Rudy. The mecha finally crossed the street and, with a scream of "Touchdown!"--though crackled from damaged speakers – Stompy slammed the butt of the Wizard Phooey Mark V onto the head of a charging rhino. The gun cracked in two, a field of black exploded and swept over the entire parking lot, with iridescent runes hanging in the air hardening the reality to magic. All animals assaulting Big Stompy disappeared. Only Charlie, Bernard, and the winged wolf remained. The field swept up to my paws.

"You look like a dog wearing tinfoil to me," O'Meara said, pulling a small pistol from the folds of her jacket.

Charlie simply stood there as O'Meara squeezed the trigger, but the black bear had come rushing forward as soon as he'd seen the gun. The first shot ricocheted off the dog's helm. The second hit him in the neck, but Bernard seized Charlie in his muzzle and ran for the border of the field. O'Meara emptied the clip into bear's back side. The wolf charged ahead of the pair, his collar flaring with purple light as he crossed the threshold. A swirling portal appeared and the wolf dived through it.

Bernard and Charlie followed after.

*Blood and ashes! O'*Meara fumed as she holstered the pistol and turned toward me. Her head brimmed full of better ways we could have handled that. Then she saw me and her anger snuffed out like a candle in a wind storm. *Oh no!*

"Hi. Sorry about losing the sword," I said, before I fell into a very dark place.

24

SCENT CAME FIRST: BURNT cinnamon along with the comforting fragrance of home. That one is tough to describe. It's my scent, mixed with all the comforts of my room, the mix of cotton and plastic of my bed, the way it gets subtly stronger when I open the shade to bask in a sunbeam. 'Course, when I do that, the AC kicks up a few notches and then I get to smell whatever or whoever's hiding out in the ductwork.

"I think we can safely say you are down one of those nine lives of yours," said a light in the darkness.

Mrrowl? A sluggish question mark occupied the entirety of my mind. The light clicked off and my single thought fell back down into the mire of blackness.

At that moment, that didn't matter because sensation came back next – a gentle pressure stroking along my spine as nails scratched at the base of my ears. If the scents were somehow not enough, that made everything okay. Charlie could rip my arm off every day if I could wake up with a double petting session each time.

Leg, O'Meara's thought prodded me. *You don't have arms, technically.*

I chirped in utter submission, as those wicked nails dug harder into my poor abused ear muscles. I flexed my claws and felt all twenty of them extend.

Yes, I had it reattached. House Morgana was happy to help with the aftermath. Simply didn't want to get involved with a mythic guild "enforcement action." Her thoughts on that had a bitter taste.

Sookay, I thought. We won.

Yes, instead of killing you, they only almost killed you. If you had been inside the anti-magic blast, the first aid spell on your harness would have stopped working. Then you would have bled out. You should have waited for me. Be more careful! The thought rolled like a growl.

Says the woman who purposely took a poisoned fang to th-uuuuh!

O'Meara's right hand switched from mere petting to plowing her fingers through my thick back fur. My argument jumped off my train of thought and swan dived into an ocean crevasse.

Thomas, you are a pathetic excuse for a cat! Midnight huffed into my mind. *I can hear you purring! And I'm sitting in the next room.*

Oh no! I was still bonded to both him and O'Meara! A wave of embarrassment washed over me, but I didn't do anything about it, since then O'Meara might stop.

*O, you want to see pathetic, do you? O'*Meara's thoughts glimmered with mischievous sparks. *You know what Thomas secretly likes?*

O'Meara, no. Not while I'm bonded to him! I protested, but far too late. She grabbed two of my ankles and flipped me onto my back.

No! Thomas! Say it's not true! Midnight begged me. *Don't let her do that!*

I'm sorry, Midnight. I can't resist this. It's a weakness, I know. I limply lay there, letting O'Meara's hands sweep up and down through the thick fur that coated my undercarriage. The relaxing strokes of her touch melted me away into the deep vibrations of my throat.

Oh, the felinity! Midnight nearly wailed. *Fight her! Claw her! Don't let her do that.*

That's right! O'Meara chortled. *The fearsome Thomas Khatt, who got himself mangled trying to save your tail, loves nothing more than a good belly rub. Don't you, Thomas? Want to tell me to stop? Uh?* One hand strayed up to my neck, making my tail lash with contentment.

I could only make a pathetic chirp in reply.

How often to you do this to him! You monster! Midnight huffed, although there might have been a small bit of envy in that tone.

Whenever he needs a reminder that he is an overgrown house cat whom I let boss me around. Or if I feel like rendering him down into a warm puddle of purrs. Whichever comes first. So at least once a week. Not that you mind, do you, Thomas?

My purring spoke for itself. Talk*... later... Midnight... You did a... good job.* Then I untangled my mind from his and rebonded O'Meara with Mr. Bitey, letting the Fey chain recoil around my neck, unused.

Instantly our minds flowed into each other. Her anger penetrated the warm fuzziness of our intimacy, and I tasted the fury boiling below her surface, at both me and herself, the fight replaying in her head like a storm-driven ocean on the rocks. The spike of sheer panic when I'd been pierced, coupled with the determination of rolling magma to make sure I stayed alive. Had we not simply let ourselves be distracted by those errant shots, then the entire fight could have unfolded differently.

The petting stopped and we rested against each other. I opened my eyes or looked through hers, it became tough to tell in these moments, and saw the aftermath of my wounds. My left side had been shaved from my chin to the bottom of my ribcage. The brown skin persisted to the elbow. A healed scar encircled my shoulder and the bottom part of my neck. O'Meara's fingers traced it. Another *inch and it would have taken House Erebus to save you. It would have cost the casino and more, but I would have done it.*

Charlie and the TAU had more power than I thought they did, I conceded.

We have to decide where our lines are, Thomas. If we had landed together, we would have had more options to deal with them.

But-

If one of those shots had hurt people, it would have been on the TAU's head. Just as it's on our head that Rudy's stray bullets hurt some people.

"What?" My body tensed, and pins and needles flared along my left foreleg. "How?"

Her fingers pulled me close. I *took care of it. Healers dispatched and contractors hired. When Rudy took out the birds. Bullets are not spells, they always hit something. That's not the point, Thomas. We're not superheroes and sometimes we need to protect our own, more than the city.*

Sometimes, I conceded. Yet there hadn't been any doubt whatsoever about what we had needed to do when that golden bomb had passed beneath the car. *Other times the world needs superheroes.* I gave her a lick on the cheek.

"Ow!" O'Meara rubbed her cheek and gave a small laugh.

I pulled away, and hopped down to the floor. My healed limb felt half asleep, but it worked. The bare skin felt cold. "Why didn't the medic grow my fur back too?" I huffed as I inspected myself in the mirror. The shaved bits looked wrong.

"I paid her to save your life, not to make you look pretty." O'Meara crossed her arms. "Maybe you'll be more careful next time."

But... My fur!

It will grow back, like it usually does. We magic it fast and you might wind up with half of it ingrown. You complained the last time we healed a wound that it grew in funny. O'Meara shook her head at me. "Lionesses dig scars anyway."

I gave her a halfhearted growl and shouldered open the door to my living room. Midnight seemed to be the only occupant. He huffed and found that his hind leg needed an urgent grooming. "Saved by a belly rubber," he grumbled, loud enough for me and everyone else to hear. Tilly and Carey sat in front of the TV, watching cartoons. They quickly rose.

"Good morning all," I told them. "What are you two doing here? Rudy didn't put you to work fixing Stompy yet? Or were you scheduled to go over to the Luxor today?"

"What? After yesterday? You want us to go back out?" Carey gaped. "Are you fucking nuts?"

"Hey, hey," I said. "Language. The only one who's allowed to swear in nut flavors is Rudy." I went to the fridge and pulled out a good chunk of bacon. "Relax, we won. They probably won't try that again for at least a week." I smiled. I had been kidding, but now she had my back up against the wall.

"You nearly got cut in half and Middy lost half his tail." Carey bounced up and down in place.

"Smelled bloody." Tilly nodded.

"Excuse me," Midnight cut in. "I lost a mere quarter of my tail length to a lucky shot by that dog. It is an honorable scar to bear." His shorter tail rose up into the air to illustrate. "When I kill him, I will have it grown back."

"You both almost died!" Carey squeaked.

"What happened to not getting put in a cage?" I countered as I carefully floated the bacon into the microwave.

"That's... different." Carey slumped for a moment.

"Charlie is a bad, bad dog," Tilly said with definitive air. "I will tell him that to his face."

The room lapsed into silence as I watched the microwave count down. Everybody else did, too, as the sweet scent of bacon slowly drifted through the room.

"Aw, nuts, smells like roasted pig in here." My ear twitched as it caught the grumble of a certain squirrel. He'd just come through the small rodent-sized hole he'd cut for himself from the main lobby of my apartment. His body froze as he saw me. "Hey, big guy! You're up!" A friendly chitter sounded as he bounded up to the countertop. "Looking good as new, too! Love that new punk look. Maybe add in some purple dye, some spiky bits to the harness and you'll be ready to face off against hordes of the undead." His smile had that manic edge that he got while assembling explosives.

"I just woke up from an injury induced from saving your over-confident tail. Gimmie a few hours before you ask me for something that is going to imperil my life," I said as the microwave beeped.

"Look, I've just been thinking about that cannon, right? We got all the bits for that now." Rudy rubbed his paws together.

"Uh huh," I said, as my steaming plate of bacon floated out of the nuker.

"Do you think you and O'Meara could take a look at it? Real soon, like? Long range ward cracker like that might be able to get us into Death's big no-no vault. And I think there's something in there that would be really nice to have."

I narrowed my eyes at the rodent, wondering what Death could have squirreled away that Rudy suddenly wanted. Grabbing a strip of bacon, I inhaled it like a noodle, pressed it against the roof of my mouth to savor the salt and swallow.

"Rudy, what—"

The intercom rang with deedledee that indicated a security risk. What now?

I padded over to look at the screen, pawed the oversized answer button next to it and stared down at the human face of my Security Chief, Cord. I nodded for him to proceed.

"Sir, there is a House Erebus magus here who would like to speak to all the partners."

My eyebrows went up. Not that the security chief would be able to see that through the camera. The spell that gave me human expressions and speech did not work over video.

"Erebus wants to talk?" Rudy exclaimed at he jumped on my head by way of my back. "I bet they're scared after seeing what Big Stompy can do."

"That would be nice. He was pretty scary helplessly pinned to a building," I said as I clicked the I'll-be-right-there button with a well-aimed and sadly broken claw.

"Wind elemental was totally cheating. You can't punch wind. I don't see you complaining about that awesome and timely touchdown that saved your bacon," Rudy said.

I cast a hungry glance at my pile of uneaten bacon. Judging from the way Tilly licked his chops, it wouldn't last five seconds without me. "Granted. Look. Go wake up—"

"Nuh huh! If O'Meara's asleep, then it's your job to wake her up. You're fireproof and I like my tail properly fluffy."

"Fine. Your tail owes me," I snagged a couple strips of bacon on my way to prod O'Meara back to consciousness.

It was the last I saw of that bacon.

25

THEY WANTED TO MEET outside. There's not that much outside to the MGM before you're standing on the streets. There's a sort of island, if you count traffic as water, off in the corner of the property. It had palm trees, a couple of cacti, and was rimmed with curb. With the packed sandy brown earth beneath our feet, you really could call it a desert island.

As Rudy, me, and a grumpy O'Meara trekked our way out there, I inspected our wards. They were in a sorry state, with fractured lines of power spider-webbing over the building. I saw a lot of work ahead of us.

The Erebus mage stood in a dark cloak, sipping from a 7-11 cup bigger than his head. At his side sat a panting husky, his fur black. The poor fella had to be dying out here. The magus waved, set his cup down on the table, and called out, "Master Thomas and Mistress O'Meara. How good to finally meet you." It was that same customer service voice we had heard on the phone that oozed from his mouth. "I am Michael and this is Albertus."

We didn't say anything as we approached, O'Meara and I swaggering as if we were ready for another fight. If *he says one thing about it's a pity our wards are so damaged, I'm going to incinerate him where he stands*, O'Meara thought.

The husky, Albertus, gave a hopeful wag before it died away. Close up I could see his color for the dye job that it was, the hot breeze folding his coat in places where it exposed his roots.

"What do you want?" O'Meara asked, with frost in her tone.

"I just came to offer my congratulations on handling our little test a few days ago. That was really quite well done. And yesterday? That was some little fight, not many thought that a single magus and familiar pair could rout Charlie without causing much more," he looked directly at O'Meara, "collateral damage. That combined with...friends in high places, indeed. Gives us some pause." He nodded.

Rudy hopped up on my head. "And that's just a taste of what we got in store for you, buster!"

Friends in high places? I asked O'Meara.

If Morrian and Esmeralda themselves show up and offer to heal my very injured familiar, I am not going to say no. O'Meara thought back and I realized that perhaps the last 24 hours contained important events nobody filled me in on.

"Hrrmumm." Michael looked down at Rudy and nodded in a patronizing manner. "Well, yes, that is what I'm here about. You see my Cabal is charged with getting the MGM back from you. It's nothing personal. We all have to do what we're told sometimes."

"And," I growled.

"And we realize that our little conflict might extend for weeks or years. We study the transition of life to death and vice versa. We, as a Cabal, find outright incineration...difficult to reverse."

"So you've learned your lesson and are going to leave us alone, right?" Rudy said.

"Alas, we have orders and House Erebus is a stickler for those. The consequences of our dropping the conflict are harsh, and then another Cabal would get stuck with the task. I'm here to suggest a quicker resolution," he said.

"You want to duel," O'Meara stated, crossing her arms. "You honestly think you can beat me and Thomas in a duel?"

"No, we're not stupid, Madam." A slight sneer leaked through his oily demeanor and was quickly pulled back. "Dueling is illegal. No house would recognize our claim if we won, anyway, deadlocked council or no. One of our members fancies himself a technomagus. We propose wagering the claim on a Golem fight."

"Yes!" Rudy nearly shouted.

"Rudy!" O'Meara and I shouted in unison. She glared at him. I twisted my neck to give him a stern side eye.

He puffed out his chest, his tail whipping side to side. "I'll hit them so hard they'll feel it in the dimension next door."

Turning back to Michael, I slapped on my own customer service smile and added all my teeth. "We need a moment to discuss your proposal."

"Take all the time you need." How does a human smile like a shark? Because he did.

We backed off and slammed down a privacy ward. "Rudy, you and Big Stompy got your tails whupped by a butterfly! Now you want us to bet the entire casino on it?"

"I can't punch wind," Rudy huffed. "Whatever they throw at me, it's gonna be in an arena and made of something solid. And it's not like we'll fight tomorrow. We'll set the date. That'll gimmie time to improve things."

"How much tass have you already sunk into that thing?" O'Meara asked.

"Less than Thomas overpaid the lioness with!"

"Rudy..." I growled.

"Do you two have peanuts for brains? Do you not see the opportunity here? This is a shot at settling House Erebus's claim. Once and for all. One and done. Finite. Otherwise, we gotta deal with this Cabal's shenanigans for months or years. Alternately, we wipe them out and then the entire House comes down on our heads," Rudy said.

"And if they cheat? If you lose?" I ask.

"I won't lose, and if they cheat, we declare the whole deal invalid. Life goes on and their rep suffers." Rudy glared up at me.

O'Meara blew a strand of hair out of her face. "If he loses, we lose the casino. But, on the other hand...we'll have our lives and we strip everything else of value out of it. We take our employees and buy or build a smaller one off the main drag."

"Are you taking his side?" I stared up at her, my jaw doing its best to hit the sidewalk below us.

"I won't lose," Rudy muttered.

"Maybe we should lose on purpose," O'Meara whispered.

Both Rudy and I stared at her. She had our bond closed. I pushed a little, feeling the swirl of anxiety and fear within her. "Look, we are one very small Cabal, playing at a level far above where we should be. We beat the TAU yesterday by a hair. If Thomas and I were a moment later coming back from Shangra-la, then it could have gone differently."

"If you had come back before I left and we had time to make a plan we could have whupped them harder," Rudy said.

"Rudy, we are very lucky. And luck runs out. We're going to lose at some point, boys. We need to plan for that day," O'Meara said through clenched teeth, worry swirling in her green eyes.

"You're such a worry wart, O'Meara," Rudy said with the tone of a forced smile. His tail had gone limp behind him. "We'll be fine."

She turned those eyes on him. "You think you can win? Then win. But I'm stating our priorities. They are this one." She poked me in the nose. "Those poor saps who are risking their fuzzy tails as Freelance Familiars." Her thumb jabbed at the three sets of eyes staring at us quizzically. "And everyone in that building. Then we worry about innocent bystanders. In that order. Understand?"

Rudy looked confused. "Am I in the building or am I not on that list at all?"

O'Meara half shrugged and put me in a one-armed hug that was hard enough to function as a headlock. "With you being

500 years old, I figure you're simply waiting around for a really cool death scene."

Rudy's tail went bolt straight. "I am not! Don't you dare think I'm Obi-wan. I'm the hero of this flick."

"Oh, then, I guess you're mostly up here with Thomas." She smiled, our bond open just a little so I could feel the heat of her determination. *If there is a threat to our family, Thomas, we crush it, then we save the bus full of school children. I will not be juggled like that again. You can bet that House Erebus will use that display today against us.*

Her grip on my neck tightened. Yes. *No more games*, I agreed.

Good Kitty. She let me go and stood, straightening her dress.

"Mostly!" Rudy squeaked with indignation. "After all I do for you guys, you gotta remind me about the age thing. No appreciation here at all."

"Well, we are letting you bet our entire future income on the outcome of a giant robot battle," I reminded him.

"Oh! Right!" The squirrel immediately grinned as he leapt back onto my harness. "Oh, I am gonna kick so much tail." O'Meara popped the ward. "You're on you black robed wacko!" Rudy shouted at Michael and Albertus, who had been watching with badly feigned disinterest. "Come back tomorrow and we'll discuss the terms!"

"Tomorrow, then." He nodded and walked toward a waiting limo.

26

"RUDY, WHY DIDN'T THE TAU hit the building with tass bombs?" I asked the squirrel the following evening. It had been an exhausting 24 hours. O'Meara and I had been working on repairing the building's wards until she had nearly keeled over into the spell circle. Everything else, from managing the trio to taunting the TAU, had to wait until those wards at least looked as strong as they had been. Yet that question had started to nag me as we worked. Those wards were really designed to prevent more subtle magics, eavesdropping, locator spells. The wards that prevented physical damage had been almost an afterthought. In case one of the local militias, human or mythic, who hated the magi, probably for good reasons, decided to shell us with military surplus. Magi did not generally assault casinos. They were valuable and a successful "terrorist attack" could chase away tourists for years.

Charlie and his cannon had been designed to take down wards without using any tass whatsoever. Efficient, but Bernard had been sitting on a pile of tass bombs that could have broken through the wards in less than five minutes.

Rudy paused the movie we were watching and looked at me as if I were an idiot. "Cuz it was a trap, dummy. I would have had Charlie roasted in that suit of armor within 30 seconds if he had set foot in the MGM. The cannon made me go to him and I thought I'd be facing Erebus goons. Tass bombs would have been a giveaway that Oric was funding the attack. In the couple hours I had to prep, I had Madam Pumpernickel ward

Stompy against Erebus' favorite tricks: conceptual darkness, hunger planes and soul-tangling gizmos. I went out with the wrong hand of cards."

I had to smile. "So, you admit we saved your tail?"

"Maybe, but I saved your arm. So you've got a long way to go if we're keeping score." Rudy turned back to the movie. "Oh, by the way, there's a package for you on the counter. It smells like a roided-out lioness."

Oh gods and eldritch entities. I had totally run off on Shina and never even given it a second thought. "She's not roided out, she's simply large," I muttered defensively as I eyed a small brown box that I hadn't noticed on the kitchen counter.

"I heard she decided it wasn't good enough to be the fifth largest cat on this side of the Veil, so she contracted some Morgana magus to splice her with a sabretooth tiger," Rudy chittered as I scryed the box. No magic whatsoever, even with my harness off.

"Can't argue with the results," I said before cutting through the tape with a fang. I'd broken too many claws on packing tape. My teeth were much more reliable, and the adhesive didn't taste that bad if you compared it to motor oil. The box yielded a note in a swoopy script.

Dear Little Lion,

Congratulations on your territorial dispute, you made them run like a pack of cowardly hyenas. I wish we could have assisted. I wish you a speedy recovery. Fredrick and I will be in Shangra-la for the next few months. Hopefully, this will remind you of me in the meantime. I noticed you already have a hole for it.

Purrs,

Shina

In the bottom of the box rattled a thick golden earring, the diameter of a quarter or so. I did have a small hole in one ear, courtesy of Rudy's teeth for something or other.

"Hmpf, cats. So formal," Rudy said as I inspected the ring. He pounced on the note as soon as I set it aside.

"Is that rodent equivalent: Miss you. Let's Boink?" I asked.

"Life's too short to plan stuff out months in advance for most of us," Rudy said in a tone that edged into sullen.

"Aw, come on, Rudy. There's gotta be more than a few rodents with extended life spans." O'Meara had been bonded to a rat for a short time, but she'd never told me the story of her familiars before Rex.

"Oh, there are!" Rudy forcibly brightened. "Don't you worry about me. Let me tell ya, I've had my fill of," he gestured at the box, "that. So, you gonna wear it?"

I was touched by the gesture. The earring had no marking and unless something proved unusual about the metal, then the faint taste of her scent on it would fade after a day. A gift that, as far as I could tell, didn't have strings attached. A rare thing these days. A few feline familiars I knew wore some jewelry in their ears. "Might as well use that hole you gave me, Mr. Sharp Needle Teeth."

"You totally deserved that hole. And I can guarantee O'Meara won't like it."

I grunted, doubting the latter and agreeing with the former. I wondered if O'Meara would prefer Noise to Shina if given the choice. Using my force hands and a mirror, several attempts later I had the thing in my ear. The gold was subtle against my tawny fur. Not bad and it didn't impede the turning of my ear at all.

"So..." I asked with a yawn. I'd be following O'Meara to bed soon. "What will Oric's next move be?"

"He's gonna push harder," Rudy said. "But I dunno when or how. I half expected we'd have heard something from him by now."

"Me too," I agreed.

"Knowing Charlie, he probably whined at Oric until he signed off on the assault. That dog is used to fighting outcasts who find familiars and bond them before the TAU can get hold of them. He had to know you and O'Meara were gone, too. So the TAU's got moles."

"Course we have moles, over fifty percent of the staff used to work for Death," I sighed. We'd needed expertise and had accepted we were going to have spies in the walls. That was the reason that our quarters were off limit to all but the most trusted of staff. Our housekeepers were all from Grantsville.

"Well, we definitely have some in security. They're the only ones that would have seen you leave with Shina," Rudy said.

"I wish Grace had followed through on her threat to join us," I huffed, my sleepy brain adding one more crucial task to the pile.

"That would be awesome. I miss Alice," Rudy said. "Ninja cow Kungfu would be great in a pinch. Look, you and O'Meara focus on the magic. I'll see what I can do to keep the usual casino stuff out of your fur. We have two weeks until our rumble with House Erebus. Get Midnight, Tilly, and Carey back out there, then we rebuild Stompy."

"What about Madam Pumpernickel?" I asked, starting to head towards the bedroom. O'Meara was in her own room at the moment, and I debated whether to slip over there or to sleep alone.

"Can't trust her against Erebus. Fine for making robots to entertain tourists while we skim a little of their hopes and dreams off the top. But against a major House? Risky." Rudy shook his head.

I paused, leaning against a wall. "What about asking the Blackwings? Gus would love it, once he stopped mourning the cars you cut up."

"They're outta town hunting beasties, but I could ask when they get back. We're getting into serious favor debt with House Morgana, though. Having Morrian herself patch you up? Gotta be careful there."

O'Meara and I had discussed that while we had worked. Once the TAU left and I fainted, Morrian and Esmeralda had walked straight out of the building Stompy had been pinned to. Gave a quick story about happening to be in the area and opened a portal to the medical facility in their tower. They'd refused payment, declaring my nearly severed limb a mere flesh wound and barely an effort to heal.

And it had been Morrian's appearance that had convinced Michael's Cabal that they were over their heads, and to sue for faster resolution of our conflict, a drawn-out conflict that perhaps favored his House in the long term, but perhaps not his Cabal. I had a feeling that there were politics playing out far beyond my perception. And like so much in my life, stuff I had no control over.

"You know what Riona wants to talk to you about?" Rudy asked, stirring me from a half dream where the Council of Merlins stood over a chess board with my friends as the pieces.

"What? No." Pushing myself from the wall I decided to go to O'Meara's room, the chance of pets outweighing the threat of her rolling on top of me in the middle of the night.

"On your Tuesday schedule. All formal like," Rudy intoned with suspicion.

"We'll see on Tuesday." I wasn't going to be leaving the building other than on bodyguard runs for the foreseeable future. With that, I headed to bed.

I saw a lot of things in the next few days, none of them tied to a certain Owl.

Once O'Meara and I finished making the wards look good, we burned an unsettling amount of tass beefing up the warded harnesses for Carey and Tilly. Of course, Midnight refused to wear any ward that he could see. The only thing he'd consider carrying were a few bomb spells. He promised to stick close to the others when out, but this was Midnight we were talking about.

Escorting the three freelancing Familiars was the only break we got in our schedules that involved leaving the building. Nothing attacked us. No mercs, no mythics, no magi. No sign that that TAU existed. It kept us all very tense. While the three were working, O'Meara and I kept ourselves bonded through the use of one of the Fey chains, allowing me to bond one of the three at any time to provide fire, advice or simply keep an eye out for trouble.

Then came Tuesday.

27

TUESDAY, WE HAD DECIDED, would be a break from magic. There were other things we had to deal with.

My appointments were booked nearly solid. O'Meara handled the human resources, meetings with the corporate employees who dealt with the Casino's parent companies and our magical politics at the same time. I dealt with mythic and four-legged employees. Usually, that was a general thing. The Grantsville employees had formed a union that handled wages and furnished solutions for living with hooves in modern Vegas. But any single employee could request a meeting with me if they so desired. They could be about anything, from requesting pay in advance, to petitioning the House for magical services.

Often, they were very serious situations, and then there were the situations that I filed under amusing. And I classified as the latter the situation where I stared across my desk at Geoffrey, the very same goat who O'Meara and I had run into when we had come back from Shangra-la.

"You want what now?" I asked watching as the little goat trembled in a rather tasty manner.

"I know it seems really odd s-s-sir. But I don't really g-g-gots anywhere else to turn to." He rooted around in a bag at his feet and pulled out a stack of paper as thick as my paw, held together by a pair of binder clips. With an effort, he placed it on my desk, the top sheet having a rough outline of his toothless upper jaw in dampness. I dragged it closer. It reeked of goat, an earthy scent made my mouth water. It read on its front, "The Underground Goat. A novel by Geoffrey Happenheimer."

"We could sell it on the dealers' floor!" He bawed. "I know it probably won't be a best seller outside of Vegas but maaaaybe here? It's a story about a goat who..." I stopped listening then, my own imagination slinking through the leaves of the forest, approaching his chatty voice unseen.

He wouldn't be tough, either. He'd be tender, his delicate neck would crack beneath my teeth.

"Sir!? Master Thomas! Why aaaaare you looking at me like thaaaat? Is the book thaaaaat bad? I didn't even talk about percentaaaaages yet."

I blinked and found myself looming over Geoffrey, my bulk nearly pinning him against the wall, my tongue frozen in mid-chop lick.

With a chirp of surprise, I sprang back from the goat, spouting apologies before I even landed "Sorry, I'm, uh it's been awhile since I ate."

"Were you going to eat me, Maaaaster Thomas?" he bleated. "You had the same look that some of the spell dwaaaags get when I talk too much."

I heard Whistler's laugh in the back of my head. "That would be entirely inappropriate. And wrong. We don't eat anything that can talk in this House." It sounded like I was lecturing myself. I smiled. He flinched, his little vest nearly bursting with his heaving breath.

He's isolated, trapped with you. No one would even know. *Whistler's* thoughts dripped with the taste of his own remembered hunts. My stomach growled on its own.

Shut up! I roared back at him. The anger must have showed because Geoffrey let out a little baa of fear.

I took a deep breath as Whistler pushed, Geoffrey became meat. "Get out!" I growled. The prey ran for the doors. He busted through with a head butt and galloped for the elevators.

The pressure on my mind eased and I found myself down on the ground, muscles tensed to spring.

You should be more polite to me, brother. Wouldn't want to ruin your precarious soft and cuddly reputation. Bone Whistler chuckled to himself.

Don't... Do that. Please. It still felt like he had his paw on the center of my brain. I desperately reached for options but found nothing, like the scheming, planning part of my brain wasn't there.

Because they're mine, and I don't have to share them while you owe me. You're so busy. All these lovely female lions giving you gifts, cuddling with that fire magus, gambling with your little pupils' lives. I'm very jealous and lonely, brother.

I'm working on it.

You are not. Start now. Or you're going to have an accident.

All my bits flooded back to me. The question working its way through my mind like blood through a sleeping limb tingled. Who did I know who had studied anchors, besides Archibald? Napoleon. He'd made a world. If he didn't know something himself, he might know who would. I wrote him a short letter inquiring about the subject.

Good, brother. Now that's a start. Wasn't so hard, was it?

No. Not that part at least.

Hunt that knowledge, brother. Keep on its trail.

Dread crept into every crevice of my soul. In Bone Whistler's world, everything that moved talked, and he had no sympathy for my ethics. He'd laugh that laugh if I killed an employee. I felt him start to recede.

He paused. Oh, *and take yourself out for a hunting trip soon, one with things you're actually capable of eating. Even pet cats need to hunt once in a while.*

Thanks for the tip, I growled at him.

Any time, brother. The image of a Cheshire grin pasted itself across my mind and he faded from my awareness. I flumped to the floor and sighed. Nudging O'Meara's mind, I found her in a glazed state of mind as the marketing and accounting people fought about how to spin this week to the parent companies outside Vegas. She hadn't even noticed Bone Whistler's visit.

Raking my claws across my desk (instead of the scratching post in the corner) improved nothing. I ordered lunch, and an apology basket of vegetables for Geoffrey, and wrote a vague note to Magus Napoleon. I pondered the Bone Whistler problem as I settled in for a nap. Maybe he still had a claw in my think meats, but I didn't see a way out. He could read my mind like a Vegas billboard, so trickery was out. He didn't view nonhuman companionship as acceptable, so I couldn't get him dating within his world. I could only play along, making progress which I couldn't hide from him. It would probably take years, decades even. And then, I'd have to do precisely what been done to me to somebody else. Rip them away from any life they had in the mundane world and plunge them into one where your life hangs in the balance on a regular basis.

My meal arrived, a tray full of slow cooked and seared pork medallions that made my stomach growl possessively. As I ate, a little voice inside my head said, Well, *it hasn't worked out so bad for me.*

And that's how it starts, I thought sourly. That's how you get magi and familiars running around with heads full of trauma. Riona would be coming within 40 minutes. Now, there was a trauma. A reminder of what happened when you forcibly awakened someone.

I needed a nap.

I closed my eyes and checked on Tilly. He sent back an incomprehensible array of scents and people. I recognized Alice and Grace in the mix.

New Friends! he thought happily.

I had him show me. Midnight stood across from a haggard-looking man as they both stared into a large spell circle. Tilly could smell the spell inside the circle, but I had no idea what it was from that. Carey perched on the armrest of a loveseat nearby, phone out in front of her. Two people in hooded apprentice robes sat talking to each other beside her.

Everything looked like it should be according to the contracts. I gave it a moment for Oric to appear, imagining his white face with villainous eyebrows and an evil cackle. Nothing. I allowed myself to drift into doze mode.

"He won't take you! I will not allow it!" Veronica's commanding voice shattered my nap.

"That's not up to you!" Another voice screeched back. Riona.

I picked my head up from my desk, wiped the drool from the corner of my mouth with the backside of my paw and licked the substance back into my mouth where it belonged.

The knocks on my door were thunder. "Thomas! Are you there? I have an appointment," Riona shouted.

"Neither of you needs an appointment with me," I called back as I hastily groomed my face a bit and assumed the I-am-very-important posture behind my desk. Anxiety drilled into my guts. I had hoped that Riona had been coming to see me about further augmentation ideas, but for something like that, she could've simply texted O'Meara. For her to come here in such a formal manner indicated a far more serious visit. With Veronica, the leader of her Cabal in tow, it meant things had broken. "Come in."

Riona stomped in, her face red and tears running down her cheeks. Veronica followed in after her, face locked so tightly in a neutral expression that her features looked chiseled from stone, cold anger radiating out from her with such intensity that my unfuzzed shoulder shivered. Behind them, their familiars, Gus, the small black cat, and Tack, a nervous German Shepherd, peered around opposite sides of the door frame, their faces textbook expressions of canine and feline misery.

Customer service smile plastered on my muzzle as the tip of my tail began to twitch, I crooned, "Good to see you, all of you." Deliberately shifting my gaze to Tack and Gus. "What...brings you here?" Although I damn well knew.

"Go ahead, ask him. He'll say no." Veronica's ice-like eyes shifted to bore into me. "If he values our friendship, he'll say no."

I swallowed. I allowed my tail to lash once but managed to still all of my own expression. Riona's lower lip sucked inside her mouth and her teeth held it there as she drew herself up to her full height. Pulling a crisp white envelope from the pocket of her patch-studded jean jacket, she walked forward and deposited it on my desk. "This is my petition for membership to House Khatt."

I gave her a tight smile. "It's House Freelance."

"Heeh," she breathed, "It's Khatt on all the official documents."

"So it is." I took the envelope, addressed to me, founder and master magus of House Khatt. No one had ever called me as magus before. Nice touch, that. I opened it with a claw and used my force hands to extract the letter. Latin confronted me, written in tight block letters. Formal, correct and somehow each character seemed to scream from the page. I had been learning Latin but reached out to O'Meara to borrow a bit more nuance than I possessed.

Ashes and dust, O'Meara swore. *Be right there.*

"Just tell her no, Thomas," Veronica said. "She is still serving her penitence for murdering Neelix. If she leaves without completing it, she will be an exile. And totally useless in Vegas." Her voice had a bit of tremble to it now, along with venom.

"Only if I refuse to complete it, Veronica. I can pay the tass. I can do the labor, but I am done living under your wing. Doing all the shit jobs while you ignore every time Dorothy tries to kill me!" I winced. Dorothy, one of the two other Blackwings, had a vengeful streak wide enough to drive a bus down.

"Dorothy..." Veronica's mouth twisted. "Is an obstacle and a challenge for all of us. You have to settle that with her."

"She's skewered me twice. Thomas was there for that one, broken both my wings, nearly electrocuted Tack, poisoned my food, and 'accidentally' wrecked all my guitars! And every time I fight back, you grab my hand and tell me I'm under penitence. I'm done!" Riona shouted as I read through her letter.

"It's all part of it. You have 4 and half more years, then you can put her in her place, if you so choose. You murdered my best friend, Riona!" Veronica paused long enough to draw in a deep breath. "I've forgiven you, but accepting your punishment is part of that."

O'Meara slipped in the back door of my office.

"It doesn't feel like it. I see you smirk when Dorothy comes after me! Let's not forget I had a fucking life before all this magic bullshit. I had a mother and three brothers who don't even remember I exist anymore because you wanted your own Cabal! I don't see you being punished for that!"

"Because it's not a crime." Veronica's lower jaw trembled; her control faltering, she spun away and faced the wall, fists clenched.

Riona looked at me, eyes pleading. "If you don't take me, I'll go to a different House."

"No one will take you. No House will take your debt on for a junior magus with a moderate anchor who's bonded to a dog," Veronica's said.

I continued reading. It was all there. Her debt wasn't huge, but she and Tack had to do spell labor for the House two days a week. Drudge work like ward maintenance and tass refining. She paid her debt by docking her tass pay to a fourth of what she'd usually get.

"I think you both need to go for a walk, in opposite directions," I said, deciding to stall for time. "I need to have a conversation with Gus and Tack."

Both magi displayed surprise in their own ways.

"Hey! Hey! Hey!" Gus sputtered. "I don't wanna get involved with this."

Tack simply gulped; his ears had already been so wilted that if they drooped any more, they'd drip off his head. He came into the room and clung to the wall.

"Tough, you're involved," I growled. "Now get your little butt in here and shut your links."

"Don't call me little! You-you ox!" Gus hissed and puffed himself up.

"I'll paint that black fur of yours yellow if you don't come through," I snarled.

"What are you doing?!" Veronica finally found her voice.

O'Meara stepped up. "What are you still doing here? He's heard you. The Petition has been submitted, your objection is noted. It's time for you both to leave."

With a sweep of her arms, she herded both of them towards the door. Veronica's eyes flashed toward Gus, who found the outlet fascinating in that moment. Tack nodded at his magus as she left. O'Meara slammed the door and activated the room's very tough wards. The walls lit up with neon. She turned to me with a pitying smile. *This is a pickle. Hope you know what you're doing, Master Magus Khatt.*

I don't, but thanks for asking, I thought back at her. *Any advice, oh fiery nuclear inferno of mine?*

None, you know Veronica way better than I. She's got a good heart as long as having one doesn't get in the way of her reputation. I don't want to be her enemy. O'Meara walked back to the door and exited the room. I like Riona, but this is the bed she made. She's a back stabber and schemer. We take her in, we're always going to have to keep an eye on her. Good luck.

28

THE SMALL, ANGRY BLACK cat and a large German Shepherd whose very identity scent was flavored with anxiety, spent some time studying the polished wood floor beneath their feet.

I took a breath and started, "Okay, I would appreciate this conversation being between the three of us. I have no way enforce this, but I think both Veronica and Riona would benefit from sweating this out a bit."

"You kiddin'? I've been cut off from her since Riona asked to leave this morning," Gus said. "This is ancient history and ain't my business."

Tack made a disgruntled noise at that. "I'll keep it private. I swear."

"Alright, Tack. Tell me how bad this is?" I asked.

"It's bad, Thomas. Gets worse and worse since you left," Tack said. "Everything she said and a lot more. Once we wake up, we never know how Dorothy's going to hit us. Gotten real good at quick wards when we're out hunting. Dorothy will knock it off if we're up against something real tough, but a collection run, she'll nail us with something or other. It's... hard to sleep."

"Well, ya murdered a guy. You're getting what's coming to ya. You heard her, six years of parole ain't bad for killing," Gus said.

"So you're okay with this, Gus? Okay with Dorothy terrorizing your family member here?"

Gus stared at the floor, which was about as guilty as a cat was capable of looking. "He ain't my family. I'm doing the job. Like you told me to."

"I told you to keep Veronica grounded," I growled.

"Don't you blame me for this, Mr. Freelance. I'm bonded to Veronica permanently. Not like I can walk away if she does something I don't like. You didn't tell me anything about Fey chains and stuff when I got here. You just said Veronica was a decent magus and a ticket out of the stables. So, what if she's mean to somebody who killed her familiar? I see the poor bastard in her head all the time."

"I see," I grumbled, I had hoped Gus would be more sympathetic.

"And I'm not done with you! Talking of murdered friends. Why didn't you tell us that Lansky killed Jet! You killed the bastard before I got a shot."

"Well, if the Blackwings hadn't been chased off by Ceres and her goons, we would have had time to catch up on that. Veronica never explained quite what happened on that day," I countered.

"We got our asses handed to us, nothing to explain," he said.

I decided to try a different tack. With a sigh, I turned to the German Shepherd, who hung his head. "So, I assume there was a specific incident that resulted in you being in my office?" I asked gently.

"Fire ants. A freak wind blew me right into a nest." I could see him wince as he remembered the pain.

"Heh. Well, you should have warded against freak winds. With Dorothy around, you should be doing that first thing," Gus commented.

"We do," Tack whined. "But we can't ward against wind when we fly, or you don't go anywhere."

"Namoi healed ya!"

"A day later!" Tack snapped, baring teeth. His entire body posture changed in an instant. I quickly stepped between them.

"Tack!" I growled.

He drooped immediately, "S-sorry, Thomas. It really hurt."

"So, let me guess," I said, not bothering to keep the growl out of my voice. "After this, Riona asked Veronica to rein in Dorothy and you two refused."

Gus groomed his paw. "They both did the crime."

"Tack, would you excuse us for a moment." The dog slunk over to a corner as I lowered myself down to Gus's level. "Well, let's game this out. What would happen if someone hurt you? What would Veronica do?"

"Get pissed," Gus allowed.

"I was bonded to the woman, Gus. I know she'd do more than get pissed."

He nodded slightly, eyes narrowed as if to scry where I was going with this.

"Riona feels the same way about Tack. She'll kill to defend him and you're letting him get hurt. You're laughing when he gets hurt. What do you think is going to happen if this continues? To you or Veronica? Riona isn't here because she can't take what you're dishing. Tack just showed his teeth to you right now. You know how far he's got to be pushed to do that? They're not angry at Dorothy. They're angry at you and Veronica for not putting a stop to it. For not doing your duty as the leaders of the Blackwings."

"It ain't—" he protested.

"How you want to die, Gus? Just like Neelix? Riona's in your Cabal, she's part of your team and when the chips are down, Veronica takes their assistance as a given. It's so bad now that Riona either knifes you from behind, or she simply doesn't save you. You've already lost her. She's gone as soon as the penance is over. Hanging onto her and letting Dorothy abuse them? That's petty shit right there, and you better put a stop to it, or one of you is going to be crying over a dead bond mate."

"We won't!" Tack protested.

Gus ignored him. "Oh, and you think I can just fucking say to Veronica, you're being mean, quit it? Cause Thomas says so?" The little cat snarled. "I ain't you, mister cat savior. You're twenty times my size and we can maybe pull down an eighth of the power you can. It don't matter. You're going to take Riona. But if you do, we're not going to help you ever again. We're done."

"Hello, Veronica," I said and Gus's tail gave an immediate twitch, his poker tell. "Remember I actually owe Riona my life. She saved me twice before I dragged you out of that hut. Once from my hunger-plane infected girlfriend at the time and again from the sand wyrms in the desert. So think on that for a bit, Veronica. I'll have my answer for you in an hour. Now get out of my office."

An hour later, with a discussion of options, we came up with a solution that might work and we were absolutely sure would make nobody happy. Riona came back early. Veronica stormed in precisely an hour after I had dismissed Gus. Both women had their game masks on, but you could see the anxiety eating away at both. The familiars came inside this time, but stayed way back against the wall. O'Meara stood behind me as I sat behind my desk, her looming presence calming the doubts that raged in my own mind. Nobody spoke for a long time.

O'Meara gave me a mental nudge, Go *on. The only way out of this is to jump through the flaming hoop.*

I looked to Riona. "Okay, we have considered your case with care. However, as a minor House with links to House Morgana, we cannot accept your petition for membership without the formal blessing of at least one senior member."

Victory flashed in Veronica's eyes as Riona's expression darkened.

"I'm not finished," I announced before either magus could turn to the other. "However, both Riona and Tack are friends of this House and we cannot simply stand by and watch our friends in an abusive situation. Therefore, we are announcing at this moment that House Freelance, or officially, House Khatt, is opening two sanctuary positions."

Veronica's lips pouted, ever so slightly. "Sanctuary? You cannot be serious. You're offering her sanctuary from me?"

O'Meara spoke, "Yes, sanctuary. A magus who claims un-just treatment by their House can be offered Sanctuary by another. All their debts and punishments are paused so long as they stay within the confines of the offering House. It does not protect against Inquisition summons, so parties are free to either negotiate or appeal the case to the Council of Merlins."

"No one's done that in..." Veronica frowned.

"Fifty-seven years. House Morgana offered sanctuary to Magus Junip of House Hermes. Her assassination is what soured relationships between Hermes and Morgana, and led to Archibald's resignation from House Hermes, paving the way for Dominicus to become an Archmagus, and led to the general shape of the council in the last fifty years," O'Meara said.

"I'm hoping this will be a lot less dramatic," I added.

Riona looked thoughtful. "It would be like being in a women's shelter."

That caused Veronica to flinch. "Fine, I will have a talk with Dor—"

"We'll take it!" Tack said in a louder voice than I'd ever heard come from him.

All the eyes in the room fell on him and the large dog seem to shrink, shoulders compressing but he lifted his head and looked right in Veronica's scandalized expression. "You don't want us! You forgave us in the desert, but Gus wasn't with us, ma'am. He didn't see the promises we made and now h-h-he doesn't remind you of that promise you forgot."

Riona seemed more uncertain and you could almost see the air fill up between them. We'd just gotten Veronica to the point of a compromise as I'd hoped. If we had offered Riona membership, we'd be a greedy House poaching a member from an ally. But Sanctuary would be more of a public rebuke to everyone involved. Her House leadership would want to know precisely what happened, particularly after Veronica herself had asked them for leniency in Riona's case. They may or may not find anything wrong with Veronica's treatment of Riona and Tack, but the fact that she wasn't able to defuse the situation would reflect badly on her. Riona knelt in front of Tack, looking directly in his eyes.

"Not one m-m-more day," Tack said, pulling away from his magus and running over to sit by my desk.

Riona stared at him, shock evident on her face. Standing, she mumbled in a daze, "Well then, I guess it's not up to me at all," and began to shuffle towards me.

"This is not wise for either of us, Riona!" Veronica said to her back. "This is limbo for you. You will not be able to leave this building."

"Talk to Tack, not me. I'm not much of a magus without him," Riona sniffed.

"Wait! Wait wait wait wait!" Gus's eyes looked like they were about to become projectiles. "Tack is telling Riona what do to? Is that what I'm seeing here? Tack is putting his paws down? Oh, come on." He looked up at his bond. "You can't believe this! It's all an act, right? The guy's a marshmallow! She's putting him up to this so she won't have to negotiate."

Veronica pinched the bridge of her nose. "Reopen the link, Gus. This is complicated."

"Complicated? Complicated! You told me this is an act. We just had to have Dorothy back off a little, and she'd come home." Gus stomped up to Tack. "And what did you say that has Riona looking like she's swallowed a can of oil? It's not like you're Thomas and can leave anytime you want." Gus shifted a quick glare at me.

"Y-yes, I could," Tack said very quietly. "You're just promising that I'm off limits to Dorothy. Well, I'm not watching MY bond get hurt anymore. I'll keep my link closed, there's no magic without me."

"That's it?" Gus snarled.

"That's all you have to do, Gus," Riona said softly. "Especially in your case. Veronica hates using her actual anchor."

Gus turned and looked back at Veronica, who had folded her arms and narrowed her lips to a stubborn slash on her face. "Are you done grandstanding, Gus? We need to go home now."

"Yeah." Gus looked over the room as if seeing it for the first time. Nothing had changed, but the little cat seemed to have more weight to his movements. Halfway to Veronica, he looked back at Tack, "I uh, I'm sorry for laughing about the ant thing."

"S-sure," Tack said noncommittally.

Veronica scooped him up. "Don't call us, Thomas." But the threat was an afterthought as she passed through the door.

"That's about as much drama as I can take today," O'Meara said. "I'll get our new strays settled."

"Sorry to drag you into this," Riona said. "I didn't know where else to go. No one in House Morgana would speak to me about this."

"I know you are, but I hope this doesn't become one of those decades-long exiles. I want you to try to resolve this," I told her.

"We'll do our best," Riona promised as she and Tack rose to follow O'Meara. Tack paused, though.

"Thomas, if we got out. Would you take us? Despite what we did?" he asked.

I thought about it. "I'm not sure I'd ever trust you completely, but yes," I said.

They left. The world seemed a little heavier.

29

AND YET, DESPITE THE constant feeling of laboring beneath a pile of bricks floating above my head, life continued. To my complete surprise, I received a reply from Magus Napoleon that was so long that I had to have the stack of paper bound before I could read it. I made a show of reading that for an hour for Bone Whistler, even though it was way over my head. A discussion of the nature of anchor planes. Rudy and House Erebus agreed on the date of the match which would determine the fate of our little House. With the wards mostly finished, O'Meara, Rudy and I spent a very long evening planning out additional modifications to Big Stompy and put out a call for referees who could invalidate the match if they saw any attempt to cheat on either side.

Rudy had originally built Stompy for show fights. He, Tilly, and Madam Pumpernickel had warded Stompy against common House Erebus attacks, coated the fist-spikes in tass to punch through wards, installed the minigun, and slung the Wizard Phooey Mark V over his shoulder. In that giant gun there had been a tass bomb bigger than the one we'd set off in Lansky's vault—the one that had ripped clean through reality and earned us the direct attention of the Veil itself, in a place where it supposedly didn't exist. The image of all those eyes within eyes would sneak into my mind whenever somebody mentioned the Veil. Most magi thought of it as a barrier. Smarter ones thought of it as a sort of eldritch entity, but that didn't quite line up, either. It had told me and the rest of us to stop blowing holes in reality.

"I wasn't gonna use that one!" Rudy claimed when we confronted him on it while we were working on Stompy the next day. "It was insurance for a Mexican standoff situation! If I go, we all go right?"

"Take it apart, Rudy." O'Meara stared the squirrel down.

"Fine, fine, fine," Rudy grunted.

"And all the bigger ones you happen to have built," I added. He caved on that way too easily.

"Aw, candy-coated cashews. You two never let me have any fun at all. What if for some reason we have to rip a huge sucking hole in reality to, I dunno, fend off a Dragon, or kill a Fey, or wipe a small, heavily armed country off the map?" He smiled.

"All of them, Rudy," O'Meara said very sweetly. "At least repurpose them into effect bombs, like an anti-magic field."

"I can see us needing to knock out all magic in the city for a few minutes," I said, thinking of how much havoc that would cause if we ever found ourselves being hunted by the entire magical community again.

"That would never work." Rudy's tail waved from side to side. "Too much power in one place. You'd need to distribute the tass, and anti-magic fields are kinda the opposite of a straight tass bomb. They harden reality, so magic can't get in. That's how Archibald hurt the Veil. Harden reality to the point that the Veil choked on it. You need a mix of hunger plane and stasis type tass."

With a little bit more prodding and the erection of a double privacy ward, Rudy began to share the basics of how to build effects into the tass bombs. It had everything to do with the origin of the tass.

Deep into this conversation Tilly screamed into my brain, Thomas! *Thomas! Help her off! Owwwiess!*

I slipped into Tilly's bewildering mindscape and peered through his eyes. Carey had attached herself to Tilly's nose, claws digging into his skin. She peered deep into one of Tilly's eyes as if she could see me inside the dog's head. "He here! He here!" Tilly whined.

"Thomas! I need help now! Bond me," Carey demanded.

Of the three new familiars, I'd spent the least time in Carey's head. Unlike the other two, who had the uncluttered mindscapes of former animals, Carey's was jagged and sharp with the accumulations of trauma. She also used those sharp pieces of herself to shield all but her surface thoughts from me. Which was fine. I was her employer and I didn't really need to have a deep bond with someone who I couldn't do much magic with. Handling her as if she were a ball of outward facing hypodermic needles had been the order of the day during our training session. I'd taught her how to share both her fleshy eyes and her magical sight with me, along with some very rudimentary spell casting.

That's all I had needed to do. Now, looking into Carey, she was anything but calm. Swallowing, I told Tilly I was breaking the connection and bonding Carey.

O'Meara had stopped talking and looked at me with the worried expression that reflected my own thoughts, as I reeled in Mr. Bitey and reached for the thin silver strand that was Carey.

This could hurt. I steeled myself as I grasped the strand and slid Mr. Bitey down it.

Rudy looked between us. "Oh, what now?"

"Carey's in some sort of trouble," O'Meara explained as Mr. Bitey rapped on Carey's mental door.

Finally! Carey screeched in my head with knife-edged desperation. *She's here! She here! We gotta get her out of here! She can't be here!* Around each thought were emotionally charged shards of memories that slammed through me.

Where the fuck are you, Carey!? The voice of Melissa, Carey's sister, burned across my mind. *Stop lying!*

Carey! Calm down, I thought at her as I desperately fended off her memories, knowing if my guard slipped, I'd be reliving the most traumatic moments of Carey's life. *I will help. Tell me, don't show me.*

We have to make her leave! Carey's thoughts pulled back, but not calming; her mind pulsed with the running of her heart, her mind whirling more energetically than a human's could.

Where is she? Specifically. In the building? In the city? I kept myself as level I could.

In the city! Looking for me! I've been trying to get her to stay out! But she keeps coming to the city! You told me she'd forget me, Thomas! You promised! Promised! Why! Her entire thought pattern threatened to explode into a storm of anxiety-induced panic attack.

I reached into her and attempted to bat the anxiety out of the way, but it was like moving a swarm of bees, stinging me with hot anger and doubt. Who was I to help her? I'd shanghaied her into this. Her vision came to me, the world a blur outside. Her body was literally running in circles over this. Snarling with my own frustration, I summoned my own tiredness, blended it with the weasel's own mental exhaustion and sprayed the mix into her mind as if I were putting out a fire.

What! No! Gotta! She struggled against the weight of our combined exhaustion, and then fell, the anxiety pinned beneath it. The vision unblurred. Tilly loomed over us, bleeding from scratches on his muzzle and looking worried.

"You okay long friend?" Tilly asked.

"I think Thomas just... drugged me." The words echoed from both inside and outside Carey's mind.

Not quite, I told her. As sleep reached up for her mind, I pulled her from its gentle grasp. *You're on a job, remember?*

"Rightss, always gotta smile on the job." She presented her vision to me as if I were the client. We stood in the corner of what appeared to be a workshop. Midnight stood across a circle from an older man in an old-fashioned suit, unlit cigar rooted in his mouth. A complicated spell floated between them. Perched on a couch were two apprentices, the first, a woman in her late thirties, rubbed her temples tenderly and the other, a teenager, was totally absorbed in his phone. Carey drunkenly approached them. "SSssorry, I gots a uh, ah, family emergency."

Follow the procedure, I urged and dumped what that entailed into her mind. O'Meara and I extracted ourselves from the scaffolding around Stompy and moved toward the exit.

"Uh huh. Tilly will finish up," she said.

"Oooo! Playtime!" Tilly bound up behind her, prancing in place.

The woman frowned. "But he's a dog."

"He's much better than me right now," Carey sing-songed amidst laughter. "I haven't felt like—"

I got flickers of needles plunging into veins, white powder on a small mirror.

"No. Not like—" She shook her head.

Burning blunts, the bubble of a bong.

"No, not quite that fun."

White and black tile, the steady beep of hospital monitors.

"Better than that," she declared.

Something soft bumped her, and Carey fell on her side. "Carey, I need collar."

I batted away a tendril of sleep that had been sneaking in and she perked up. "Right, right." A mental push and the Fey chain came free of her neck. It eagerly snaked around Tilly's foreleg and wrapped around his neck.

Carey excused herself as Tilly bonded the reluctant apprentice.

Okay, now what's this about Melissa? I asked as soon as Carey found herself in the hallway.

She can't be here, Thomas. She has a good, important job. She a doctor, but she's been coming every weekend looking for me since I changed. Her anxiety made feeble buzzing noises as I balled it up in the thick taffy of the exhaustion and looked for a spot where I could shove it. Unlike O'Meara, Carey didn't seem to have much in the way of holes to hide the painful memories; instead she lived among them as a prisoner whose cell had been carpeted with shattered glass. *We've been texting. I keep on trying to tell her I've got a good solid job, but...*

A swarm of tiny text windows popped into existence.

Stop lying, sis!

You want me out of your life? Tough tits, miss!

Stay there! You can spare five minutes to see me.

Oh god! She's coming here! No no no. The anxiety shook her like an earthquake. I built a wall of calm thoughts, but it wouldn't hold for long.

We're on our way. O'Meara and I were climbing into her car. *Tell her you'll meet her outside.*

Oh, crud, my phone! Carey ran back toward the room.

Melissa paced in front of the Picitrix Tower, glaring up at stomach-churning heights occasionally before glaring at the very normal sidewalk. Specializing in magi who are anchored to the planes of concepts, the tower showed off by being abstract, featuring decorations right out of an MC Escher drawing, except being wholly three dimensional and moving. It was not uncommon for tourists to cluster below it and then lose their lunches. Melissa wore jeans, a pink tank top and large-brimmed hat.

Carey watched her from the bushes. Okay, *you see her?!*
Now magic her home! Get her out of here!

It would be better if we can convince her to take a plane,
*O'*Meara chided as she pulled the car up to the curb and
shouted. "Melissa!"

The woman's head jerked up, her eyes narrowed into slits.
Her hand slipping into her purse. She waited until she was
right beside the car before hissing, "Where is my sister?"

"She's fine," I said from the backseat.

Her eyes met mine, she flinched, half pulling her hand from
the purse, clutching the handle of a gun.

"Doctor, we aren't here to hurt you. We are Carey's em-
ployers. We'll take you to meet her," O'Meara said.

Okay Carey, get over here, I thought at the weasel.

You can't tell her the truth! Carey nearly screamed in my
head.

Carey, we need her to know that you are safe. Then the Veil
should be able to make her forget when she's less obsessed with
finding you. Now get in the car, I thought in what I hoped
would be a commanding tone.

Melissa hadn't moved, starring hard at O'Meara. "Where
is she? She said she worked here. I had her phone tracked.
It's right here. And I'm not leaving until I see Carey and that
phone."

"Oh, fine. You're not going like what you see though,"
O'Meara said. "She's right behind you in the bushes."

Melissa spun. Carey ducked down into the hedge she had
been peeking out of, but far too slowly. There were plenty
of bushes for a human to hide beneath. "Carey! Game's up!"
Melissa's roar would have impressed the lions, I caught a spark
of something in her aura. "Come out now."

"No!" Carey called back before slapping her paws over her
muzzle so hard that I felt her nose sting. *Dammit, Thomas!*
Nonono!

"Carey?" Melissa rushed the bush, grabbing it with both hands and opening it up, exposing Carey, who clung to the branches, paralyzed as her anxiety burst free of the restraints I had made.

"I don't need your help! I'm fine!" Carey shouted up at her sister.

"Carey? What?" Melissa arm shot downward. I winced pre-emptively, waiting for the resulting bite. Carey surprised me. Carey wasn't crushed, and Melissa didn't get bitten. Instead, Carey hung limply in Melissa's grip. Both of them glaring at each other. "This has to be a joke."

"It's not." Carey was turned this way and that, her harness that held her cell phone to her back examined.

"Satisfied? Perhaps you two would like to catch up over lunch?" O'Meara said, reaching over the passenger side door and popping it open.

We took them out for tacos.

"See, I'm safe. I'm employed. I'm fine," Carey said after O'Meara and I had sketched out a vague version of the situation, making the magical world out to be simply parallel to the mundane. A happy Harry Potter land.

"You're a weasel, Carey. That is not fine," Melissa countered.

"She's doing the best she can with that." I was about to add, and she's clean, but I received a mental foot stomp from her.

Melissa ignored me. "There are warrants out for your arrest, Carey. Court dates you skipped." Then she looked at me and swallowed back some details of those arrests.

"Misunderstandings. I was going to take care of it. Then this happened." Carey looked away. "It doesn't matter.

"It does, Carey!" Melissa snapped, and around they went, Melissa highlighting Carey's broken promises and Carey insisting everything had always been fine.

O'Meara got sick of it first. "Look, girls. Clearly you two have some issues to work out, but Carey is on the clock at the moment, and she's got solid bookings for the next two weeks. We'd be happy to give Carey some time off after that so you two can catch up. Maybe see a therapist together." Two weeks should be long enough for the Veil to do its work. Most people forgot about the wonders of Vegas ten minutes after takeoff, leaving a hazy sensation that Vegas was a magical place. The mind quickly filled in the gaps with adventures lifted from movies and books.

Melissa pushed her mostly emptied tray away. Arguing with her sister hadn't diminished her appetite at all, but then, these were really good crunchy tacos. "Fine. I'll get a room."

"You can't stay here!" Carey said. "You're still a resident. They'll kick you out."

"I can use medical leave or something. I'm not leaving without you. I can't believe you're okay with being a weasel. We'll get it fixed. I'll use the medical facilities at night or something," she huffed.

"You're going home," I said.

"And if I don't?" She glared defiantly at me. "It's a free country. I'm a doctor. I can find work. What are you going to do to stop me? Turn me into a frog?"

I decided there was only one way to get her to cooperate. "You are a distraction to Carey's important and lucrative work. If you do not go on your own power, then it will be in a magically induced coma." I looked at her with a calm stare. "This not the place for you."

You wouldn't! Carey gasped in my brain.

Course not, but play along, I thought at her.

Melissa turned to Carey, who nodded solemnly. "Sis, I'm safe. I'm employed, just like you wanted me to be, but you're not safe here. Best you go home."

"I see," a sudden sweat broke out on her forehead.

We took Melissa directly to the airport and booked her on a chartered plane home.

"Thanks," Carey said as I broke the bond and the exhaustion hit her full force. Minutes later, she was asleep.

*Think that worked? O'*Meara asked as we pulled into traffic, her mind pondering how far away from the airport she had to go before blasting off.

Maybe? Does travel between Vegas and the mundane world make someone more prone to awakening? I thought of the spark I had seen.

Not usually, no. O'Meara touched the crystal between the seats and the car rose into the air. *However, awakenings can run in families sometimes.*

Let's hope this one doesn't, I thought back.

O'Meara's phone let out a red alert klaxon, our ascent paused as she swore and fished out her phone. I peered through her eyes at the screen—a text from our security team.

Archmagus Morrian and her familiar are here.

They demand to see Riona.

"So much for a quiet afternoon working on a robot," I said.

30

WE MADE IT BACK to the casino in less than a minute. The elevator up from the parking lot took more than twice as long as the flight, a good thing in my opinion, as it gave time for my guts to catch up with me.

Morrian had the air of someone who we'd kept waiting for hours, instead of five minutes. To my surprise, she wore a white suit jacket and flowery skirt instead of the green robes of House Morgana. This made her look a little less like a grumpy frog and more like one of those high society women who willed their millions to their dog.

She did not, however, have a dog. She had Esmeralda. The calico draped over her magus' shoulders as if she were a furred scarf. The lids of her eyes opened a tad as O'Meara and I approached to the beat of Morrian's shoe tapping impatiently on the tile. "Hmpf. The head of House Khatt, here to escort me?! You both have some nerve."

"Those are the rules, Archmagus Morrian. Welcome to House Freelance," I stated formally, coving my paws with my tail respectfully. O'Meara curtseyed.

"You two are a fine pair to talk me about rules. I'm sure your quarters are piled with law books, which you use as scratching posts. Renting out familiars to House Picitrix!" Her deep eyes narrowed. Morrian and Esmeralda had very similar eyes, deep set within folds of skin.

"And House Morgana. You get them next week," O'Meara said, in her diplomatic tone as mentally she rolled her eyes at Morrian's performance.

"At a scandalously high rate! While you brawl in the street with the TAU, of all things. Tangling with a mythic guild. The Council does not approve." Her seemingly permanent scowl lifted for the briefest moment before she advanced on me, the wooden staff she used as a cane thumping. "Now let me see that wound, cat."

"It's been fine," I said quickly, but there was no warding her off. Her aged hand hooked behind my formerly-detached limb and pulled my paw up into the air. Esmeralda stirred to cast her eyes at me as the Archmagus pulled my limb this way and that. I endured the examination, only letting my annoyance show in rapid sweeps of my tail.

"No pain?"

"Tingles sometimes," I admitted.

"Good," she said without a trace of mirth. "This is why you come to House Morgana for healing, not Hermes. They'll put you back together backwards." She stood, although she didn't gain all that much height. "Now, where is this girl? Riona."

"And Tack," I corrected softly.

"Watch your tone with me, Khatt," she said, but didn't follow it with a threat. I had to count that as a victory. "Don't make me ask you again."

"This way." I turned to lead her to the elevator that hotel residents used. *I cannot see how this woman could make the situation between Veronica and Riona any better. If my tongue is sandpapered, hers is composed of caustic acid,* I thought at O'Meara as we rose to the 13th floor.

Funny, I think she's warming up to you, O'Meara thought back.

Like a nuclear furnace, I thought.

Riona's door opened before we reached it, Riona stepping out wearing her multicolored hair in a ponytail, a denim jacket festooned with patches, and black jeans. For a moment, I thought she'd bolt down the hallway, but instead she steadied herself, swallowed, and forced a smile. "Hello, Archmagus Morrian." And bowed.

"Where are your robes, girl?" Morrian snarled.

Riona winced. "Back in the tower. I didn't bring them."

"Why's that? A magus in Sanctuary should wear their robes. Makes it much easier for visitors to point at you and say, "See, there's the first magus who's claimed Sanctuary in half a century!" Morrian welded her voice like barbed whip.

Riona's head snapped to the side as if she'd been struck. "I didn't come here asking for sanctuary."

Morrian's voice wavered minutely. "No, you didn't. And you're very lucky the master of this House has a half a brain in his pointy-eared head, and didn't grant you that petition. This should have been taken care of internally. This is rotting ridiculous, girl!"

"Archmagus Morrian, please, there is no need to shout," I said.

She turned to me. "Oh, yes, she's under your protection, not one hair will I touch. Let me warn you now, there will be plenty of shouting. First, I will shout at her. Then I will shout at Veronica, then I will shout at the Crones who did not see this coming. Finally, I will shout at the sky because I blew a hole through the roof of my house when I heard about this mess."

Rudy's school of anger management? O'Meara quipped behind a solemn mask. I snorted to avoid a chuckle.

Morrian shifted focus to O'Meara, "Why don't you two get me and Riona some tea? We are going to have a very long, very private conversation." The chills O'Meara got from that glare jumped through the link to crawl down my own spine.

O'Meara swallowed. "We be happy to, so long as Riona is agreeable."

"Of course," Riona said before we could even look in her direction.

We set up the pair in a conference room with a steaming pot of tea from the coffee bar downstairs. O'Meara and I debated waiting outside the room, but decided against it. If the Archmagus decided she wanted to break the rules, we had no way to stop her. All the remaining Archmagi had stellar reputations when it came to their word, even Michael the Second, the corpse in charge of House Erebus. We both headed to our standard waiting hangouts, O'Meara for the bar downstairs, me to a hidden napping spot above the casino floor, a small ledge only accessible via a hidden cougar-sized passage in the upper-level security center.

I watched the tourists and regulars amble below through a one-way mirror, both worrying for Riona and trying to guess the outcome of their meeting.

"You should know that I am a very astute referee." The raspy voice of Esmeralda startled me from the sleep I had been drifting towards. I looked to the side to find her standing in the middle of the access tunnel, which meant she had passed through a room full of spell dogs to get to it.

"What?" I asked, peering past her. The tunnel itself had been warded as well, nothing more than an alarm, but it had not been triggered. "How did you get up here?"

"We should go up to the balcony in your private quarters. I would like to see your roof pool." Her ancient eyes twinkled with some unseen amusement.

"You going to tell me why?" I asked.

""Naaah," she drawled with the tone of a meow. "Humor me. You cannot make Morrian happy now, but you can make me happy." She turned and walked back down the tunnel at a dignified pace, forcing me to follow.

"Hey, care—" I started as she approached the alarm ward, but it simply winked out as she passed through it.

"This bet with House Erebus interests me. I want the best seat in the house. Judging people and people-like things is what I do," she said as we passed through the security booth. The guards looked at us quizzically, but shrugged.

"I'm not sure that's a stellar idea at the moment, Esmeralda," I said as I managed to catch up with her outside the door to our personal elevator, which opened without me pressing the fob on my harness against the panel. I scryed her and found her in a nest of dim wards, but didn't see anything that could override electronics.

"Are you afraid that House Morgana would allow a minor fight inside our most junior Cabal to influence our judgment?" she asked.

"Morrian didn't act like it was minor," I said, as the elevator began to lift.

"Morrian is Morrian. She is not me," she said.

"It's not your judgment I worry about, it's your politics," I said.

"And you think I would let that interfere?"

"Well... yes. I do."

"You do learn." She sniffed, wrapping herself in her tail. "It would be a great show of trust that House Khatt and House Morgana continue to work together, despite this small issue."

"And I suppose you will promise to be a true referee and not purposely endeavor to make us lose the MGM?"

"I will make no such promise," she said. "Our actions will be in whatever direction we please."

"That's not a very compelling argument for the job."

"Without a show of trust, Thomas, then our relationship and support for you over the TAU will come to an end. With Hermes about to withdraw from the council entirely, you need us more than ever."

"Picitrix has come around," I countered. "We have contracts with them right now. Paying contracts."

"And you think they came around without our influence?" Esmeralda   studied the tiny squirrel-sized elevator buttons.

I actually attributed that to Doug and Ceres, by proxy, but I kept that in my harness pocket for now. "I think the entire community is seeing the benefit of familiars being able to choose their bonds. And has seen that we are more than capable of defending ourselves."

"You... three are proving quite the stubborn spot to remove. I enjoy watching others try," she allowed as the elevator door opened. We sauntered through the antechamber. Distantly, I heard Rudy haranguing O'Meara to come back with him to the mech bay. The clock was definitely ticking.

"Sooo, what happens with Riona and the Blackwings next?" I opened the office door for her.

"Nothing until after this fight, this bet. If you lose, you will no longer have the resources to continue offering her sanctuary, and there is no decision we have to make. Should you win? Well, then decisions will be made. If you want her, you can have her, provided she completes the terms of her penitence. No one in the House besides Veronica and Naomi will be sad to see her leave."

"That is, of course, if you are our referee?" I asked.

"Oh? Have we not settled that matter?" A mock surprise temporarily widened her tired eyes.

"I'm still not entirely convinced you will have our best interests at heart, Esmeralda. I don't like to be toyed with and that sounds like precisely what you want to do over the next two weeks."

She tsked. "My, oh my, that would be amusing, watching your little family scramble around to my every whim. Do you think we are so petty, Thomas?"

While her magus certainly had a rep—cantankerous, sharp-tongued, and able to reduce the most powerful magi in her own House to simpering children—nobody gossiped about her familiar at all. At functions where she strayed from

Morrian's side, people either ignored her or swiftly left the room. "If you were, we probably wouldn't win the match. There is a lot to prepare."

A simple nod. "That would be counterproductive. You have to look at things from the larger scale."

My brain started thinking; we were a minor unaffiliated House in the big scheme of things. While minor Houses were technically unaffiliated, most had primary patrons among the Major Houses. Taking in Riona, and then still having Esmeralda as our chosen referee…that no longer made it look like trouble they couldn't contain, but instead as if they were pawning off a problem magus onto us. "It wouldn't make much sense for House Morgana to allow one of their assets to go to House Erebus, would it?"

"Mrrrowl," Esmeralda exclaimed as her tail snaked up into a question mark. "The wheels do turn. Like I said, a show of trust between us."

"And ownership," I grumbled as I shouldered the door to O'Meara's balcony.

"Being House Morgana's minor House is not a bad thing. We need a place for the male apprentices we find and, since we lost the Grove, a large portion of our Cabals travel to gather tass for the house. We find many of the awakened animals that go to the TAU, and while we get tass bounties for them, we are outbid for the strongest ones. If they go to you, we will not lose access to them." That last bit had the air of an order to it.

"We'll need more Fey chains."

"A kitten does not grow within the space of a day," she chided, hopping up on the balcony railing. "You need many things."

O'Meara's balcony didn't look over the street. It looked over the building, specifically over the rooftop pool that existed as a pale blue oasis in a sea of concrete and metal vents. I had no idea what Esmeralda wanted to see up here, but she looked at the pool with a very intense gaze. Our wards extended over the roof about twenty feet and, if her magical sight was far better than mine, she might detect a few very minor enchantments over the pool. "What are you looking for?" I asked.

"Possibilities," she whispered. "Potential."

"Are you time-scrying my casino?" I asked in a very tight voice.

"Never. Time hates that." Her ears flicked in feline amusement. "Thank you for the view. It is enlightening. I will let you return to your struggles."

"I have to discuss this with the others. I cannot consent to this on my own," I told her.

"O'Meara will agree because she is feeling very vulnerable, and Rudy will say no for reasons he will not explain because he has forgotten them. You'll have to lean on him a bit." The elder cat began to walk towards the door.

"How do you know that?" I asked, feeling a bit like a checker who'd ventured onto a chess board.

She didn't pause in her slow slink. "I'm merely good at watching."

"Liar," I said.

She laughed as the door opened for her as if there were an invisible butler opening it. I didn't even see the faintest hint of magic, and there should have been a dozen wards on that door.

The wards flickered back into existence a few seconds after the door closed. I let my head rest against the nearest wall and simply closed my eyes for a moment. The invisible pallet of bricks floating over my head seemed to tremble.

A warmth slid through my mind. It's *okay, Thomas. She's scaring you on purpose.* O'Meara had been watching, after all.

It's working.

Morrian's known for waltzing through wards. No one knows how she does it. If she wishes to visit you, for good or ill, there are very few ways to stop her. There are reasons

Archmagi earn the title. But...Esmeralda is offering mostly carrots, O'Meara concluded.

That reflected my own thoughts. You want me on your side, not on theirs, seemed to be the bulk of the message. And they had turned their own management error, Riona's alienation, into leverage for closer association with House Freelance. Healing me had no doubt been part of that. Riona had merely stepped up the timetable.

She didn't ask for a cut of the casino, at least, O'Meara thought.

Not yet. She could hardly claim to be a third party if they took a cut.

Come on back and let's talk it over with Rudy.

31

ESMERALDA'S PREDICTIONS WERE SPOT on.

"Have your skulls been cracked open!" Rudy shouted at me after I explained the cat's offer. "Because I think some brain must be leaking out somewhere! You can't trust Esmeralda!"

"Why not, Rudy?" O'Meara asked. "Logic's sound. They don't want House Erebus to get the MGM and it will keep the Riona problem from blowing up into an actual fight. Otherwise, we lose both House Morgana and the Blackwings."

Rudy grabbed his ears and tugged as if they would come off. "Nrrrugh! You two didn't even ask me about the Riona business! I'm planning on asking Naomi to whip up a focus for big Stompy! That's one nut that's got tossed away from the tree."

Naomi was only really good at one thing: turning herself and other things into birds. It was actually fairly useful, particularly due to the healing side effect. "You wanted to turn Big Stompy into a bird?"

"Exactamundo! Be a whole you-have-not-seen-my-final-form thing! The crowd would have loved it," Rudy said.

"Please say that's not integral to the plan," I said, looking to O'Meara.

"It's not. He's just stalling," O'Meara said.

"Look. Esmeralda and Morrian are grumpy old hags with no sense of humor. Nothing's more fun for them than when everybody's dancing to the tune that only they can hear. We let that cat referee the match—the only ones who are going to win are them!"

"Do we have anyone else in mind? Who are the Erebus putting up?" I asked.

"Not yet, and I dunno," Rudy said. "We both got six days before we announce the refs. Then seven more till the match. Me and that sly bozo, Michael, are still hammering out the rules. So far, it's a battle to the death of the bot, which is totally in their favor since I'd bet the entire crop of cashews that theirs can rebuild itself. Or number of knockdowns within thirty minutes. Still working on round lengths and what precisely Death means."

"It would help a lot if we weren't entirely guessing that what they're going to field," O'Meara said.

"Stop distracting me!" Rudy made shooing gesture at O'Meara. "Look, we could ask somebody from House Hermes? Maybe invite that fella who's been sending Thomas treatises through the fax? Naple or something?"

"Speaking of people we don't trust," I said.

"Well, maybe, Doug then?" Rudy said hopefully. "We could threaten to expose him if he's reluctant."

"Got a way to mitigate the withdrawal of Morgana's support then, Rudy?" O'Meara asked.

"Find something else they want. A cut of the casino income. Give them Midnight for a year?" Rudy grasped at the air around him. "Something to apologize, maybe? They're gonna hold the entire casino in their hands, and if Erebus has something in trade, it's theirs."

"Rudy, the refs can only invalidate the match, they can't change the outcome if you win. They force a rematch. And if they do it without cause, we can replace them in the next match," I said. "Am I wrong?"

"No," Rudy grumbled. "Friends don't put friends in positions they can't say no to."

"I believe the term we're looking for here is 'business associates'," I offered.

"Or...ants infesting your cashews?" O'Meara grinned, prompting an even more sour look from the squirrel.

"Fine. But when they stab us in the back, I get to say I told you so real loud."

"Deal!" Me and O'Meara said at once.

"Now, let's finish Stompy and then we have an owl to feed firecrackers to." Rudy hopped down from the table and we all got back to work.

A day passed, then a week. Days were split between escorting the trio to either House Picitrix or House Morgana, stuffing magics into Stompy, strengthening the building's wards, and any down time I had which wasn't spent sleeping, Bone Whistler insisted I plow into the strange correspondence with Napoleon about the nature of awakenings. The casino stayed packed, not only in terms of mundanes, but magi, too, floated through, mostly lower-ranking ones who then attempted to break or bluster their way into the mech bay. We eventually contracted a minor House to move the entire operation into a folded space we had initially sealed off. Less secure against Oric and space bending magi, but much more secure against the casually nosy.

Riona and Tack couldn't officially help us with anything, but after three days of subsisting entirely on room service, she apparently couldn't take it any longer. By the end of day four, a two-page list of magical 'bugs' found throughout the casino 'magically' appeared on my desk. Inviting Riona to 'tour' the supposed secure sections produced a four-page list and a night of indigestion.

On Wednesday, the familiars' day off, O'Meara and me finally decided that the three of them would be safe enough on their own inside the Casino while we did a bit of saber rattling of our own. The TAU had gone to ground; their usual offices had been shuttered. They had sent out an invitation to an auction to be held in two months, but that had been the only official communication from the organization since the assault. Unofficially, Oric had been moving among the Houses. Napoleon made an offhand comment that the owl had been in Shangra-la. In my head, Oric was stealthily replacing the pallet of bricks floating over our heads with anvils and landmines.

It wasn't much of a plan. Head over to one the shuttered offices, break in and use a locator spell to figure out where they were hiding. If we had to burn through a hundred groat to do it? So be it. Just for a lead. Charlie and Bernard's main office operated out of a residential neighborhood. It was the only custom house on the block, a three-story McMansion with two small medieval turrets flanking the round front door. Wards glowed over the property, but compared to the ones we had over the MGM, they might as well be made of paper.

O'Meara and I opened them with the ease of a locksmith unlocking a car. The wards' security were no more than an illusion to those in the know. We got to the door and O'Meara paused, squinting at the sweeping script engraved on a strip of metal that encircled the circular doorframe. What *language is that?*

I groaned. *Elvish.*

What? Elves and fairies had two origins to a magus, either they were some sort of mythic or they were projections or avatars of the Fey and not to be messed with. Neither possibility had their own written language.

Tolkien elves. I'm guessing Bernard's a fan. Or maybe Charlie? He had been the one wearing plate armor, after all. I chuffed in annoyance, that puffed up husky had no similarity to me.

What's it say? She bumped me with a knee.

*I don't know. I was more of a gamer when I had thumbs...*I looked up at the doorway again. *What bonds gives strength.* A pang of loss struck as I remembered the time I had hobbies. I'd read those books ten times during high school. Getting my

Master of Library Science had been a bit of book overload. Once I'd worked with them, I'd shifted to video games. *Are we breaking into his building or not?*

Right. O'Meara nodded, and we undid the totally mundane lock with a spell. The round door swung open on its one strong hinge with a loud squeak. Stale scents greeted us; Bernard's scent marks, along with a half dozen others I did not know. The first floor had an entirely open floor plan and it had been stripped down to the polished floorboards.

I took a chance and dropped all but one of my wards to scry. Nothing. Magically sanitized. Nothing but the background purple of the Vegas shallowing.

"This doesn't look promising." O'Meara stepped into the house. As if we had hit a tripwire, her phone filled the place with that Klaxon ring. My guts, already off balance from our breaking and entering, took a swan dive off a cliff face.

"They've taken Midnight!" The tiny voice declared when O'Meara lifted the phone to her ear.

32

O'MEARA AND I RUSHED back and arrived to find Rudy already clustered with the security team.

"Give us the details. Rudy, get us a Fey chain now," O'Meara said, and to my surprise, the squirrel rushed off.

The chief started talking. "We barely caught it. Midnight was watching a craps table and this magus plucked him off the edge of the table and shoved him in a bag. Then just causally walked out the front door. Doorman caught a whiff of something funny, and then watched the man disappear as soon as he stepped beyond the wards. I just reviewed the tapes."

"How long ago was this?" O'Meara asked, pulling a pencil, a bit of tass, and a small vial of blood from her purse. After a minute of spell work, the pencil spun around aimlessly. "Well, they're not complete idiots," O'Meara said. "They've warded his location."

We could burn through that, but they'd notice if we did it, fast.

"Got your Fey chains here!" Rudy declared, riding in on Tilly. Carey followed in behind him.

"Cat friend hurt?" Tilly's brow had developed a worry wrinkle.

"We'll get him back, just gotta find him. Rudy?" I said.

"Got it!" Rudy leapt on to my back, chain in tow.

I nodded to O'Meara, and we did the bond switch, breaking my bond with her as the Fey chain wrapped around both our necks. As we settled in, Mr. Bitey snaked out into the universe, found Midnight's thread and connected me to his mind.

Heeeeeelllooo, Thomas! Ha ha ha. Midnight's thoughts came like puffs of smoke.

Where are you? I asked. What had they done to him?

I'm in a velvet bag! It's so comfy! I looooove it, he thought, everything in his mindscape remaining hazy and indistinct.

Is he stoned? O'Meara asked, peering through my mind and into Midnight's.

It's catnip. I sighed, recognizing that dreamy haze instantly. I'd even felt it. Midnight must be extra susceptible to it.

We considered feeding Midnight O'Meara's anchor, but that might simply leave him vulnerable, like in the duel with Charlie. The tabby hadn't even been wearing his pared-down harness when he'd been snatched by the overconfident idiot. Anger flowed. As soon as we got him back, I might skin him.

"How'd they snatch him?" Rudy asked the security chief. "You can't even notice that cat half the time."

O'Meara hoisted her hand with the spinning pencil. "He hates his wards. Once they're inside the building, they could have used something like this to find him, even if he's got some sort of natural don't-notice-me magic."

"Let's go look at that spot where the guy disappeared." Not waiting for them, I rushed outside.

It took a few more precious moments to find the doorman who had seen the kidnapper, but he knew exactly what I wanted. "Here, here, boss." He made a slashing motion of his hand. "Just, just walked through something here, and gone. Wish I had my nose on, boss. Coulda told ya more."

"You did good," I told him, mentally making a note to reward the man with additional vacation as I glared at the spot.

See anything? O'Meara asked, catching up.

No, not yet. Only seeing the glare of my own wards. A queasy fear slid through me. My eyes lifted to the rooftops across the street. Nothing there. Trying not to envision Oric

waiting to pounce on the other side of the rift we were searching for, I lowered my wards. All but one.

I've got you, O'Meara assured me, her mind coiled like a cat
about to strike as she grasped the sword at her waist.

With a shaky breath, I turned off the last ward, the spider
web of purple that prevented any sort of teleportation within
ten feet of me. If this was a trap, it would spring right now.

And be met with a tass-infused plasma blast, O'Meara reminded me.

Nothing happened, and for the first time in months, nothing
blocked my vision. Squinting, I focused on the air in front of
me. It took time, like waiting for night vision to return after
a flash of light, but there it was, a purple scab in space itself.
A standard portal spell. I saw the whispered remains of the
straggled runes. Coating a single claw with tass, I ripped it
open. Space rippled as if in pain around the portal, revealing
an alleyway. The scent of burned rubber tore at my nose.

O'Meara and I stepped through. The purple background
didn't change. We were still in Vegas.

"North east Vegas." O'Meara looked at her phone. "Right on
the edge of the Shallowing. Two more blocks north and we're
in the desert."

This was not an area where magi or mythics went. Upper
class humans lived up here. It also meant that a warded hide-
out would stick out like a fat lip. I looked all around for the
trace of magic. I fletched, tasting the air. The night was coming
with the promise of cooler air. The choking taste of exhaust
and oil. A particular herby note that played like a fiddle in my
brain. Catnip. "This way." I ran out of the alley and down the
street following the scent. It quickly faded. They'd probably
shut the doors to the vehicle, but I had direction. Away from
the highway. O'Meara blasted off from the ground to keep up.

Then I saw the ripple. I never would have seen it if I'd had
my wards up. Down a side street. Another portal scar, this one
big enough you could drive an entire car through.

More powerful, too, O'Meara observed as she caught up, landing beside me. *Probably sunk a bit of tass into it, if they know what they're doing. They're going to have an alarm ward on the other side of that. How's Midnight?*

I touched the cat's mind. He giggled at me, floating in his herbal bliss. Midnight, *Gimmie your senses.* I pushed myself into his brain.

Mmmkay. He pushed the scent of herbal bliss at me. *It's good!*

Not that sense! Hearing and vision!

Ooooh. Right.

I heard the roar of an engine along with its vibration. Still driving. Voices, too.

"Master, why are you driving so fast?" a small, timid voice asked.

"The faster we get away from that portal, the better," a gruffer voice answered. It was a voice I hadn't heard in two years: Whittaker, O'Meara's original and abusive master. We'd questioned him briefly when she and I had first met. It hadn't gone well.

"The TAU ain't coming for us. He ain't a member," a third voice. Another male. "Fair game, and Tylus said he ain't bonded.

The engine revved. "Not worried about the TAU."

"Can you bond him to me? Now?" the original voice asked. "Please, master."

"When we get home. Quiet now."

"The nip won't last that long. I want him to be happy when we're introduced."

A flare of seething heat washed over my mind and I separated from Midnight enough to look at O'Meara beside me. The pavement around her feet had begun to boil. "He's done it again." Then she swore as she wiped the slag of her phone from her fingers.

Uhhh, O'Meara, you might want to let go of your anchor. Or you might get a view of the sewer.

We're getting my car.

33

IT TOOK ABOUT TEN more minutes to go back and get the flying car. We ran into Rudy and Carey, riding Tilly, coming out to meet us, with the Wizard Phooey Mark II on Tilly's back.

Both Tilly and Carey insisted on coming along. So Rudy sat in his cupholder seat, Carey clung to the dashboard, and Tilly stared out from the back seat between O'Meara and me. The plan was that once we reached them, Rudy and Tilly would circle around while O'Meara and I made a frontal assault. I was less sure what Carey would do, but O'Meara was so eager to make an example of her old mentor, she probably would've invited more of an audience, if she could.

Rudy sniffed the air as we rolled through the portal. "Smells like Canada to me. That's a lotta pine." The car sat on a patch of gravel by the side of a road that went north and south while the on ramps to a maple leaf-marked highway stretched east and west.

"Okay, which way from here?" O'Meara asked.

I slipped into Midnight's head. The nip was finally wearing off. Thomas... *what's going on?* He pawed uselessly at the fabric that surround him.

Be quiet and listen.

"Somebody breached the ward," Whittaker announced.

"They'll give up. They have no idea which direction we went," the minion said.

I heard gravel crunch under the wheels. "They're not on the highway." I announced. Midnight also didn't hear any more traffic, but heck if I knew how busy highways were in Canada.

"Why are we stopping, Master?" the timid voice asked, definitely female.

"Ted, I want you and Freddie to whip up three portals we can fit the car through."

O'Meara was rolling. I pulled halfway back in surprise. We pulled onto the road. I shot her a thought that consisted of little more than a question mark.

"He's heading north," O'Meara said. "There's only one thing south, the US border, and he won't be hiding there. If he's opening decoy portals, then that will take them at least twenty minutes. Bastard is underestimating how fast we travel." *Got you this time...Master.*

"Uh boy," Rudy said as he sank deeper into his little seat. Buckle up, everybody!"

"Err. How do you do that?" Tilly asked. "Again? Are there more straps somewhere?"

"You're already bundled in, sweetie," O'Meara soothed. "Carey, you're going to have go to the back and squeeze yourself between the seat cushions." She revved the engine as she seized her anchor. "Thomas, you have Midnight watch for us, the moment he sees a hint of my light, we'll kill it."

O'Meara gave Carey a moment to scrabble into the back seat and burrow back down between the seat and the back cushions. She touched the white crystal. Flames leapt out of the back of the car and it screamed down the country road. Wary of the Veil outside of Vegas, she stuck to the road, following its lines as we flew a foot from its surface.

Midnight clawed at the fabric that held him. The catnip had begun to fade, and a vague sense of unease crept into his awareness. I could give him the fire now. He'd burn right through the floor of the car, but that would tip them off that he was our spy. Magic was being worked outside the car.

The purple glow of space-tearing magic lit Ted's smaller figure and his small familiar, Freddie, I assumed. The truck's cab heaved upwards as a great weight left the flatbed. The bear, Loki, probably. And that hunch was confirmed by an irritated huff that rolled right through the closed windows.

Give me the heat, Thomas, Midnight thought. *Just a bit to get out of his bag.*

They'll notice. I thought back. *And where is the girl?*

As if in answer she spoke, her voice very nearby. "Sit tight there, kitty. It's a good life out here, we're going to have lots of fun. It will be way better than that city life. You and me. Master's gonna teach us all sorts of stuff. You'll see."

"Kitty?!" Midnight huffed. "My name is Black Shadow Who Strikes at Midnight! And I insist you open this bag."

I pulled back a bit, opening my eyes to the world outside my own body. Walls of green blurred on either side of us, illuminated not by the headlights but by the corona of orange flame that enveloped the car. All the occupants made various noises of distress as the g forces of the curves alternately slammed us against the sides of our harnesses. Even Rudy's gleeful whoops of enthusiasm had given way to calls of, "Woah! Aw nutcakes, watch the—! Never mind."

A glance at the speedometer made my claws dig futilely into my seat. It had redlined at 250 miles an hour as O'Meara's face had been distorted into a fearsome grin. I didn't dare ask if it were the speed or the prospect of confronting her old mentor that drove her, but I didn't dare poke her, mentally or otherwise.

I wasn't entirely sure we were going in the right direction, but wherever we were going, we were getting there fast.

Midnight had continued to argue forcefully for his release, but the girl wasn't having it.

"I think you need another dose of catnip. It would relax you, you don't need those mean nasty words."

I heard the pop of a plastic container. Outside a portal flared to life. "Just give a little bit of a boost," she said as pale light flooded Midnight's vision.

There was a light kerchunk of a car door. "Izzy! What did I say about channeling!" Whittaker barked.

The girl squeaked, her light blinking out. "Sorry, Master! He's saying mean things."

"You don't open that bag, Izzy. We'll teach him manners later, like Freddie. Now get out of the car. Bring the cat, too."

What does he mean by that? Midnight growled as someone lifted the bag.

Steady, we have to be almost there, I counseled as Whittaker did something in the front of the truck. Then the doors were closed, and Midnight felt cool air bite his ears and nose.

"What about the gear?" Ted asked.

"We'll get it later. Bring anything magic you can't hide. Push it, Loki," Whittaker said.

A huff and a resentful growl rolled through the air. The crunch of gravel sounded as the portal flickered. Pushing the truck through it? The portal closed and faded out.

Another portal slash appeared but did not open, starting to fade immediately. Right next to the first. "I hope they try this one first," Ted giggled, in the manner of a fourteen-year-old troll.

"Why don't we just go home, Master?" the girl whined.

"Because we cannot have it found. Come, into the woods. We'll take a different route. Ted, use the last of that tass and do another false porta—"

A tiny blip of blue appeared in the sea of Midnight's dark vision.

"Huuurgh!" Loki bayed.

"They see us!" I told O'Meara as Whittaker announced.

"She's coming. Everyone into the woods. Now!" he said.

I slipped Midnight a thread of O'Meara's power. He clutched it, but did not channel it into his body yet, his mind shifting into a hunter's patience.

"Why aren't you killing the rocket boosters?" I asked O'Meara.

"Because if I stop, he'll know that we know where he is. We're not going to slow down until we're on top of him. Everyone brace for a screeching stop, as if we noticed the portals on the side of the road. Everyone out, but Thomas and I will be out first. Be careful, they'll be able to see your wards if they look. Hopefully, we'll shine so brightly, they won't notice. We'll back up, get out, and pretend to inspect the portals while you circle around. The man we're up against is Magus Whittaker. His anchor is the concept of breaking and it's very effective against wards that are not specifically designed against it. The wards on your harnesses can probably take one shot. The next hit will break your legs. With the spell ripper, we can block it, and he will focus on me. Watch for the Bear, he's faster than you think he is. Be careful of other two. Neither is likely to be as experienced or dangerous, but don't dismiss them."

"And we're just gonna rush them?" Carey squeaked.

"Nah huh," Rudy said. "We, as in you and Tilly, circle way around the thunder dome."

I looked back. Tilly stared straight ahead, ears back, breathing hard as his nostrils flared. "You alright, Tilly?" I asked.

"Who has my sneaky friend?" he asked in a sort of faraway voice.

"The girl," I said.

"I get her," Tilly said, his lips pulling back in a snarl that seemed utterly foreign on his normal dopey face. My heart winced at the golden retriever's loss of innocence.

It happens..."Less than a minute," O'Meara warned.

We waited. "Everyone ready?" I tensed.

"Here we go!" Rudy said.

34

"HERE THEY COME," WHITTAKER said.

I listened through Midnight's ears and watched through his magical sight as O'Meara's blue blaze shot past his perspective, then burst anew as she slammed on the brakes with a counter-directional thrust. The seat harness bit into my chest as the wheels touched down, the tires squealing as O'Meara swung the car around, pivoting it about the driver's seat before we came to a complete stop.

"Go!" O'Meara and I activated every ward we were wearing as she pivoted and thrust her hand back, jabbing at Tilly's buckle. I released myself, slipped down into the well of the seat, my force hands jabbing and pulling. The door opened and the seat back swung forward. Tilly leapt out, Carey clinging to his back, the metal domes of the Wizard Phooey Mark II shining dimly in the light of the nearly full moon. Rudy launched himself from the dash and landed on Tilly's neck. He scrambled up onto the weapon's perch, shooing Carey further down.

"I get her," Tilly said and took off into the dark wood with so much speed that both Carey and Rudy gave squeaks of surprise.

"Give me the cat," Whittaker said. "You so much as squeak, cat, and the first thing I do is I break every bone in your body.

Not answering, Midnight simply thought, Wonder *how well you'll do your magic when you're on fire?*

O'Meara hit the gas before I had time to close the door. We'd overshot Whitaker's pull-off by about a thousand feet, and we rolled up to it with caution. I couldn't see the portals through my wards, but I hoped they didn't know that. Midnight remained still, about two hundred feet into the woods. The wards covering us and the car gleamed like halogens in the darkness. Tilly's and Carey's were still more distant, candle-like. The magic was so much crisper and clearer out here compared the glare of Vegas.

On the shoulder, a large truck was pulled off of the narrow two-lane road. A barrier of steel posts and thick cables divided the road from a dark wooden expanse. I tried not to look in Midnight's direction as we rolled to a stop.

Make like we're inspecting the portals, O'Meara thought as she got out of her door.

I slipped out the window.

"Look at all those fancy toys you've got there, Sammy girl," Whittaker muttered under his breath.

Ted giggled again. "Come on, kitty, get a little closer."

Closer to what. The portal? The one he hadn't opened? From the tracks in the gravel, we had parked roughly in the same spot as their truck. If I got too close to it, the portal wouldn't work at all. That didn't matter.

I am the Black Shadow Who Strikes at Midnight! The tabby screamed into my mind and, before I could tell him to wait, he seized hold of O'Meara's heat. Her red light burst into existence from deep in the woods.

"The hell!" Whittaker screamed, as he and all his companions lit with the light of their anchors. O'Meara and I whirled. As O'Meara opened up a beam of heat straight at Whittaker, a purple ball materialized in front of him. The beam diffracted and several trees burst into black ash, skipping the flaming step entirely.

*Space-bender! O'*Meara swore in my mind as her hand went for her sword, but a lash of power flicked out from Whittaker at the fleeing fireball that was Midnight. I heard the snap of bones in both his ears and mine.

Growling, I ran forward, planning on using my wards to gum up the magus' tricks.

The second dummy portal opened, and a jet of water slammed into my side. My kinetic wards activated from the sheer crushing force of the water, channeling it around me in a circular dome. Things splattered against the ward like bugs against O'Meara's windshield. Little bastard had opened a portal to the bottom of the ocean.

"Bend this!" O'Meara shouted as heat flowed. An explosion of steam disrupted the ocean jet, and I pushed forward out of its path

However, the distraction had worked. Whittaker, a bear of a man, stood next to his Kodiak bear, heat wards shining. He was as I remembered him, 'bout seven feet tall, long beard. A roided-out Gandalf. One hand was a smoking ruin. Presumably, it was the one that had been carrying the bag with Midnight.

Midnight himself lay on the ground about twenty feet in front of Whittaker. Both his back legs were broken and he snarled with agony.

The rest of Whittaker's crew were hiding behind trees, but I could see them by the light of their power.

"Drop the sword. One more spell and the cat is dead, Sammy," Whittaker said with a charming smile.

"You think I can't pop that ward?" O'Meara shouted back. Behind us, the sea still roared through the portal, which had begun to close.

"I'm sure the Veil would have something to say about you starting a forest fire. Call off your friends circling around the back and nobody has to die, O'Meara," he said. "No harm, no foul." I could see Tilly and Carey moving to cut the party off.

"Nobody's dying today," I said, smiling. Together, O'Meara and I channeled the plane of Stasis into Midnight. White light flooded his body. Whittaker flung one of his sickly bolts at the cat, but it bounced off, deep cracks appearing in the tree trunk he hit.

He's the entire reason I found that plane, O'Meara thought as she swung the sword, releasing the battery of magical missiles directly at Whittaker. He responded with a white blast of his ichor-like energy. The bear roared, charged. We both lit with the energy of our magus' anchors, me in a nimbus of flame, him in a miasma of this-is-going-to-hurt.

"RRRUUUUGH!" Salivating jaws snapped in front of my nose, spittle splashing against my wards as I pulled back. I ducked under a swipe and raked a fiery paw across his muzzle. The ward snuffed out my fire, but claws ripped into skin. But beneath the skin? Iron. Utterly ignoring the scratch, he slammed his head down on me. The Kinetic ward, the one that had saved me from being smeared into bloody water, shattered with a burst of that ichor.

Don't get sloppy! O'Meara chided as I danced back to avoid a clap of his paws that would have crushed my skull like a grape.

Working on it.

Loki half stood, swinging a storm of swipes that would knock me into another time zone if I allowed them to connect. Channeling a blast of heat through my feet, I leapt. His jaws tried to follow, snapping an inch away from my tail. I landed behind him; he spun a tad too slow. Springing forward, I got my teeth in his shoulder. Coating my teeth with tass, I tore at both flesh and his ward. His bellowing scream echoed as his flesh started to sizzle.

O'Meara marched toward Whittaker, alternating between the stored magic in her sword and fiery blasts, both Ted and Whittaker barely fending off her assaults. Rudy would be here any moment. Just had to hang on.

Then the girl stepped from behind a tree ten feet away and threw a cloud of something into the air, her anchor burning as she did. I leapt away from the smoking bear. The scent hit me midair and something warm and gooey exploded in my brain, like tasting a brownie with every pore of your body. My limbs fumbled the landing and I staggered, falling against a tree, which promptly ignited.

Catnip. Really good catnip.

Dimly, I saw Loki smother out his flaming shoulder and rush at me. I *should probably move,* I told myself. Also, way back behind the bear, I saw a small object with a lit fuse drop between Ted and Whittaker.

The bomb went off a split second before the bear hit me. Which is good, because I only got hit by a 700 pound bear, instead of a magically enhanced 700 pound bear. Jaws clamped down on my neck and hauled me up into the air. My body did nothing to stop it, even as parts of my mind screamed impotently. Oh, *is this how I die?*

Another piece of me kept drinking fire.

Perhaps the heat searing his mouth and tongue prevented him from biting quite hard enough to shatter my neck, or maybe the simple fact that feline skin is loose and stretchy, so it scooted far enough away from the strongest teeth. I didn't die. Instead, I was hoisted into the air and flung, legs splaying out like a flaming pinata from hell.

I went through two tree trunks, the wood vaporizing before it touched my skin, and I landed in a tangle of limbs and steam.

Hang on! O'Meara thought. I felt her in my head pushing something. *WAKE UP, THOMAS!* she shouted at me, along with a chorus of authority, my mother's authority. Instantly my body sprung from the bed—I mean ground. I heard the distant *thoomf!* of the Wizard Phooey and a cry from the wizard named Ted. He had stepped out of the anti-magic field only to get caught in the chest by an anti-gravity round.

I shook my head out, the world and my limbs re-solidifying. Feeling the weight of bloody fur, but nothing seemed broken.

Where'd the bear go? Or the girl? Or Whittaker? I only saw Ted and a Pomeranian, who had to be Freddie.

They're running! O'Meara replayed an image of Whittaker seizing Ted's shoulder and shoving him towards O'Meara as he spun on his heel, disappearing into the trees behind him.

"I surrender!" Ted shouted as he whirled helplessly in midair.

"You bet you do!" Rudy snarled from in the tree. "I got these two. You get the rest!"

"Alright! Be careful." I began to trot in the direction Whittaker had run. A mountain lion's trot is about the same speed as a normal human's flat-out run. Mortification started to claw at my mind. I'd nearly been killed by catnip. Tilly came out of the murk and joined me, his teeth bared, an expression of anger I'd never seen on his dopey face. To my surprise, Carey wasn't on his back. I didn't have time to question it, though. The wind shifted in our favor and brought with it the scent of freshly-cooked bear.

We poured on the speed and we heard them. Moving at speed, the bear was breaking through the brittle twigs that barred their path, Whittaker jogging with more speed than a man his size should be able to. The girl hobbled after him with a limp, probably having twisted her ankle in the dark.

Circle around in front of them! O'Meara thought as she crashed through the forest behind us, the flames of her hair lighting her way.

"I get them," Tilly growled, then charged off toward the trio before I could object. I sprinted to keep pace. Crossing over a swelling, I saw them. Still distant, a thousand feet away, too far for me to keep up a dead run.

I had to cover Tilly's charge. Splitting off from him, I lit my fur up as O'Meara gave me every bit of power we could slam through the Fey chain's link. The forest lit up with the light of a noonday sun.

And in that light, I saw what they were running towards. Dead ahead of Whittaker were a pair of Grecian columns standing among trees of equal girth. I didn't need O'Meara to tell me it was a gateway of some sort. That was the only thing it could be.

The bear immediately rounded and roared a challenge, but his magus just kept running. Tilly shot by the bear, a golden-furred missile.

The girl saw him. "Master!" she called out in warning and he spun, ten feet short of his goal. I saw the whites of his eyes. He grabbed the girl's arm and flung her into Tilly's path. "Loki! Heel!"

The bear's collar lit up with a massive kinetic force and he was flung backwards toward Whittaker. The girl and Tilly impacted with a chorus of her screams and his growls.

A portal opened between the pillars. "See you later, Sammy girl!" Whittaker called out, as the bear sailed into the portal. O'Meara, behind me, launched herself skyward with a blast of fire. A beam of heat pierced empty air the moment after Whittaker followed Loki through the portal.

"Blood and ashes!" O'Meara kicked at the leaf litter and vaporized it to ash. Anger boiled through the link along with bitter memories that I very purposely did not look at. *You let him get away, Thomas! All we needed was a solid hit and that heat ward would have failed. You could have rocket boosted to get him! Or—*

"Master!" The girl threw Tilly off and rushed toward the pillars. Or tried to. Tilly latched onto the back of her jacket and hung there, growling fiercely.

"Stay down! You-You Bad Girl! Very Bad Girl!" he said with vehemence. "You're in trouble! So much trouble!"

"Let me go!" She struggled forward, but Tilly stopped her five feet from the pillar.

O'Meara gave a heavy sigh, "You can't open that, child," she called out, straightened her robe, and tramped toward the girl.

I dimmed my flame down to something not quite so bright. "He never showed you how."

"I can! I can!" the girl insisted, reaching. Tilly tugged and she fell on her butt. "He wouldn't have—"

"Tossed you at us to slow us down, while he threads through a long-abandoned realm he knows well? Yes, he would. He did it to me and he's done it to you," O'Meara snapped, the anger had turned toward herself now. How she should have seen this coming.

"But—" the girl stared up with wide eyes.

"He figures I'll kill Ted and Freddie, but he knows I won't kill you, an unbonded apprentice. You're a trade if someone had reached the rift within a minute and flung it open." She looked at me. "No, now, he's well away from the entranceway and I am not chasing him through a half-broken realm. So now we have to make an example out of this girl and this Ted fellow, instead of a well-known outlaw who slipped through our fingers."

"Ah...right," I said, finally cottoning onto precisely what she was truly pissed at me for. "I guess I could have tried a little harder? I blame the catnip?"

The girl had stopped struggling. Tilly still shook the back of her jacket like a tug toy. "Example of me?"

Maybe we can make an exception? I thought at O'Meara.

You know what she intended to do. You heard her. She knows, O'Meara responded. *She's a child, but even children need to know when they've done wrong. It's your House. Your rules, Thomas. You gonna back down now?*

"No," I said.

"Got one, I see." Rudy dropped out of a tree and onto Tilly's back. "Good boy, Tilly."

Tilly sprung up, tail wagging as he let go of Izzy. She sprang up, leapt at the twin pillars, and absolutely nothing happened. She clawed at the stone, fingers tapping in various patterns.

Rudy watched her as he fiddled with his phone. "She a mentalist, then? Looked like she got Thomas pretty good back there."

"She's an enhancer." O'Meara reached forward, grabbed the girl's neck and hauled her out from between the columns. "Very rare, almost as rare as space-bending. I don't know what her range is, but she can take a mundane object and make it more potent. Either House Morgana or House Picitrix would have snapped her up if Whittaker hadn't found her first."

"Soooo?" Rudy asked as he fiddled with his phone. The Wizard Phooey spun and with a sizzle, a bottle rocket shot straight up into the air. It exploded with a dull pop.

"She enhanced an entire container of catnip and flung it on me," I told him. "Aren't you supposed to be guarding the other two?"

"Eh, Carey's got him." He looked at the girl appreciatively. "Nearly killed by catnip. That's one way I haven't even tried." Rudy chuckled as droplets of rain began to fall.

A small giggle rang out from above me. I looked to see Carey on a branch right above me.

"And what are you doing there?" I asked her.

She sat bolt upright on the branch. "Uh, I was curious what happened."

"Hey, no shirking, my shirk! You were supposed to be watching that Ted fellow now," Rudy scolded.

"Well...I really don't think he's going anywhere." She attempted to do a hair flip and failed, since her head fur was short fuzz, and instead groomed her long side.

35

SHE WAS RIGHT: TED wasn't going anywhere. Rudy had somehow taped a tass bomb to his head and told him that it was motion-activated. He was sitting very still, as was Freddie about a foot to his left. We directed Izzy to sit on the dog's left.

"He left us, Ted," Izzy said as she sat down. Her eyes were staring at something distant. She wore a long black coat that she gathered into her lap; her short black hair seemed to be recovering from a recent buzz cut.

"Yeah. He does that," Ted said glumly.

We had them sit there while we pulled Midnight out of stasis. His rear legs were broken in multiple places. We healed them all, one by one. The girl watched, Ted didn't. Freddie had his eyes closed, pretending to be asleep. The rain had snuffed out all the fires we had lit during the fight. We made sure no one was troubled by the rain.

Bones freshly knit, Midnight was a sneezing, bleary-eyed mess and he glared at the three of them; no pity existed in his mind towards any of them. "Do you have anything to say for your sorry selves?" he asked them.

"Just get it over with," Ted said.

"Are they really going to kill us, Ted?" Izzy asked, her body shaking.

"They're not TAU, so we're not getting a trial, and they're not summoning the Inquisitors, so we're not getting fined. So yeah, we're dead. Unless the boss has some sort of plan other than leaving us here. Nice knowing you, kid," Ted said. "Bye, Freddie."

Freddie did not look either displeased or pleased by this prospect.

"You see, Thomas! They agree they should die for what they've done," Midnight said.

"And if they had killed you or succeeded in bonding you against your will, their lives would be forfeit to you, Midnight. But since they didn't get that far, they get the lesser penalty, as stated in your contract," I said drawing myself up formally as O'Meara took her place opposite me on the casting circle we'd drawn around them. Izzy and Ted looked at me, confused. "For the crime of kidnapping a member of House Freelance without consent and conspiring to bond him against his will, I, Thomas Khatt, current master of the House, sentence you to two years of stasis, during which you will be displayed at the MGM. You will not be conscious for your term as decoration and will be assigned penance and parole after your term is up. Freddie, we will discuss your options at future point in time."

"Stasis? What—" Izzy began to speak as O'Meara and I filled them with the strange energies of the stasis plane. Color faded from them until all three resembled the most detailed statues that the world had ever known.

Still, I can't say I felt satisfaction as we stilled the life in Izzy and Ted. They were helpless now. And Izzy—

Needs to pay for what she attempted to do, O'Meara thought at me. *You heard her. She was eager to have Midnight broken to her will. If she feels she paid for her mistake, it will not haunt her.*

I mentally nodded. This was responsibility and protecting those we cared for.

Midnight strode up to Izzy. "I would urinate on you, but you do not deserve to have my scent upon you." He turned to O'Meara. "Will this Whittaker come back?"

She shook her head. "Doubtful. And certainly not without a new crew. If we had gotten him, then we might not have to worry about another kidnapping any time soon. Whittaker is one of the most powerful outlaw magi by reputation, if not actual power. With him on our wall, Oric wouldn't be able to find many to go against us, no matter how well he pays."

Carey approached Freddie, the Pomeranian, who hadn't said a word. "What about this guy? He wasn't saying much."

"He can't. Never could," Rudy said. "If you look hard at him, there's no talking spell. Can of cashews says he's not TAU and he might have a pain lash bond."

"Pain lash bond?" she asked.

"Before the TAU, there were lots of ways to bond a familiar. And most of them were nasty. Pain lash is a simple one. It's similar to the one the Council and the TAU use, but the magus can inflict pain on the familiar at will. Oh, and it's lots more fragile and its bandwidth is horrible, but it's easier to do," Rudy explained, shaking his tail as he tilted his ears in Freddie's direction.

"We'll have to sort that out, then," I said.

"So, the TAU put a stop to that?" Carey asked. "The TAU's not all evil?"

Rudy made a disgusted sound. "Not too many things start evil. The TAU were lots better in the old days. They really were a union, instead of a mafia. They forced magi to use bonds that were more akin to equals, in their heads at least. There used to be far more awakened animals than magi. Magi as apprentices just used to go out and find one. Ask them if they'd be interested in living longer and getting fed every day. Those that said yes, joined the TAU and were bonded. Those that said no were free to hop, fly, or whatever on their merry way. Then, about two hundred years ago, something shifted, and awakened animals became rare, while awakened humans became more common. That's when the finding fees and auctions started. That's when Oric decided that every awakened animal who says no to a bond is simply a misguided fool who doesn't know what they're missing."

"Will that happen to Thomas? If we pull this off? Defeating the TAU? Killing Oric?" Carey asked, shooting me a worried look.

"Eeeh." Rudy waved at me dismissively. "Probably, I reckon he's got a good hundred years of justice before he rots." The squirrel winked.

"Rudy!" I said, I wanted to tell him something like, *not in front of the kids*, but alas, I had no mental link to Rudy.

"Hey, prove me wrong, buddy. Prove me wrong. You guys woke up the old ghost in my head and he's being noisy. And when he's noisy, I remember stuff. You know I hung out with Death for a bit? He changed a lot about House Erebus in his first twenty years. Vengeance and Justice. Didn't have much in common with the guy who Lansky ate."

"You got a point there, Rudy?" O'Meara asked. "And don't you worry about Thomas going evil on you. He's way too big of a softy. No force on earth will make Thomas ruthless enough to actually make an evil empire. He'll get offed by the first psychopath that pulls the helpless innocent act on him." She scuffled my head.

"Hey!" I protested.

"Come on, let's get our new decorations on display and have a pint. Or treats," she gestured with her hands.

"Treats?" Tilly answered with enthusiasm.

"Whittaker got away. But we won," O'Meara said, looking over the three statues in front of us, her gaze resting on Izzy. *Two years and then you are going to be a handful, girl. I'm still unlearning what Whittaker taught me.* Her thoughts were focused as a prayer, even though Izzy couldn't hear her. O'Meara's attention shifted towards me. *No matter what happens, she comes with us. In two years, we have to be in a place where we're ready for apprentices. Casino or no.*

We will be, I swore to her. Then I took a deep breath. "Alright, I want everyone to look at this. We're all safe. We've captured several of those who sought to hurt us. And we didn't kill them. That's a step in the right direction. Yeah, it's weird." I looked at their sightless eyes and shivered a little. "But think about the alternative. We want there to be a day where there is an authority we trust to serve out justice. Till that day, we're going to do the best we can. We won today, and now we keep winning, until justice is something that everyone can expect in the magical world."

I looked over the little crew. Rudy and O'Meara smiled; Tilly wagged his tail, slightly uncertainly; Carey looked up into the trees; and Midnight finished grooming his hind paw, as if to say, "Of course, we will win! You cannot lose when you are the Black Shadow Who Strikes at Midnight! Next time we will do it without breaking my legs. Or losing my tail."

"Maybe you should wear a ward?" Rudy chuckled.

"You don't wear wards, and I am braver than any rodent," Midnight declared with the toss of his head.

"Sure!" I jumped in, cutting Rudy off. "But notice Rudy's always hiding behind people who do have wards?"

"I do not hide!" Rudy protested. "I simply stay where my weapons are mounted."

"Come on!" O'Meara clapped her hands. "Let's go home and celebrate!"

"Treats!" Tilly barked.

36

WE DID CELEBRATE. STEAK tartare was Midnight's and my "drink." Tilly contented himself with a prime rib bone. Rudy broke out some ultra-fancy chocolate-coated cashews. Carey made moon eyes at O'Meara's whiskey, but grudgingly accepted a cup of warmed raw duck with a blend of seasoning that was favored by the spell dogs.

Freddie was placed in my quarters, as a reminder to me that we needed to thaw him out and see what he had to say.

Ted, Izzy, and Grugar were installed overlooking what would be the main door to the fight stadium. O'Meara and I spent the morning working on wards to make sure they would stay there and remain undamaged.

As we were wrapping up, I noticed a black cloak among a small cluster of magi watching us. "I have to say, Mr. Thomas and Mistress O'Meara, that those are some very interesting decorations," that smarmy customer service voice called up at us.

"Aren't they charming?" I growled from the top of the extended platform or whatever the portable elevator thing was called.

"I dunno. I guess I'm simply a traditionalist." He tapped his chin.

O'Meara pulled the lever and the platform began to lower as her mind fingered her anchor. "Not many people can look at a skull and see the person it belonged to, Michael."

"But the skulls of your enemies are so much more elegant and cheaper. Are you not worried about someone coming in here after you fill out your gallery a little, and waking up a small army of people who don't like you?" He smiled.

"I like gnawing bones," Michael's familiar, Albertus, added.

"Maintaining stasis isn't very expensive at all, particularly in Vegas. It doesn't like to move. A full gallery won't even cost a groat a month," O'Meara said with a sly smile of her own.

Michael cocked his head, a furrow of confusion on his brow. "Mistress O'Meara, that sounds like a sales pitch."

"Maybe it is. It could be a service that House Freelance provides," O'Meara said as she opened the door of the platform for me to hop out.

"Provided you are still a House next week?" He smirked. His dog smiled and gave a little wag.

"Why are you here, Michael?" I snapped, suddenly irritated.

"I need to talk to the rodent." He smiled wider. "We are supposed to announce our referees today. I intended to go to his office but this," waving a finger in the general direction of Izzy and Ted, "distracted me. Is he in?" The fact Michael used 'I' while his familiar stood at his heel annoyed me.

Rudy was doing something in his lab, I was pretty sure. "He's upstairs. Follow us."

Michael paused as the elevator opened. "Is there any way we could do this in a different room? Albertus has difficulty with heights."

Both O'Meara and I chuckled as the dog's facade of cheerful vacancy flashed to annoyance for a moment. "You're the one who agreed to meet on his turf, Master Michael," O'Meara said as she strode forward to the wall that hid Rudy's office, the small door, no bigger than a cat, was the only obvious entrance. O'Meara rapped a hidden panel with her knuckles and a large section of the wall slid away. "Did he open this for you last time?" she asked with an air of innocence.

"No comment," Michael said with a haughty coldness.

"Hey! Michael, buddy! Come on in!" Rudy called from his throne inside. My office was comfortable. Rudy's looked like something from the mind of a deranged imaginer with a very large budget. He perched on a squirrel-sized throne carved into the trunk of a massive oak tree. Acorn and firework motifs alternated in the ornate carving around his seat. Two chrome robot arms bolted to either side of the throne held the latest iPhones at an angle that only Rudy could see. Beyond it extended the tree's branches, with two thick ones running to the door that supported human-sized visitors, but branches of all sizes swept around the edges of the room, providing amphitheater-like seating for more diminutive visitors. Beyond that, sunlight streamed in between broad leaves. Below, between the branches, stretched out the busy traffic of the Las Vegas strip.

The husky sniffed deeply, shot a glance at his magus, and trotted in. Michael took a deep breath and followed with very careful steps. I tried not to smile. About two feet below the branches was a floor of borderless ultra-high-res digital displays connected to a very expensive camera on the outside of the building. They were not magic, and if a magus wasn't hip to digital technology, it'd be easy to make them think Rudy's office extended outside the building. Fooled me the first time, too.

O'Meara and I circled through the back to join Rudy on either side of the tree.

"...yeah, we got our ref," Rudy said in a tone that broadcast his unhappiness with the selection. "The great Esmeralda of House Morgana."

Michael gave a slow nod that gave no hint of his thoughts as to the ancient familiar. "That is acceptable. She certainly has talent for finding untruths. We do not veto that selection."

"Nuts. Come on, help a buddy out here," Rudy said.

Michael shrugged and offered a smirk. "Due to political considerations, we must put forth Oric as our referee."

And there it was. The TAU had circled back to Oric's usual modus operandi. He'd given Charlie his shot at taking us out directly and now the bird was bending every lever of power he could wrap his beak around. He'd put some sort of bounty on Midnight's head and now wormed his way into a contest with the casino at stake.

"Veto," Rudy said with a dismissive gesture.

"You would at least know where he was during the match," Michael countered.

"Yeah, he'd be inside the casino, which is not allowed. Veto," Rudy said.

Michael raised his hands in a gesture of helplessness. "Then the entire deal is off."

"We have a veto. It's in the contract." Rudy's tail quivered as his black eyes bored into the magus in front of him.

"Sadly, we cannot provide a substitute if you use your veto," Michael said. "He is applying pressure from higher levels of the House. If we cannot use Oric for this initial bout, then we must withdraw."

"You withdraw, you owe us five hundred groat, Michael." Rudy stood up.

"My Cabal is not happy about this railroading, Rudy," he said. "We invested time and resources that are not easily replaced or salvaged."

"With Oric reffing, there's no chance we can win. He'll invalidate the match one way or another," Rudy said.

"According to the contract, no ref can serve in consecutive bouts. The second bout, Cherri of House Picitrix has agreed to referee. A much more neutral judge. Makes the first round a sort of exhibition match."

"For you!" Rudy chittered. "Esmeralda won't simply invalidate the match if you get the upper hand."

"I know it's unfortunate. But surely you can see this as an opportunity, either way. No one gets put on display in either of our House's styles." Michael smiled.

"Me and Stompy will smash whatever you've cobbled to-gether to its component atoms, but I'm not gonna waste my time performing like a monkey for that bird brain," Rudy growled.

"Hang on," I said, an idea occurring to me that might put Oric between a rock and a very pointy stick. "What exactly are we fighting over again?" I asked Michael.

"The MGM and all the magical assets that are part of the property." Michael said.

Translation, O'Meara thought, *if we relocated everything that isn't nailed down on the night of the fight, we keep it. We'd have to leave the forbidden vault and the tass collection, but everything else we could keep. But we'd be out of any income besides the Council's payments on their loan. And they'd probably attempt to weasel out of that.*

Rudy looked at me as if I'd grown a second head. "One moment, I have to conference with a cat and a magus who are out of their rotten, peanut-brained minds." He pressed a button and a privacy ward activated.

"You cannot be thinking what I suspect you're thinking!" Rudy glared at me.

"Look Rudy, if we lose the casino, then we don't have to be House Khatt anymore. We can be a mythic guild," I said.

"And then the Inquisition would have to keep the peace between us," O'Meara joined in. "It would put Oric in a worse spot against us, if Archmagus Fibalt's vote flips. The loan we gave them would give us income. We wrote it in Thomas's name, not the House's."

"That's a lot of ifs!" Rudy hissed. "We'd need a commitment from Cherri, and that's not something we can go get while Michael and his totally innocent looking familiar are standing here."

"Oric must know he's an unacceptable choice, Rudy!" I answered. "He's trying to stop the fight entirely."

Rudy paused, eyes looking down at the screen in front of him. "Cause he knows I'll win."

"Oooor," O'Meara said loudly, "Win or lose, it removes an element he can leverage against us. He cannot convince the entire House of Erebus to march against us if the claim is resolved. If they're no longer hostile, they might look to us for familiars instead of to Oric. They're the only House still in his pocket."

"None of this win or lose, nutcake!" Rudy fumed. "I'm gonna feed them their skulls and crossbones three times in a row if I have to!"

The ward went down and Rudy jabbed a digit in Michael's direction. "You're on! Owl or no Owl. I'm gonna punch whatever you got straight into orbit!"

"What?" Michael blinked, but recovered quickly. "Of course. This will be instructional to both of us."

"Just remember, if Oric don't show or he has a mishap during the fight, you guys fight without your ref. We got no terms for pinch hitters in here. And we're not amending it," Rudy said.

"Engineering a mishap would be quite rude on the host's part." Tightness gripped Michael's voice.

"You best be sure he's coming to judge a fight instead of starting one, then," Rudy said.

Michael went still for a moment before giving a very small bow. "Very well. In a week, you get to meet Gargantua. See you then."

He and his dog left.

Rudy huffed. "Dang it. Now I gotta go see Cherri."

"You know her personally, Rudy?" I asked.

"Do I know her?" Rudy shivered, then folded his paws in an imitation of the raccoon on the council. "The way we's see it...uck. Leave it to me. I'll get that oily raccoon to commit to your make-Oric-behave plan."

37

IT'S RATHER FORTUNATE THAT the MGM has an arena. It's usually used for concerts, but they do use it for lots of fights, boxing, and mixed martial arts. So, it already had most of the equipment to provide seating and cameras to watch the show. However, it took a bit of work getting it ready to handle fighters two stories tall in a ring the size of a basketball court. We used the same minor House that created my anti-Oric wards, House Fendosa, to protect the floor and the watchers from anything that might escape the ring. I spent a long time checking their work—both by inspecting visually and by hurling everything we could think of at it. Riona and Tack pitched in where they could. The ring was essentially the same as a panic ward. Nothing got in and nothing got out. Which makes the ward much simpler. A personal ward is much more complex because it has to tell the difference between your spells, the environment around you, and the stuff that could actually kill you.

We kept Midnight and Carey very busy. House Morgana had requested Carey for the entire week, an assignment I only found out later was because the magus' own familiar had been refusing to set foot in an abandoned realm that the House was harvesting for tass. Something about monsters with mouths for eyes. Tilly got a few rounds with curious apprentices, but mostly watched over Midnight's work with the House Picitrix magus as they assembled more efficient hope and dream gathering spells for the casinos that they had acquired from House Hermes.

The day before the fight, we recalled everyone. There were two more days until the full moon, when we'd lose more than half our security.

It felt unreal. This would be the first big test of House Freelance. And it came down to giant robots. The work was all done, so the morning was spent snoozing and running through combat scenarios with Rudy. We'd packed Big Stompy with everything we could think of to counter House Erebus' tactics and a few more besides. The robot seemed to shine with eagerness as he waited in his bay.

We had not advertised the fight, but the casino was filled to near capacity by three in the afternoon. No tourists, but locals, humans and mythics, were elbow to elbow, with a seasoning of magi and their familiars. This felt so much different. Yes, the stakes were high and yes, Oric had stacked the deck against us, but they were all in our House. O'Meara scratched my ear as I watched the security cameras like a house cat perched outside a mouse hole.

Good turnout. Somebody's promised a show.

Oh, it will be that, I agreed.

We watched and waited, as did the crowd, clustering in every available space with a view of the stadium doors. Magi with magi. Mythics more interspersed, satyrs dominant, clusters of humans who kept sniffing the air, off duty spell dogs, trolls, and goblins flickered between the groups, as well as more varied mutants who were letting their unearthly qualities shine.

Two hours to go and Rudy said, "Hey, Thomas, check out the street."

We switched the monitors to outside the building. The strip had been cleared of traffic somehow and a hulking silhouette marched down the road. Gargantua. House Erebus was coming for their practice bout; for us it would be for our very home. No details were showing through the hulking figure, other than that it was massive. Twice the size of Stompy.

"Idiots," Rudy chuckled. "They went for the absolute size limit. This is gonna be fun."

Purple flashes, Midnight thought through the bond. *I see an owl, a bear and a white husky. They are pausing outside the wards.*

On our way, I responded. "Rudy, you've got the watch. O'Meara and I have to extend our welcome."

I'll give them points for politeness: they waited at the ward's edge. "Hello, Oric," I said, pitching my voice up near the chipper range. "I had begun to think your tail feathers had turned yellow. So nice of you to yield the city to me."

"Simply because you cannot find a target to strike does not mean we have left," he hooted softly, tilting his head to match the angle of the scar across my shoulder. Stubble had just begun to recolonize my former wound. "Thomas, you are looking well, as is your pet magus."

"Oh? Pet?" O'Meara said. "Is that all you have, Oric, a petty insult at *our* doorstep? Running out of magi stupid enough to come after us?"

Oric's feathers ruffled. "I apologize, for now. For as long as it is your doorstep, at least. I suspect you are about to be evicted."

"Can't even play at impartiality, Oric?" I asked, as I felt a pressure step into the back of my mind. *Back off, Bone Whistler! This is not the time,* I snarled mentally.

"Why bother? I'm sure you'll cheat. Just as you did at Death's game. I merely have to point it out," Oric said.

I could make you lose it all right here, brother. The Owl would make such a nice snack. He'll be at our mercy in a few steps. A quick tasty snap and it will all be over. He laughed.

I stepped back behind O'Meara, blocking my line of pouncing with her body. If *I lose access to the resources of the casino, then performing that favor will take longer than my lifetime,* I growled.

Just a reminder of our priorities. Bone Whistler backed off a hair, still watching, although not treading on me.

O'Meara covered for my distraction. "Regardless, you have our hospitality for tonight's event. So long as you obey its rules, you have nothing to fear. Your associates however..."

"They come with me," the Owl said.

"So long as they swear they are coming in unarmed." I glared at Charlie, who sported a scar on his neck where O'Meara had shot him.

"You gonna pull out my teeth, cat?" Charlie snarled. "I don't need nothing else for you. If Esmeralda weren't sweet on ya, you'd be a tripod cripple now."

"Now, now, Charlie. What did I tell you about manners?" Oric chided. "You two had your fun. Now, it's simply business."

"I'm so glad you see it that way, Oric." I smiled at the bird. "I simply want to remind you that if, say, we were to lose the casino, we would then be in a prime position to reclassify ourselves as a mythic guild. With all the protections that comes with." We'd reviewed the laws and, truth be told, I'd rather hold on to a place of power like the MGM than rely on Inquisitors for protection, but we'd be able to call on them if Oric threatened us.

He didn't blink, but the owl's head rocked back a fraction of an inch. "Maybe you are growing up. Making backup plans instead of digging in your claws and screaming at the unfairness of the world."

"Whatever works," I said and called out for Tilly.

Tilly stepped out from one of the pillars, tail wagging. "Yes, friend? You need help with not-friend?"

"Do your trick, Tilly," I said.

Tilly bounded up to Charlie in a doggy greeting, "Hi! Hi! Hi!" each syllable accented with a sniff.

"Hi, yourself." Charlie's tail gave a half wag and he stepped back.

Tilly didn't slow, moving to Bernard, "Hi! Hi! Hi!" and then popping up on his hind legs to greet Oric as well. The owl fluttered as Tilly circled back to me. "They got tass bombs! I think!"

O'Meara handed Tilly a crunchy treat. I had not seen any of them. Not the faintest bit of tass shone through their auras. Fortunately, dogs are much more sensitive to trace amounts of magic.

"Still think he's simply a very good boy, Oric?" I asked.

"I'm not so good anymore," Tilly sighed. "Can I have another treat?"

"Now," O'Meara began. "Unless you can prove that those devices are purely defensive, then you must hand them to the doorman on your way into the building. Tilly will check."

"Since you don't need them anyway." I winked at Charlie, who glowered back.

"Have a good evening." O'Meara waved and we turned inside. *One threat defanged*, we sang in our heads.

Now we just had to grapple with House Erebus and whatever they were planning.

"Thomas. O'Meara." Esmeralda greeted us as we stepped back into the casino. I managed not to jump.

O'Meara recovered first. "Esmeralda, did you just arrive?"

"Oh, no. I've been here for hours. I came by tram." Her watery slits that contained eyes twinkled as a bolt of shock traveled through us both.

Hours? She's been here for hours? What the hell has she been doing? My mind nearly wailed as I slammed up the customer service smile. "So good to see you. Is Morrian not joining us this evening?"

"Liar," she drawled before stretching. "As for Morrian, she sees it all through me, if she's not napping. Robots. She doesn't see the appeal if they don't bleed. Death used to host some glorious combats here. A Minotaur vs Cerberus once. Now that was a fight." Esmeralda smiled, displaying fangs that age had worn down to nubs. "Too bad we bet on the minotaur."

"You made a bad bet?" I asked, sliding between O'Meara and the ancient cat.

"Oh, you're cute. Not I, Morrian. You never gamble on the promises of prophecies. They dislike it." Her nose drifted up as if something beyond the ceiling tiles held a mystery.

"Do you know what's going to happen tonight?" I asked.

"You're going to lose something," she said, as if it were the most casual thing in the world.

I froze. "The match? Aren't you going to help us with that?"

Her tail curled across her legs and her head tilted. "Thomas, you've done so well. You are a king among the pawns, but still only see the squares ahead of you. It's a very small part of the board."

A growl flowed out of me. "Then what am I not seeing?"

Suddenly, she was as large as me. A paw whipped through my wards and slapped me across the muzzle so hard that my head snapped to the side. "Do not growl at me, youngster!" Teeth grabbed the scruff of my neck; my limbs went slack as I was lifted like a kitten.

I blinked, and everything was back the way it had been. Except my cheek stung.

"You're blinding yourself with all those wards, kitten. All they do here is tell me what you are not defended against. They advertise how afraid you are," she cooed.

"Almost every magus in this city uses wards like this," I muttered defensively, my breath heaving as adrenaline kicked in far after the point of usefulness.

"Yes," she said and disappeared into the sea of legs.

I leaned into O'Meara's legs. What *the hell did she just hit me with? Did she suppress my wards like she did the security system?* I babbled possibilities.

I don't know. She hit you fast and I felt her teeth, too. A mind attack? We have a ward against it, but it's not a big one.

It felt physical to me. We cycled through my wards, but nothing looked touched.

Is she right? I wondered. Here I was, warded in my own house. Or was it some sort of ploy for me to go before all those magi without my wards? So I could see what they were really doing?

O'Meara rubbed my neck. You *keep those wards up, especially through the demonstration. If we're losing something tonight, it'd better not be you.*

38

GARGANTUA ENTERED THE ARENA as a hulking beast of pure shadow. Conceptual darkness cloaked its features like the reaper's own cloak. Stompy stood at the other end of the basketball court, utterly still and as silent as the death house's golem. Its eyes glowed like embers in the night. O'Meara, Rudy, and I stood in a glass box overlooking the court from Stompy's end. Michael's Cabal gathered in an identical box opposite, as people filtered into the seats. Oric and his bodyguards were in a suspended cage at half court, Esmeralda sat in an identical cage across the way. Both of Oric's bodyguards were channeling lightly, nervously, as they scanned the crowd below. I had finally gotten Oric and his cronies in a cage. Too bad I had to let them out again. Still, the pictures would give me some joy.

"We ready, Rudy?" I asked as seats around the edge of the stadium filled to capacity. We'd blocked off several rows of seats closest to the ring just in case. Nobody seemed to be pushing past the rope barriers.

"I was born ready!" Rudy bounced in the window. "Go do your blah blah speech stuffs. Me and Stompy are gonna show them all."

"Okay." O'Meara slipped a headset over my ears and the window in front of us swung outward. It would boost my talking spell to fill the arena. The top of the arena's ward flashed into view and I walked out onto it. The magic tingled at my paw pads as I slowly walked out to the center spot of the arena.

A hush fell over the crowd. "Welcome, One and All, to House Freelance, aka House Khatt. I am Thomas, the master of the House. We stand six months to the day," O'Meara finally pulled my speech in front her eyes so I could read what I wrote, "of the night Vegas was nearly lost to the hunger, to grief and pain. Magi and familiars in this room, remember it. You gathered to watch me die, and yet we saved you all. In return I asked you for a home, and the MGM was the place you granted me and my family."

Across the way, Michael finally figured out how the latch on the window worked and stumbled out onto the ward. He was hurrying while attempting not to appear hurried.

"And yet, we are challenged, again and again. We have met them all. For this particular challenge, we have chosen a more sporting contest!" I looked to Michael, who had just joined me at center court. "State your ridiculous challenge!" I snarled for the cameras.

Michael opened his mouth and was startled by a loud chorus of boos. Not surprisingly, the House that bought the corpses of the city's dead were not terribly popular among unaligned mythics. "We," he tried again but was confronted by his own unamplified voice. A microphone dropped from the ceiling and he grabbed it, his eyes flashing with anger. The contract hadn't specified about speeches and smack talk. Apparently, he didn't watch much wrestling. "We, the Cabal of Resplendent Decay, and the entire House of Erebus contend that Death's House, the MGM, is House Erebus' and was illegally claimed," he stated formally.

The crowd mostly booed. I noted a cluster of satyrs cheering and chanting, "Whup the kitty! Whup the kitty!" I wonder how many of their names started with the letter G. The magi in the audience were keeping themselves quite neutral and still. Are *there any other House Erebus here?* I asked O'Meara.

Just one other Cabal, younger than the Resplendent Decay, and a few more scattered through the crowd. Looks like the House wants to distance themselves from this. We've got a smattering from all the Houses. There's a big shape in the back, too, that Midnight noticed, might be Napoleon? Or Cerberus is back in town.

I waited for the crowd to die down. "We refute this in the strongest terms. But to prevent the messiness of two weeks ago from spilling out into the streets, we're going to settle this here. Today. In combat."

Michael pulled the mike down to his side, "You couldn't have gotten a neutral announcer?!"

I couldn't respond, my mike didn't have an off button, so I introduced the rules. There weren't many. No spells that targeted the pilots. Then, I turned back to Michael. "And what fights for House Erebus?"

He sucked in breath between his teeth and glared briefly down at me. With a roll of his eyes, he brought the mic back up to his mouth. "Behold and tremble, cat! Today you face Gargantua!" Finally getting into it, he made a dramatic sweep toward the black shape. With a rushing roar of wind, the darkness spread like wings across the back of the arena. A figure of bone and black iron, its face a gaping skull set on broad metal shoulders. Twice the size of Stompy in every dimension, black hungry magics flowed within its limbs. One arm ended in a black ax while the other had bone white talons that could sever cars in half. "Piloted by my familiar, Albertus!"

The dome of the skull lifted to reveal the darkly dyed husky. The crowd cheered and he preened, thrusting up his chin and howling. Lap *it up, dog,* I thought.

The stadium quieted some. "Well, that's mighty impressive there," I said. "But today you face, Rudy—" my ears caught tiny voices cheering above me and I forced myself not to look up, "piloting Big Stompy!"

A chorus of hard metal guitars boomed out through the stadium, accompanying a spotlighted Rudy as he slowly leapt from spiky bit to spiky bit up the robot, posing for strobe lights each time.

"You never mentioned we needed theme music!" Michael hissed.

"That little toy will be stomped on and there won't be a next time," he huffed.

Rudy headbanged to the music and played the worlds tiniest air guitar before leaping into the hatch. Rudy's voice came over the loudspeakers. "BIG STOMPY, GO!"

Then there was the sound of a struggling engine, the red lights of the mecha flickering with a putt-putt-putt. It didn't start. Rudy tried again, then a third time. "Aw, nuts."

Laughter rang out, and I heard gasps of concern from above. I continued to smile. "I guess we need to give it a quick jump start. Excuse me, Michael." I tapped the ward below me and a circular section of it dropped smoothly down into the arena. With a brisk walk, I joined O'Meara as well as Carey, Tilly, and Midnight, who came in via the rear. Stealthily, I broke my bond with O'Meara as I took my place opposite her on the casting circle drawn around Stompy. Midnight and Carey were at the other compass points, with Tilly right by O'Meara's side.

O'Meara lit up with the power of her anchor. Mr. Bitey manifested with extra shine to his links, and slithered through the air, dramatically encircling O'Meara's neck before breaking apart and completing the bond.

Hi, again! I thought, giving her a mental lick.

Hello, Thomas. It's going to get a little crowded in here. She gave me power, and I felt the now familiar swoosh of my fur bursting into flame.

One by one, Tilly, Midnight, and finally Carey bonded with O'Meara. Their thoughts burst into excitement. We *did it! Yay! Of course, we did. This is easy.* Mostly Midnight and Tilly.

O'Meara wobbled. Quiet *please, still. Still.* Everyone pulled their thoughts into themselves as O'Meara fed everyone power. The trio's fur glowed and then all of us were the source of a pillar of flame. *Now get to work.* Four views of the circle overlapped with mine as we began to weave. With this many eyes, I didn't have to imagine the bits of the spell I couldn't see. We could see it all at once as we built a tiny sun and bound it into a core of metal. It was completely unnecessary to Stompy's function, but we all helped on the weave, even Tilly holding bits in place. In under a minute a fusion-powered ball of light hovered above us, completely self-sustaining for the next hour or two. Stompy's belly button telescoped open and the sun floated into the socket.

Flames flooded across Stompy in a tiger-striped pattern as the screaming guitars swelled back into existence. All of us not inside the mech ran for the exit as Rudy's voice came over the loudspeakers, "Awww, yeah! It's go time!" as Stompy pulled a metal cylinder off his leg and it burst into a blade of pure plasma with a trademarked woosh.

"Let the battle begin!" I shouted as the arena ward closed behind us.

Okay, everyone break but Thomas, O'Meara thought, gasping. *I got too many cooks in my kitchen.*

Yes! If you wish! Aww okay. The three thoughts blended together.

"Thomas!" Rudy cried out into my headset. "I need your eyes!"

I ran upstairs into our viewing box as O'Meara untangled herself from the others.

Did it work? Did the magi see that anyone can be assisted with extra familiars? O'Meara asked, as she shook out her head, mentally slumping against me.

I couldn't tell, I just had to hope. Fatigue leaked from her mindscape as I parked myself in front the window, prying off my headset, jabbing the channel over to Rudy's private one and pulling it back on. It pinched one of my ears, but I ignored it and stared down at the fight. Michael might not be up on wrestling, but Albertus clearly knew how to put on a show. Gargantua advanced cautiously chopping arm up, slashing fingers splayed out as if the fingers were ready to catch a blow. "I'm here, Rudy."

"Bout time. Here we go! Geronimo!" Ports on Stompy's back bloomed open, twin cones of fire blasting the mecha into the air. Gargantua's hand came up to meet Rudy's slashing blade. Fire and kinetic wards flashed at the impact. The axe answered. Thrusters flared. Stompy slammed into the ground with the ax whistling through empty space.

"He's got heat wards and kinetic wards mounted on that hand, they're not full-body," I said. *Why are they not full-body?*

"I hear them!" Rudy shouted as the sword whirled in a figure eight against the shield. "Is it weakening?"

The shield ward held as Gargantua braced against the blows. The shield's flashing was not dimming. "Not as far as I can tell."

It's a one-way ward that will be much stronger, O'Meara said.

Stompy danced back. We'd known whatever opponent Rudy would face would be heavily warded against heat, so we'd instead used O'Meara's talents to make Stompy more maneuverable. Wiring the mecha in the same way as the flying Porsche, a focus at his heart was channeling her very anchor into jets placed all over Stompy's body.

Gargantua's dark wings fluttered, the darkness coalescing into a half dozen thick cords of shadow. The top one struck down at Stompy. "Hope ya got sunglasses!" Rudy cried, the star in Stompy's stomach brightening tenfold. The tentacles withered in its glare before being chopped in twain with the sword.

Yet the green of summoning flowed along the remaining tentacles, pearly white debris coating the darkness, mixing with the gray of tass. "Rudy! Tass weapons!" I shouted, as the bone tentacles lashed out with wicked barbed spears at each end.

Stompy's own shield sprang out from his forearm, blunting two of the strikes. The sword parried the third, but the fourth bounced off Stompy's kinetic armor ward, cracking it with the force of the blow. "I thought we agreed no long-range weapons," Rudy sputtered.

The crowd Oooed. Above I heard thousands of high-pitched voices begin to chant. "Go, Uncle Rudy! Hit him high! Hit him low! Hit him in the nutsack, go!

"I think it was worded no guns," I replied, "Did you invite your extended family?"

"They shouldn't be here!" Rudy hissed and snuffed the plasma sword. "You just warn me if they use those death magics I hear in his core. I'll handle this doc oct act fine." Big Stompy brought up its fists as Gargantua reformed the top two tentacles in their boney configuration as the majority of its bulk hid behind that thick shield. I squinted, looking for a weakness. Rudy had the spell ripper on board, but he'd have to get close again. "Buster bomb time."

The tentacles struck. Stompy's fist met them all, his punch bursting into a cone of brilliant gray. The wards of the arena flashed gold as the tentacles were flung against them, their tips shattering with the impact. Tass bomb number one.

Stompy charged forward on columns of flame as the snake limbs slid down the magical walls.

"Hey, nice shield!" Rudy called out over the loudspeakers. "I think I'll take it." Stompy grabbed hold of the shield as Gargantua started to rise. The kinetic ward rippled around Stompy's fingers as he yanked on it. The tentacles stilled as the two began a tug of war. The ax came up and Stompy twisted. The ax hit the inside of the shield, striking off two of Gargantua's own talons. With a bellow, Gargantua rose to his full height and pushed, slamming Stompy into the wall ward and pinning him against it.

"Get up, Uncle Rudy!" A lone voice screamed out from above.

"Hit him in the nutsack!" The rest of the rowdy rodents answered.

"Ahhh!" Rudy screamed out frustration as Stompy's front armor began to bend from the pressure. "Those idiots are going to expose the entire warren!"

"Ignore them! Focus on the fight!" I shouted back at my friend.

"Premium California cashews flushed down the drain!" Rudy swore as rear rockets fired. Stompy shot up and over Gargantua, carrying the shield and the arm with him. Overextended, it appeared Gargantua would topple backwards.

The tentacles, which had never retracted, had dug into the floor and pulled the mecha out of the way. They swung Gargantua down to the opposite end of the arena, green and black energy swarming in the craters Rudy had left in its leg and side. White bone filled wounds as Gargantua settled into another defensive stance. "Well, there's the resurrection function," I growled.

"What is summoned, can be banished," Rudy said.

A blue flare burst in my magical vision. Carey's trouble signal.

You see that? O'Meara asked.

I'm on it, I said as I broke our bond.

39

TILLY, MIDNIGHT AND CAREY had been deployed to watch for any magical trouble in the crowd. Each was equipped with a magical flare to signal if they needed assistance. I could hear O'Meara running up the stairs toward me as I found Carey's thread and connected to her, only to feel Mr. Bitey slam into a wall as she refused to accept the connection. Whaa?

The weight of a weasel fell onto my back. "I'm sorry," Carey whispered. My vision lit with grey and my wards winked out as purple flared. I turned and saw O'Meara's face, eyes wide, Fey chain clasped in her hand.

I fell. I fell a very long way through a purple tunnel. Long enough to run out of breath for screaming. Mr. Bitey recoiled. I searched and found O'Meara's thread and sent Mr. Bitey down it. He raced along it as fast as he could. And he kept going, and going, and going. Finally, I felt a jerk on my mind. The spool in my head that held Mr. Bitey's coils had emptied. O'Meara was out of range. Just how far had I fallen?

I stopped falling. Blackness greeted me.

"Welcome to the edge of the universe, Thomas. Where I bring my most treasured and troublesome competitors." A light flickered in the distance to illuminate a small Owl who wore a bowtie. He perched on what appeared to be a skull, on a skeleton that hunkered in a small rowboat. A lantern burned on its prow. "We'll have a lovely conversation in a bit. I imagine you'll plead for your life again, try pleading for food and water. There's none out here. I do, however, need you alive to ward off your fire witch, so float tight." The owl winked out of existence. A slight pale blue afterimage remained. A magical illusion. The real Oric was still in the casino.

The lantern still shone, and by its feeble light I found I was far from alone in this patch of void. Twisted shapes spun lethargically through it, the emaciated shapes of withered individuals, mostly larger individuals—the faded fur of a tiger, the twisted wings of a golden eagle, a mummified snake longer than three of me stacked nose to tail. A few humans. Many of the corpses had fatal wounds, slashed throats. Others sported wounds that appeared to be self-inflicted.

One floating shape lived. A shivering donut of fur rotated out into the void, the momentum of her jump carrying her away from me.

"Wards are advertisements of what you cannot defend against." I echoed Esmeralda's warning and growled. "Carey," I said, my voice a whisper in the void.

The little donut flinched, but did not respond. I reached out with my force hands. They chased after her, their magic little more than a feeble glow. Carey struck out at them. The force of her teeth disrupted one, but the other swatted her from behind. It applied enough force to start her floating towards me, spinning like a hot dog through the lens of a slow-motion camera. She hissed in blind rage, snapping at the surrounding emptiness.

I examined the wrist where the spell focus for the hands was hidden. The weave appeared to be strained; the threads frayed as I watched. I looked at the interlocking wards on my harness. The same thing. Fraying spells. We had minutes, hours? What the hell was time down here? I reached for anger, but I found mostly the cold wet noodles of fear.

"W-Why, Carey?" My voice wavered, and for a moment I wondered if my talking spell would give out, too. "Why'd you do this?"

"Because you're an idiot!" she shouted, still clawing at the air, totally ignoring the futility. "Because you're never going to win! You took me out of that cage and slammed me into a new one."

"We're working on it, Carey. If you were unhappy with the hours or something, you could have said. But change doesn't happen easy," I said. "Look, we can get out of this. Together, we can make a spell circle. I...I still have tass with me." There was something like a knocking on my brain, something I'd overlooked, something I really did not want to realize.

"You. Are. A. Total. Fucking. IDIOT!" She spat each word as she orbited to face me and then waited for her body to come around again for the next. "I'm not the only one in the cage! He has my sister! He and that bear were waiting for her when she got home! She's chained to a wall somewhere between Vegas and Washington DC!"

Shiiit. Several things clicked together. Carey hadn't complained at all since we'd sent her sister home. I'd been too busy to pay attention, but there was the anger. I snarled. "You could have told us! We could have fixed it! Rescued her. There are ways to find her." Or were.

Carey spun within a paw's grasp. I reached out and jerked my paw back as her white needle teeth snapped at it. "Kill me! Kill me now! I betrayed you, Mr. Boss. And that's the punishment, right? I'm a weasel in every sense of the word. Not that you're worth anything. Midnight believed in you and got his legs shattered. How many times is that gonna happen under your protection? That whole outing almost got us all captured because of a jar of catnip! You have any idea how depressed Tilly is? Any idea how often he's staring at walls, wishing he was just another dog!"

I hit her. "Shut up!" My paw slapped across her backside and sent her into a high spin.

She puked in-between hurled obscenities.

Purple flared in the space beyond the boat. I activated the force hands and gave myself a shove towards it. I clapped two paws on Carey. If we could reach it in time. I'd managed to start a slow drift towards the rowboat, barely perceptible.

The flare closed, Oric appearing. He hooted with amusement. "Is this a bad time?"

"Kill me. Kill me now," Carey hissed. "Crush me. It's the only way to save her."

"Tsk. Well, he definitely won't kill you now, you silly weasel," Oric said, settling on that very same skull that his image had been on previously.

"You coward," I growled. "O'Meara will burn you to ash."

"Thomas, come now. Think rationally. I have no idea what you did to provoke your own student or familiar or whatever you're calling Carey there to attack you. I certainly didn't violate your generous hospitality. I even agreed with Esmeralda to recast the fight as an exhibition match. It will be rescheduled. Perhaps after your funeral," Oric laughed. "O'Meara will look interesting in black, I'm sure."

"She'll find me. Just like last time," I said.

"O'Meara is a bright spot on your horizon, but she's no Merlin. This was our special spot. The place where secrets were hidden." He tapped the skull he stood on. "Meet Gawain, the finder of the so-called Holy Grail. Fenrir is somewhere around here, as well as various others whose talk was far greater than their power."

He pointed at a single speck of white in the black expanse. Both my eyes and my mind saw it. "That, that right there is our finite universe. A constant tangle of overlapping realities. Infinite possibilities there but here there is nothing. No spell that's not specially designed will sustain itself long. Even our souls feel the stretch out here. Those that survive too long simply go mad. After that happens, I will consider returning you to your lovely magus, if she behaves. And speaking of behaving," he looked at Carey. "It's time to go."

I squeezed the weasel tighter. "Do it!" she begged.

"Maybe I'll keep her for company," I said.

"I'll kill her sister, then. More blood on your paws," Oric said.

I released the weasel, letting her sit in easy reach. "Carey betrayed me and she'll suffer my fate alongside me. Come and get her," I sneered, pulling up a tass bomb I'd had stored in my stomach and displaying it between my front teeth. It was an anti-magic bomb. It would do very little out here, but you can't tell what the bombs are before they go off.

"Those wards of yours won't last more than a week," Oric hmpfed. "I will retrieve you and Carey when those are gone. You both can eat corpses till then. Bon appetit."

"No!" Carey screamed as Oric disappeared into the portal.

"You idiot! He'll kill her!" Carey screamed at me.

"Relax," I told her. "If he kills her, then he won't have any leverage on your cowardly tail." Oh there was my anger at her, passive aggressive as usual. "My guess is he's planning on keeping that for the rest of your sister's natural life span."

She fumed, hurled insults, and struggled in the air as we slowly drifted ever closer to the rowboat.

"Are you ready to be bonded? You can scream at me directly into my head that way. You might actually hurt my feelings in there," I said, as my paw could just about scrape the edge of the boat.

"Why the hell would I do that? We're stuck out here!" she fumed.

"Because I have precisely one idea to get us out of here and we'll need to do magic. Which is not possible without a bond." At least not yet.

"I'm not a magus!" she exclaimed. "My anchor's in some finite treetop plane and all she cares about is eating squirrels!"

"You talk to your anchor, too?" I asked, wondering how common that experience was.

Carey reached for the side of the boat, extending out her claws as far as they would go. Still short by about an inch. I tapped her gently on the rear, and she grasped the edge and clung to it.

"You're welcome," I said.

"Fuck you," she snarled, still hugging the wood.

Ignoring the insult, I explained, "You don't need a magus with a channeling plane to do magic. It's really helpful to have those as power sources. Fortunately, I have ten groat of tass on me, so if we can put together a circle, I can place a call to someone who might help."

Carey stood unsteadily and pointed her nose at the small distant light that was our universe. "I don't know much about magic yet, but that's going to be one hell of a long-distance call." After a pause, "And I'm not helping. I'm going to be a good weasel and wait for Oric to come back. He has my sister, and unlike you, he can make sure she goes back to her job and lives her life without getting dragged back into the madness here."

"O'Meara and Rudy will find me." The words sounded with more conviction than I felt. Space was not O'Meara's specialty. "They have resources and allies. O'Meara saw me fall into the portal. It's going to be a war down there. What if O'Meara gets Oric in the next week? Or Rudy. I notice he didn't talk much about Rudy."

"And if you had let me go with him, my sister would have been released. What kind of shining knight are you?"

"I'm not a shining knight. Sometimes I tell myself I am, but it's not true. I want to make the world a better place. But I'm a selfish cat who protects his family first, and right now you are standing in my way, little weasel." My voice sawed up into a growl. "If we work together, we can get out of this, make sure everyone is safe. Your sister, my magus and our friends."

"And if it works? What you gonna to do to me? Will you kill me then?"

"We will make sure your sister is safe. Then I'll let you run away. Or if you prefer, we'll leave it to Rudy and O'Meara, since I'm a softy."

"You make me human again. Then I'll go back to being my sister's deadbeat burden." Her voice was bitter.

"No. I'm not promising things beyond my ability or power ever again."

"Fine..." She stared off into the darkness. "I want to get high again. You can do it with catnip any time you want, but nobody knows what will just kill a weasel. I want you to find me a vet who will tell me what I need and give it to me because this life sucks. I'm done with it."

"So, you're just going to go Brave New World on life?" I asked her.

"What's that?" Her eyes narrowed.

"Librarian joke," I muttered, "Okay. I'll agree to that." The only thing that'd cost would be money and a blind eye.

40

IT WAS THE THINNEST bond I've ever made, a pinhole into each other's minds. Thoughts had to push through, and even then, the words echoed through like tin cans on a string. Still, even this didn't hide the magnitude of Carey's sullen anger. I tried to ignore it as she climbed up onto my back and I launched us to the nearest human-proportioned corpse.

You could smell the despair on the thing. A Hermes medallion floated on a leather thong around the withered neck. Carey crawled down my leg very purposely putting her claws into my skin. What *am I looking for, Boss?* she thought at me.

"Metal string or chalk. Something we can make a casting circle with," I said.

She crawled around outside the robe, grumbling. "Where the hell do they put the pockets in these things?"

Nothing there. We moved on. Two more human corpses, one that felt vaguely fresh. I made a note in case this took a while. Out here, there'd simply be a line between meat and not-meat. None of them had anything useful. They'd been stripped clean. Probably before they were tossed in here.

We hit pay dirt on a tiger. He had a large chain collar on, the steel was totally unrusted, but it pulled away flakes of mummified skin and clumps of fur as I unwrapped it.

"Eww," Carey said as it swung over to her. My magical hands had given up the ghost and I was once again thumbless.

Put it together, I told her.

She examined it in the dim light, then took one end in her mouth, shimmied up to where the other end protruded out of my mouth, and hooked them together. There was our circle.

I spat it into the void and carefully, using the tips of my claws, got it spinning as a hoop. So long as all the metal bits touched, it would work. "Okay, unhook my harness."

She paused. "Aren't you afraid Oric will show up again? You can't defend against him without those wards. Haven't you seen this guy's eyes?"

I looked. Dried blood caked the fur around the tiger's open eye sockets. No hint of the eyes within. Had Oric plucked them out like some sort deranged raven? I pushed the question aside. "Just unhook the harness."

Not having the strength to undo the clasps, she chewed through the nylon straps. And a weasel's teeth are not made for gnawing. It took her over an hour of pensive silence. Then I maneuvered the harness's top piece into the middle of the circle.

"Okay, you're going to need to open up a bit, Carey. I need your eyes for this part," I said.

"Not like Oric needed this Tiger's eyes, right?" she snorted.

I put the half joke into the victory column. "No, we've done this before. Let's get it over with."

"You're not going to like it," she announced as the pinhole be between us grudgingly opened. Working with Carey had been delicate before. Now, it felt like pushing through a room full of gun barrels with every single one pointed at my head. *I don't trust you, Thomas Khatt.*

This the best chance we have, I thought at her, *for everyone.*

Then what are we doing?

We're calling someone.

Who?

The thing that made me.

As soon as I had bonded Carey, she had stopped shivering. And for me? Other than it being dark and spooky, I wasn't uncomfortable here. My eyes had adjusted to the gloom, and I could see details on the dark bodies that orbited nearby. Cautiously, I slipped behind her vision and saw myself. A dim aura shimmered above my fur with undulating patterns overlapped in a ghostly kaleidoscope of muted colors. I hadn't seen it at all with my eyes.

What's that? You still got a focus on you? Carey asked.

Not sure anymore, remains of an old enchantment, I answered. Maybe I was about to find out what the Veil had meant when it had addressed me as an embryo. *Now, let's get to work.*

It took time to find the thread among all the others. It actively avoided my attention, but I knew it was there. I sorted through them one by one...Rudy, O'Meara, Alice, Noise, security chief, Midnight, Tilly, and everyone else I'd met since I grew a tail. Until I had it cornered. While the silver threads that connected me back to earth were thin and strained, this thread gently waved, as if it had plenty of slack.

I brought it into the circle and build a small spell around it, molding the spell from tass and empowering it with the remains of my wards. It was similar to the one time Noise and I did magic together as we struggled to find the Blackwings' prison. Yet, not. I knew far more this time and received zero help from Carey. Still, I found the memory of that night comforting. I wondered what Noise was doing these days.

The spell shuddered. I let it go. It zipped out of the circle and disappeared like a captured songbird fleeing an open cage. A warm tingly sensation spread out across my scalp.

And I knew. The Dragon had heard me. Not like the bond. Not like a thought at all. A certainty, knowledge that came from my very center.

It didn't arrive all at once. Space around us bent, as nothingness gained colors like those of the oily sheen on the surface of water. That same, scaly aura that flowed over my fur rippled into existence, coalescing into a much more solid shape. The eye, one of its many, opened first, a solid red light.

What the hell? Carey's animosity for me fell away like a sheet ripped off a window as naked fear drove her into my side.

You could say you're meeting my parent, sort of. Whatever happens, don't let go of me, I told her.

*That's your mom?!*Carey's head filled with expletives and awe. The Dragon continued to pull itself into the plane of our perceptions, impossibly long, like a gator stretched out to the length of Florida. It coiled around us, its serrated teeth lining a maw that had no hinge, the jaw merely separated from its body. And eyes, filled with colors and stars, decorated every few feet of its marvelous and horrifying length. They had become so much more since the last time I had seen them.

HAPPINESSDISAPOINTMENTCONFUSIONCURIOUSI-TY! The world exploded, pain hitting my head like a lightning strike. I screamed, every limb went rigid. Agony faded into a harsh tingling in every nerve I had. Like swallowing cold water on an empty stomach, but pain was inside of every neuron.

"Softer! Please!" I begged.

An expression rippled through the face that spiraled around us. Happiness-Disappointment-Confusion-Curiosity!

Owie Owie Owie. Carey whimpered next to me.

"Please, a little more linear. Let me separate it?" I asked.

Happiness—you called upon us. Disappointment—you called upon us. Confusion—why are you here? Curiosity—why are you here? the Dragon clarified.

"I am very happy to see you have recovered from your ordeal. I've been stranded out here by an enemy. And I was hoping for a lift back?" I asked.

Never. Anger. Know better than to ask that. Its voice slipped back into the one I remembered, its mind palming mine and peering into it. Reassembling the "hand" that gripped me to reflect my thought processes.

I winced. The Dragon would never come close enough to my reality unless it had zero choice. The pain inflicted had been very real. Sorry, I thought at it.

Stay. Reintegrate with me. Abandon your life, it suggested.

The memory of the Dragon pulling me apart made me recoil and growl, You *granted me independence.*

"Haaaaa." The Dragon's laugh rolled over everything at once. *Understand now.*

It doesn't have to be all the way to earth! Simply closer than this. Within range, I can rebond O'Meara. She can pull me the rest of the way. Somehow.

No. That is the lair of my kind and I am not welcome there. To be torn asunder by the Lords of Dragon is an honor for some, but not this one.

So, you won't help?

The Dragon smiled. Do *your young need to be taught how to crawl?*

Before I could answer, the maw opened. A thick tongue slapped into me from every angle. It pulled in a direction that made my brain whimper, leeward. The fourth direction.

Swallowed and spat.

My paws hit pavement. Fear of pain wailed through me as I recognized the impossible internal structure of the Dragon. Tessellations of me and Carey spiraled out along the ceiling and walls, each facet acting out a different possibility of what I'd do. In some, I killed her. In many more, she bit me and I threw her away. And in others, we went inside the house in front of us.

Archibald's house. The entirety of it, a single-story ranch house. The white paint peeling, the pink shutters bright. The place where this all started.

"Okay, I'm really confused now," Carey stood on my back, staring up at the reflections of ourselves.

"We're inside the Dragon," I said.

"It ate us!?" Carey squeaked.

"Yes, but it isn't digesting us," I said.

"I thought we were calling for help. When is getting eaten helping?" Carey fumed so hard her tail waggled.

"We have to learn how to crawl, apparently," I said, and walked up the front steps. The wards that guarded the house were all gone. I gripped the doorknob with my teeth and after a few attempts, managed to grip it hard enough to twist it. It still tasted of old man sweat. *Blech*. The door opened, revealing the house's living room, still crammed from floor to ceiling with books, with the ancient lazy boy recliner in the center of the room.

Curled up in the chair, a small ball of fur appeared to slumber. My ears went back. Surely the Dragon hadn't...? I advanced with a small hiss as I tasted the air.

A single eye opened, not where it was supposed to be, but rather in the small cat's shoulder. "I'm dead. Go away, lad."

"Scrags," I said, sitting in front of the recliner. "This is a surprise."

"Oh man, that's so gross. It's moving." Carey shivered, watching as the eye seemed to realize it was in the wrong spot and slowly flowed up the neck toward the spot where it should be.

"It's not surprising. A Dragon ate me and the house. I got digested which killed me. Now I'm dead and was enjoying a nice loooong nap. Which you interrupted! That's the least surprising part." Scrags yawned, his entire head flipping in half to display a mouth crammed with long needle teeth.

"That makes no sense," Carey said. "Dead don't nap. And would you pull yourself together! Eyes on the face, not the neck! That's totally messed up and rude! You're trying to gross me out."

"I've been dead for... I don't know! You try remembering how everything is supposed to be put together after not existing!" Scrags snapped, huffed, and screeched. The formless mass of dark fur gained limbs as he did so. His eyes reopened in the right spots and peered at Carey. "She's a weasel."

"Through and through," I agreed.

"And you're an idiot, Thomas," Carey said.

"Aye, that he is," Scrags agreed.

I shrugged and looked at the masses of books around us. "Okay, Scrags, tell me which of these books are going to help us get home from the outer edges of reality. I assume that's what you're here to help us with, because I don't see any magic in this house."

"Then you're blind. We're inside a bloody Dragon and you don't see any magic?" Scrags jumped up. He'd almost gotten himself put back together, but his ears were facing backwards and his tail stuck out of his right thigh. "Follow me." He jumped down and headed toward the hallway.

The ranch house only had one hall, proceeding down the length of the house. The last time I'd been here, I'd seen two versions of his hallway: one restricted to the physical limits of the outside walls, and the other that stretched on like an infinity of doors on either side.

The Dragon had preserved the longer hallway. Even fixed it up, no more decaying seams of purple at the edges. Scrags started to march down it and I felt the slightest hint of Bone Whistler's claws in my mind.

I paused outside the first door. "Hang on. I have to check something else first."

41

MY FACE STARED BACK at me from the paper. My human face preserved in the graphite of Archibald's drawing. Vaguely handsome, if you liked chubby cheeks. And it was all over the room. Stapled up to walls were charts of progress. I could read them now. Scattered throughout the room was the progress of my own awakening. Latin notes scrawled in the margins had been incomprehensible the last time I had been here, but now I paced around the room with brand new eyes. O'Meara herself couldn't have understood it. She couldn't see the silver threads, didn't know they existed.

"Is looking at pictures of this dude really going to get us home?" Carey watched impatiently as I pored through the charts. I ignored her and continued. A lot of them were documenting what Archibald called culling the threads. Working with my old girlfriend, Noise, to socially isolate me. This was apparently standard procedure to force an awakening. Veronica had done it to Riona to force her awakening, magically sabotaging her singing career. If your strongest connection is on the other side of the Veil, it loosens its hold. But it always takes something more. It had been done for a long time to get pupils but not many magi had put that sort of resources and time into getting familiars.

"That's him. You still think you can undo your awakening, lad?" Scrags laughed. "Still dreaming of the days when you couldn't reach your balls with your tongue?"

"No." I landed heavily on my front feet. It was all about connections. And I could see mine; to undo it, I'd have to give them all up. Forget them all. Never. Not lie with my head in O'Meara's lap ever again? Or gossip with Rudy as we walked through the streets with him riding my back? But understanding this gnawed at me. Even more than Bone Whistler's teeth in my mind, urging me to focus on this alone. We were too far apart for me to hear him, but he'd see this when I got back. I had to at least try to understand while I had the chance.

I looked at Scrags. "There's more to this. Show me."

"It's where I was gonna take ya in the first place," Scrags said, and started walking down the hall.

We followed.

"How long is this gonna take, Thomas?! What happens when Oric comes back and finds the Dragon sitting there? Why don't it just wait for him to pop through that portal and kill him?"

Scrags answered before I could. "We're far away from where you were picked up. We're hunting for food and being hunted. We can't afford to stay in place."

I nodded, knowing everything Scrags spoke of before he said it. "And even if we did somehow jump Oric, we'd be right in the middle of his turf with no wards. If there is a way back on our own terms, that will be much better. It would be much safer for me to simply rejoin them." I blinked and growled up at the ceiling.

The Dragon laughed.

Carey looked up at me with a wary expression.

"Staying here long-term isn't an option," I told her. The Dragon apparently missed my company and I could feel its desire to keep me growing. It could sever all my silver threads with the barest flicker of effort.

"In here." Scrags stopped outside a door that looked like all the others and flowed beneath the door. Literally liquid kitty. A wet squelch sounded and the door swung inward, revealing a cavernous room. A marble slab inlaid with a golden casting circle dominated the center, a pillow marking Scrags' usual spot. Yet beyond that, at a small bench in the corner, magic glowed. The color of which I had no word for. The same color that the traveler disappeared into. Time.

I walked directly for it. The glow emanated from a basin of a sort. Its rim etched with jade runes, the pattern of the scrying spell, but repeated, spiraling down into the infinite.

"That is not the answer you want, Thomas!" Scrags hissed at my feet. "It's never the answer. You can't change the future."

Next to the basin stood a photograph. The smiling face of the traveler greeted me. The man outside Morgana Tower, who spoke to Magus Napoleon before O'Meara and I. Who babbled about the threads.

"Who's this?" I tapped on the glass with a claw.

"Our avatar, Nick Fessbender. During our exile in Grantsville, Archibald used a spell to take possession of a mortal man. For brief periods, at first, and then for much longer periods of time. Sabrina, our jailer, took a decade to find the threads."

The desk the basin rested on had drawers with the corners of papers sticking out through the cracks. I took the knob in my mouth and wrenched the drawer out. Too fast; the contents of the drawer spilled out across the floor. Polaroids rushed out like a flock of drunken pigeons. They were all shots of Nick. A younger one than I'd met, playing guitar in a band, selfies with women. One woman, in particular, seemed all over. Green shone from one. Green scrubs, the woman holding a wrinkled infant and beaming at the camera.

Scrags' eyes closed and he seemed to melt a bit as Carey drifted closer. Squinting, she pawed one of them and pulled it closer. "Who this kid?"

I peered at the photo. Nick stood, aged but in his rocker regalia, black leather jacket, hand posed for a wild strum. And next to him, with her own guitar stood a little girl proudly mimicking her father.

"Wow," I clicked, gnashing my teeth together as I pawed through the pile. There was a lot more of that little girl and the resemblance grew in my mind. "Riona is Archibald's daughter?"

"That chick you gave Sanctuary to?" Carey asked.

"In every sense other than biological," Scrags conceded. "Sabrina and the council cut us off from seeing her. Or using Nick as our avatar."

"So, you switched to using time magic to keep tabs on her. This Nick, he woke up. Walked out of her life?"

Scrags nodded.

I gazed at the basin. "You'd scry into her past, but what creepy remote-viewing father doesn't want to see what he can do about his daughter's future?"

"And saw the disastrously short life she had. We didn't know how the rulers of time guard their territory. You can dabble in vague prophecies all you like, but to see it is to invite the worst upon you and yours. Leave that basin alone, lad," Scrags said.

But that wasn't what was clicking into my head. "Then I'm..."

"The frikkin tool," Scrags growled. "The only pathway that prevented Riona's death, either at the hands of Veronica or Dorothy, was your intervention."

"And he had to die to awaken me," I said.

"We went on journey after journey through time. Looking for other ways, but every pathway ended in disaster."

"So, did you see this? See us sitting here?" I asked, reimagining my life as some sort of play, sculpted and planned by unseen hands.

"Ha!" Scrags barked into laughter. "Why would we see this? Your role is done. Archibald didn't care about anything but her. No matter how the time demon enfeebled his mind."

"That explains how I saw you after I freed us—I mean the Dragon; I saw you both. But how is it I've seen Nick twice now? Ran into him after I think he visited Riona and then again outside Napoleon's tower. The second time he definitely used time magic."

"What! That's impossible!" Scrags sputtered. "He can't do that without me! He wouldn't! He would have told me!"

I thought for a moment. "You're dead, Scrags. Maybe he is, too. Could a mind ghost of Archibald woken up in Nick's head?"

"Then he must die, as well." Scrags' mouth moved, but the voice came from everywhere, including me.

"That is just, like, freaky." Carey stared at us both. "Could you not talk in unison? Definitely bad."

"Sorry," I pushed the Dragon's anger out of me. Somewhat surprised I could. "We still need to get home. Scrags, where's the section on anchors and planar travel?"

"You have to kill him," Scrags said.

"I'm not chasing him through time!" I said.

"Then our deal is void," Scrags said as I felt the Dragon try to slide into my mind.

I shoved it back. "It isn't! He's still dead. There is apparently a piece of his mind running around mucking things up," I growled. "That's not my fault. You want to drop us off, maybe we can come to an agreement. You're free. That's the important thing. Isn't it? Or do you get some pleasure out of adding people to your sock puppet collection?"

"It is Archibald who imprisoned me. To have a piece of him experience what he did to me is justice. Not revenge," Scrags said. "He possesses this Nick against his will. Makes a...sock puppet—no, a *meat* puppet of him. We will save Nick. You like saving people."

"You have to save my sister first," Carey reminded me, "then you two freaks can do what you want."

"Okay then. You will drop us off at earth? Our earth?"

"No, we will tread closer to the universe, but I am too weak to travel the populated planes, I would risk capture or death. The court for Archibald's crime must persist. You will open your own way. I will provide power as needed," the Dragon spoke through Scrags' mouth.

"What keeps us from getting eaten, then? If you're afraid of going back," Carey asked.

"The Fey that rule those waters are the sharks. I am a bleeding pike." Scrags looked hard at Carey. "You are proto plankton." Then at me. "He is a microscopic mite. As long as he doesn't make them itch, we will be fine. Get to work," the Dragon commanded and his attention withdrew. Scrags promptly melted into a fuzzy puddle.

Apparently talking was over.

I searched the room, looking for anything of actual use. I quickly found my curiosity piqued in a different corner of the room, where stacks of handwritten journals had my name on every page or so. I started scanning them.

"Are we reading that entire stack?" Carey shoved herself between my eyes and the journal. "How is *Controlling Anchor Attachment* going to help get us home?"

"You can read Latin?" I asked, double-checking the spines of the books. Yep, Latin titles.

"I was a liberal arts major in college and you're leaking it into my brain," she said.

We were still bonded; our connection was so light, I had forgotten all about it. "Carey, this is how we're going to get home. Archibald was able to change or create a connection between the planes. A magical anchor, one you can pull on. If I—if we can figure out how he did it, we can make a connection long enough to reach the universe. Then, we simply reel ourselves in. If the Dragon spares us the tass, we build a harpoon."

"You have another reason. What is it?" Carey asked, her tail beating against the floor.

"A personal interest in my own creation," I lied. I shoved the book at her. "If you can read this, then help me find the part where he got it working." She stared at me for moment before pulling another volume from the pile.

"At least he had good handwriting," she grumbled.

Hours passed, my nose inhaling the musty scent of the paper as my eyes squinted at the Latin. The visions had given the magus the task of awakening me without revealing how to do it. I could barely follow most of the early volumes which were scattered and tangential, mostly the Archmagus thinking to himself. The trouble with anchors and planar travel is that it fell outside typical spellcraft, where you built a receptacle from tass and pulled power or information from a different reality to power the spell. The closer the energy was to what you wanted to accomplish, the less tass you needed. To toss a lightning bolt at someone if you had a plane of lightning, then you barely needed a spell. In order to use the same plane to charge your cell phone without it melting into slag, then you needed a spell to step down the power. But Archibald had thought a lot about the how the universe had been put together. He had, after all, developed a Dragon trap and constructed a weapon that severely injured and might have killed a Fey, the Veil itself if the Council (and Rudy) hadn't stopped him. I began to see what Esmeralda had been getting at. O'Meara, with her powerful anchor, and I could knit spells together quickly, but this, this meant keeping the 4th dimensional structure of the universe in mind at all times, sneaking a hand into the dimension next door and fiddling with the settings.

Now what we wanted to do was shoot something through the many realities. Leeward, a propellent and harpoon, had to not get stuck in any three-dimensional spaces.

"Hey, Thomas," Carey said. "You think a tass cannon is what we need?" She pushed one of the later volumes at my nose.

Excitement leapt off the page, a redesign of what he called a dimensional defense weapon, still a massive spell. "That is exactly what we need."

I took the book over to the still puddle of fur that had been Scrags or at least the Dragon pretending to be Scrags. "We need to build this."

Feline eyes opened in the puddle and looked at me.

"Is he bloody lying to me, lad?" Scrags asked. "Did it really feel like that?"

"What?" I asked, confused.

Scrags pulled himself up from the puddle, ears and mouth looking melted. "Did it really hurt that badly in the pit?"

"I've been through a lot of pain this past couple years; shot, burned, and broken a lot of bones, and I've never run into anything that holds a candle to the pain I felt when I first bonded our Dragon. Are you not his mouthpiece right now?" I asked.

"Do this accent sound like a bloody Dragon?" he hissed, a familiar spittle dripping from his fangs, but it did not hiss when it hit the floor.

"Not at the moment, but I do need to talk to him," I said

But Scrags ignored me. "He wants me to hunt Archibald. If I don't, I go back to being flotsam in his blood stream, being dead." Scrags' stare went off into the infinite. "Fook it. I'll do it." His body reformed the rest of the way, everything snapping into its proper place. "You don't know him. He'd wipe the floor with you."

"You helped him build this cannon then," I dropped the book in front him of.

Scrags glanced at it. "You want to use that to get home?

"In part. We'll need two shots."

42

SCRAGS SAVED US DAYS of work trying to build the spell from Archibald's drawing, and the Dragon sped things along, as entire components rose from the ground into our circle. We had no elemental planes to power the spell, but Dragon's blood proved to be an able replacement.

My design, while less elegant than Archibald's, should be sturdier. I'd built multiple redundancies into the spell. Seemed prudent since we were going to be traveling inside it.

"This is, as Rudy would put it, nuts," Carey said as we both stepped back from our handiwork. "Inside a Dragon, we built a spaceship." Her head shook as she marveled at the glowing spear inside the circle.

"It's a dimension ship," I corrected. "We are literally billions of light years away from everything if we had to use physics."

"It's a hamster ball with a double-barreled harpoon gun mounted on it," Scrags huffed.

"Well kinda," I had to concede, the glowing ball had a large abstract arrow jutting from it. I noticed a shifting sensation. A note sounded in my mind as tension among my silver strands began to ease. We were moving.

The tone stopped. I was tempted to test our distance to O'Meara but that would require breaking the bond with Carey.

"It's time," Scrags announced. "Thomas, bring me that basin."

I hesitated. "You sure?"

"Lad, unless you got yourself another time scryer, I'll need that to find Archibald. I don't need a magus anymore to use it," Scrags said.

Turned out, time spells are really heavy. I had to drag the basin across the room and it settled into the base of the sphere. I wound up sitting on it. Its chilly stone bit right through my butt fluff. The sphere had not been made with cougar comfort in mind, so the central shaft of the seeker spell was in my way. As I curled around it a sense of Deja vu whapped me in the back of my mind.

I'd been in a similar apparatus before. "This seems familiar," I blurted out as Carey and Scrags sorted out whether my ribs or my thighs were more comfortable perches.

"We had to stick you in a very similar spell five months before you actually changed. Noise doped you up so much, you actually saw her through the Veil." He chuckled. "She was pissed you called her a good doggy." He looked around, squinting. "You built all those parts, too."

"Why mess with perfection?" I said, carefully closing the link between me and Carey, forcefully shoving away the guilty thoughts. When I had first bonded to O'Meara, I'd found it impossible to hide things with a telepathic link, but I was getting better at it now. It helped to know that Carey had been able to hide stuff for weeks, so I knew it was possible. I reopened the link and smiled at her. "Ready to have your mind blown?" I asked.

"Do I get a choice?" she asked.

"Like many things in life, that's a solid nope," I said.

"Hit me, mister dealer man." Carey pointed her eyes down the barrel of the harpoon.

I swallowed and stilled my twitching tail as my third eyelids flicked over my vision. "Do it."

Sixth dimensional life. Where my reality was ribbon without mass, an elementary particle.

It hurt. Both Carey and I screamed. But I saw it. The universe as a whole, realities weren't layers of some onion. They seethed and slid together, forming webs and strands of worlds and lives. They flowed and churned, forming structures, bones, muscles. The universe was an organism. Dragons, Fey and who knew what else, were parasites and symbionts within it.

"Fire the thing!" Carey shouted.

"I don't know where!" I called back.

"Anywhere!"

I pointed the barrel of spell toward the universe, pulling it from the narrow pocket of three-dimensional space within the Dragon's stomach thing. The mouth opened. Together, Carey and I pulled the trigger on the spell. A clot of Dragon's blood ignited and with the sound of an echoing whoosh, the other harpoon shot out into the ether beyond.

We shoved the Dragon's sight away and both went limp, panting. Still, the vision of the universe stayed on inside my mind as if burned on the inside of my skull. Yet deeper, as if I were swimming in it. My tongue strayed up to my nose. Tasting blood. Instinctually, I reached to my bond mate for comfort and only found more shock.

Owie, owie, owie, owie. And then, *Why am I even doing this? What's the point? I'm dust. Just dust.*

I composed reasons as the spell's massive amount of inter-dimensional cable spun out into the void. Your *sist—*

An echo of a ker-thunk sounded. Purple blasted our vision as the sphere lurched into a tunnel of space.

Goodbye, stubborn offspring, the Dragon whispered into the dark of my mind as the distance between us grew. The purple around us grew textured, undulating with light and dark patterns as we sped through.

"Aw hell," Scrags said. He had both paws pressed against the back of the bubble and stared. Turning my attention, I saw a pair of black shadows swimming after us.

"What are those?" I asked, futilely turning my eyes toward the pursuers. Only blackness greeted my meat eyes.

"If Fey are sharks, and Dragons are pikes, then I'm guessing those are the minnows!" Scrags said.

"What do minnows eat?" Carey asked.

"I'm guessing us!" I responded. We had no way of defending ourselves. If the sphere was pierced, we'd be dumped into a nearby reality with no protection. If we were lucky, we'd simply be vaporized instantly.

We did, however, have a way to maneuver. I checked the reel. We had about fifty percent of our line reeled in. Halfway there, we were probably in the area the Dragon hadn't wanted to go, a sea surrounding the universe. "Help me with this, Carey!" I shoved my plan into her mind.

"We'll lose one of the harpoons!" she hissed as she ran around to the other side of the apparatus.

"That's why we made two!" I said. The second had a much shorter chain, a third of the length of the first, intended for moving within the universe.

"I hope you know what you're doing!" Carey took her place and lent her vision to me. Using it, I set the second harpoon at a leeward angle to our travel vector. It would anchor in a separate reality.

"They're getting closer, lad!" Scrags called out from a mouth on the back of his head, face squashed up against the rear of the bubble.

"I see them!" Not entirely true. I saw their shadows in the purple tunnel, long pointy shadows of wickedly hooked teeth. They were gaining. I checked the reel; were we close enough? The spindle had thickened.

A maw opened behind us. I fired. The second spindle spun with the loud*vvrrrrrr* of a cast fishing line. The open maw loomed up behind us. The other shadow struggled to catch up.

Tink! The reel stopped with only a few loops of thread on it. I switched it to reel in and we were jerked to the side just as the teeth snapped closed. We slammed through the purple wall into another tunnel. This one had great gaps in the purple walls. Each a window to another world. Greenery in some, others spat flaming lightning into our wake.

"We're traveling between the two strands, crashing through the realities instead of between them," Scrags hollered.

A giant banana-colored blob leapt into our path. I paused the winding of the main reel and we swung around it.

The closest shadow disappeared to avoid it and reappeared farther back.

"Whatever! It's working! Eat giant banana-slug thing!" Carey took over the secondary reel and together we started swinging our little craft around the bits of realities that were leaping into our path.

"You bloody idiots! It's making a lot of noise!" Scrags said.

Yes, the shadows were falling back, but there were a lot more of them now.

The lines in front of the sphere were at about a 30-degree angle to each other and the angle began to widen. The feeling of speed began to wane.

"They're gaining again!" Scrags said. "Drop into a reality! Anywhere!"

"We need at least one of those harpoons back!" I cut the secondary line and we whipped forward. Contrary to my expectation, however, the windows into realities widened. We rammed through one. I made eye contact with a surprised looking fire serpent's eight wide eyes. Purple flashed, an erupting volcano. A woman made of lava gracefully ducked out of our path. "The hell!" I cried as the speed of the transitions increased.

"We had too much speed! We're swinging like a ball on a pole through the realities. The more we shorten the rope, the faster we go. Hang on." Scrags flattened himself against the wall. Carey grabbed onto my thigh as centrifugal force pressed in on us from an angle my brain screamed couldn't exist.

Outside dimensions and transitions flashed into a solid strobe of light. Above, a shadow grew.

With a final flash, we fell into a world of fire and flame. Why *can't I ever visit some place nice?* I thought to myself as we bounced across cracked blackened soil and skidded to a stop on the bank of a river of lava. The glowing harpoon was embedded in the trunk of a gnarled tree with five-fingered leaves of flame.

We sat there for a moment, stunned to be alive.

"We gotta—" I panted, "We gotta reload the harpoon." I reached for the hatch.

A sharp pain bit into my thigh and I flinched away.

"What was that for!" I snarled at Carey as she spat out my skin.

"Open that door and we're all toast," Carey snarled right back.

"Oh right. No O'Meara." Blinked and checked my threads. They were all there, I was close enough. I could rebond O'Meara right now.

"That doesn't help us! Unless you can make heat wards with her on a different plane of reality," Carey said.

"Right." I slumped down and stared at the glowing harpoon. I'd be fine from the heat, but we had no way to spellcraft unless we nearly merged and who knew if that would work across realities.

"Better do it soon. Looks like we're attracting the attention of something." Scrags slipped under me. Up in the sky, in the purple scar of our entrance to the world, a black spot hovered. A single eye.

"Is that?" I asked.

"Yep, lad, that's a Fey," Scrags whispered. "Told ya you made too much noise."

I turned on the main reel and it pulled us right up to the base of the tree. Carey and I mentally grasped the cord.

WHO? The voice boomed into our minds, vibrating up from the cord itself. The tree's branches rippled above. I swallowed. The harpoons were designed to find an anchor. They went right through reality, they only stopped if they hit a being capable of serving as anchor for a familiar, an intelligent being.

We terribly sorry to bother you, but I need that spear back, I thought at it while urging Carey to start wiggling it. She did, tugging at the line.

What is spear? the tree asked.

I skipped the explanation by balling up a very brief story of what was going to happen to us if the tree didn't let go of the barb in its trunk and slam dunking it into the tree's mind.

OH! A moment. *MAY YOUR FIRE NEVER DIM, STRANGER.* The spear slid free from the trunk as a crimson ooze flowed from the hole.

"How'd you get it to do that?" Carey asked as the harpoon was pulled back into the firing tube.

"I asked nicely, apologized profusely, and added that we would probably die if they didn't give it back. It's a nice tree."

"Focus!" Scrags said. "We're spotted."

An eye looked down on us, and several buddies were appearing alongside it. Black orbs adorned with bright pink irises, their pinprick pupils glowed with golden light. They were drifting down in our direction.

Swearing under our breaths Carey and I packed another charge of Dragon's blood into the harpoon's chamber. "Okay, stick to the plan. Think of everything about your sister. Hate and Love."

She licked her lips and closed her black eyes as I stared hard at her aura. "She's got an annoying voice. And is really pushy. Always telling me how I gotta live my life. Always better than me." Her breaths were getting deep. I scryed past the magics that surrounded us, keeping us alive, slid my vision along our bond.

"What else? Loves too," I said.

Her long body trembled and dug in front of her, claws scratching through my fur. "She shows up when I'm in trouble. Bails me out. No questions asked. Every time. Every single time."

There, there I saw it for the second time on another person. A silver thread, glowing with emotion.

Interlopers. Aliens. The presence in my mind made my concentration wobble, but I managed to hold on.

"Scrags! You talk to it!" I growled as I gently pulled Carey's relationship into the mechanism built for it.

"Uuuh. Bloody Mary in hell fire," he moaned before broadcasting thoughts. *Ah hello officer, we were just passing through. Had a bit of a break down. We'll be right on our way.*

You have made work for me. I do not like work. And you are not worth chewing.

The spear began to rise as the harpoon swung out of this reality and oriented itself toward home.

I heard tension in the surrounding sphere, as the harpoon fired. Its reel only whirred for a fraction of a second.

Stop. Die. Darkness surrounded us.

Scrags blurred.

*AAAAH!*A cry of pain rocked my head as purple exploded around us. The sphere filled with the scent of burned fur.

Scrags slid out of even a vaguely catlike shape, spreading out across my shoulder, all of his fur blackened and smoking.

"What happened to you?" Carey shook herself out of her fugue.

"I bit him," Scrags groaned. "It's really hot out there."

"How did it even feel that?" I asked.

A grin spread across the blackened surface. "I have a lot more teeth than I used to."

43

WE BARELY HAD TIME to brace for impact. We shot through the tunnel so quickly, I barely registered that there was a tunnel before we slammed right into a tree. Damn, *another forest!* I thought, as our hamster ball played pinball among the tree trunks. Even as my body spun through the vomit-inducing ride, I smoothly disconnected from Carey and sent Mr. Bitey sliding along to the warm embrace of O'Meara's mind.

Honey! I'm home! I called out.

Thomas! O'Meara's warmth hit me with the force of a gooey volcano. *Bloody Ashes! Where the hell are you! Are you alright?!* Invading tendrils of thoughts slammed through my mind, some trying to rip the answers right out of me, others doing their level best to squeeze me with imaginary hugs.

I'm okay, I thought at her, pushing back with what I could but I couldn't let her pull me from my surroundings. I still had work to do.

Dammit, Thomas! We have to stop this from happening! Do you have any idea how worried I've been? What I was about to do?! There were dark thoughts there, sharp plans that she kept out of my reach.

I know, I gave her a mental lick. *I'm sorry, hadn't expected Carey to—*

She's with you now, isn't she? The ungrateful tube rat, O'Meara growled as a new mind nosed into the connection.

Thomas friend! Boss friend. Tilly mentally wagged his tail at me.

O'Meara pulled herself together. Among *other things, we were trying to sniff out where Oric had stuck you. We weren't having much luck with that part.*

How long was I gone? I asked.

Five days. Only one more day to comply with Oric's terms. Rudy's so pissed. Carey stole his show. He's convinced he had Gargantua on the ropes.

The ball skidded to a stop in a clearing and I had to smile. The line of the harpoon traced across a field of weeds and into a small ramshackle house. The roof looked partially caved in, the gray siding flaked and bubbled. It was a sad thing.

The side of the bubble opened and I poured myself out onto the ground.

Charlie, his shiny armor the only spot of cleanliness in my view, sat on the front porch, teeth bared as he sniffed at the air.

Can I have some heat? I asked O'Meara as I took a moment to stretch.

My fur ignited. All *you want. Where are you now?*

I painted her a picture.

I'll get a locator spell up. Hang tight, stall until we can get there.

"Hello Charlie," I called out. "You have someone in that house who's under my protection. I suggest you move out of the way."

Charlie shook his head in disbelief. "Oric say stay with the girl and keep your armor on. And doesn't tell me why. And here you are, two days later, crashing down stinking of space-bending." He sniffed. "You got no wards. Pity. To worm your way back from the great beyond only to get plastered all over these trees."

"I'm not alone," I taunted, drawing on O'Meara's power, creating a shimmering layer of super-heated plasma over my skin. The grass flared and fell to ashes in a five-foot radius.

"Shall we find out how much heat the ward on that tin can you're wearing can actually take?"

Without the glare of my wards, I watched Charlie's power spark within him, coiled my legs as it built and launched myself upwards as he exploded into motion. He charged beneath me, my super-heated tail coming within inches of his back. I twisted, landing on my feet as several trees that Charlie had blown through remembered that gravity was a thing and began to fall. Charlie himself skidded to a stop and turned to face me, the back of his armor smoking, its shiny metal surface dulled from my intense heat. His wards sprung back into existence almost a full second after dropping out of his cannon-shot technique.

I felt O'Meara grin as Charlie's trick flared. I sidestepped, flicking the tip of my tail into his path, shining with sunlight.

He yelped as my tail was blown to the side. The expected sting of a broken bone hit me as he tumbled to a stop. I hissed with annoyance. My poor tail tip had been torn off and white bone shone from the end.

"YERRRGH!" Charlie screamed as he pawed desperately to get his smoking helmet off his head.

Something in the window of the house moved and the cough of gunfire erupted. The bullets liquefied a foot from my skin, hit me like the spitting of heavy vertical rainfall. Charlie staggered up to his feet, finally free of the helmet, one of his eyes a total loss of charred flesh. "Hit them now!" he called out.

A gray spot in my vision flared from inside the house, transmuting into the golden glow of a ward. Tass bomb. A heat ward surged up from the wall of the house and rushed outwards. I moved, charging sideways, out of the firing arc of the gunner. My fur snuffed out as the golden wall passed through me.

"Dead meat now!" Charlie lit with power.

*Never! O'*Meara called out, reaching for the plane of Stasis.

My body went totally rigid in mid-leap as the dog crashed into me. An audible crunch of his bones as his unstoppable object met my immobile one. I spun off in one direction and he ricocheted off. I pulled the power out of my body, twisted out of the spin and landed on all four feet. Too fast; my back ankle snapped.

Charlie lay twenty feet away, his front legs at crooked angles, whimpering softly.

Teach them to think I'm a one trick pony! O'Meara laughed. *Hold that ankle still while I heal it. Tilly and I can do any spell, so long as you're the target.*

What about the—I cut off the thought as a horned man with an assault rifle stepped out of the front door and lifted the gun in my direction. O'Meara grabbed hold of the stasis plane a moment too late. The shots fired and I braced myself for pain. But it was the man who started screaming, his hands clawing at the weasel latched onto the side of his face.

"Well, that about wraps it up," I said and instantly regretted the words as purple flared across my vision. Oric! I flung myself to the side, dodging a pair of tiny talons that had been aimed for my rump. My ankle flared in pain as I rolled up onto my feet.

Purple flared from behind. I sprang forward. Flare! Side. Flare! Leap! Twist! He passed under. Adrenaline flared. If he touched me, he'd hurl me somewhere I wouldn't survive. There was no speaking, no gloating, he was just doing his damnedest to kill me. My eyes closed, world narrowing to the movement of my body and flashes of his magic. The flare of the magic gave me the barest moment to dodge out of the way. He had entered a single dive and was whipping through space at an increasing velocity.

Then I made my mistake. Landing hard on the injured ankle, the leg crumpled. I watched as those talons streaked toward my nose. And I flung myself, my entire body, leeward. It wasn't far, not even an inch. The purple haze of the between washed over me. I saw Oric streak through the place I had been, but I also saw into a dozen other realities where Oric hit me and both of us disappeared. My paw lashed out through the haze and tagged the bird from behind. He squawked and tumbled into another portal; I watched it burrow through reality up into the branches of a nearby tree.

I leaned the millimeter back into reality. Both our chests heaved. Oric gaped at me, sucking in oxygen through his tiny beak. His little bowtie had been knocked askew, and he grasped it with a claw as pins and needles flared in the bones in my ankle as O'Meara and Tilly knitted them back together. My eyes narrowed as I resisted a mighty urge to sneeze.

"New trick, I see," Oric observed. "You have a lot of those."

"And you're running out of them," I said. "We don't have to do this, Oric. You had a good run, a hundred and fifty years, was it? Ever thought about retirement?"

"Longer than that, cub. And that's all you are. A soft-hearted cub who won't do what is necessary. You bully your way through with power and luck. No real skill. No idea of the bigger picture. Magi know how to awaken others; the practice is getting more common. But what holds them back is the scarcity and expense of obtaining a good, acceptable familiar. You think our world can handle many more magi?"

I sneezed.

He flashed. I stepped leeward, the muscle wasn't in my body. Yet I felt it all the same, part of the hidden stomach where I could smuggle tass or anything. Oric streaked through where I stood and reappeared on his perch without a ruffled feather.

He continued, "They'll rip this place apart. Already, magical resources dwindle, not because there's any less of them. There are simply more who want it."

"So, it's all a noble act while you keep the prices high and stockpile it?" I asked. "Yeah, right."

"Mankind was blinded for a reason, kitty. The Fey will crush this entire reality to dust if we repeat those sins," Oric said, as I felt the prickly bite of his scrying. Looking for a focus or something that was allowing me to sidestep his attacks.

He's stalling for something, O'Meara warned.

Well, let's give him something to worry about. I have work to do. I scoffed in Oric's direction and turned my back on the bird. "What happened to this being all business, Oric? Why's it gotta be a zero sum game?"

"Don't you dare turn your back on me, Thomas!" Oric called out.

"I'm not afraid of you anymore. And I'm not going let you waste my time. Why don't you do something useful like get Charlie to a vet?" I said, walking back towards the house.

"I'll show you useful!" Oric disappeared in a flash.

Flash. Bernard appeared, Oric on his shoulder. "Uh?" the bear asked. The owl disappeared.

Flash. A coyote looking just as confused appeared. One by one all the officers of the TAU appeared before me. A corgi in plate armor. A cobra with rainbow scales, a Chihuahua that jittered so hard sparks were coming off his ears. A large fluffy house cat. That huge wolf with eagle wings. And more.

I didn't wait for him to finish. I stepped sideways and ran through them. Watching the various parallel mes do the same. I had one more charge of Dragon's blood left, and I needed it for Melissa.

"What's this, Oric?" Bernard finally raised his voice. "Charlie!"

All ten arrived. The final officer being a crocodile with diamonds for teeth.

"First one to kill the cat gets 500 groat!" Oric huffed from the back of the crocodile. The recent arrivals looked toward the overly fluffy cat.

"What you do, Harold?" asked the Crocodile.

"Not me, you pea brain!" the cat turned to glare at me as I stepped back into the world on the front porch. "The mountain lion."

"Get him. Or it's a trip to the great beyond!" Oric hooted, bouncing up and down.

"Now there's a threat." I smiled. "I just came back from there. All by myself. A certain squirrel taught me how do to that." I couldn't survive all of them. I had no idea what they could do. The sidestep effect saved me from Oric's trick, but I knew his trick inside and out.

Options, O'Meara? I thought at my bond.

Stasis armor. It would slow you down, though. I could give you an air of authority, but they'll see it for what it is. We could try to overwhelm the fire ward. Tilly and I could channel other energies, but you won't be immune to them like you are to fire. We could alter it to block specific spells. I'm making a bond-tracking spell now. Hang on. I can do conceptual light. Make you much faster.

Get that one ready. Speed would help. *In fact, start layering on enchantments, it doesn't matter what they are.* I had an idea and scryed hard at the area. Oric was still breathing hard. He was injured, my back slap had hurt him more than he was letting on.

"Alright Cat," the wolf growled. "End of the line."

"You have it wrong. You're all here to celebrate Oric's retirement," I quipped. "Which of you is second in command, anyway?" There, the purple scars marking the Oric's passage shone. I shouldn't have moved to the porch. I'd have to get to their line. "Is it you, Bernard?" I started walking toward him. "Did you know that between you and Charlie, Rudy is far more wary of you?"

"You promised me no trouble, Thomas," Bernard grumbled, eyes flicked toward Oric as he levered himself up on two feet. That sickly green anchor of his shone and two bears stood side by side. Then two German Shepherds budded out of the bear on the left. More animals continued to step out of his body.

"What is your knack anchored to, Bernard? The concept of the zoo?" I snarled.

"As long as he can't use his Magus' fire, he can only shield himself, Bernard! Hold him down." Oric screeched.

Some of the others chuckled as I circled around the growing menagerie. "I am not the one you should challenge first, Thomas."

"I'm not challenging you. I'm beseeching all of you. Why work for a despot? The TAU's a union. Do any of you remember the days when you actually helped people?" The rift I was targeting was now in the center of them. I could see gray beginning to illuminate the teeth of Bernard's bodies, tass. Apparently, I wasn't the only familiar who knew how to pull someone out from a leeward step. But if I could step sideways, then maybe I could do something else there.

Not without practice. You'll fall on your face.

What if I just climb?

Do it, O'Meara thought and I stepped out of reality. Two canine Bernard's with teeth of tass charged me. I leapt upwards. O'Meara channeled the stasis into my front paws, fixing them in place. My body swung back. I kicked out. The stasis let go. Back into reality I went. Crashing onto the roof. O'Meara and Tilly supplied me with the tass to coat my claws as I got my legs beneath me.

I leapt, muscles launching me through the air, arching out toward the Bear's original body. My own claws glowed. Bernard opened his jaws and paws rose to clap me into a very painful hug. I raked my claws down.

My claws snagged not on flesh but on space itself. Purple flashed as they tore open the very space Bernard had been brought through. Shifting leeward, I saw the holes. Oric had made swiss cheese of reality, a chain of portals stacked through space, and by shifting to the side they formed a tunnel with a fat owl at the end of it. Kicking off the side of a bear's head, I flew into that tunnel. Oric tore open another rift, his power flaring.

Crunch.

Not fast enough.

My mouth tasted of feathers with a fabric seasoning. Dammit. I looked over Vegas at midday. My head sticking through a hole in space, my body in about ten different locations. I pulled my head back and dropped the bloody body on top of the crocodile.

I looked back to see my tail thirty feet away, hanging out of a portal right above Bernard's head. They didn't say anything as I delicately extracted myself. Any one of them could have finished me off. Nobody moved.

I stalked towards the house, letting their silence settle. I could smell mixed emotions rising from them.

As I reached the door Bernard called out, "He'll come back, you know. He can do that."

I paused. "It takes time, right?"

"Few weeks," he said.

"That's time enough for you to decide what you're all going to do about that," I said.

"Oric is the TAU," the crocodile spat. "He's what transports all of us as well as supplies all over the country."

"By the time he's back there won't be a familiar shortage anymore. You all need to think about what that means. Now get out of here. My people—my family will be here soon. We'll get Charlie to a vet."

"We're in upstate New York. I can't walk back to Vegas," Bernard huffed with one voice again.

"Well, my House does have openings." I shot him a cheeky smile and pushed open the door, stepping over the cooling corpse of the gun satyr. I found Carey and Scrags waiting outside a wooden door with a magical lock on it.

"You killed Oric," Carey looked up at me and swallowed.

I took a deep breath of my own. This was gonna hurt.

44

*O'Meara, I have to take care of something. If I run into trou-
ble, I'll rebond, I* thought at my bond.

*You still have ten TAU officers out there, Thomas! Tilly and
I are burrowing through the wards that are hiding your location, but we still have at least a half hour, O'*Meara thought
back.

*And if they give me any trouble, you'll be the first to know.
But, Carey and Melissa have to have a chat in private. I* sent a
mental lick and broke the bond, leaving me alone with Scrags
and Carey.

"Hello?" A voice called from behind the door. "Who's
there?"

"I could have used your help, Scrags." I said, eyeing the
small cat, who looked mostly like the kitten sized grump I
remembered, a little fatter, maybe.

"You handled yourself fine, lad," he said. "I'd rather everyone think I'm still dead."

"He ate about five guards in here," Carey said. I noticed she
wasn't standing very close to Scrags.

"But you missed the sixth?" I asked.

"I got full," he protested, then burped.

"So, I had to do that one," Carey hung her head and
groomed her whiskers, no trace of blood left on her face but
her white stomach had a rusty color.

"I don't suppose you found a key on any of those guards?"
The magical padlock was from a minor House specializing

in defensive enchantments. Fortunately, the hinges looked mundane. The harpoon's tether went beneath the door.

"Allow me," Scrags announced and he flicked out a paw. The padlock split and fell to the floor with a clunk.

"You could have done that this entire time!" Carey exploded at Scrags.

"And have her run into a magical fight that she can't see? What do you take me for, lass?" Scrags said.

"There's a back door!" she hissed with exasperation.

The swinging open of the door stopped Scrags' retort. Melissa sat on a bed, dressed in dirty scrubs with dancing panda bears, and an iron collar around her neck connected her via a thick chain to the metal bed. The harpoon stuck out of her belly, but she didn't seem to perceive its being there.

White went all the way around her brown irises as she spotted me. "What now?!" she moaned. Her aura was sparking like a short circuit, a little glimmer of power that threatened to ignite any moment. I could see her fighting with the Veil itself, its threads in her head fraying.

I like this one, brother. This one is a fighter. My mate will like being bonded to this one. Bone Whistler's thoughts were so eager that I felt him salivating into my mind.

"Hello, Melissa. Do you remember me?" I asked her, trying to push Bone Whistler away, but he didn't yield one iota.

She shook her head and buried her face in her hands. "No... you don't talk. You can't talk. No no no! This is insane. I've gone insane. Fucking insane."

"Don't talk to her!" Carey squeaked. "You're just gonna freak her out. Where's O'Meara! We need her to talk her. Get her home."

Bone Whistler, it doesn't have to be this one. I can do this on someone in Vegas. I can get their permission, I pleaded.

Do it or you'll spend the next decade getting very in touch with your instinctual side. The favor is long overdue. His senses bled into mine, blood coated his tongue. He had fought his own battle recently.

I took a deep breath. Mr. Bitey uncoiled from my neck, the chain knitting into his cobralike form.

"What are you doing?" Carey hopped up and down. "Are you insane?"

I nodded at Mr. Bitey and he nodded back me. There seemed to be something more in his jeweled eyes than there had been. He didn't strike, but flowed across the room, gently wrapping himself around her torso.

My mind opened into the negative space that I hadn't felt in some time. Someone! *Anyone, help me! Please!*

We're here to help. I thought. That was all it took. She opened wide, my mind spilling into her darkness. I did my best to project warmth and safety, but, like her sister, her mind was full of sharp objects, despite being far more focused. The only thing she could rely on had been herself and she had applied that to the max. *It will be okay*, I assured her, as I slipped into her vision and put my human face there, remembered from Archibald's sketches. The Veil was eager to accept my suggestion and where I sat on my haunches a human stood in living color. Another bump and I wore a police uniform.

"Oh, thank god!" She surged up from the bed, clotheslined herself on the collar and fell back on the mattress, choking.

"Easy, easy," I said. "Let's get that off you. Scrags?"

"You need to sharpen your claws, laddie." Scrags scooted up, his legs merging into a rippling pad beneath him. I hurried to mirror him, rushing up to Melissa, taking her hand in my mouth and letting her think it was enclosed in a human hand as Scrags bounced up onto the bed. "Hold her still! I don't wanna miss." He stretched up into a narrow fuzzy pole to peer at the collar. A blur cut through the air and the collar fell open. A lock of her hair fell with it. "There!"

"I've been here for about a week," Melissa began to blubber as she stood. "They grabbed me right off the street. They had a dog and an owl! They talked to them as if they were people!"

That's totally crazy, isn't it? I thought at her as I guided her towards the door, trying to not to let my river of guilt flow into her.

Carey danced from side to side, claws skittering as she followed in her sister's wake. "Thomas, whatever you're doing, do it again. I need to talk to her!

"This is about my sister, isn't it? She's mixed up with some bad people in Vegas. They put me on a plane. Did my sister call you? Did she tell you where I was?!"

I guided her out the front door.

"Thomas! The TAU is out there!" Carey whined. As she did Melissa's soul sparked. I could feel it, an untethered part her of desperately seeking something, anything. She was going to awaken, whether or not I did this. Probably. Her mind clung to mine, wrenching herself free of the Veil's lies about the reality she actually lived in.

The TAU officers had not moved far. Clustering in a circle. Several had pulled out cellphones and were nosing them. Heads turned to watch me and I could feel their scrying gaze. They might be able to tell I had bonded Melissa, who stared right back at them.

Ignore them, I urged, but she stopped moving.

"Do they have cell phones?" she asked in a small voice.

The croc smiled.

"Bullshit," she said to herself as she nearly leapt down the stairs. "Goddamn fucking bullshit. This is Carey's fault, isn't it? She's a little weasel! Nothing but a backstabbing weasel!"

Carey squeaked and froze on the porch. I could hear her little sniffles get more distant.

The memory of Carey jumping on my back and setting off the portal bomb replayed in my mind and Melissa seized it. Drinking it in she pushed into my mind, the Veil scrambled in vain to refute everything as totally impossible, farcical. The best it could do was, I*'m drugged, aren't I? She hurt you. She double crossed you. And you're going to do something to me now.*

She still walked with me towards the bubble. I wished she'd pull away, try to gouge out my eyes, something. But she held onto me with a dreamlike clarity, pawing through my memories until we stood right outside the bubble, which in her eyes looked like an ambulance.

For what it's worth, you can blame me for this. I have to do this. It almost doesn't matter that she betrayed me, I thought at her.

I don't understand. You owe someone and I'm the price? But you're not going to kill me? Torture but not?

You will. I also promised to protect you. I can't really do that if you live outside Vegas. I pulled her into the bubble and she fell in next to me. It sealed itself closed. The grass outside rippled as a 9-inch-long tube of fur and muscle charged over it. Carey pounded against the transparent shell. "Thomas! Don't you dare! Don't you dare do this!"

I activated the apparatus we had built. Well, mostly the Dragon had built, the modifications had left the spell's original purpose intact and needed even less intervention than the original. Runes began to spin around Melissa's head as interdimensional loops of tass captured the seeking part of her soul and bound it to the spiritual harpoon that the apparatus drew back into itself. I offered it my own anchor as a guideline. A silver glow shone out of Melissa's pupils as her mind stretched along the cord. Memories altered by the Veil vibrating and glitching into their true forms.

Ready on my end, I snarled at Bone Whistler.

I'm not giving you any choice, why be so harsh on yourself? Bone Whistler answered. *Ready.*

Carey, still beat and clawed at the side of the bubble. "Sorry," I said as I released the mechanism. The point of the spell twisted leeward, pointing into the universe beyond. Melissa screamed as it fired off along the cord of my soul, pulling a thread of her spirit along with it. A shiver went through her, and everything in my magical vision showed cracks for a long moment before reality seemingly noticed and fit itself back together.

"Wow," Melissa breathed. "They...they...must have drugged me good."

Okay, that's all I do on my end. If or when she awakens, she might swap bodies with your mate or she might be a shaman.

Do not worry. The favor is repaid, Bone Whistler announced, and a weight lifted from my mind. I felt lightheaded. *Go, your magus is arriving.*

How do you—

A purple portal opened into the clearing; with space already shredded by Oric, reality offered no resistance. O'Meara stepped out, Midnight perched on her shoulder, followed by Riona and Tack. The remaining TAU moved out of her way. "Thomas!" O'Meara called out. I pawed open the hatch, totally forgetting about the irate weasel.

"Mel! Mel! What'd he do to you?! I kill him! I kill him." Carey dashed into the bubble and climbed up on top of her sister's head and emitted highest-pitched hisses you could imagine.

Melissa screamed blue bloody murder, batted Carey off, and scrambled out of the pod, kicking me several times in the process. Bare feet slipped in the tall grass and she fell not five feet from the bubble.

Carey followed. "Sis, Sis! Are you okay!? What he do!"

Melissa pushed herself up and stared at Carey. "No... not... possible. Carey?"

A spot of light appeared over Melissa's head before flowing down over her body. A light purple in hue.

"Transition!" O'Meara shouted. "Get back!" Even as she said it, O'Meara launched herself into motion. Sprinting forward, she snatched up Carey by the back of her head and hauled her back as the width of the transition widened from where Melissa knelt, and bled into the ground, its area widening.

Bone Whistler's laugh was so clear that it was as if the spirit was standing right next to me. Don't *be surprised, brother. I wouldn't leave this to chance. My mate is getting her proper body today. Melissa has a beautiful one. Not that you noticed.*

As the transition spread, I saw a figure standing over her. Waving four of her eight legs in a dance over and through Melissa's body. "Weaver!" I exclaimed. The spirit that Bone Whistler had lent to me in return for the favor I owed him to save the life of someone who had backstabbed me the next day.

There are many other things that can force two planes together, but I only hire the best, Bone Whistler said. *I learned that from you, brother. Less complex than favors.*

Weaver's shadow form drew something taut in Melissa, and I saw her, a cougar overlaid on Melissa's body. They'd been pulled into a similar pose, the cougar sitting, while the woman squatted on all fours.

Their features and forms began to slide into each other. They met briefly, becoming a blend of cat and human before continuing past each other. Until a human figure was lifted away by Weaver's arms and the purple light snapped out. Leaving a tawny colored cat quite a bit smaller than me in our world.

Her yellow eyes blinked once. She gave a surprised chirp. And promptly fell over. True exhaustion flooded her and threatened to overflow into me. I closed the link and broke it.

"Noooo! Mel!" Carey screamed and thrashed in O'Meara's grip, but made no progress in freeing herself. "You promised to protect her! You promised! I helped you build that thing! I hate you! I HATE you! I erk!" The weasel went still as O'Meara moved her thumb across her throat.

O'Meara brought up Carey to look her in the eyes. With her voice thick with both accent and anger she said, "You listen well, missy. I'm sure you and Thomas made some sort of deal. But... I want you to understand that you hurt my bond. We would have helped you at any point, if you had been honest. We would have done our damnedest to help you. You deserve nothing."

"I think I've done enough to her now, O'Meara," I said.

"Thomas, I love you." She gave me a little smile. "Now butt out. You're going to have your paws full with that sister. This one "killed" you in front several thousand mystics. She goes on the wall. Midnight."

The cat jumped down off O'Meara's shoulder and tossed down a casting circle. O'Meara placed the trembling weasel into its center.

"Midnight?" she pleaded.

"You broke Tilly's heart, Carey. He howled for two days straight. You are the unfriend," Midnight said with coldness.

"Wha—" was all she got out before the spell turned her pure white.

O'Meara picked her up and placed her in a black velvet bag. She turned to the TAU officers who were watching with interest from a fairly safe distance away. Raising the bag, she brandished it at them. "If you're tired of the TAU, come talk to us in Vegas. But we're going to be more careful from here on out." She looked at me, her green eyes hard. "Aren't we, Thomas?"

I stood quickly. "Well, yes. It worked out. Except for Melissa." I looked guiltily at the unconscious cougar.

"We'll take care of her. Now get over here. I owe you a very rough noogie."

I accepted the noogie with all the grace and dignity that one can.   Protesting loudly despite the purring.

45

"AND THAT'S THE PLAN. Agreed?" Rudy glared at me.

I raised my paw. "Is it really necessary to encase O'Meara and me in concrete?"

"Dude, I am gonna put you up on the wall myself if I gotta go rescue you," Rudy huffed. "I had them on the ropes two weeks ago! Now they've had two weeks to tweak Gargantua, and we've only had one, because we were trying to find where Oric stashed ya."

"You didn't come to my rescue," I chuffed in reply. "O'Meara did."

"Well, we didn't have a portal big enough for Stompy. Now we do. As I was saying. I'm gonna bash somebody's head tonight." Rudy's tail swung behind him, stiff and puffy.

I opened my mouth to respond but O'Meara put her hand on my head. "We understand. No bond breaking and we stay in the bunker," she said in an overruling tone.

"You're asking me to sit on my paws all night!" Plus, having to watch the fight with so much at stake through a magically blind camera feed was gonna be awful.

Yes, but it would make me feel better, O'Meara thought. *Midnight will be do a fine job of spotting for Rudy, and Michael agreed to let Riona be the announcer.*

I huffed and puffed a little for show, but I know when I'm beaten. "Anything else? Or am I free to wander a bit before the show?"

"Just don't get catnapped again. Seriously," Rudy said. "Take the morning off. Stompy's ready."

"Come on Thomas, let's get a drink," O'Meara said.

"It's ten in the morning," I grumbled, already following on her heels towards the exit of my office. "Good luck, Rudy," I called back.

"Don't worry, I got this," Rudy said.

O'Meara endured my mental complaining that the threats were really minimal now, as we rode the elevator down to the casino floor. Oric was still dead and most of the TAU officers were still en route back to Vegas. They'd stolen a trailer truck, but it had 'mysterious' engine trouble in Kansas. Then they had started fighting and split up. Rudy's agents (aka a pack of rats) had lost track of most them then.

Really, the biggest worry was that House Hermes might lose their council seat next week if they couldn't come up with the tass to pay for it. If that happened before a fifth Archmagus was confirmed, the Council would fall to three members and be dissolved entirely. Nobody knew what would happen then.

One day at a time, O'Meara thought at me as the doors opened right into an ambush.

"Hello Melissa." I swallowed. The cougaress stood smack in the center of the elevator door and displayed her teeth. I stilled my instinctive backpedal. Interactions with Melissa where her teeth didn't make an appearance were rare. She wore a tailor-made white lab coat that covered her torso and forelimbs. A stethoscope hung from her neck, along with a pendant that bore the mark of House Freelance, a paw with coins in place of the toes, signifying our protection. "How'd the interview go?" I asked, steeling myself to not dodge a slap to the face.

Her sawing growl overlaid her voice. "They took one look at me and said they're not interested. When I protested, they told me no hospital in Vegas would hire me."

Whatever you do, don't say 'I told you so,' O'Meara thought very unhelpfully. She hadn't been very sympathetic when I explained what Bone Whistler had forced me to do. In fact, she had spelled out that if my relationship with Melissa ever reflected Bone Whistler's relationship with her anchor entity, then O'Meara would flay me alive personally. So far, it hadn't been an issue. I'd given Melissa every resource she requested to "overcome the disability" that I'd inflicted on her, of being a 150-pound female mountain lion. A personal assistant, force hand foci and custom personal protective equipment.

"That's too bad. Maybe a smaller clinic? One that specializes in mythics?" I suggested, covering my paws with my tail.

"I'm a resident! I can't practice in a clinic. I need to finish my residence and get my license," she snarled and continued to sit in my way.

"Do you want me to do something about it?" I asked.

"Don't you dare bribe them, if that's what you're asking." Still, she didn't move, glaring at me, tail lashing. "I want you to unfreeze my sister and let her go." She took a deep breath. "Then I will consider this familiar bullshit. That's what you want me to do." Her head turned to the side.

"No," O'Meara said, her voice firm. "You're not bailing her out. She owes me at least two years on that wall. You want to be a familiar, great, but we're not trading for that decision."

Melissa stood up and arched her back in a threat display. "Then let me talk to her! Prisons have visiting hours."

Right or wrong, O'Meara simply crossed her arms and looked at me to back her up.

"In a year's time, she will have experienced a day," I said. "A day to think about the situation. Then we will consider giving you that conversation. It's her punishment, not yours. I promised her we'd protect you. And other things, but O'Meara's punishment stands. House discipline is her prerogative until we reach the size where tribunals can be conducted. You can make an appointment with her if you want to argue."

"But it would be a waste of both our time," O'Meara said. "Is there anything else?"

Melissa sat back down, hackles smoothing. "A magus offered me a spell yesterday that would make me appear human if I served as his apprentice. I want you to buy it from him."

"Illusions will be obvious to any magi," I sighed.

"I don't care. I want to see my face in the mirror again. He was Cordite of House Kampos." She turned to go.

"I'll see what I can do," I said, mentally adding it to the list as my words addressed her tail.

Kampos. Now there's a cluster of misfits, O'Meara thought as she strode out of the elevator. *And she didn't hit you. Already at bargaining, not bad for a week. She might even forgive you in a few years.*

I didn't comment, guilt washing in on my mind as I followed through the casino, heading to the bar we had renamed the View. From it, you could see the entrance to the arena and above that, our rogues' gallery with Grugar, Izzy, Ted, Carey and Charlie. Plenty of room for more, too.

Tilly sat outside the bar, big sad eyes looking up at Carey.

"Hey Tilly," I greeted the dog with a light head butt.

"Oh! Hi Thomas," he shook himself and started up his wag.

"What you doing here?" I asked him.

"Thinking about long angry friend. I done with angry friends. Angry friends are bad." He nodded as if he had discovered a universal truth.

"Tilly, it's not that simple," I said as O'Meara leaned against the wall a bit behind us. Tilly had been delicate this past week.

"I know." The dog ears wilted. "Why it not simple, Thomas? Do good, not bad."

Not really wanting to delve into doggy moral philosophy, I simply shoulder checked him. "Come on into the bar and have a drink. Get a round of pork broth for us."

"Okay, liquid treat is good, warm. I come." Tilly got up as O'Meara let out a mental groan.

Blood and Ashes! she exclaimed as she reached for her anchor.

I looked down the hallway to see the tourists rapidly clearing out of the way for a black bear, a crocodile with diamond teeth, and a chubby orange cat carrying a little white flag between his teeth.

"Thouuumas!" Jowl called in greeting around the stick in his teeth.

"Quiet, tubby." The crocodile growled at the edge of my hearing "You da page, remember?"

"Yus ser." Jowls nodded meekly and the three of them remained silent until they drew up within five feet of us.

"I see you made to Vegas faster than I thought you would. What can I do for you?" I slapped on that trusty customer service smile.

The croc and Bernard looked at each other. The bear glanced up at Charlie before sighing and looking at me. "You mentioned that you are recruiting." He reared up and spread his paws. "We are here to apply."

The croc nodded. "Jowls here is a peace gift. You can put him on that there wall, if you wish."

Jowls puffed himself up and trembled slightly. "I can take it."

I blinked. We did it. We'd fractured the TAU.

Acknowledgements

First, thank you for reading *Aggressive Behavior*. Without readers, a book is a useless pile of words. Only when it is read does come to life. To share these pieces of whimsy, thought and emotion, to know they'll dance around in your brain and (hopefully) bring you joy and release, is one of my life's greatest joys.

That said, getting a book to this point is work, plus much gnashing of teeth and emotional support. The person who bears the brunt of that, as well as maintaining my website, performing alpha readings and providing limitless love is my spouse, Amanda Potter. I love you.

Support also comes from a bevy of writer friends, whether it's discussing (arguing) how to assemble a story, listening to lamentations, figuring out the endless minefield that is marketing and social media, or simply hanging out on Zoom. Thanks go out Taya Latham, ML Spencer, Dryk Ashton, Matt Presley, JC Kang, and Ben Galley, to name a few of the TT crew. And to my formerly local peeps in the Bay Area: Mike Ryder, Alan Petersen, Jame Beach, Killian McRea, and the rest of the San Francisco Bay Area Self Publisher meetup. I think I'm going to need a credit scroll for future books, because I'm not nearly done here.

Thank you to everyone who's helped in making this book better. including my beta-reading team, Andrea Johnson, Pseudo Sapien, Sarah Whitney, Seria MeCreary, Loren Foster, Sarah Patsaros, Nathan House, Peggy Brandt Brown, and Jo Lucas.

And a special thank you to my Patrons who encourage me with a little extra financial support every month.   Every little bit helps.   Thank you to the members of the Freelance Familiars Headquarters on Discord for hanging out, being awesome, and being a good sounding board for wacky ideas.

Thanks for reading and I hope to hear from you soon!

Also by Daniel Potter

Freelance Familiars
Off Leash
Marking Territory
High Steaks
Aggressive Behavior
Pride Fall
Apex Familiar
Rudy & the Warren Warriors (a FF short story)

The Full Moon Medic
Emergency Shift
Midnight Triage
Twilight Run (Book 0 short story)

Rise of the Horned Serpent
Dragon's Price
Dragon's Cage
Dragon's Run
Dragon's Siege